*True North*

# ANASAZI VISION

PROFOUND WISDOM
FROM THE FOUR CORNERS DESERT
AND ONE WOMAN'S JOURNEY TO PEACE

## ALSO BY TRUE NORTH

<u>Anasazi Vision</u> - Return To Third Mesa  *(Winter 2025)*
<u>The Anasazi Vision Companion</u> - Navigating The 30-Year Reset:
A Guide The Lessons And Tools  *(Winter 2026)*

*True North*

# ANASAZI VISION

True North is the award-winning author of the Anasazi Vision series. She is a lover of nature, connection, and growth. She believes in traveling life with curiosity, saying yes, then leaning in and allowing soul to lead the way.
She lives in Oregon.

www.truenorthauthor.com

*Copyright © 2024 by True North*
Anasazi Vision ™

All rights reserved. No portion of this publication may be reproduced in any form without prior written permission from the publisher or author, except as permitted by U.S. copyright law.

The story, all names, characters, and incidents portrayed are fictitious or used with knowledge and permission of the individual. For privacy reasons, some names, locations, and dates have been changed and timelines altered.

The information given in this book should not be treated as a substitute for professional medical advice; always consult a medical practitioner.

ISBN: 979-8-9920599-0-8
Book Cover: True North

www.anasazivision.com

First Edition
Printed in the United States of America

For Joshua McDaniel

And for my children,
Cedar, Denver,
Stewart, and Clint

## CONTENTS

| | | |
|---|---|---|
| | Author's Note | 7 |
| 1 | Accepting Change | 9 |
| 2 | In The Wake | 19 |
| 3 | Four Corners | 30 |
| 4 | San Juan Campsite | 44 |
| 5 | Hovenweep | 61 |
| 6 | Vision Quest | 69 |
| 7 | Oliver | 83 |
| 8 | God's Van | 97 |
| 9 | Cortez Diner | 108 |
| 10 | Red Rock | 117 |
| 11 | Two Infants | 128 |
| 12 | Raven Creek | 145 |
| 13 | Leaving Campus | 154 |
| 14 | Chihuahua | 166 |
| 15 | Spirit Eyes | 191 |
| 16 | Veranda | 213 |
| 17 | Appendages | 222 |

| 18 | Lolita | 249 |
| 19 | Chaco Canyon | 262 |
| 20 | Cantina | 277 |
| 21 | Medicine Man | 285 |
| 22 | Vera | 299 |
| 23 | Hotevilla | 308 |
| 24 | Crows | 322 |
| 25 | Turtle Island | 328 |
| 26 | Guardianship | 339 |
| 27 | Digging Holes | 355 |
| 28 | Prophecy | 381 |
| 29 | Journal | 399 |
| 30 | Ceasefire | 410 |
| 31 | The Voice | 420 |

| Epilogue | 429 |
| Afterword | 435 |

| Acknowledgement | 437 |
| Book Club Topics | 439 |
| True's Playlist | 445 |
| Biscolli's Tee Shirts | 446 |

## AUTHOR'S NOTE

This book is part fiction, part channeled storytelling and part memoir. It is a story birthed from a vision quest and the experiences that followed. It is a unique, immersive experience that blurs the lines between fiction and memoir—and author as protagonist, because, as you will discover, the events in this book were experienced by the author in one form or another.

It is perhaps because the story belongs each reader that it needed to be written from such a personal standpoint. It is a journey into our shared human experience, and a decades-long collaboration from both sides of the veil—a beautiful tale with profound wisdom from the Four Corners desert, the people who call it home, and spiritual guides. Enjoy the journey.

— True North, 2024

# 1

# ACCEPTING CHANGE

An unusual thing about my mother is that she doesn't cry. Not when my father sold the only home she wanted, not when she entered menopause, not when her mother—whom she deeply loved, died, and not even when her leg was amputated. She saw emotions as a nuisance. They were complicated, unpredictable, messy, and something she simply wouldn't yield to. Crying was unthinkable. So when a tear escaped her eye today, I scarcely knew how to respond.

Unlike my mother, I live life through my senses. My shoes are rarely on, my feet connected to the cool earth. I bend to touch flowers and pause to feel the breeze on my skin. I've been climbing trees and wading in creeks since I first discovered them at the age of three. I love the outdoors. It is my home.

My mother is genuine, kind, thoughtful, overly compartmentalized, and logical—she works crossword puzzles in ink. It's safe to say that my mother and I travel in two very different orbits, but where our worlds do touch, there is love, and a mountain of understanding that's taken decades to build.

She lives in Southern Oregon. Her home sits on forested land along the Rogue River, about seven miles from town. The country road to her home is lined with fenced properties—home to cattle, horses, mules, goats, and sheep. It's rural, but neighbors know neighbors and are there for one another.

Two weeks before Mama's amputation, I came to live with her. Of her three kids, I was the one who swore I'd never move back to Grants Pass, yet here I was. The three of us had been raised to be responsible, but I was the oldest and had the most flexible lifestyle, so I moved home. As long as I had a laptop and Wi-Fi, I could continue to design websites and lead women's self-development circles.

I remember the phone call when Mama told me she'd be losing her leg. Without hesitation, I said that I'd be there for her. Of course, our family had no idea what her care would entail. Mama had melanoma. Surgery had removed the cancerous cells and radiation gave her a clean margin. Unfortunately, a follow-up biopsy of the radiated area never healed, and the open wound grew worse. In the year preceding the amputation, recurring infections plagued my mother, and months of antibiotics to treat the wound left her antibiotic-resistant. That's when her leg had to come off. Post-surgery, her attending physician explained that Mama had flatlined twice in the ICU.

Sepsis.

She was lucky to be alive.

The threat of dying from sepsis was very real. Mama was fragile and needed a home nurse, but we were at the height of a pandemic, so she got me. Mama arrived at her three-bedroom home on a gurney in a medical transport van. I didn't recognize her. She could have been anyone's mother. Mine was strong-willed, independent, and sturdy. The woman being wheeled into Mama's house was a ghost.

I was terrified.

## ANASAZI VISION

No one was allowed into her home for the first two months, not her neighbors, not her church community, not even my sister, who had also moved to Grants Pass. Everyone was "sheltering in place."

A nurse came to visit once a week, signing in upon arrival for her scheduled visit, dressed head-to-toe in a sterile clean suit and hood. To this day, I couldn't tell you what the nurse looked like.

Eventually, the facial mask mandate eased, and my sister could help more. She was working full-time though, so she took over the extra tasks of managing Mama's finances, appointments, medical transport, and picking up supplies and prescriptions.

In the year I've been here, I've learned to capitalize on the things that make Mama smile—for her sake and my sanity: cutting flowers from her garden, morning cocoa, and brushing her curly hair, because the reality of diaper changes, 2 AM medications, oxygen tanks, blood pressure checks, and complete dependence of one human being on another is a long list of wont tasks that no child, no matter how much they love their parent, looks forward to. I was exhausted. And yes, I cried.

And then it happened. In an attempt to alleviate the stinging nerve pain in Mama's stump, her doctor—who truly did care, prescribed a new medication. A side effect, however, was diarrhea. Mama was bedridden, and bathing her was interesting. It was a time-consuming process of laying plastic under her head, shampooing and rinsing her hair, washing and sponging her off, then rolling her to one side, removing the soiled sheet, scooting it towards her, laying down the fresh sheet and pad, rolling her onto it, then completely removing the soiled sheet and tucking in the fresh one. By the end of the laborious process, Mama required a nap.

## ANASAZI VISION

At the onset of the diarrhea, and diapers unable to contain it, the cumbersome task—now foul, was performed four to six times a day. Five days into the nightmare, both my mother and I were spent. She suffered from dehydration, discomfort, and being shoveled from one side of her bed to the other. I, from a lack of sleep, the sheer physical exertion, and the mound of things I still had to accomplish—because my tasks didn't stop just because Mama and her bed needed cleaning. I called her doctor, and he prescribed yet another medication for the diarrhea.

The day my mother cried was especially brutal. I remember waking to her moaning, the bedside clock reading 2:07 AM. With a sigh, I peeled back the thin hide-a-bed blanket, slipped on my robe, and covered the short distance to Mama's hospital bed. The monstrous bed had taken over her dining room, claiming most of the space once devoted to family meals, game nights, and the occasional dinner guest. Our once-joyful activities had been cleared to accommodate this chapter of Mama's life. There was no need to flip on a light to know what had stirred her awake. I could smell it. I was sure I could manage the chore in my sleep now, but for Mama's sake, I lit a dim light and leaned towards her.

"I'll be right back, Mama," I assured her, but before I could rise, she reached for my wrist. Her bony fingers were cool on my skin and conveyed what she could only whisper. "I love you too, Mama," I said. "We'll get you cleaned up and back to sleep in no time."

But she didn't let go.

"Mama?" I asked, feeling her squeeze my wrist firmly enough that I sat on the edge of the bed. Her bedding was disheveled, and she had somehow managed to tangle a blanket around her only leg.

"What is it, Mama?" She was silent. I placed her hand on her chest and ran my fingers through her hair. "I'll be right back. I promise."

As I stood and turned toward the stack of linens, I secretly prayed that Mama might find a comfortable position after her bed bath and nod off easily. I knew she was tired, and honestly, I couldn't take another night without sleep.

I gathered supplies and returned to Mama, washing her and changing her bedding. When I had finished, I kissed her forehead, turned off the light, and made my way to my bedroom. I'd been sleeping on the hide-a-bed nearby to hear her easily. But tonight, I needed to be in my own bed, where I wouldn't hear her, and finally get some rest. I loosened my robe, let it drop to the floor, and collapsed naked onto my bed.

The sound of a barking dog startled me awake. Had sleep actually lifted the exhaustion and brain fog, I might have realized that hours had passed and my mother was lying in a mess, but it took a moment to come awake. I slowly pulled myself from bed, stepped into panties, and moved like a wrecking ball down the hallway towards the dining room… and Mama. The smell met me before the disaster did. I inched closer; leaning in. She was distressed and the sight of her pained face gripped my heart and shoved a knife blade into it. I wanted to take her pain. I wanted to make it go away.

I reached for her shoulder and began to cry. Mama shouldn't have to suffer like this. When would that prescription finally kick in? I swallowed and could feel bile rising in my throat at the smell. I wanted to be strong for her; to be healthy for her. I needed to be strong and healthy. If I was, maybe she could be too. But I was failing. I was a wisp of myself—tired, too wrung out to be strong, let alone healthy. I could barely see straight, and it didn't help her. Nothing I was doing was helping her.

"Oh, Mama, I'm so sorry. I'll get you cleaned up," I said as I stood. "I'll be right back. I promise." But my words sounded hollow… scripted; the ones I'd repeat every time she needed to be cleaned. I felt like an imposter. Was I a daughter, a caregiver, an angel, a failure? Mama wasn't getting better and I knew it. Failure pretty well summed it up.

Mama stared up, her eyes fixed on me, heavy in their sockets. And then I saw it; a tear. Never in my life—not once, had I seen my mother cry.

I pushed myself away from the hospital bed. I couldn't bear to see—to feel, my mother's distress. I headed to the kitchen sink and turned on the water. Washing my hands—that would ground me, and bring me back to sanity. As I waited for the water to warm, I glanced out the window, and my eyes landed on the rafters of Mama's carport. A strange, wonderful, terrifying, exhilarating thought came to me: I wondered if the aging rafters could support my weight. The rafters would end all this. They'd bring sleep. Oh, glorious sleep. I stared at them affectionately. No child should have to choose between sleep and a parent. Screw this pandemic. I just couldn't do this alone. Not anymore.

Through tears, I turned towards Mama and then returned my gaze to the window. Could I do it? How would I do it? Familiar tears returned to my eyes. I wept for her—and me. At that, an insatiable burning filled my throat and I lowered my head just in time to vomit into the sink. Stunned, yet relieved, I cupped my hands beneath the stream of water—now warm, that had been flowing in the sink, sipped it, and then washed my vomit down the drain.

## ANASAZI VISION

"I'll be right back, Mama," I called over my shoulder, then toweled off my mouth and entered my room to pull on some clothes. I'd slept on top of my bed, and though wrinkled, it was made and the throw pillows were untouched. The small joy raised a smile on my face. I stooped to pick up my robe and hung it on the door peg. Oh, how I loved this room. It was my sanctuary—a sliver of solitude and restoration within this foreign world of prescription charts, bed pads, and pureed foods. Here, I could retreat and meditate, read, write, talk with a friend, or, at least, exhale.

It was a beautiful room. Its single window faced east and in the mornings, the rising sunlight would touch teardrop crystals I'd hung between swags of sheer fabric draped above my bed, casting a panorama of rainbows onto the walls.

The meditation cushion was well used. Books, crystals, and candles rested on the tidy shelves, and the framed photographs of friends and grown children, filled my lonesome heart with the memory that these people remained in my life, though I was far from them and the world they lived in.

I glanced at the wall clock: 7:20 AM. God, not another day. Please help me. I opened a dresser drawer and absently pulled on a sports bra and leggings, grabbed some tissue from the Kleenex box, and walked to my bathroom.

I stood at the sink for a moment, thoroughly dried my face with a hand towel, and took a deep, measured breath. Thirty seconds at a time is how I'd made it through the most intense moments of Army basic training. I could do this—I just needed to get through thirty seconds, and then, another thirty seconds.

I grabbed a can of disinfectant spray and medical gloves, then walked to the stack of linens, collected what I needed, and gathered supplies for a bed bath into a bucket. As I neared the dining room,

I reminded myself that I could do this. Like a parachute that had opened 500 feet from death, the mantra caught me. Hope that lived within some invisible speck drifting aimlessly in the air settled on my breath and found its path to my tired heart. It fed fresh light to my weary soul, propping me up.

The decision to place Mama in the dining room was a conscious one. Natural light, even on drizzly April days like today, streamed through the large windows, and from there, she could watch the world, and I could keep an eye on her. My siblings and I had decided that Mama did not belong tucked away in a bedroom, away from life. It was out here, where the cooking, laundry folding, and conversations lived that filled her heart and lifted her mood, which lifted mine.

Usually.

A canopy of white mosquito netting hung from the ceiling above her bed, separating her space from the adjacent living room. It cascaded onto the rails of her bed and to the hardwood floor. It was lovely—airy and feminine, and she often remarked that she felt like the "Queen of Sheba," sleeping beneath it.

Nearly a dozen orchids lined the windowsill and her most treasured mementos sat on the shelves of a built-in dining hutch, repurposed to hold medical equipment and hygiene essentials. The room was beautiful, and it delighted Mama. The orchids were my touch and had arrived with me from Portland.

Truthfully, there were few days when I didn't question my decision to move back home. Once the reality set in, the choice felt hasty—reckless, even. It was a gamble I seemed to be losing. This new life had taken me by surprise, crashing into me like a tsunami, sweeping away the life I had so carefully built. I had worked hard to create a life that allowed me space—space in my home, in my relationships, and in my day. There was a reason my life had the flexibility it did. Now, all of that was gone.

For months, I fought to hold onto the remnants, guarding the sacred parts of my old life. But the tsunami of change would not allow it—it took everything. This decision was demanding that I release my grip on everything familiar: my livelihood, my purpose, my relationships, and enter an unknown world. I could have gone quietly and surrendered to what was, but I resisted, caught in the tension between my past and future, never fully living in the present. Deep down, I knew that clinging to my old life, wishing things were different, was draining my soul. And yet, I held on, refusing to let go. It came at a cost—I suffered, and the suffering was of my own making.

Finally, after months of fighting reality, I let go. I softened. I began taking walks along the river, finding solace in its steady flow. I rested my soul on its grassy banks, watching blue herons, bald eagles, ospreys, egrets, and ducks as they went about their lives with calm patience. I kicked off my shoes and placed my bare feet on the earth, wading into the creek, and watching the clouds drift by. I listened to the crickets, frogs, and geese.

In the evenings, after washing the supper dishes, I slipped out the backdoor and walked the country road, listening to Sarah Blondin's meditation, "Accepting Change," on repeat. I sat on the front steps, pouring my heart out to the evening sky, and she sat with me, listening in quiet companionship.

I lay beneath the branches of an old mulberry tree, free of judgment, and it whispered its wisdom to me. Gently, it urged me to step out of my restless mind and notice the fertile ground I had been given. Mama wouldn't always be here, but while she was, I could embrace this time with her—be present, fill her days with joy.

Nature—my first mother—became my redeemer. I spoke with her often, feeling her strength and resilience, her rhythm and divine timing. She knew how to let go, unaffected by delays or imperfections. Slowly, my perspective shifted and softened. And at last, I embraced the days that made up my life.

And then, there were mornings like this.

I returned to Mama, comforted and cleaned her, then placed the soiled bedding into a large plastic bag, tied it off, and set it just outside the back door. I'd deal with it later. I pulled off the medical gloves, tossed them into the garbage, and washed my forearms and hands. When I looked in on Mama, she was already nodding off, so I stroked her hair.

"Sleep well."

# 2

# IN THE WAKE

With Mama bathed and settled, I slipped into the shower and ran the water warmer than usual. Streaming over my head and skin, I became aware of my body for the first time today. I felt detached—bereft from my own life. Naked, I leaned against the tiled wall and just let the water have me—hold me.

"Help me, please," I said, surrendering my tears to the rushing water. My life felt unremarkable. Unimportant. Unsustainable.

I hoped this thought would pass. I needed to be strong—needed to continue. A neighbor would be coming in tomorrow to relieve me, giving me a few hours of respite, and I fantasized about the sleep I knew this would afford me. Toweling off, I took inventory of my day. It would be a day like every other.

Until it wasn't.

Mama went into cardiac arrest, and the flurry of calls, paramedics, and neighbors' concern at the sight of them became the cyclone tearing through our day. My sister, Linda, arrived within minutes.

You know, it's strange what is remembered in the final moments of a person's life. The paramedics were working on Mama. Linda and I were seated, cupping her hand in ours. It still had color. I remember turning it and studying the veins beneath her skin. I stroked the back of her hand and thought of the million things these hands had done for me during her lifetime: they had washed my hair, ironed the dresses she'd made me wear, prepared my lunch, and reached across the passenger seat to protect me. They had sewn a comb into my bridal veil, and they had held my newborns—her grandbabies.

Her life passed before my inner eye. I saw her as a little girl, wild and carefree. Then, the moments of her life shuffled quickly through my vision, eventually slowing, until all I saw was her frail frame and her hand in mine. I gently brushed my cheek against her hand. Not a moment later, she was gone. My sister and I turned to one another in disbelief, and we wept. The paramedics noted the time, completed their work, had Linda sign some paperwork, and then carefully transferred Mama onto a gurney, wheeling her to an ambulance.

As dangerously close as Mama had come to death in the ICU, nothing quite prepared me for how quickly she actually passed, or the sudden realization that I had no parents on the planet. However fragile she was, she was our matriarch, and now she was gone.

Linda pulled me close and we held one another for a long minute on the driveway. I lowered my head to her shoulder and strengthened my hug. She had no idea that I had started the day wanting to take my life, and by its end, our mother had given hers.

In the days that followed Mama's death, family and her church community swooped in, assuring me that my only task was to rest, which I attempted with marginal success. My brother was the first of visiting family to arrive. As executor, Dan pulled me aside and asked if I would like to stay in the house. As picturesque as the setting is here, that was an easy "no." This was Mama's town, Mama's people, Mama's life.

He stayed ten days, arranging Mama's funeral and burial in the Veteran's cemetery alongside my father, and managing estate details. He was the last to leave town. Standing before the double doors of the airport, Dan hugged me longer than I had ever known him to hug another human.

"Words seem inadequate," he said. "You've been our hands and feet, Sis." I felt him take a breath. When he spoke again, it was slower and gentler.

"I know you gave up your life for Mom—for us, to do this. You need to take care of yourself now. Okay? I mean it, True. Don't just work. This has been a lot. I'm sure I don't know the half of it."

My brother was a meteorologist, and a fine one, at that. His specialty was hurricanes, and he was one of nine meteorologists at the National Hurricane Center in Miami. It's safe to say that, as a scientist and a lover of all things math and numbers, he navigated life using his intellect. I admired him as a man and looked up to him. He had known since childhood that he wanted to be a meteorologist. I had changed my major three times before deciding on journalism. What we had in common, was our love of nature. As kids, we were usually together and were either wet or covered in dirt.

Dan was an incredible human—caring and wise, and able to keep emotions in check. I had not known him to lead with his heart often or to extend such empathy. I wondered if his own grief had given rise to it. Standing there, I became keenly aware of his strong arms around me. I gave my weight to them, wept, and let my brother just hold me.

"Thank you," I said. "Thanks for being here—for handling arrangements, and being here for me. It means a lot. I love you."

"Of course, Sis," he said, looking at me. "I love you and am here for you. It's time you take care of yourself now. Okay?"

He pulled me near again, this time holding himself a little straighter, ready to step back into his own life. I squeezed him one final time, let go, and watched as he turned and entered the terminal. The drive home was silent as I pondered what caring for myself might look like.

Later, alone in Mama's house, I walked the simple floor plan. The house felt cool, so I eased up the thermostat. It was oddly quiet—still. Afternoon light streamed through the large windows and lit dust, swirled by my entry. The specks danced in the sunlight, unaware that life no longer lived here.

At the doorway between the kitchen and dining room, I paused. Mama's bed was gone. Church members had apparently moved it in my absence so this moment would be easier on me. I studied the vacant room and sighed. This was as easy as it was going to get, I suppose.

I mindlessly opened one of Mama's drawers: adult diapers. Oh, how I'd cursed these things. I could still feel the stinging resentment of changing diapers in my bones, and I felt embarrassed. I closed the drawer. What else needed attention? I scanned the lonely room.

"Oh crap, the orchids."

On cue, I picked up a dutiful pace and filled a bowl with ice cubes. This was a weekly ritual of mine, and each week, I would humor myself, as setting the ice cubes in the pots felt like hiding Easter eggs. I grinned, grateful for the small joy. These fine orchid ladies were holding up well, even with my neglect.

# ANASAZI VISION

Orchids are vain, you know. Many people cannot grow them because they don't understand them. These ladies need to be reminded of just how beautiful they are. With attention, and verbal compliments to prevent them from dropping their blossoms, and grown in the company of other orchids, they'll flourish.

I walked to Mama's closet and ran my finger along the clothing I knew well, then turned away. Honestly, I don't know why I stopped in the hallway. That only happened on really bad days. But there I was. Or, more accurately, there it was.

Before me was a familiar family portrait—likely no less than eighteen by twenty-four inches. It depicted my brother and me. I assumed because Linda wasn't in it, that I must be about four, with my brother at two. On desperate days, I would stand right where I now stood, and look into the eyes of that little girl. I would wonder what she wanted for the grown-up me—the sad me, the frustrated me, the one who felt trapped, and alone.

I would look long into her eyes. They were so bright, so full of wonder and curiosity. So blue. So eager to play—to giggle. She would pull me into her imagination and whisk me away. I would be with her, and this foreign world of medication and decline around me, nipping at my heels, would fade, and her bright eyes would fill me. Sometimes, I would find wild, spontaneous joy with her; sometimes wonderment at tiny seeds discovered in a simple pinecone—sometimes delight in dunking toast into hot cocoa, or swinging high from the branch of a tree. Wherever she took me, I always returned able to meet another day. In return, I would pour so much love into her—maybe because I knew what she would face in her life, and she would find a way to meet it. But mostly, because I love that little girl with all my heart. I love the woman she became. Standing there, I felt urged to speak to her.

"Bunny?" I said. "I'm not doing so well. This tiny world swallowed me whole. I don't know how to not be sad—how to not have one eye and ear open—how to not be on alert. I'm always 'on.' What happened to me—the fun me, the deep, soulful, inspired me? Where did I go? I don't know how to find my way back. I'm so lost, Bunny. Help me, please. Help me."

I then took a long walk along the country road, stopping to pet the horses and speak with a young couple I passed as I returned home. I stepped into the kitchen, prepared a simple meal, readied for bed, and pulled the covers over myself. Stillness punctuated the house as I lay there alone in the dark. A bamboo water feature in the living room was the only thing moving in this deserted place.

I thought of Mama and the wide arc our lives had traveled. There was a reason I'd left home; a reason I said I wouldn't return to Grants Pass and live near Mama. I didn't trust her. Not in an outright dishonest way, as though she'd taken something or deceived me, but in a covert dishonest way. Because she couldn't—or wouldn't—respond to life, she felt two-dimensional. Even as a kid, it didn't jive that my mother was always "fine." She may have considered overriding human emotions a superpower, but as a child living through my senses, it felt dishonest—counterfeit. And I didn't trust her because of it.

My siblings and I were forever guessing Mama's mood as if it were our job to figure it out. Was she fine or frazzled? Were we measuring up? Were we just meeting or surpassing her expectations? We were always "adjusting fire," looking for a clue we had Mama's approval—had her love. Lord knows how my father survived. Mostly, I didn't like the person I was when I was around my mother, ceaselessly seeking acknowledgment, approval, and affection; even as an adult—especially as an adult.

I left home and truth became my religion. I excavated life for truth and meaning. I pondered what lived in the murky waters beneath conversations and behavior. I developed a nose for things that didn't quite smell right. I would ask questions—I'd speak up. And, I excavated for truth, deep within myself. Truth became my North Star.

Unfortunately, trust wasn't so easy to excavate, especially when it came to Mama. Decades of unpacking my own "stuff," eventually opened a space where I could see my mother for the rare human she was, and the pain she endured keeping everything hidden, locked away from herself and everyone who loved her. It took years and a dozen trips back home to rewire the way I behaved around her. When the call came about her amputation—and my subsequent move back home, I prayed that I could hold my own and not get sucked back into seeking her approval.

I placed both hands on my chest and let out a deep sigh. What a ride the past year had been. Only my soul would have thought to plop me into four walls with my mother in the midst of a pandemic to open my heart to her. Oh yeah, she triggered me, and God knows I swore and squirmed, especially in the beginning. Seven months in, though, the winds changed and damned if it didn't soften me. I suppose I should trust that the Universe knows exactly what It's doing—knows how to time things just so, but death is a tricky thing, and tonight I just hoped for peace. I hoped that Mama was at peace… and at peace with me. I hoped she knew I loved her.

I turned my attention to my hands resting on my chest, and let my thoughts fall away. I paid attention to the rhythmic rise and fall of my ribcage. It expanded and fell with no effort on my part. It was a simple reminder that my heart knew to beat and my lungs knew to breathe. I sensed an intelligence living within them—living within me and everything that exists.

I then closed my eyes and sensed that life force energy moving in and through me—supporting and loving me without question or obligation. It felt light, full, intimate, and divine, and I spoke to it.

"This hasn't been easy. Still, thank you for the time with Mama. Help me grieve. Help me heal— whole and healthy. I feel spent; I feel like I've tapped into my Chi—my life force. Help me know how to restore it, care for myself, and feel vitality again. Help me come back to myself—to the peace, joy, and awareness I know myself to be. I am here, I'm yours, and I am listening. Thank you."

As I closed my eyes, it occurred to me that I was living a moment I knew would one day come. Mama was gone. My work here was finished. The only thing I needed to do right now, was sleep. But sleep didn't come that night. Or the next. After a third restless night, I asked Linda if I could sleep in her guest room. My sister and her pets were what I needed. I lay on her guest bed at 11:30 AM. She woke me at 10 AM the next day with tea. I smiled at the sight of her, sat up in bed, and propped a pillow behind my back.

"I know you want coffee, but I don't know the first thing about making it. I hope this will do," she said, putting a steaming mug in my hand. "Did you sleep well?"

"Yes, thank God, finally. Oh, this is good," I said, lowering the cup. It felt wonderful to be with my sister. Linda possessed a calmness that infected those around her. She could rise to the surface in situations like a buoy, knowing what to say to soothe, nurture, or ground people. A good thing that had come from my time at Mama's was that my sister and I had grown close—very close. I loved moments like this with her.

"Chai with a bit of milk. You know, almond milk," she said.

"Well, it's good. Thank you, and thanks for the room."

"It's here for you whenever you need it," Linda said. She looked at her mug thoughtfully and sipped from it. "You need anything, Sis?"

"Actually, do you have a minute?" I asked.

"Of course," she said, the interest rising on her face. Linda lowered herself to the corner of the bed and faced me. I took a long sip of my tea and then looked at her.

"I need to get away. Someplace where I can be alone for a while, let go of all this, and just take care of myself."

Linda's face softened and she smiled.

"I was hoping you'd say that. It's been a hard year for you. You need to unplug, rest, and take some time for yourself."

"Yeah, I know," I said, then swirled the remaining tea in my mug. I wasn't sure the enormity of the year had caught up with me yet. I was still in it. I'd been grieving with—and for—my mother all along. Now, a fresh grief had found me.

Still, as hard as it had been on me, Linda wasn't far from the impact zone. She'd assumed everything—business, medical, and financial—regarding Mama's affairs and was my rock. Dan, thankfully, supplied the funds for Mama's ongoing needs so I could focus on her round-the-clock care.

As resilient as I knew myself to be—knowing that I would be all right once I regained some balance and normalcy in life—I knew that Linda would right herself quickly. She had stayed with the Church, and it made her buoyant and sturdy.

"Where are you thinking?" she asked, with heightened curiosity.

"Someplace quiet. I need to be in nature, be still, and figure out what's next."

"I thought you might go back to Portland—back to your close friends. I know you miss them."

I looked at my sister fondly. Her male Shih Tzu puppy had wandered into the room and was at her feet.

"Yeah, maybe, but not yet," I said. "I'm thinking of heading to the San Juan. Some time on the river will do me good. You know I love it there."

She smiled.

"That sounds perfect."

"Yes. It's been three years. I might even take my fly rod," I said, smiling.

"That's even better! Oh, I'm so glad to hear it. Take all the time you need, Sis. Dan and I have things covered here."

"Thanks. The San Juan feels like home and it's calling me."

"I understand that. How about I bring your orchids over here and swing by Mom's periodically, just to check on things?" Linda asked.

"That'd be great."

"Okay. Let me know if there is anything else I can do to help you get out of town."

"A ride to the airport?"

"Done. You go do you, and don't give this place a second thought."

"Thanks, Sis. I love you," I said, then tossed back the covers, crawled towards her, and wrapped my arms around her. She laughed, which roused her puppy. He jumped onto the bed, toppling Linda onto me and igniting more laughter.

Over the next few days, I unsealed boxes that had been stored in Mama's garage and sorted through my belongings. I found my camping and fishing gear and felt alive for the first time in a long time. I knew this was the right choice.

I booked a flight from Medford, Oregon, to Albuquerque, New Mexico. Two weeks on the water, that's what my soul needed.

# 3

# FOUR CORNERS

It was early May, a perfect time to be on the river. From the grassy riverbank, I studied the current. Just above the tumbling waters, hundreds of tiny midges danced aimlessly in the late afternoon sun. Long shafts of low sunlight caught their miniature wings, magically transforming the insects into swirling specks of silver.

About a stone's throw downstream from where I stood was a beautiful stretch of water known as the Upper Flats. I knew it well. Here, a mile-and-a-quarter below the Navajo Dam on the San Juan River, the water calmed and spread to form several channels, pools, and back eddies in its main body. It is a favorite spot of mine for its deep holes, ledges, and flats, each guaranteed to be full of trout. This stretch of the river is also home to a fish known throughout New Mexico as the San Juan football trout because its thick, dust-colored belly is as fat as a football.

I scrambled up a boulder and spotted a reef of rock, just below the surface, that sent up a single wave. The dark green water fell upon it then circled back, dizzy on itself, forming a bottomless eddy. Only a hint of breeze was in the air, so I knew the fish would be feeding.

"He's in there, all right. Are you going to pull him out, or should I?"

I jumped with a start and turned to find an old fisherman, stuffed inside aged neoprene waders standing near the edge of the boulder. In one hand he gripped an Orvis bamboo rod, similar to one that my uncle taught me to cast with. His fingers were swollen and cracked, something too much stream water would do. Over a freshly-pressed cotton shirt, he wore a fully-zipped fly vest tacked with all the standard flies for this leg of the San Juan: orange midge larva in a size 18, emergers in gray, black, and olive, and of course, a variety of baetis.

He offered me a broad smile. "Go on, dear. He's in that slow backwash, fillin' his belly with bugs."

I glanced toward the water and back to the wrinkled face.

"You know your water," I said. "But, he's yours."

"Alright then," he agreed.

I carefully backed down from the boulder and onto the dirt trail. I watched the white-haired fishing veteran work his way downstream and out onto the broad shelf of slick rock covered in shallow currents. He knew where the trout would be, and why.

When he had reached the flats, he widened his stance to steady himself but wobbled on a loose stone. I leaped toward him, sure he was about to lose his footing in the brisk current. He managed to steady himself and then freed the fly that had been secured to the cork shaft of his rod. The fishing line glistened in the sun. I anticipated a cast. Instead, he raised his tanned face to the sky, kissed the antique rod, and added two feet of line to his roll cast. I sunk my hands into my pant pockets and looked on. God, it felt good to be on the water.

# ANASAZI VISION

The old man's first cast fell short of the foam, so he drew back his line from the pool and laid it down again, perfectly. He flashed me a grin after the trophy cast and I gave him a quick wave. In an instant, the trout struck the artfully placed fly with a fury. My fingers itched for my fly rod. I retrieved my gear from the tree I had propped it against and set out to find my own fishing hole.

Spring runoff from the Rockies had brought high waters, changing the face of the stream over the years. I had my heart set on a generous hole where I had caught and released a beauty three years ago. I hoped it hadn't been destroyed.

In a rolling river such as the San Juan, the trout tend to seek shelter in the slower currents where they don't have to exert any more energy than necessary to load up on bugs. I knew there wouldn't be a single fish in the middle of the stream. Instead, they would be hugging the bank or in one of the newly formed eddies behind a rock, out of the swift-moving current.

Five yards from my jackpot hole, my head snapped toward the sound of a trout splashing back into its watery bath after a skyward leap at the insects flitting above the surface. My hands shook with anticipation as I slipped on my waders and boots, glancing around to decide which fly to tie on.

A midge hatch speckled the warm air but the water was clear, so I opened my wallet-sized fly box—a gift from my late husband, and picked through it until I found an annelid. High water forces these little worms from the crevices between river rock and into the current, making them easy prey for hungry trout. I tied an orange one onto my leader and secured an additional red one to my cap.

I took hold of my fly rod, and it came to life in my hand. Without so much as a thought, it was above my head, sweeping through the sunlight in a metronomic cadence as natural to me as breathing. The years it had been out of my hand seemed to vanish.

My first cast coasted to a soft landing on a quiet bath of shallow water and disappeared beneath its surface. I stepped into the chilly water and the cold water washed over my feet, instantly cooling the lightweight waders pressing against my thick socks. It felt delicious.

With another step, the water lapped onto my calves, and my felt-bottomed boots gripped the slippery rocks beneath. I gave a little flick of my wrist and the fishing line gently rolled above the current, coaxing the fly upstream. A few more steps and I was in an isolated world of floating green.

This was my third trip to Four Corners—an area located in the southwestern section of the United States, named for the point where the state boundaries of Colorado, Arizona, Utah, and New Mexico meet.

I first came to Four Corners seven years ago. My husband had died from Leukemia a few months earlier, and I traveled to San Juan for some solitude and fishing. Roger and I had always talked about stealing away to the San Juan River to fly fish. He never made it, so I was there for both of us that year.

I'd had my heart set on a stretch of water in southeast Utah called Grand Gulch. It's a labyrinth of rocky terrain in the heart of Cedar Mesa, bordered to the south by the San Juan. The tributary flows across the high mesa, goosenecks some fifty-six miles, and finally pours into the San Juan. The west-flowing river then zigzags another sixty miles through deep canyon gorges, past Mexican Hat, and eventually empties into Lake Powell. Spring runoff can lead to Class III rapids through Grand Gulch, but off-season water levels are generally low and rapids are few.

It's gorgeous country, with buttes, mesas, and canyons as far as the eye can see, in hues of soft reds, ambers, rich loam browns, and bleached tans. It's tough water to fish, though, completely unforgiving and not very generous.

I'd spent many summers of my life in trout streams. The year I lost Roger, I brought a new Sage fly rod with me that I was eager to put to the test. Feeling ready for a challenge, I decided to take on Grand Gulch.

The hike into it was quite an adventure. I passed a remarkable dry falls, where water, when it had once thundered through, had carved out hollows and holes, staining the walls with ribbons of purple and gray. High above me on the canyon walls were tiers of milky-white and pink-colored rock, faulting into layered ridges. The pinyon and junipers spread their fragrance throughout the canyon, rising out of the parched ground in contorted shapes, their gangly roots reaching into the cracks and crevices in the rock.

After hours of hiking in the sun, the beauty of the country turned ugly. By noon, tremendous heat was radiating off the rock walls. I decided to turn back. A cloud of biting gnats swarmed just above the ground and attacked my unprotected legs. Finally, out of desperation, I snapped a branch from a pinyon pine and began swatting my legs with it to ward off the pests. I had seen no fish, which made the hike out of the canyon even less tolerable.

My heart was pounding and my muscles were beginning to fatigue. I was particularly concerned about dehydration, as I could feel its effects creeping up on me. I ducked into a thin overhang of shade to drink water from my Camelback. As I was ringing out my bandana to tie it around my forehead again, I saw something move on the far side of the canyon.

I wasn't alone.

Closer observation revealed a figure—a man, hidden among the rocks, slowly picking his way along the ridge. He was level with me, but far enough to put a soccer field between us. I took a short sip of tepid water and watched him carefully choose his steps. From my vantage point, I could see no sign of an established trail, so I scanned ahead of him to see if I could determine his destination. As far as I could tell, he was heading toward a dead-end ledge, or so it appeared. Needless to say, he held my attention.

I put down my gear and took another sip. What was he doing here? He wasn't a fisherman—of that I was sure. He had no fishing gear. The man pushed on, too sure of his steps to be a novice hiker. A few minutes went by as I cooled in the shade, slowly sipping my water. He was at the dead-end ledge. A bead of sweat crept its way down my cheek. I untied my bandana, then poured a trickle of water into my cupped hand and splashed it onto my face. I dabbed it dry and retied the bandana around my forehead. When I refocused my eyes on the ridge, he was gone. I scoured the canyon wall. There was no sign of him.

I backtracked the pencil-thin trail, criss-crossing every possible intersection. There was no one. Dear God, where was he? Had he fallen? I stepped close to the drop-off and looked into the deep canyon. It made me queasy. I returned my gaze to the beige wall, examining the ledge again, looking for something—anything. My heart was pounding fast now. Where was he? My eyes swept upward and I froze in an instant.

"Oh, my God!" I'd been looking at eye level—too low. There, about twelve feet above the trail, were four or five masoned stone buildings tucked under a cap rock dome. He was wandering through them. But how had he gotten there? How had the buildings gotten there?

I'd never seen anything like them and had certainly never come across ruins in America. Lewis and Clark historical sites dotted Oregon, but they are barely a century old. These looked ancient. Just how long had they been there, anyway?

Curiosity trumped my plans to fish. I knew I couldn't miss this opportunity to check out the ruins. Exactly how far the cliff rooms were by foot, I couldn't tell. I only knew that I had to get to them. If the man had found his way to the cave, so could I. I broke down my fly rod and stowed it near the trail with a note, checked my Camelback for water and fly vest for food, then slipped it back on and set out. As I neared the drop-off ledge and my vantage point shifted, I could see that the canyon rock face formed a large arc. The man I'd seen had hiked in from the South. I'd be hiking from the North.

I spent the remainder of my afternoon picking my way across the jagged rocks toward the cave. It was a weary, meticulous trek, keeping one eye on my goal while pinned close to the canyon wall, selecting just the right rock to grab or step on. I dared not look down as I worked my way across the ridge.

The heat held by the rocks radiated off the steep wall face. The temperature was tolerable, but I continued to sweat. Fat beads of sweat formed along my hairline and crept down my face, neck, and back, but with my hands gripped onto the rocks, I had no way to swipe away the pesky beads, which made the trek even more nerve-wracking.

The night was closing in when I pulled myself into the alcove. My time as a fitness trainer was still paying off, and I was glad for it. There was no sign of the man or animals—only rodent scat, which eased my concern that big cats might frequent the area.

The first thing I noticed was how cool the cave was, and how wonderfully soothing it felt to my skin. I was tired, but that soon gave way to excitement. I was here. I sized up the alcove, estimating it to be sixty feet wide and fourteen feet high. Towards the back of the cave was an impressive row of neatly mortared rooms made of various-sized beige-colored stones and clay mortar. I admired the craftsmanship and was sure it must be ancient. A few of the walls had collapsed, but it was remarkably well preserved. The structure had small windows, no larger than a basketball, and extremely low, narrow doors that linked the rooms. Who had built these? And why here, high on the canyon wall?

Since daylight was thin, I decided I'd better look for a suitable place to bed down for the evening. The floor of the smallest room would do. I sat, removed my fly vest, and opened its pockets. My supplies amounted to a bag of almonds, trail mix, a granola bar, a first aid kit, fly-casting paraphernalia, and a half-full Camelback. I sighed. Had I been over-confident? Was this reckless?

I was no stranger to demanding conditions. Fourteen years of Army bivouacs and five months thru-hiking the Pacific Crest Trail found me sleeping on every ground surface imaginable. But it had been a while and I was out of practice. I'd spent the past several months in the leukemia ward at Wilford Hall on Lackland Air Force Base with my husband. He was active duty Air Force—a flight surgeon, and, in the wake of a leukemia diagnosis and then not surviving the bone marrow transplant, my own Army commander placed me on "reserve status," so I could focus on my (then) teenaged children, manage estate details, and grieve. This first trip to Four Corners was my way of taking care of myself. I smiled. Roger would have appreciated finding these ruins.

The ground of the cave was hard and unforgiving. Fortunately, night came fast and exhaustion pulled me easily into sleep. Staying asleep, however, was the real challenge. Since Roger had died, I'd only been sleeping four, maybe five hours each night.

I lay there until it became apparent that it was going to be another short night. From my pocket, I pulled a tiny flashlight, and carefully made my way to the belly of the alcove where a half-moon, hanging low in the sky, could be seen. I shined the light around until I was satisfied I was safe, then clicked it off and stood in the dim moonlight.

I had no experience with grief, and losing Roger thrust me into an unfamiliar territory I had few skills to navigate. I'd never lost anyone close to me before. My father and grandmother would soon follow, but when Roger died, I had no idea what grief was or where it would take me.

Without skills to navigate grief or an awareness of the internal terrain that I would cover, I saw grief as something to steer clear of at any cost. It felt like a deep, dark hole—one I was terrified of falling into. I had no idea where I'd go, how long I would stay, or if I'd even come back.

Standing in the alcove, I looked at the dark canyon and wondered who had lived in this high mountain perch. Why had they chosen such an inaccessible spot? Did several families live in the rooms, or was it generations of a single family? What did they do with their days? What troubles did they have? Which one of them stood right here because their troubles kept them awake at night too?

The thought was fleeting, but I pictured a Pueblo mother, her spirit heavy with grief over the loss of a child, staring into the mournful night. The image sent a wave of anguish crashing through me, tearing at my heart. In my exhausted state, my own sorrow spilled over. My grief-stricken heart was so full that her imagined tears broke my levee, unleashing a flood of my own.

For weeks, I had been paddling with one oar—coming precariously close to the levee's edge. Now, the flood carried me over the falls and I took a nosedive, sinking like a chunk of cement into my sorrow. Nothing could stop this pent-up grief.

I dropped to my knees and fell onto my back, pinned there by a loss that could no longer be shushed. I sobbed. I wailed like a mad woman. I prayed for my man to come back. I yelled at the dark. Was anyone listening? I needed my husband. I cried and cried, and begged the dirt to swallow me. I curled into a fetal position and sobbed.

That's when I detected a hint of stillness within. It fluttered—barely noticeable at first, and then, softly, it came into my awareness and quieted me. As I became silent, I felt a presence—not next to me, but in me. I can't say that it was God. This didn't feel like the God the priests had warned me of. This was a Presence, and it felt soft, yet strong. It felt big—immense even, and yet, it felt as though it was nesting in my heart, like a tiny bird's nest, cradling life.… my life. I felt a sensation of calm, and it reminded me of a place I couldn't quite pinpoint—someplace familiar, yet far away. This far away, familiar place felt like I belonged there. It felt like home; safe and secure, where I was loved and anything was possible.

I lay motionless for several minutes. The Presence remained and comforted me. Eventually, I stirred and sat, hugging my knees, in the dirt. Roger crossed my mind, and as I sat there, recalling him, I felt a new presence. A chill passed through me and I detected Roger's aftershave. It took a moment to register the scent, but there was no question that it was his. And then, I sensed my lover, my companion, my husband, and the father of our children, near me. He kneeled, facing me, and in my mind's eye, I ran my finger over his lips. I traced his closed eyelids, his brow, cheek, and chin, and squeezed the lobe of his ear, just the way that made him smile. I brushed a lock of blonde hair from his forehead and smiled at this handsome man.

I then sensed his eyes open, and felt his gaze meet mine—his crystal blue eyes piercing and steady. The warmth of his breath enveloped me, and I felt his touch—his caress that had intoxicated me from day one. He kissed my lips, and a shiver ran through me. I felt his love, his patience, and the spark of our eternal flame.

He moved, sat beside me, and we spoke of life, of love, and of letting go. He told me he was happy and that I wouldn't believe him if he told me of all that awaited us beyond.

"I know. It can seem like we're insignificant specks of dust in the galaxy," he said. "But that's not true. Each soul is unique. Each gains its own unique experience, adding to the larger expression of life itself."

I smiled again, hearing his voice, and the passion in it.

"We're stars. No, really—it's true. We are made of the components of heaven. We are stardust. Did you hear me? We're made of the same stuff as stars. We are light beings. If you could see things the way I do now, you'd see just how much light you're giving off. You are beaming with light right now."

I imagined seeing myself the way he was seeing me and leaned on his shoulder.

"All souls were made in the same moment, so technically we're all the same age. What varies is the number of lifetimes we've lived and the experiences we've grown through."

I listened, amazed at what he was saying.

"We grow on both sides of the veil," he continued. "I love my life on the other side; I'm constantly growing and learning. But here's the deal," he said, and paused. "We choose to come to Earth because of the contrast it offers. See, fear doesn't exist where I am now. Earth is the one place in the universe where love and fear are present. We choose to come here because we can grow so much faster with contrast—with the dicey dance between fear and love. It makes for exponential growth, so we choose to keep coming back to Earth." He smiled.

"Really?"

"Yep. What's hysterical about the whole thing is that when we're on Earth, we keep dreaming of the other side, and how wonderful heaven seems without contrast—without all the human emotions and choices to be made here. You're navigating love and fear, but it truly leads to exceptional growth."

He went on to say that we choose what experiences we want to have each lifetime; the lessons we want to learn, and the people who would best allow all that to occur. He said that we have a life path and an exit point—that there are no mistakes when someone leaves this planet—that the time and means of death was on their life path. We could take solace in that… and that those who pass are happy on the other side. Sometimes the way that person dies is for the growth or life lesson of those left behind.

I told him that the kids and I miss him so much. He replied that he could see that from the other side, but it felt different for him. He immediately started living a new life there and didn't feel sorrow or grief.

He then placed his arm around my shoulder and pulled me close.

"You are not alone, Darlin'. If you ever feel that way, remember it's just a thought. I didn't 'go' anywhere. I'm right here," he said and placed his other hand on my chest. "Don't you dare let our best memories break your heart."

I began to cry and attempted to dab the tears from my face with the back of my hand.

"Souls can't die," he said. "The way it works on the other side is kind of like a flashlight. When you think of me, I see your thought as a light, and can energetically be with you, just as I am right now. When you think of me, I become aware of you. It's how souls connect. However, this little sit-down of ours won't always happen. Your 'flashlight' was blinding tonight, like the beam of the Lexor in Vegas. I couldn't miss it. I came because you needed this. I needed it too, actually. Do you have questions for me?"

I looked into his eyes: flirty, ambitious, wise. This man knew me better than anyone on the planet. He knew how to crack me up with his crazy antics, how to tease out the best in me or talk me off a ledge. Oh, how I loved this man.

"How do I pull the pieces of life together again?" I asked. "I feel fragmented, lost. And the kids… what do they need?"

"Feel what you need to feel. Life—living, dying, failing, rising… and doing it all over again, is the essence of the human experience. You're soul, yes, but you've got to be human. You came to Earth to be human—to grow, learn, expand. So let it happen. As far as the kids go, never let them guess or wonder if they are loved. If they know that—if they feel your belief in them—and you allow them to gravitate toward whatever ignites their souls, they'll be just fine."

We stood, faced one another, and hugged.

"Darlin', you've got a lot of life ahead of you… you have no idea. I can't tell you about it, of course, but you'll bring so much light to this world. Remember, I'm with you, and you are so much more than you believe you are. Don't you forget that."

I felt him kiss my forehead and he was gone.


I awoke in the morning on my back, staring up at the uneven roof of the cave, blackened by long-ago fires. In the narrow chasm of Grand Gulch, the early morning sun had touched the massive cliffs that plunged to the canyon below. I felt like a newborn, opening my eyes to this world for the first time.

I sat up in the dirt. Breakfast was a granola bar and a handful of almonds. I was spent, but felt a calmness that I hadn't known since childhood. I suppose at that moment, the cave became sacred ground to me. Hiking out of the canyon that cool morning, everything in my life seemed changed—though, in reality, nothing had changed but me. I made a silent pact with myself and God that I would return to the San Juan often. I'd been back just once—three years ago, so this trip seemed especially poignant. Mama was gone. It had been seven years since that sacred night with Roger in the cave. The San Juan wanted me, and I was happy to give myself to her.

# 4

# SAN JUAN CAMPSITE

I had worked my jackpot hole for two sweet hours and watched Venus rise in a pale blue sky. I stole a long look at the San Juan River and felt content. It was a moment I wanted to hold onto forever.

By 6:30 PM, I had caught and released eight gorgeous trout, and not a single thought of Grants Pass had crossed my mind. Stepping out of the water, I pulled off my boots and waders, stowed them in my backpack, and slung it over my shoulder. I cinched my cap tight over my long, dark ponytail, broke down my fly rod, and made my way up the footpath toward the rental car.

It was a half-mile hike and not overly steep, but the 5,600 foot elevation of the San Juan, unexpectedly caught up with me. In my haste to get on the water after flying into Albuquerque and the drive north, I had forgotten that it could take a couple of days to acclimate to this high desert. Quickly winded, I realized I had completely overestimated my lung capacity.

Two young fishermen, effortlessly outpacing me on the trail, started to pass but paused when they heard my heavy breathing. They offered to carry my backpack, and, seeing their genuine intent, I accepted. It turned out they were brothers who lived not thirty miles from Powder, Montana—my birthplace. Grateful, I handed them my pack and waved a thank you. When I finally reached the parking area, I found my backpack hanging from a post with a wildflower tucked into an outer pocket. I glanced around, but the brothers were nowhere in sight. In the fading sunlight, I checked my watch and realized I needed to hurry back to my campsite.

Night was nudging the sun from the sky when I crawled into my tent to unroll my sleeping bag. It took only moments, but in my brief absence, the pale sky magically turned pink. I backed out of my tent and read the sky. It had all the makings of exploding into the fiery palette that draws both poets and photographers to this land.

Anticipating a show in the sky, I scooted onto the hood of the car and leaned back against the windshield, slipping my hands behind my head and gazing at the sky. Pink clouds streaked with orange stretched the length of the sky above me. I watched with delight as a shimmering glow seeped between the apricot-colored clouds and ignited the sky into a blazing heavenly inferno as if an angel had accidentally toppled pots of molten gold onto heaven's floor.

I lay there for a long time, watching the subtle transformations and breathing in the evening air, which carried the scent of juniper and my neighbor's campfire smoke. A single cricket chirped, and then a second. Soon the air was filled with their mesmerizing primal chant. From far off, distant coyotes joined the ancient song. I felt wonderful. This was the desert I remembered. The desert I loved.

Darkness, unwilling to dally another moment, smothered the last bit of color smoldering on the horizon. At that, the coyotes' calls turned long and thin, announcing that night had arrived. Their primitive call swept me away. Half a day in the desert and I had nearly forgotten Oregon. Somehow, none of that mattered right now.

I eased off the car and, after an extended shower in the campground's ladies' room, I wormed my way into my chilly sleeping bag. My eyes ached from tying on flies and the three-and-a-half-hour drive north from Albuquerque. I squirmed deeper into my sleeping bag and dreamed of sleep. But the clouds had parted and a huge moon, just a sliver shy of full, had risen in the night sky. Its bold light filtered through the tent roof. I scooted myself towards the tent door and poked my head out, just enough to see the moon.

On either side of me, the campfires were dwindling to embers, and the surrounding camps had grown silent. Smoke from the fires hung over the tents, dense and lingering like thick soup. The stillness of the desert was interrupted only by the gentle rustling of cottonwood leaves, stirred by a wandering breeze. I turned toward the sound, watching as the white moonlight shimmered off the leaves, which swayed and danced aimlessly in the soft, night wind.

I gazed up at the moon and considered why I'd made the long trip. Of course, there was fishing—always there was fishing. What set this trip apart was that I'd be doing something monumental—at least, it felt that way to me. I'd be doing a vision quest.

Nowadays, we scarcely hear of vision quests, but in ancient times, each young person within endogenous tribes was encouraged to seek a sacred vision. Visions were known as powerful medicine, that provided the young person with the discernment and direction they would need throughout their lifetime. A vision quest was an extraordinary inner journey—done in solitude, that could last from a few days to several weeks. They frequently took the form of a retreat into nature, away from the life of the village, where one would sit in quiet introspection and call forth a sacred vision, which would reveal their service to the tribe or their life's path.

When the idea of a vision quest first came to me, I wasn't sure I wanted to do one. I was opening boxes of camping gear in Mama's garage and had the thought. I told myself it was unrealistic. Vision quests were done as a rite of passage—a coming of age. I was forty-three. Why seek a vision now? What good would it do me in my forties? But the thought persisted. It worked its way into my imagination, and I found myself noodling on the idea until it became possible, maybe even doable. I gathered supplies for it—a journal, a drum, some sage as if I was truly going to embark on one. It was the oddest thing. Finally, I decided that the quest wanted to happen and I'd best agree to it. Once I'd committed, I was all in.

What I knew of vision quests I'd learned in Joseph Campbell's books and from an elective college course, where we'd identified North American native tribes and studied their cultures. After taking the course, I attempted a vision quest but had no idea what I was doing. It became a guessing game that fizzled out.

Once I decided to embark on a vision quest during this trip, I went online to learn what is typically done—and perhaps more importantly, what isn't done—on a vision quest.

I decided to hold mine at a place called Hovenweep. While exploring the southeastern corner of Utah during my second trip to Four Corners, three years ago, I came across a six-foot boulder in the Hovenweep National Monument park and thought at the time that it felt special—sacred.

I penciled out a few simple ceremonies that I might perform. Admittedly, I'd only read about such practices or studied them in class, and going into it, all I truly knew was that a vision quest was a time of solitude and surrender. I had determined that a successful quest wasn't so much about the ceremonies themselves as it was about the open-hearted faith with which they were performed. I could do that.

I was excited. Still, questions and doubts assailed me on the drive up from Albuquerque. I wondered if I was too old to call in a vision. Was I prepared? Would it feel anything like the presence I'd experienced at Grand Gulch seven long years ago? If so, could it find me again? I'd been meditating for several years and often reached a state of inner stillness. Yet, how could I be sure any of that would translate—or have any correlation—to calling in a vision? I was secretly worried.

Lying there in my tent, mulling all this over, I began to have the oddest sensation that I was being watched. Not by just one person, but by many people. I had no idea what to make of it, so I lay very still. Then, in my mind's eye, I saw boys and girls, men and women—likely a hundred of them: hunters, farmers, priestesses, warriors, and medicine women and men, in the dark.

Who they were? I have no idea. But, they slowly drew closer, until they encircled me, standing shoulder to shoulder. I felt their presence, their power, their strength, and love, and it shored up my courage, faith, and hope. Whoever these people were, they were with me—supporting me. Protecting me.

I woke up once during the night. It was dark and I was lying on my side, my head still outside the tent door. I inched myself just inside, coaxed myself back to sleep, and woke to sunlight and a pair of dark eyes studying me inquisitively.

"What the…?" I queried, in my half-dream state, "Eyes in my tent? How can there be eyes in my tent?" It was a preposterous idea. Who had heard of such a thing? I rolled over, pulling a corner of the sleeping bag onto my shoulder, pondering the strangeness of the idea.

"Wait," I thought. "I am awake and those are eyes!" I flipped onto my back and opened my eyes. In an instant, it hit me—doggy breath.

"What the…?"

That is when the calamity came into focus. Eyes. Dark ones. Set in fur. Black fur. Black fur? It was a dog and it was hanging over me, panting. Drool had collected along its gum line, ready to dribble. There was nowhere for me to go.

"Oh God!" I yelled.

The startled dog pulled its head away. I flipped onto my belly in time to see a puppy take two or three steps backward and then bolt into the brush.

"Damn dog," I called after it, raising my voice so I could hear it over my pounding heart. Exactly how much drool had landed on me, I couldn't know. I rolled onto my back, pawing at my face. My heart was a wreck—no doubt, one of the more unpleasant ways I have been pulled from sleep.

I took a deep breath and then listened for other sounds of life. A camper was stirring on the other side of the dirt road and a couple of birds were chirping. No sign of the dog. I found my jeans and pulled them on in the sleeping bag, then shimmed out of it to pull on chilly socks and a shirt. I tied on one hiking boot and, discovering the mate missing, backed out of the tent to track it down.

## ANASAZI VISION

I figured the puppy had probably run off with it to God-only-knows-where. Sure enough, I found it under the camp table, the heel gnawed on. I pulled it on over my dirty sock and sat on the camp table to tie the slobbery lace. This was not how I had hoped to start the morning of my vision quest.

I visited the outhouse and returned to my campsite. The sun was up, still low in the east. I looked up to study the sky—cloud cover. What luck. Conditions were perfect for the four-mile hike to the boulder today.

Hovenweep was an hour's drive from here. I figured the hike would take another ninety minutes, plus time to check in at the ranger station. That would mean I should break camp and leave here about…

"Excuse me," called a voice from behind me.

The interruption startled me, and I nearly slipped from the table. My head turned toward the voice, and found a man about twenty, in a red University of Utah sweatshirt and sweat pants, standing beside my car.

"Excuse me," he repeated, almost apologetically. "Sorry to disturb you, but I'm looking for a black lab. A puppy. Have you seen…"

"Yeah, she's been through here," I said, straightening myself.

"He," the man replied.

"Excuse me?"

"He. Smurf is a male."

My heart was still recovering and he wanted to argue.

"Smurf? What kind of name is that?" I asked without weighing my words.

"A perfectly good name," the man shot back.

Aw, crap, I had done it again—spoken before coffee, and I could see there was no room to back out of this one without an apology.

"No, no. I'm not trying to insult you. I'm just wondering who names their dog Smurf. I mean…" The apology hadn't come off as smoothly as I had hoped, and there were clear signs that I was digging myself a grave.

Suddenly, there was a commotion behind the outhouse. We both turned toward the racket, just as the puppy circled around it and came bounding toward the man. This changed the focus of our strained exchange, and I was instantly glad to see the dog. I didn't really expect the man to forget the would-be apology, but I was hopeful the puppy would at least warm his mood. I was quick on the uptake.

"Well, there's your answer," I said.

The man braced himself against the front fender of my car, anticipating the impact of Smurf's arrival. The dog skidded to a stop and then attempted to leap on his master.

"Down, Smurf," he commanded.

"Yep, you've got yourself a puppy there," I said, then laughed.

Since I was dressing myself when company arrived, I wasn't quite sure what I had on and what I didn't. I swept my hand across my head to determine whether I was wearing a cap. I felt bed hair.

"My last dog was a Chocolate Lab," I said, as I slid from the camp table and slowly walked towards the car, keeping my eye on the puppy. "I'm True. True North," I said. "Sorry for the misunderstanding."

"Quite alright. I didn't mean to startle you. They call me CJ," he said. "Talk about names? How'd you get that one? Were your parents smoking something?"

I laughed.

"No, they weren't that clever," I answered, raising a generous smile. I slid my hands into my pockets and, considering our rocky start, thought a story might lighten the air.

"About ten years ago, I hiked the PCT. It's a long trail that runs from Mexico to Canada. Anyway, friends gave me a ride to the Southern Terminus where I signed the hiker's register. After our goodbyes, I began looking around for the trailhead."

CJ was looking at me and appeared interested, so I continued.

"They told me to follow the road we drove in on, and I would find it. Well, the next thing I knew, they pulled up alongside me and asked what I was doing. Apparently, I had already passed the trailhead. So, I turned around and eventually found it. Later, I learned they had named me True North, so I could find my way to Canada because I couldn't even find the trailhead. True North became my trail name. When I finished the trail, I legally changed my name. Trust me, it doesn't mean I don't get lost," I added, grinning.

"Cool name and that's a great story," he said, lifting the first smile I had seen on his face. "Are you camped here for long?"

"No. I'm leaving this morning. How about you?"

"I'll be here another two days, I think." He appeared puzzled. "This is Thursday, right? Imagine that. I'm losing track of time. Bad sign."

I thought it funny—losing track of time was the very thing I was hoping to do.

CJ was more man than boy, though not by much. Perhaps he was a student at the University of Utah, I guessed from his sweatshirt.

"True, do you drink coffee?" he asked, combing his unruly hair with his fingers. It was the first clear view I'd had of his face. His features were almost delicate, unlike his first words to me. A gymnast, maybe?

"Uh, yeah," I answered. "But I'm fasting today."

"Fasting? You don't have food?"

"No, no. It's nothing like that," I reassured him.

"Oh. Well, mind if I get myself a cup?" he asked, his smile noticeably warmer.

"No. Go right ahead."

I wasn't sure I really wanted the company. I was anxious to get on the road and hike to the boulder before the day turned warm. He turned to retrieve his dog and I ducked into the tent, slipped on my cap, quickly threaded my hair into a loose braid, and secured it with a hair tie. At least, now I was dressed.

"Come on, boy," he called.

Smurf lifted his head toward his master without getting up. He looked reluctant to go. CJ and I exchanged glances. Mine said I wasn't exactly keen on having the puppy stay here and chew on something else I might need. CJ persisted. The puppy leapt to his feet and onto the path in front of his master. With each step toward their camp, CJ labored to move the gangly body of his puppy, who had pressed against his legs. When they returned, Smurf was on a leash.

"We're right over there," CJ said, pointing towards the next camp with his coffee cup. "Are you from New Mexico?"

I noticed that he was glancing at the license plate on the rental.

"Oh no, Portland Oregon is home."

I was still weighing the cost of visiting with a stranger. Did I want company? With the apology out of the way, I remained warily neutral. I frankly have no patience for chatty conversations of no substance.

"Long way from home," he said.

"I suppose. And you?" I said politely, still weighing the cost of a conversation.

"Oh, I'm from here. Well, not far from here. Blanding. Ever hear of it?"

"Of course! I'm headed in that direction this morning. Hovenweep." His answer tipped the teetering scale toward a conversation. A short visit. What could it cost? Twenty minutes?

"Oh yeah? I've been there a couple of times," he said. "Not many campsites. But then, not many people camp there either." He lifted the leash so I would notice it, and motioned toward the mirror on the driver's door of the car.

"May I?" he asked.

I shrugged my shoulders. It was a rental. CJ looped the leash over the mirror and sat on a bench across from me at the camp table. Campers in the park were beginning to stir. At the campsite across the road, an older man was breaking twigs to be used as kindling for a morning fire.

"You think that will hold him?" I asked, eyeing the pup as he panted and walked in dizzy little circles. CJ didn't seem concerned.

"Oh, he'll settle down. What takes you to Hovenweep? If you're planning to camp there, there aren't many facilities—not even trash cans. You have to pack out your trash." He paused. "Are you going to see the ruins?"

"Not exactly," I answered, testing the interest on his face. "I saw the ruins on my last visit. I'm going there to do a vision quest." As soon as I had said the words, I could feel them hanging in the air. Clearly not what CJ expected I would say.

"Really?"

"Yeah. I've been thinking about it. I love the high desert and I've had some amazing experiences here. I just thought it was time to have one. Back in college, I did something of a vision quest, but didn't really know what I was doing—just kind of made it up as I went along." I realized that I was sharing more than I had planned, so tested his expression again.

"My mother just passed away," I said. "It's been a hard year, so thought I'd come here and do a vision quest."

"You can do that? Have more than one vision quest in a lifetime?"

His question surprised me. I had never thought about it in that way. Could it be I had already had my vision quest? Is that what I had done years ago? Suppose you only get one go at it and, if you fail? Is that it? Had I wasted my one opportunity? His question made me wonder. As I sifted through the concerns his inquiry had raised, it occurred to me that, perhaps, I'd had a vision—only it had been so insignificant that I hadn't paid attention. Had my expectations been too high coming into this? Heck, maybe I wasn't going to have a vision because I couldn't.

"I don't know," I answered, bewildered.

"I'm not sure either. I was just wondering, that's all." He placed his coffee cup on the table and passed the dog a fleeting glance. Smurf had collapsed in the dirt with his chin resting on his fat paw.

I was actually pleased that CJ had come to visit. He was easy company and I was enjoying myself. He was an intelligent young man. Something about him reminded me of my son, Stewart, and I suddenly missed him. We drifted into silence.

The camp next door was now stirring with activity. CJ sipped his coffee and stole glances at the campers. I tried not to stare at

CJ's frame, but it was hard to ignore. It was a fitness trainer's habit that I had fallen into. Clearly, he had a trained physique.

"So, exactly what is it you do on a vision quest?" he asked, abruptly.

I wasn't sure I wanted to get into it. There was nothing secret about it, but it was sacred. I hadn't shared my intentions with anyone. Not Linda—not even my best friend, Lidija. I pondered why that was. I'd come to share everything with Lidija. We were relatively new friends, but we shared everything. She was gentle, open, vulnerable, forthcoming, and transparent in our conversations and, unlike me, her outer and inner worlds lined up. She was unapologetically, Lidija, and filled life with her essence.

We'd met the week her mother was released from the hospital, following a massive stroke. I was on vacation in San Diego, visiting a mutual friend, and she introduced me to Lidija when we'd stopped by with lunch.

My reaction upon seeing Lidija's overwhelm at caring for her mother was that no woman—whether I knew her or not—should have this responsibility alone, so I told Lidija I was available to help if she would teach me how to care for a stroke patient (which she was just learning to do herself). The following day, I moved into a room adjacent to her mama's, and together we cared for her. Unlike other friendships, ours began with no initial chit-chat, no small talk, or getting-to-know-you moments. We literally held hands and jumped in the deep end together. We had each other's back, and that cemented our friendship. We've been like sisters ever since.

It was within the trust of our friendship, that I began to unwind what I had tightly coiled and protected since childhood. Emotions had no soft place to land in our home. As a young girl, I was forever spouting off about the rainbows I saw around people or talking trees and ladybugs. My parents shook their heads and handed me a coloring book.

It was only when I was alone, with my grandmother, or now, with Lidija, that I could explore the full spectrum of myself—that I could peel back, open, and expose myself. Within the safe, trusted container of Lidija's friendship, natural abilities I'd abandoned in childhood, resurfaced, and sensitivity to subtle energy all around me returned. I opened up and grew tremendously within our friendship.

Lidija often found it humorous, however, that I had no problem saying what was on my mind, but when it came to quiet, sacred things—things of the heart, I had a hard time trusting others with my truth.

I refocused my attention and looked at CJ.

"I suppose that depends on what you want to accomplish," I said. CJ frowned, and I could see he wasn't going to be satisfied with a short answer. "Are you sure you really want to hear this?" I asked.

"Yes! Please go on," he said.

"Well," I sighed, "I'm calling in a vision. My plan is to go into it fasting. Food has a lot of emotion attached to it. Changing that pattern affects other patterns and habits—things I rely on every day, like coffee. Taking food out of the equation frees up energy. Besides, digestion is the most labor-intensive thing our body does. It consumes energy that could be directed to spiritual matters. I simply feel better fasting, so, that's my plan."

"That's it?" CJ said, clearly disappointed.

"Well, yeah."

"You don't do anything?"

"That's pretty much the point," I said.

"Excuse me for saying so, but that seems pretty lame," he commented.

"Well, it's not like I won't do anything," I added. "There's about half a dozen ceremonies I'll do. I'll meditate and focus on my breath. I'll stretch and dance, beat my drum and chant."

CJ smiled and nodded his head. Seeing his interest, I softened and decided to share what was really in my heart.

"A vision is an extraordinary event—certainly something beyond the reference of our normal, human senses. I wouldn't go so far as to call it supernatural, but it lifts us out of everything we think we know, and gives us sight of what's possible for our life."

"I like that," CJ said. I took a sip of water and continued.

"There's no particular spiritual beliefs someone needs to hold in order to have a vision. You just go in with intent, surrender control, and open to the possibility that there's more—something unknown or unpredictable, we don't even know is possible for us. Taking my hands off the 'steering wheel' of my life... now that'll be the challenge for me," I said.

It was more the answer he was looking for, and the little confession about taking my hands off the wheel felt good to share.

"Anyway, that's me. What about you? What's in Blanding?"

"Blanding? Well, I'm checking out a law firm there. I'm a senior at the University of Utah Law School. Spring term just ended and I drove up earlier this week to discuss an internship with their firm. Blanding is home, too. My Dad is there. It sounds like I'll be working at the firm by this fall. After that, it's the Bar exam, and then, who knows?"

"Busy guy."

"Yeah, too busy. But I like it. I like the intensity, you know? Not much else to say. I've got ol' Smurf here. Right, boy?" he said, smiling at the puppy. Smurf perked up at the sound of his name, rose to his feet, and tugged at the leash, begging for attention. CJ combed his fingers through his hair again. It was a nervous gesture, but if he was nervous, it didn't show. He would make a fine lawyer. He then stood, unleashed his puppy from the mirror, and walked him back to the table. He sat on its corner and patted Smurf's shoulder. Smurf pressed his face affectionately against CJ's leg.

"I've got to ask," I said. "What's the story behind Smurf's name?"

"Oh." CJ turned and looked me in the face. "It seems we both lost our moms recently. I was raised on The Smurfs," CJ said, then grinned. "Mom and I used to watch the reruns together. Ol' Smurf here, he kinda fills the hole she left. Yeah, boy, I'm talking about you," he said, patting the puppy.

"I'm sorry, CJ. You're so young to be losing your mom."

"Thanks. I appreciate it." CJ stood, then sighed, looking at me. "Well, I think I'll walk him. I'm sure I've kept you long enough. Anyway, you probably want to get on the road."

I wasn't aware of the time. In fact, it was the first I'd thought of time since he had sat down. But, he was right; I did need to go.

"It's been great visiting with you. You're an interesting woman, True. I hope you have a great trip, and good luck on your vision quest. You'll find what you're looking for. I know you will."

CJ smiled at me one last time, picked up his cup, and then smiled at Smurf. The gangly animal leapt up on him. He corrected his dog and steered the puppy away from the table. The two headed toward the dirt road and I watched them walk away. Just before CJ was completely out of sight, I saw him lean over to pat Smurf's dark coat. Then, they were gone. I suddenly wanted to say goodbye again and wish him well.

"You too, CJ," I called after him. I pictured CJ turning his head and waving goodbye.

# 5

# HOVENWEEP

When Spanish Conquistador De Vargas first began his journey across the American Southwest in the 16th century, his expedition found a vast territory inhabited by native people, dwelling in multi-story homes of stone and clay. They worshipped strange gods and performed exotic ceremonies and dances. It was a visual feast for the fair-skinned men who, upon witnessing the amazing sites before them, asked if it was all a dream.

Two centuries later, Spanish Friars Anastasio Dominguez and Silvestre Veléz de Escalante, traveled southwest through unknown territory in search of a route to Monterey, the capital of Spanish-occupied California, and its missions. The two mapped a large portion of the untamed interior west and encountered a mysterious city of stone, which had been abandoned for centuries. The friars inspected the ruins with amazement and, upon sharing their findings, sparked one of the greatest fascinations of a culture known to man.

The native people that the Spaniards encountered and those who occupied the plateau homes discovered by the friars, were one and the same. They were called the Anasazi (ah-nah-sa-zee), and for 5,000 years they made the southwestern desert their home. The communities of the Anasazi were spread over some 10,000 square miles. One of these pueblos is Hovenweep.

Discovered in 1854, Hovenweep was set aside for protection and preservation in 1923 as a National Monument. It is believed that the Anasazi—also referred to as Ancestral Puebloans, occupied the pueblos here between 500 and 1300 AD. The structures here are fascinating, varying in shape: some are square, others D-shaped, round, or even four stories tall. Towers also stand among the ruins, but their purpose remains a mystery. Were they observatories, defensive structures, granaries, communication towers, or civil or ceremonial buildings? Only the Anasazi knew, and they left no written record of their culture.

Not a single word.

The mesa that Hovenweep sits on is nearly 5,600 feet above sea level and is home to six known archaeological sites. In the canyon below, a series of rivers and streams snake their way through the sandstone landscape. They feed into McElmo Creek, and eventually the San Juan River. This broad desert valley is a windy, desolate place. Hovenweep straddles the Utah-Colorado border and is accessible from the east by way of Cortez, Colorado. I was driving to it from the west, by way of Blanding, Utah, along the San Juan Mountains.

I had stopped for gas at a service station along the lonely two-lane road. As I pulled away from the gas station, I surveyed the road ahead. Nothing but parched, open desert. It looked like I felt. I gave a heavy sigh. All morning, I had been gnawing on CJ's question about a "second" vision quest. Now, a knot sat in the pit of my stomach. A wave of loneliness and melancholy followed. For the first time in a long time, I felt spiritually bereft. Lord knows I had covered tremendous ground since Grand Gulch... and leaving the Church.

Stepping away from church was, at first, like breaking a long-held habit, but I had to know if what I had been taught was what I truly believed, or if it was something that I'd adopted. My first hurdle was my family. They are devout in their religion, and couldn't fathom that I would question what had been the backbone of our family for generations. They were understandably puzzled.

I had plenty of skin in the game when I pulled away. I was a Young Women's Advisor, and my church community was stunned—alarmed, even—that I would be in youth leadership if my devotion was in question. What they didn't understand, is that my devotion and my faith were intact. It was the limitations of religion that I struggled with. That's when I learned the extraordinary, experiential distinction between religion and spirituality.

I found myself in a world where God was external—a being bestowed human characteristics and emotions, to be read about, worshiped, and obeyed. Whereas, my experience was very internal—extraordinarily intimate, moving, and experiential. I felt connected with God. I was an intrinsic extension of God and of everything, as it all came from the same source.

I cared about the person next to me because we were the same, not because they were a "brother" or "sister." It was a subtle, yet profound, difference. It explained the inner struggle that I'd been unable to put into words. I felt no judgment. Religion has its place, and it certainly did in my life. It helped shape me into who I am today. But, it no longer resonated with me.

When I chose to step away, I was the one and only family member who had ever done so. The dominoes fell from there. So here I was, a family oddity, driving a desert road in the middle of nowhere, heading toward a vision quest I wasn't even sure of anymore. Had I blown my one chance at this?

The Hovenweep Ranger Station lies mid-way between Cortez and Blanding, forty miles in either direction and sixteen miles of it must be traveled just to reach the nearest conveniences, such as groceries. Hovenweep is, literally, in the middle of nowhere. It is without a doubt, the quietest place I have visited on the planet. Tourists are scarce and the scenery is magnificent. It was everything I was looking for.

From Route 262, the remaining sixteen miles to Hovenweep went quickly. I slowed the car at the sun-bleached National Monument sign and turned into the unmistakable intersection that sets Hovenweep apart from any other intersection in the country. Peacocks were casually strutting the intersection and wild turkeys were pecking the hardpan. It was just as I had remembered. I eased up on the gas and gave the peacocks plenty of room to exit the intersection.

During the ten days between Mama's funeral and my flight to Albuquerque, I'd called the ranger station and discussed my plans. They were less than enthused. The grounds were sacred and not for just anyone to rove. And, it was a National Monument. They slowly came around when I told them that my intention was to hike on an established trail and to sit on a boulder, not to touch the ruins, not to camp at them, or hike over the grounds. No trace would remain of my having been there. I was coming just to sit on a rock.

Archeological sites are extremely fragile and very prone to damage. Federal laws have been passed in recent decades that prohibit artifact hounds from digging among the ruins. Regulations restrict handling or climbing on the ancient walls. At Hovenweep, hiking was limited to established trails.

I stopped at the ranger station to sign in. The ranger was expecting me. I provided the emergency contact phone numbers she had requested during our call. When I asked about parking the car, she pointed her ballpoint pen to the campground area. The car could be parked at one of the campsites. I read her name tag, thanked her by name, and then backed into one of the more visible sites.

I sat in the car and calculated what ten days of camping fees amounted to, then slid cash into a strongbox and strolled the camp area. Hovenweep is immense but lonely—a deserted place where, as far as I could tell, none of the campsites were occupied.

Back at the car, I pulled my backpack from the trunk, along with five one-gallon jugs of drinking water. After removing them, I locked the car and stowed the keys, along with my phone, in one of the outer pouches of my pack. I wouldn't need either for the next ten days.

There were only a few items in my pack. Not much for venturing into the desert. But then, I wouldn't need much. The jugs of water that I had picked up in the last town, accounted for most of the weight. The remaining contents included enough clothing to layer in case the temperatures dropped, sunscreen, a flashlight, toilet tissue, a hand trowel, a sunhat, a drum, my journal, and a pen.

In my emergency kit, there was a whistle, compass, snakebite kit, extra flashlight batteries, and insect repellent. The repellent had been upgraded to emergency status after I'd forgotten it three years ago, and been nearly eaten alive by biting gnats. I hate those blasted things!

# ANASAZI VISION

The backpack was heavy, a far cry from the ultra-lite pack I'd enjoyed when hiking the PCT. With four gallons of water in the pack, I estimated my load to weigh about forty-two pounds. I would be carrying the fifth jug of water in my hand, so I could sip from it during my trek to the boulder. It would be the longest I had gone without food in my life, but I was committed to doing whatever was necessary to call in a vision.

I hefted the pack onto the camp table and slid my arms through the straps. Then, just like that, it was on. I buckled the waist belt and, gradually, the weight settled onto my hips. I double-checked to make sure the car was secure, then braided my hair, rolled and tied a bandana around my forehead, slipped on the sunhat, and turned toward the trailhead. As I walked through the vacant camp area, I noticed that the ranger had stepped onto the porch. The woman, neatly tucked into a freshly pressed green uniform, was standing with her hand to her forehead, shielding her eyes from the sun. She lowered her hand and waved at me. I was glad someone knew where I would be. I questioned again why I hadn't told Lidija of my plan.

There are three major hiking trails at Hovenweep. Two originate at the ranger station and are relatively short and lightly maintained. The third—an eight-mile trail, connects two of the outlying ruins and becomes little more than an animal path. My boulder would be two and a half miles along this trail.

The ranger had warned me about "the locals," as she referred to them: cacti with thick-skinned leaves and piercing needles, sagebrush with twenty-foot taproots, rattlesnakes, scorpions, and biting gnats. Black-tailed prairie dogs, hawks, kangaroo rats, jackrabbits, antelope, and coyotes also called Hovenweep home, and I could expect to see any of these during my ten-day stay.

The grass and scrubland that make up this high plateau seemed almost surreal. These lifeless grasses on this mesa come alive during early spring and late summer with the onset of thunderstorms, and the rains they bring. It was early May, and I was surrounded by vegetation. As I scanned over the ocean of grass and brush before me, bright red-orange patches of Indian paintbrush, tall white plumes of yucca, and blue tracts of lupine and sego lilies carpeted the landscape with color.

A shower had passed through here days before and blessed the ground with moisture. The resulting bouquet before me would last mere days if the weather held, and the thunderclouds remained stacked against the Colorado Plateau to the east. But that wasn't to be. Rain was no longer in the forecast, and the coming week promised to bring rising temperatures to the mesa. The arid heat would soon fade this visual feast. I was glad I'd seen it while it was in bloom.

Life in the high desert is hard, not only for the plants but for the animals as well. They retreat underground and live within a carefully organized network of burrowed-out tunnels, or hide between the seams of boulders and under rocks. I knew the desert was alive and active, though it wasn't visible. It's the sun that drives life underground here, and the sun was now directly overhead.

Within minutes of starting the trail, my shirt was damp with sweat. One by one, beads of sweat slowly crept down my neck and spread across my shirt. The backpack was bulky from the jugs, and the water sloshed with the rhythm of my cadence. I settled into an easy pace, not wanting to repeat my debacle walking out of the San Juan River two days ago. The pack was heavy, but not terribly uncomfortable. At least, not yet.

I stayed hydrated with sips of water as I navigated the trail, which soon narrowed and drew within fifteen feet of a dry gully. The recent showers had done little to impact the ditch that spun in all directions, before disappearing over a ravine.

I stopped to adjust the load on my back. The jugs had shifted and the weight was unbalanced. Suddenly from overhead, the cry of a red-tailed hawk caught my attention. It swooped low and plucked a jackrabbit from a snarled piece of dead wood beside me. The rabbit twitched just twice as it dangled from the hawk's razor-sharp talons. I watched as the majestic bird flapped its twenty-inch-long wings and climbed effortlessly into the sky. I noted the sun's placement and judged it to be about three o'clock.

The adventure of the hike was waning under the rising heat, pack weight, and scratchy underbrush. It had become a bothersome task to stop every few minutes and pull out the stickers that had needled their way into my socks and boots. Time dragged on, and I became anxious to get to the boulder.

A quarter-mile further, and the trail leaned slightly toward the west. I continued around the slow bend and at once recognized something familiar. In the distance was a mesa, and before it stood a boulder with a lone pinyon pine tree growing beside it. I caught my breath, overjoyed. This was it. I was here.

# 6

# VISION QUEST

Rituals and ceremonies used to be external, awkward attempts to attune me to God. Each Sabbath, we partook of bread and water in remembrance of a sacrifice made for humankind. This was my understanding of ceremony as a child.

I took to religion easily. It was the scaffolding that gave my life structure. There were scriptures to memorize, awards to earn, programs to participate in, and parables to fill my young, hungry imagination. My home life was similarly structured, with chores, expectations, and standards to meet. All of which I owned and polished like a precious stone. Outwardly, I'm sure I came off as ambitious or competitive, but my pursuit was decidedly inward and personal. I sensed a need to grow into something and challenged myself mercilessly to stretch—to do better and be better.

This wasn't always appreciated. I was an energetic eleven-year-old, with lofty ambitions and questions to match. Life was a giant puzzle to me—one that I was determined to solve. Learning became my passion, and I became good at it. One of the happiest days of my young life was when I got a library card. I was teased by classmates because I was the "smarty-pants." Honestly, sometimes I was a showoff, but mostly, I just wanted to understand what this place called "Earth" was.

## ANASAZI VISION

Ceremonies had taken on a whole new meaning since childhood. They were now deeply personal, intentional, and something I entered into with reverence—perhaps at the time of Equinox or Solstice, and I often incorporated cacao, incense, or burning a bundle of dried sage to energetically clear a space.

Their counterpart: rituals, were a whole different ball game. Rituals were everyday things: lighting a candle before I would meditate or write, brewing tea before calling a friend, or offering gratitude when I ate a meal or stood at the riverbank. These things were woven into the fabric of my daily life, performed routinely with intent and awareness.

Simple rituals, such as these, have brought consistency and stability to my life. Nothing could be truer than during stressful, demanding, unpredictable, or strained times of my life, like the year I'd just experienced, caring for Mama. I needed ritual.

It would be ceremonies, however, that would play a role in my vision quest. Several that I had penciled out were new ceremonies—ones that I had either heard of, read about, or intuitively created. I would perform them over the coming days as I felt guided to. My hope was that, in performing them, they would lift me from the mental, physical, and emotional confinements of my normal routine, and prepare me—separate me—from my known and patterned life. This was my hope anyway.

Finally, at the boulder, the last thing I felt like doing was organizing myself to death. Unloading the pack could wait. I was exhausted and needed to hydrate. In the narrow shade of the boulder, out of the direct sun, I swung the pack from my shoulders and dropped it to the ground with a thankful sigh. I then pulled off my shirt and hung it from the pinyon tree to dry.

The gallon jug that I had been carrying was still two-thirds full. I took a long drink from it and then leaned my back against the boulder in the warm shade. Was it really as warm as I imagined, or was I just feeling the effects of the hike and elevation? I sat and rested for several minutes, sipping the tepid water.

From a clump of nearby grass, something moved. Probably a lizard or brown snake, I surmised, but I quickly forgot about it as I rose to my feet. The backpack felt like concrete when I scooted it further into the shade. I kneeled, half-crouched, and unloaded the jugs of water, stowing them out of the sun in the shade of an adjacent rock, then spread my bandana and sun hat on a warm rock to dry. The rest of my clothes, drum, journal, and emergency kit could stay in the pack, which could double as a pillow.

I studied the boulder—its cracks and thin crevices, its seams, buckles, and contours marbled along its rough surface. I quickly discovered a deep groove in the rock that would serve as a foothold. With a six-foot climb to the flat surface, I would need more than a single foothold, however—something I could grab onto. But what? After careful observation, I found a second foothold and, hopefully, the means to hoist myself up onto the boulder. This was looking good. I tested it and scaled to the top. Yes, this would do nicely.

The view from here wasn't much to look at. In my travels throughout the Four Corners area, I'd seen some magnificent sights. This wasn't one of them. There was nothing particularly picturesque about this spot. It had no cliff looming in the distance at which to gaze. No interesting rock formations to inspire me during the long hours I would sit. And yet, I'd never questioned that this was the place I wanted to call in a vision.

## ANASAZI VISION

I stared across the sea of grass and desert before me. The brush became considerably greener just west of where I stood. Was it a ravine? It had been a good year for rain and the recent shower may have left water there—a trickle, anyway. Now curious, I backed myself off the boulder, slipped on my shirt and sunhat, and headed in the direction of the green grass. As best as I could calculate, it was one hundred feet from the boulder. Above me, the sun had escaped behind a lone cloud. It was white and puffy. The weather forecast had been accurate—clear skies and not a chance of rain.

It was a gully all right, but the stream that flowed through here was dry. Cracked earth was all that remained. I kicked my boot against something solid, embedded in the hardpan. At first, it appeared to be just a rock, but I dusted the pink earth from it and found a small animal skeleton. Near it were several small stones, each about the size of a women's belt buckle. They looked like something I could use for one of the ceremonies, so I stuffed four into my pockets.

The land showed no trace of human impact, and I was glad for it. Actually, little had changed from the time I had first walked this trail three years ago. I could appreciate why the Rangers were emphatic about keeping it this way, undisturbed and natural.

Years ago, I had learned from a Zia Native American, that the number four is sacred to them, as it represents the harmony of the universe. The Zia believe that the sacred number four is embodied in the earth—with its four directions and elements; in the year—with its four seasons; in the day—with sunrise, noon, evening, and night; and in life—with childhood, youth, adulthood, and old age.

## ANASAZI VISION

"These things of the universe," my Zia friend had said, "are our guide to life's sacred obligations: a strong body, a clear mind, a pure spirit, and devotion to our Earth Mother."

I returned to the boulder and climbed up. I retrieved the stones from my pockets and, using my compass, placed them on the boulder's flat surface, positioning them with care so that they marked the four directions. When I had done this, I stood at the boulder's center, extended my hands over my head, closed my eyes, gave thanks, and officially began my vision quest.

"Grandfather Sun, Grandmother Moon, Father Sky, and Mother Earth, I come to this sacred place in this sacred moment within the span of time and space to give my thanks. Thank you for your generosity which sustains life; for your wisdom that lives in and teaches us through the elements of air, water, fire, earth, metal, and the great ether, where the formless exists."

I placed my hands on my chest.

"Thank you for my body. Thank you for the life force that moves through it and sustains me here on Earth. Thank you for the love and support I have in my life. Thank you for my family of origin, my children, and my chosen family—my tribe. Thank you for the wisdom my years here have cultivated. Thank you for my shortcomings and mistakes; they have been my greatest teachers."

I placed my hands on my belly.

"Thank you for my life as a woman. Thank you for the intelligence of my body to create life. Thank you for my intuition, my inner compass—my True North. Thank you for my angels and guides; I rely on them daily. Thank you for my ability to reinvent myself again and again. I dedicate this time, all that I am and will ever be, to being of service to the greater good of all. Thank you for this opportunity. I dedicate this time to your guidance and grace.

And so it is. Aho." It was done. My invocation had been spoken and carried by the wind to the ethers.

I then faced each direction, in turn, bowing to honor and deliberately contemplate what that quadrant represented. I faced east and drew in a deep, purposeful breath. The air was clean and fresh, carrying the combined scent of sage and pine gum. I contemplated Earth's easterly direction—its element of air, season of spring, climate of wind, hour of sunrise, archangel Raphael, emotion of anger, color of red, aspect of illumination, and life phase of childhood. I bowed to it in respect.

I then turned and faced south. I contemplated Earth's southerly direction—its element of fire, season of summer, climate of heat, hour of noon, archangel Michael, emotion of joy, color of yellow, aspect of innocence, and life phase of youth. Again, I bowed.

I turned and faced west. I contemplated Earth's westerly direction—its element of earth, season of autumn, climate of dry, hour of evening, archangel Gabriel, emotion of melancholy, color of black, aspect of inner-knowing, and life phase of adulthood. I bowed.

Finally, I turned and faced north. I contemplated Earth's northerly direction—its element of water, season of winter, climate of cold, hour of night, archangel Uriel, emotion of fear, color of white, aspect of wisdom, and life phase of old age. I bowed in reverence, completely absorbed in the ceremony, and felt at peace.

I contemplated the delicate balance between each aspect of life, each honored and equal. I had to admit, I had favorites. I think we all do. We honor youth over old age and autumn over winter. I thought back to my early childhood, when there was no concept of age or race, politics or religion, no time, directions, or seasons. Is this what it is like to hold all things in equality?

## ANASAZI VISION

As I concluded my first ceremony, I felt grateful—honored, to have such aspects as context and companions in my life. I let myself have this moment.

I was actually here.

My vision quest was no longer an idea or fantasy. It was no longer something to consider, plan for, and dream about endlessly. I was here! All at once, I began to giggle.

The image only lasted a moment, but I saw my four-year-old self standing next to me, holding my adult hand. She looked up at me and smiled. I gazed upon her round little face. Her eyes were crystal blue, so clear and bright, like her daddy's. A thought then came to me—this little one had made sure that I arrived here. She'd heard my plea while standing at the hallway portrait, shared it with heaven, and helped me get to Four Corners.

My heart swelled with so much love for her. In my mind's eye, I saw myself bending down to scoop her into my arms, hug her little body, kiss her plump cheek, and point to the land before us. I then felt her small arms find their way around me. She leaned onto my chest and buried her head there. I closed my eyes and smelled her hair. I then gently swayed, holding her close to me. Never had I felt such peace. I wanted this moment to last forever and continued to stand in place, taking in the sweet moment and the love that hung in the air.

"Thank you," I whispered to the desert.

After a few minutes, I backed off the boulder and removed my clothing, carefully spreading them over the limbs of the pinyon pine tree. The four full gallons of water had been neatly stowed in the shade and were intended for drinking. The open one that I'd hiked in with, was now christened "Bath Water." Actually, I did need a bath. But that wasn't why I was bathing. The intent was to symbolically remove the world from me, as I symbolically removed myself from it.

Now, I was under the impression that the sun could heat water left out in plastic containers. I thought wrong. The first trickle of water on my head sent a chill down my spine, and I let out a "Whoop" into the still air. The water ran down my bare shoulders. I helped spread the thin stream over my chest and arms, down my belly, and along my back, all the way to my hips and legs. Beneath me, the dry, chalked, pink earth caught the falling beads and bounced them in its dust before swallowing them up. I skimmed my hands over my body and flicked droplets into the warm air. I was dry within minutes.

I stood there naked, my skin white, except for my tanned extremities. I was in decent shape, I suppose, for having had four children. The bodybuilding and yoga had helped, and I still ran, though only on hiking trails now. My hair had grown very long during my year at Mama's. It was brunette and was usually pulled, either to the side or back, in a loose braid. Some called me petite, but because of my strength, I felt larger than my actual size. The crazy thing was, I had big feet. I have no idea where I got them but, the sheer length of them could have added inches to my stature.

So there I was, buck naked and feeling wonderful about it. I grabbed one of the full-gallon jugs and tossed it, along with my backpack, onto the top of the boulder before climbing its warm face, still naked, to the top. It was a relatively easy climb now that I had figured it out. Still, nothing I wanted to do repeatedly.

I rifled through my pack and pulled on panties and a sports bra. The view from my perch was totally blissful, a regal throne in an untamed wilderness. I pulled in a deep, metered breath, closed my eyes, and stood absolutely still. The air was silent. On my next inhalation, I gave thanks again for the opportunity to be here and then opened my eyes.

Nature is my first home. Even as a young child, it was not unusual to find me up a tree or wading, calf-deep, in the shallow creek near our home. I can't tell you the number of times my mother would shake her head upon seeing me and send me to the bathtub. I was clean and dirty, clean and dirty—and I was happy.

It was the backyard forts, the frogs, the birds, and the woolly worms that I loved. It was geese, flying in formation overhead, that made me squeal in delight. Mine was a wonderful childhood. And, it was done in dresses. I was a girly tomboy, if that's a thing. I loved being a girl and I loved romping.

I unfurled my sleeping bag, folded it in thirds on the boulder, and centered myself between the four rocks. I sat cross-legged and took in my new surroundings. In this quieted state, I recalled a poem that I had written as a young mother. Single lines came at first, and then, it became alive in my memory. Remarkably, I remembered each word crafted years earlier. I spoke it aloud to my beloved desert:

"If I could, I would sleep under the stars every night.
I would fly fish and talk to God and talk to people.
I'd ask God where to fish and what to say to people that would do them some good.

I would read a little and write a little.

## ANASAZI VISION

I'd walk with my best friend each day, just so we could be together.
Sometimes we'd walk. Sometimes we'd just talk and never move, but we'd always go just where we needed to that day.

If I could, I would make love just as the morning light overtakes the dark.
I'd work in the dirt without gloves and set my work boots, still caked with earth, just outside the back door.
I would sit with old folks and little folks. I'd ask them things and wonder how they got to be so smart.

I would put on a full skirt and dance and twirl to my favorite song.
I'd drink coffee on the front porch late Sunday morning, then take a nap.
I'd wade in the creek and spend time with the kids each day, doing their stuff.

If I could, I would learn to play music, paint, or sculpt.
I'd spend afternoons at a potter's wheel or just working on photographs in the darkroom.
I'd practice my putt and sometimes my shot. I'd tie a fly for the morning cast if I needed one.

I would study history and civilizations, world cultures, and myths.
I'd study folklore, tribal rites, and rituals.
I would learn about the earth and I'd be good to her.

If I could, I would live naked and skinny dip in the river.

## ANASAZI VISION

I'd curl myself into a human cannonball and hurl myself into the water.
I'd jump in puddles and catch raindrops in my mouth when they fell.
I would take hot baths until my skin wrinkled and the mirror fogged up.
I'd lather my hair and shape it into all sorts of horns and hats on my head.
I would fish for slippery soap between my legs and scribble on the foggy mirror before I left the room.

If I could, I would climb hills and sit in trees during the day.
I would pick wildflowers and put fresh sheets on the bed.
At night, I would pull my best friend close and explore him all over again.

I would eat the bottom out of ice cream cones and lick the sweet trickle from my arm.
I'd ride a bicycle real fast on streets covered with leaves, just to feel them swirl around me.
I'd count the stripes down the center of the road and watch lightning storms from the front porch.

If I could, I would play 'Oh Holy Night' over and over again.
I'd sleep by the Christmas tree on Christmas Eve and still believe in Santa Claus.
I'd forget all about gift giving and give someone something, just because I wanted them to have it.

## ANASAZI VISION

I would build things out of wood and make things out of clay or cloth.
I'd have a box for tools. I'd have a box for makeup too, only it would be a pretty box.
I'd put on makeup and get dressed up every once in a while, just because I like to. After all, I am a girl!

If I could, I would have back rubs, candlelight, and story time every night.
I would cuddle the kids and whisper how special they are just before their eyes closed.
I'd sleep with them sometimes, just to hear them breathe.

I would hike and camp. I'd float around on an inner tube wearing my purple Vans with the toes kicked out.
I'd watch the wind play with branches and ponder the shapes of the clouds.
I'd discover quiet, reverent places and just sit there and listen to the birds… then the crickets.
If I could, I would sleep out under the stars every night."

I smiled, completely satiated—at home on this planet in a way I'd not quite known before. Earth was my mother—my first mother and I was grateful to be here with her.

I never knew either of my grandfathers. It was my grandmothers, and in particular, my maternal grandmother that I adored. She was my favorite person on the planet. She knew and understood me as no one else did. She was a spitfire until the day she died—the first in her small town to bob her hair. The one who snuck into the trunk of the family car as a child, to hitch a ride to town. The one who climbed into a wooden flume used to transport logs to the valley, some 200 feet below, and took the sloshy, harrowing ride. The one who, later in life, turned Gypsy, and traveled wherever the mood struck her. This woman's blood runs through me.

My maternal aunt is my favorite person on the planet now. I adore her. She, like Grandma, understands me. Aunt Carol was the girly one in my mother's family. Age aside, we are like a couple of school girls when we get together. We stay up nights, talk, paint our nails, and can fall into laughing fits. It was also her husband, my Uncle Claud, who taught me to fish. I love her for that too.

Uncle Claud once shared a story with me about the Mayans. Where he'd heard the story, he never said, so I don't know how much truth there is to the tale. Whether it is grounded in fact or not, this story has stayed with me all these years, if only because I want it to be true.

I was about twelve when I traveled to the Smith River with my Uncle Claud. He was explaining the river's current when he turned to me and asked, "Bunny? Has anyone ever told you the story about the Mayans and water?" Of course, no one had.

"Water is power," he explained. "Water has the power to wash the old and decaying away. The Mayans knew that and they would come to streams of flowing water, much like this one you are standing in. They would stand and talk to it. They would tell the water all their cares, all their angers, fears, sorrows, and troubles."

"Why?" I asked. He pointed to the water rushing past us and continued.

"Water, you see, is moving life energy, and when the water had heard all the emotions they had poured out upon it, the stream would take them into its current and carry them away," he said. I thought it a beautiful tale.

Sitting quietly on the boulder, I remembered Uncle Claud's story. It was the first time I'd thought of it in nearly thirty-one years. Why had it come to mind? What river could wash my grief, anger, heartbreak, regret, and woes away in the desert? And then, a second thought followed the first.

Wind.

Of course! Wind is a moving energy as well. I would "brain-dump" everything into my journal, then leave the book open and let the wind, symbolically, lift and carry my heartaches away. I pulled the new journal and pen from my pack and began writing every thought that came to mind. Every one.

Every.

Last.

One.

The exercise must have taken hours because when I finally looked up from my writing, the sun was low in the sky. I thumbed through the pages. Impossible! How could that be? I'd filled thirty-nine pages! I was mentally spent. The exercise had, literally, emptied all the babble and quieted my mind.

Freed of its cares, my mind went still. I couldn't raise another thought, even if I tried to. An indescribable sense of peace and stillness came over me. I was clear-minded and keenly aware of everything around me. I simply had no interest in interacting with it. All I sensed was stillness. I laid the book open in front of me and waited for the wind.

# 7

## OLIVER

There was one thing I knew I couldn't do, and that was fall asleep on the boulder undressed. If last night was any indication of the daily temperature swings, I knew that it might dip into the forties tonight. I pulled on a pair of leggings and a long-sleeved shirt for warmth.

It had been a long day, but I felt glorious. If there had been a sunset this evening, it had escaped my attention while I was "brain dumping" in my journal.

I looked around the boulder for the most feasible sleeping area, then moved my four ceremonial rocks, spread out my sleeping bag, and crawled into it. I repositioned myself a couple of times until I found a comfortable position, then turned my awareness toward the night sky.

It was hard to believe that it had been just last night that I'd felt the presence of young warriors and watched moonlight dance on cottonwood leaves from my campsite. The San Juan, CJ, Smurf, and the drive here, all seemed forever ago.

Above, a million stars shimmered like a jeweled rainbow against the clear black sky. The desert air was cool and still. I knew the moon would be full tonight, so I waited expectantly for her arrival and then watched as she slowly rose to take her place in the heavenly canopy. She was magnificent. From my Hovenweep home, it appeared that every star in the Milky Way had come to greet me tonight. I was spellbound. It was a magical night—the kind of night created for the soul, or lovers.

The thought transported me. I wanted to believe that someone was missing me tonight, but there was no one. No lover anyway. I breathed in the cool air, surrendered to the moonlight, and let it carry me into the embrace of imagined strong arms. I softly closed my eyes, feeling his presence so vividly that the warmth and weight of his hold became my world.

My head found its home on his chest and I eased myself closer, taking in his scent. I felt his hot breath on my skin; his hands in my hair, tousling it. I heard myself flirting with a man I deeply loved. I called his name and felt our legs entwined, our fingers interlocked, and our lips pressed. I gently traced the contour of his face in the afterglow—his eyes passionately, lovingly, fixed on me. I heard our laughter, felt our breathing, and surrendered to our closeness, finding myself wrapped around him, our worlds merging in a timeless embrace.

I swiped an insect from my face, and reality backfilled my fantasy. I attempted to linger just a moment longer in the experience before it faded, but it belonged to the moonlight, and she had willed it back home. I sighed. The reality was that my life had become narrowly thin in Grants Pass. The last thing I had time or energy for, was a man. And now… well, the dreamy, fantasy man in the moonlight was as far away as a man in real life.

I sighed again, though this time, glad the past year hadn't stolen the memory of being in love or smothered the heat that fueled it. Maybe one day, there'd be someone again.

I attempted to adjust the lumpy contents of my backpack and made a dent in it for my head. I zipped the sleeping bag around me, pulled it over my shoulders, and tried to get comfortable again. I gazed up at the moon overhead and listened to the coyotes. The night had turned lonesome.

Moments later, the distant howls ceased. The night fell still and lonely. I waited for their cry to return, but it didn't. Something had silenced it. I had never given thought to having a weapon with me. However, at the moment, I seriously challenged the logic of that thinking. It would have been easy to buy a knife or pepper spray in Albuquerque.

In all my wanderings in the wilderness, I'd never been afraid of an attack; not even on the Pacific Crest Trail, where bears are known to run off with hiker's food sacks. Why now? Why here? This was an open landscape. I could see forever, and the moon was full. Anything approaching could be seen long before it ever reached the boulder—or me.

What was I thinking? What could possibly scale this enormous rock? An attack would have to come from the air, which was unlikely. A creature on the ground would have to have haunches powerful enough to leap six feet, and that was unlikely. Yet, my uneasiness steadily grew.

This could be my last dance—my final breath. Was I being irrational? Overcautious? Or simply realistic? I couldn't know. What I did know, in that moment, was that I wanted a weapon—and I didn't know why.

A shiver shot through my body. From the cold? Or was it something else? The thought left me empty. I rolled onto my belly and rifled through my pack, feeling around for the flashlight. At the very least, I should have this. Was there anything else in the pack that I could use? Anything that might double as a weapon?

There was nothing.

The trowel was below, lying near the pinion tree. The long-handled flashlight was it. 'Some weapon,' I thought, my heart pounding.

I laid there alert, straining the night for answers. But it had nothing to give me, not even the sound of a passing breeze. This was crazy. There was nothing out there. My imagination was having a field day. I set my head back onto the lumpy backpack, one hand on the edge of my sleeping bag and the other on the flashlight. Both the boulder and I were lost in the dark.

Night fell heavy and I eventually slipped into a deep sleep. Moonlight blanketed the land, surrendering not a sound, though something moved through it—silently, steadily, it crept, closing the distance, until nothing separated us.

It gave no warning. There was no evidence of its presence. But it was there. In a split second, I was awake. My eyes shot open. I sat upright, instinctively scanning the night, probing it for anything that might explain the movement I sensed—the eyes I felt upon me.

There was nothing, just scattered rocks, and a few shrubs. The desert floor might as well have been dead. Still, something out there was keeping it alive. I was sure of it. My skin crawled. I could almost feel its razor-sharp claws tearing at my skin.

My head went straight to work, examining the situation from every conceivable angle. I could die here, I reminded myself. I would either be ripped apart or be eaten, but it would be here, on this boulder.

Then, right there, I boldly decided that this Montana girl wouldn't go without a fight. The flashlight would have to do.

Still seated, I quickly devised a plan as I reached my fingers toward the flashlight, deep within my sleeping bag. My eyes were on the desert—scanning. I waited on the edge of fear, motionless, braced for an attack. I understood that once I moved, even slightly, I was committed. The victor had already won.

My blood raced. I asked myself if I was ready for this. Then I thought, "I only have a stinkin' flashlight to defend myself. I'm going to die."

Now, with the flashlight at my hip, I slowly, silently, unzipped the sleeping bag so the corner could be easily flung back and… What the…? I ran my hand across the inside of the sleeping bag. It was cold—no, it was wet!

"What?" Closer inspection confused me further. My sleeping bag and my leggings were soaked. "What the…?"

It was a costly distraction. In a split second, I lost whatever minute advantage I may have had. My attention diverted elsewhere, the thing closed in, until it was over me.

"Oh, my God!" I screamed.

That instant, both of our bodies bolted in opposing directions. Where it landed, I wasn't sure. I landed on my back. Panic-stricken, stumbling to right myself while struggling for air, I fumbled to recover the flashlight.

"Sweet Jesus, what is this?"

Nothing in my life could have prepared me for what was over me. I considered leaping from the boulder to the ground below. It was no more than a six-foot jump. I might get injured, but I'd be alive.

I quickly came to my knees, stealing a look at the thing under the moonlight. The creature stood just a step away, draped in its own shadow. A wild mane framed its head, and it appeared hunched and round-shouldered, standing about four feet tall.

It moved slightly and faced me. It was then that I got a better look, and gasped. This must be a dream. That's it… I'm dreaming.

'Wake up, True. Wake up!' The command changed nothing. There was no escaping this nightmare, and it continued to play itself out.

In the clear moonlight, looming before me, stood an extremely old man—small, round, and stooped, his face marbled with deep folds, eyes barely visible. Long, unruly white hair floated about his head, topped with a strange, dark cap; oddly shaped, and trimmed with a material that caught the moonlight. His white whiskers fell onto a long raven-colored cape. Beneath the heavy cape, he was clothed in a dark, loosely woven shirt that hung over heavily textured pants—full through the thigh and tapered to his ankles. Everything about him was bizarre. Even his dark boots were odd, as if from some forgotten place or time.

And he was trembling.

I couldn't take my eyes off of him. The more I stared, the less aware I was of anything else. Every detail of this creature was enough to make me forget even why I was here.

The very idea that this old relic could move through the desert with such agility and silence—especially in a cape, was totally absurd. I couldn't begin to wrap my mind around the possibility. Still, something had been out there. Was it still out there? Was the old man a diversion? Was I being toyed with? I was confused.

He was ghastly, yet intriguing; alchemistic, and punishing to my eyes—and, I was mesmerized. As I regained some composure, he removed the cap from his head, and in one long, slow sweeping motion, painstakingly shifted his weight onto one leg—bent and creaking with age, stepped back and bowed to me. I gasped.

"Greetings, True. You need not be afraid," he said slowly but distinctly, in a shallow, gurgled whisper. "My name is Oliver, and I speak for the Mother you rest upon."

Slowly, he slid out of the bow, replaced the cap to his head, and recovered his stooped posture. I followed his wrinkled hand, which he extended toward me. An earnest, toothless smile emerged from the deep creases of his face. I was dumbfounded, caught between wonder and apprehension.

Where had he come from? From out there? But, how? What could he possibly want with me, and how did he know my name? "Wait… he knows my name. How is that possible?" I squeezed the flashlight in my left hand. Though somehow, I felt I wouldn't need it. This old wreck could barely move. What could he do to hurt me? Hurl wads of phlegm?

Now I was acting nuts. This was just some old geezer out in the desert in the middle of the night, probably lost or homeless. Yeah, that's it. Still, there was something about him—his presence, his mannerisms, and the fact he knew my name. That's when it hit me. Wait!! How could he know my name? And, who is this "mother" he is talking about?' Questions spun wildly. Of all the questions that I could have asked, not one had a voice.

"Huh?" I said, finally.

"True," he repeated. "The rock you rest upon wishes me to speak for her. She weeps. You have felt her tears?"

What?

Wait?

What?

# ANASAZI VISION

Why, of course. It was all coming back now—my sleeping bag. That's what distracted me. My sleeping bag and leggings were completely soaked. But with tears? No way! I didn't understand what was happening.

He continued.

"Because you have honored, reverenced, and cared for her ground, it is you she has chosen. This is a great honor, yet it bears a heavy burden. You, True, have a choice to hear her words or not."

My ears must have been the size of Texas. How could this be? This was insane. A little man? A crying rock?' And, still…

"Tell me, please."

I couldn't believe it. What was I saying? I heard the words come from my mouth and couldn't stop them, as if they volunteered themselves from deep within my soul.

He nodded.

"Earth Mother has been silent for many centuries. She now speaks."

I blinked, astonished at what I was hearing.

"Listen closely, True," the stooped man chastened. "Hands, heavily soiled with greed, have put her essential balance at risk. Earth Mother has cried. All life has felt her tears as exceeding rain in diverse places. She has sighed. All life has felt her great sighs as strong winds upon her land and seas. She has trembled. All life has felt her trembling beneath their feet—in her oceans and on her mountaintops. She has warned. Now, Earth Mother speaks…"

He cleared his throat and continued.

"Her balance is not to be disturbed. Advanced civilizations have perished when her balance has not been honored. They lost sight of her needs in pursuit of their own. They did not uphold the balance. You still have time."

I couldn't believe what I was hearing.

"All who call her home will feel the impact if her balance is not restored. The key to her survival—living with her and the peace sought by all life she sustains, is here, beneath this ground."

"Impact?" I questioned.

"Listen closely," he reminded me. "Man has discounted this desert as nothing more than worthless miles to cross. They are blind to the power it holds. Yet, their blindness has been a protection for this land. Do you understand?"

"I think so. Earth is crying. You are speaking for her. She must come back to balance. The desert has a power?" I answered, bewildered by what I was repeating.

"True," he continued with great effort. "The power and support of Earth Mother is with you. The Ancient Ones of this place hold a secret, as does the land. Learn this secret and you will unlock a floodgate that will renew the world, restoring it anew. Man will learn to use the elements they have, and remember they are all the same."

A secret? Here? I couldn't imagine such a thing.

"Find Leo Biscolli. He excavates the earth in this area, searching for the Old Ones that came before. Remember these words. Earth Mother is with you."

That was it. The gnarled, old, troll-like man was gone. I blinked.

Wait!

What?

Where did he go?

I looked everywhere. I scanned the boulder. I edged to its lip and searched the ground and the surrounding area, but he was gone—completely vanished without a trace!

"What the…?"

I eased backward and then rolled onto my back. I was a wreck. Dazed. Confused. Exhausted. I was alive but felt heavy as cement. 'What had just happened?' I asked myself.

A thought came to me that this wasn't a dream—that I'd actually seen the old man. It was a strange, loaded idea with ramifications—and I had to think about it carefully.

No, it wasn't possible. I had been imagining this. Little men don't appear in the night and rocks don't cry. I must be dehydrated—perhaps I had heat stroke. That could stir up things that weren't there, right?

My mind raced and tumbled these thoughts until I decided that I'd imagined the whole thing.

"Whew," I sighed aloud and laid down in my sleeping bag. It was wet. "My God!" I gasped.

I lay there, awake, and my mind went straight to work. I'd planned for ten days of solitude in the desert, and I intended to use every minute of it. This was my vision quest and it was going to go how I'd planned. Getting a vision takes time; it's a lengthy process of cleansing one's body and mind of the toxins and tears put there by daily living.

I don't know what this "thing" was that just happened, but it couldn't be a vision. A vision would never come this fast, and not like this—not with some little, hunched-over man. My imagination was getting the best of me. I'd been so bent on having a vision—because I thought I couldn't, that I'd invented this. No, this wasn't a vision.

# ANASAZI VISION

I nestled deeper into my damp sleeping bag and tried to get comfortable enough to sleep, turning and lying on my side. Maybe it wouldn't be as wet there and I could get some sleep. In the morning, this whole nightmare would have ended, and I could get on with my ceremonies.

The evening labored on but, eventually, I dozed off. At daybreak, a chill was in the air, and despite the fact that I was lying in a wet sleeping bag, I was reluctant to start my day. For a moment, I lay perfectly still listening to the air, thinking of no particular thing. I didn't want to think about "it" yet.

I was inclined to ignore the matter as an untimely intrusion—a nuisance. The whole idea behind a vision quest was to be alone, someplace isolated from life, where I could go about my simple ceremonies undisturbed—someplace secluded where maybe—just maybe, I could have a vision. That was the reason why I nearly broke my back yesterday, hiking to this dang boulder. All I wanted was a little peace and quiet, and solitude! And now this had to show up.

A brown bird flew to an upper branch in the pinyon pine tree. I watched it without a thought, as it wrenched its feathered head and groomed itself. I rolled onto my back and stared into the sky. The whole idea was preposterous—finding some archaeologist. There had to be at least a dozen ruins currently under excavation in Four Corners; a hundred or more archaeologists, chipping away at rocks, or whatever it is they do.

Where would I start? What did the little man expect me to do?—drive all over the desert looking for this Leo whoever? For that matter, if I did find this Biscolli character, he was sure to think I was some sort of crackpot. I didn't even want to imagine how that little drama would play out. I could see the whole thing in my mind:

I would say, "Hi, my name is True, and some old, toothless geezer told me to track you down."

"Oh yeah? Why?" he would ask.

"Well," I'd say. "I sure as heck don't know. If you have any ideas, we would both like to hear them."

It was true. I had no idea what to ask him. What had the troll-man said? I had to remember his words. He specifically told me to remember his words. What had he said? If I couldn't remember them now, how did I expect to remember them when I met this Leo Biscolli face-to-face?

Looming in the back of my mind was the fact I was already having a conversation with this fictitious Leo character, as if I'd somehow made up my mind to find him.

Which I hadn't!

This was not what I wanted to do. This wasn't why I'd come to the desert and it sure as heck, didn't fit into my plans. No way was I going! Do you think I don't know how ridiculous I'd look if I actually found Leo Biscolli? Lord knows I hate being embarrassed. Consider my ego. No way!

I sat up and pulled a long drink of water from the plastic jug. Oh, how I missed my coffee. A cup of steaming java right now sure would make my morning. I was itching for something—anything. A little diversion, perhaps.

I would go for a walk. That would do the trick. I flung back the sleeping bag and peeled the wet leggings from my legs.

"Ah heck," I argued with myself. What a sissy I was, fretting over some little man with sinus problems. What could he do to me? This was nothing compared to the real dangers I'd faced in life. I'd survived a winter on a crab boat in the Bering Sea, earning money for college. Now that was dangerous! This old geezer had nothing on that.

I'd felt a bullet graze my head at age fourteen. A state trooper was target practicing on his property when my friend and I decided to cut across his land. The bullet went through my hair, for God's sake. Now that's what I call shaking in my boots!

I'd had my share of scrapes and tangles: repelling, rock climbing, whitewater rafting—heck, there'd even been skydiving, descending headfirst while repelling, and racing triple digits on a motorcycle. I'd learned early on to acknowledge fear, then to tuck it into my back pocket when my life depended on it. At 5'4" and 115 pounds, size was never in my favor. My stronghold had become leaning into something, rather than away from it. It was going with the energy, rather than away from it, that gave me an advantage when I was staring danger in the face.

Still, that was years ago, and certainly before my very unremarkable life at Mama's. Had I lost my taste for risk-taking and adventure—my curiosity for the unknown? Or, was it that I was afraid of discovering something that would rock my little world? Something that I couldn't explain—even to myself?

'Oh, sure!' I argued as I pulled on dry clothing. If that were the case, that had already happened last night. I slid on my socks and tied my boots. I eased myself off the boulder.

"Ugh…"

I pouted and stomped around for a moment, then took a walk along the trail that I had hiked in on, arguing with myself—and the desert—the entire time. By early morning, it appeared this thing wasn't going to give me a moment's peace until I'd settled the matter, so I decided to try to find this archaeologist.

Perhaps it was out of curiosity or, perhaps, to prove myself not insane. Either way, my mind was made up. Where I'd look for this Leo Biscolli, I hadn't a clue. Heck, I wasn't sure he even existed, other than in my head.

Doubt raised its ugly face a dozen times as I stuffed everything back into my backpack. I was confused, but curiosity had won the argument. This question had to be settled. I had to take care of this before I could do anything else. Besides, it was now pointless to try to continue my vision quest with wonder and doubt nipping at me. I had to go into town.

I poured out the water from three of the jugs, crushed and stowed them in my pack, and carried one in my hand to sip from on my way back to the car.

The hike out gave me plenty of time to wonder about this Leo Biscolli. Would he be excavating close by? I was curious what the archaeologist would look like. What did archaeologists look like? Where would he be digging? Is that what he would be doing, digging? Heck, I didn't know. What did archaeologists do anyway? How would he react to me—to my crazy story? Would he even talk to me? What would I say to him? With each step, I became more anxious.

This was all wrong. I didn't want to leave. I'd just arrived and wanted to do my vision quest. I still had the whole thing in front of me. There were ceremonies yet to do; drumming and chanting…

# 8

# GOD'S VAN

Asking seemed a simple enough plan until I pulled in front of the first market that I came to along the road. I'd seen it from a distance, off the side of the road on a patch of dirt. From two hundred yards, it appeared to have all the markings of a store: roadside signage, gas pumps, and a grocery "specials" board. Now that I was upon it, I began to wonder if it was in business. The little Mom & Pop grocery had seen better days.

Rusted remains of a 1960s-era gas pump stood decaying in a parking lot, riddled with potholes and weeds. The sad building looked as though it had weathered a century of storms without a single shingle replaced, except perhaps for the two lengths of timber that had been cut to prop up the sagging porch.

I pulled the car in through a blaze of dust, then sat inside as I waited for the heavy cloud to settle. I was frustrated and confused. While sitting there, I concluded that if this query turned up nothing, I could at least get something cold to drink. Fasting was now out of the picture.

There is an order to life, and I decided that fasting was meant for a vision quest. Since I was no longer on one, fasting could wait until I'd delivered a message to this Leo character. Then I could return to my boulder, resume my fast, and my vision quest.

I took a deep breath and stepped out of the car. The desert air tasted like dust. My goal was to make it through the dilapidated screened door. I feared that if my feet stopped moving, I would spin right around and drive away, so I hurried to the warped awning and pulled open the gray, splintered door.

It was a death march. I was sure of it. The owner would hear my loony story and hang me from the rafters right there. I argued with myself for another second and then finally concluded that I was nowhere without some information. I entered the store and raced to the beverage cooler against the back wall.

"Morning," I said, pulling a bottle of cream soda from the cooler. "Any chance there's an archaeological dig around here?"

The question was innocent enough, nothing to tip off anyone—nothing too demanding. At worst, I could get some information without committing myself. I liked the sounds of that. I looked at the pop bottle and knew that I was nervous. I hate cream soda.

Behind the counter was a slight man, tall and thin as a broom, with a few strands of fine, whispy hair that moved as he stood up from a deep chair. His face was narrow and his cheekbones protruded through his loose-fitting skin. I watched as he freed his hands from behind the chest compartment of a pair of coveralls. From the dust on the canned goods and sparse boxes on the shelves, I concluded that sitting in the store must be a hobby—and this must be Pop.

At some point during the morning, Pop must have read a newspaper. Remnants of it were strewn in a pile beside him. The man stared at me for a long time through his glasses, and when he had decided it was time to greet me, he was chewing on something that looked disgusting every time he cared to show it. Some of it went on his lip when he spoke.

"Missy," he finally said, "In case you haven't noticed, you're in an archaeologist's paradise. We got plenty of 'em. Whatcha looking for?"

"Well, it's not exactly what, it's who. Leo Biscolli. Ever heard of him?"

"No, can't say I have. Is he an archaeologist? This Biscolli fellow?"

"Yes, I hope so."

"Then I'd be lookin' in Cortez. Last I knew there were some active sites 'round there. Some'n there should be able to help you." He stared at me again, and after a long silence, asked, "Missy, you buyin' that soda or just holdin' it?"

"Oh. Oh, yeah."

I slid a couple of dollars across the counter and pushed open the screened door.

"A big, fat zero. This is ludicrous. It's crazy," I said, as the door slapped shut behind me. I walked quickly back to the car and was about to start my, "Let's get real" lecture, when I remembered the wet sleeping bag, airing out on the back seat.

"Okay, you win! Which way from here to Cortez?"

Spectacular stair-stepped landscapes of deep canyons and high plateaus stretch across southwestern Colorado. To the far south, is Shiprock, a remarkable solitary peak of red rock, carved by eons of wind to resemble a 25-foot-high lighthouse. The Navajo claim that it is home to the mythological winged monsters of their tales. To the north, lay the La Plata Mountains, which form a natural barrier along the northern border of Navajo country. To the west looms Sleeping Ute Mountain, where, according to Ute tradition, is the place the Rain God collects clouds from the sky and puts them in his pouch.

The green valleys nestled between these landmarks hold a beauty all their own. Sparkling creeks meander their way through the lower mesas, plateaus, and hills, blanketed in high desert flora. It is some of the most breathtaking country I have ever laid my eyes on, and with each advancing mile I traveled east along the road separating Hovenweep from Cortez, I was tempted to surrender myself to it, and spend the rest of my life here. In all the exploring I'd done throughout the Four Corners area, I had somehow managed to overlook the southwestern tip of Colorado. From the Navajo Dam, the San Juan flows west, through New Mexico and into Utah. My day trips off the water were spent exploring the surrounding areas. I'd heard of Cortez, and knew it was in Colorado, but had never been there.

The winding fifty-five-minute drive helped take my mind off the "situation," and I managed to avoid the thought of what I'd say to Leo Biscolli, if and when we met until I reached the outskirts of Cortez.

Whatever I did say, it would have to be something believable—which was going to be hard, since I wasn't sure I believed any of this myself. Leo would be an educated man, a scientist. Scientists want proof, of which I had none. Unless, of course, you count a wet sleeping bag, which I easily could have hosed down myself. What kind of proof was that?

As I approached the city limits, it occurred to me that I could turn around before it was too late, and return to Hovenweep. Heck, for that matter, I had my backpack, fly rod, and all my gear in the trunk. I could shoot south to Albuquerque, catch a flight to Grants Pass, and be sleeping in my own bed tonight. Oliver could find someone else to track down this Biscolli guy. My dilemma would be solved.

"No," I said, as I shook my head. As much as I wanted to forget my spontaneous commitment, I'd said yes, and I'm a person of my word. No one else may have known I'd said yes, but I knew, and that was enough to keep me in the game.

I needed a plan—of that I was sure. I had no clue who I was searching for. If there was such a man, where would I start? Several ideas came to mind, each more desperate than the one before. I shrugged them off and noticing a gas station a couple of blocks ahead, decided that I would deal with the "Leo Biscolli problem" later. Right now, I needed to gas the car and eat a meal. A cafe was just ahead on the left. I could drive to it after filling the car. A meal would buy me some time to think this through and come up with a plan.

Cortez is a cowboy town, and a short look around would have told anyone with eyes, why. Women. Pretty women. Lots of them. Of course, everything else was there too: feed stores, clothing outfitters, and restaurants, but it was clear that the women outweighed any other commodity that the small cowboy town had to offer. One of them greeted me at the gas pump.

"Morning, ma'am. Fill it?"

I suddenly felt old and off my game. I'd been sleeping on a rock, looked a mess, and was searching for a fictional character I'd likely fabricated in my mind.

"Yes, regular. Thanks," I said, refocusing my attention.

The brunette went right to work.

"Nice town," I said.

"Yeah, it's okay. You must be from out of state; license plate says New Mexico."

"Oh, no. A rental. I'm from Portland—Oregon, that is, not Maine."

"Still, a long way from home."

"Yeah, sometimes it feels that way."

I was just about to ask her if she'd ever heard of a Leo Biscolli, when a dirty white passenger van with a deep cargo rack on its roof, pulled up to an adjacent pump. A young man stepped from the gas station office. He was wearing a set of work clothes that matched the ones Miss Brunette was wearing, except that his was cut in half by a saucer-sized silver belt buckle. He slid a cowboy hat over his tangle of red hair as he emerged into the sunlight. From the looks of the hat, he'd done the motion hundreds of times with grimy shop hands.

"Leo! Hey man, where have you been?" The cowboy-turned-mechanic, put one hand on the van and leaned toward the passenger's window. "Yeah," I overheard him say, "There was a fellow here lookin' for you a couple of hours ago, askin' questions and all. Seemed pretty anxious to find you. I'd seen him around town before. I think he's with Collier's outfit, though I could be wrong."

'Leo?' I thought.

It was safe to say the silver-buckled mechanic had my attention. I stuck my head out the window and strained to look beyond the pump between us, to see who was in the van. Miss Brunette must have thought I was looking for her because she came to my window.

"Not quite," she said, looking at the gas pump. "You must have been running on fumes."

"That man," I said, pointing to the white, four-wheel drive van. "The one in that van. Who is he, please?"

"Him? Oh, he's one of the field supervisors over at the RAC Campus."

'The RAC Campus? What was that?' I would ask her, but first, I needed a name.

"His name, I mean. I heard your friend call him Leo."

"Yeah, that's right, Leo. Leo, uh...."

I was dying here. If it was Leo Biscolli, I couldn't let him get away. If it wasn't, well... I decided I could live with the consequences, and leapt from my car. I guess that I startled Miss Brunette because she reached for the edge of the gas pump.

"Sorry miss, didn't mean to surprise you," I apologized.

A blonde man wearing sunglasses had gotten out of the dirty van and had taken his conversation with the cowboy mechanic into the garage. They appeared to be arguing. My legs instantly went weak. I didn't like the looks of this. Cautiously, I approached, keeping my eyes on them both.

The men faced a greasy shop bay. Hoisted above them on an unattended lube rack was a newer GMC pickup truck. I walked across the service station lot and stopped ten feet short of them at a vending machine, located between the open shop bay and the office door. The cowboy had turned by now, and I could see his face. His expression told me that something was wrong. Words broke out again and suddenly the agitated blonde man grabbed the cowboy's arm. My eyes widened. Anxiously, I fed the pop machine all the change I had on me and leaned toward their conversation. I got an earful and it worried me.

"Look man, why you so spooked?" the cowboy asked, pulling back his arm.

"Earl, shut up," the other voice hissed.

"What?" the cowboy said. "What was I supposed to do? I told him I hadn't seen you in a week, maybe more. So where you been hidin' yourself, anyway?"

"Earl, shut up. Don't say a word to anyone. In case anyone asks, you haven't seen me. You hear? Don't say anything!"

"Sorry!" the cowboy replied, clearly shaken.

My pulse was racing. I jiggled the coin return, kicked the vending machine once, and acted irritated longer than necessary for a measly two-dollar drink, then slowly backed toward the car. None of this felt right. I wanted to leave, but darned if I didn't change direction mid-step and started walking right back toward them.

'Okay, let's be rational,' I argued with myself.

By now, they had seen me. Both glared and put their strained conversation on hold. Cowboy Earl looked terrified. The other man's expression was unpleasant, at best. He pulled off his sunglasses, and I watched his eyes narrow with each step I took toward him. There were clear signs that I should stop at the edge of the garage. His eyes burrowed through me.

He was probably my age, though it was difficult to put an age on features I could barely see. It was his chin that led me to believe that there must be a handsome face under the untrained mop of blonde hair. He wore a torn blue tee shirt that read: "If women are from Venus, why don't they go home?" paired with faded khaki shorts, intentionally cut off mid-thigh to accommodate his legs, and a pair of well-worn, dirty boots.

He was waiting.

This was it. We were face-to-face. I was committed. I felt three sets of eyes on me: Earl's, Miss Brunette's, and Leo's. I broke into a cold sweat.

"Leo?" I asked sheepishly. "Leo Biscolli?"

"What the…? Who are you?" he said and sneered.

A wave of panic shot through me. I remembered the rental car. It was within sprinting distance, a source of security—a means of escape; a way back to sanity, to my boulder and my vision quest. I could jump in, floor it, and no one would be the wiser. How had I gotten into this mess?

"I'm looking for… I mean, are you Leo? Leo Biscolli?" I asked.

"You've got to be kidding," he said, eying me up and down. He frowned, then turned to Earl, jabbed him in the ribs, and began violently shaking with laughter. I was clueless.

Earl chimed in. I followed their eyes down my legs, to where their gaze was firmly fixed on my feet, or rather, on my hiking boots. They had a fresh coat of mink oil on them and, aside from the dust and the teeth marks Smurf had left on one, they looked straight off the shelf. They were nothing like Leo's boots, which were even unlaced.

Leo had all the information he wanted. He shook his head, spun toward the van, and walked away.

I couldn't jeopardize the chance to talk with him, so I scraped together what was left of my pride and chased him, taking two steps for every one of his.

"Don't think I'm crazy or anything," I blurted out, "But, jeez, I don't know where to start."

Leo abruptly stopped at the van and turned to me, his face stone. For a long second, he glared, then shook his head again.

"You're not a digger. You're not even a local. You're a damn tourist," he said, coming dangerously close to being cruel. He looked toward the garage. "Hey, Earl?" he called, "Get a close look. This here's no Collier snitch. She's a damn tourist. Can you believe it?" He brought his attention back to me. "Yes, I'm your Leo."

It was a moment of lucid joy, swallowed up by a garbled jumble of emotions.

"God, it's true. You're actually real!" I walloped, my eyes all over him.

"That's it, I'm out of here."

Leo hopped into the van and slammed the heavy door behind him. He rolled his eyes and then slid on his sunglasses. "Sorry, can't talk." From the dashboard, he grabbed some loose money and slapped it into my hand. "Here, do me a favor, would you? Give this gas money to Earl. Thanks."

The engine turned over and the van lunged forward. Without thinking, I grabbed the half-open window. No! He couldn't go. Not now… now, that I had found him. Where was he going? I couldn't let him leave.

There was a quick jerk under my fingers and then the glass slipped from my grip. A cloud of dust lifted from the pavement. I panicked and ran after it, chasing the dirty white van into the street. It sped around the corner and disappeared. He was gone.

For a long minute, I stood there and took a wide-angle snapshot of the disaster, and pressed the whole sorry scene into my memory. In the forefront, was a parked Chevy Malibu and three Chevron gas pumps anchored to concrete. Beyond that, were two cowtown folk with their mouths open, hands fixed on their hips, staring at the gawking tourist who had just chased after a rangy old van, as if God himself were driving it. No one spoke. I think none of us wanted to believe what had just happened. Reluctantly, I walked back to the car, opened the door, and dropped to the seat.

Folks in Cortez were barely finishing their pancakes and I felt spent for the day. I asked Miss Brunette where I could get a room at 10 AM, and she pointed to a yellow and red sign down the street. Some nice folks at White's Motel fixed me up with queen-sized comfort and Wi-Fi. I parked the car and moved in.

# 9

# CORTEZ DINER

I tried as best I could to forget Leo Biscolli over an egg salad sandwich while watching Wheel of Fortune. As if it wasn't bad enough I'd put myself out on a limb, Leo had left me dangling there, feeling like a fool. I didn't like him, and I was confident the feeling was mutual.

I made a couple of phone calls to family and friends, just to check in and let them know where I was. I didn't go into my debacle. It was too recent—and painful—to recall yet. That could come later when the bitter pill wasn't still in my mouth. It was with Lidija that I spoke of my vision quest. I told her of my "warrior experience" at the campground. I told her about Hovenweep. I described my boulder and the ceremonies that I'd just begun before my vision quest had gone awry through a strange encounter with a little man.

I told her about the wet sleeping bag and Oliver, and that I didn't know what to make of him, or his strange message about "Ancient Ones," a secret in the desert, and some archaeologist named Leo Biscolli.

Confiding in Lidija felt like the most sane thing that I'd done all day. She assured me that coming to Four Corners had been a good decision and that now was not the time to try and comprehend the little man's visit. That could come later.

I bought a paperback from the motel lobby catchall rack—which was conveniently displayed next to the aspirin and buried myself in it for most of the day. Around dinnertime, I took a short three-minute walk to the diner that I'd spotted. Seated in a booth facing Main Street, I mindlessly watched people as I dined on the first square meal I'd had in days.

Once I had eaten, my melancholy heart retreated to a dark, lonely place. I asked the waitress if they had a house red, and she slid one in front of me as she cleared my plate from the table. I swirled the glass, regarded it thoughtfully, and then took a sip. I hadn't had a glass of wine since before leaving Portland to care for Mama.

My first taste of alcohol came in my mid-twenties. I was headed off to college, and the gym where I taught fitness classes was giving me a sendoff party. I was offered "tea." How was I to know that it was Long Island iced tea? I nursed the wretched thing for hours and still, half a glass of it remained when everyone went home.

Alcohol had never been a temptation. I routinely had 5 AM personal training clients, it was counterproductive to my own training and perhaps, the most driving reason: I did not want to lose a day of my life recovering from the night before. That just made no sense to me.

Alcohol had been a ceremonial cheer a couple of times a year—or a lively "zivelee" when I traveled with Lidija to her home country of Serbia in Eastern Europe. I'd planned on savoring a glass of wine after the completion of my vision quest. This Red—the one intended for the end of my quest, somehow belonged in my hand now—perhaps, for no other reason than I'd survived meeting Leo Biscolli. What a disaster.

Slowly, the smooth wine brought back a day far kinder than the one that I'd lived just a few hours earlier. I slowly sipped the mellow Red in the glow of a neon "Open" sign above my head. Daylight was waning, and the cowboy town was collecting long shadows. A handful of cars lined Main Street and a dozen more were parked in a grocery store lot. I stole glances of Cortez and daydreamed.

Now, any fisherman will tell you that they despise wading upstream. Caught once in a dark green hole with no way out but a hard walk against the current, cures you from wanting to go there again. A good part of me wanted to abandon this idiotic crusade, even though Leo had been found. What had driven me this far anyway? A promise? A promise to whom? Certainly not that little man. He was speaking for the earth. He had called her "Earth Mother." Was my promise to her?

These questions and more assailed me, and my head hurt from it. If I'd only not said those dreaded words: "Tell me."

The little man had given me a choice. I could have refused right then and been done with it. Where had my reply come from anyway—volunteered from some inner voice unknown to me? Not possible. And yet, the words had practically said themselves. What else might I agree to if backed against a wall? Could I trust myself? The thought terrified me. Sure, I'd done things spontaneously: Grand Gulch, helping Lidija with her mother… and then caring for my own. But this—this was different. Some inner voice had volunteered me.

I could see that I was putting myself at the bargaining table, hoping a second round of negotiations could be made, but with whom? With Oliver? With Earth Mother? With Leo? I gave a heavy sigh. No, it wasn't going to happen. I sipped the wine and considered what to do.

A couple entered the diner, stirring me from my musings. I caught the waitress's attention and stepped out, walking along the sidewalk with no specific destination in mind. Why make me promise to find some smart-mouth jackass, who couldn't be bothered to tie his own shoes—much less listen to what I had to say? What makes Earth Mother think this self-centered, sorry-excuse for a man, would listen to her?

I had barely finished that thought when it dawned on me that I was in no position to judge anyone. Forget Leo. Why did Earth Mother want me? I held onto that thought.

Who was I, anyway?

I was of no importance or influence. Nothing about my life felt remarkable; in fact, it'd become insignificant. Heck, three weeks ago I was changing adult diapers. Surely someone more capable could find Leo and give him this message. My argument wasn't whether or not I loved nature—loved Mama Gaia: this earth, but what qualification is that?

This was a crazy story: a little man, a crying rock, a smart-mouth archaeologist, and me? Nobody was going to accept any of this as real. One could logically conclude that the whole thing had been brought on by exhaustion, grief, or sunstroke—it was all an illusion. Coincidence. Heck, even I didn't believe it.

But now... now I knew otherwise. Leo Biscolli was real, which meant that this was somehow real. I slowed my pace.

Leo is real.

I stopped and stood very, very still.

"Leo is real," I repeated, this time aloud. A cold chill ran through me. I raised my hand to my mouth and held it there, contemplating. 'Wait. How can that be?'

I took three steps, then stopped again and stood very still. I quickly replayed this morning's debacle through my mind and gave myself a moment of quiet.

As much as I didn't like this Biscolli character, it was hard to quit, knowing that I'd found him.

Or, maybe...

Wait! Could it be?

Maybe... What if, Leo had found me?

The strange idea scrambled my thoughts. Was it possible, I wondered? What were the odds that Leo and I would be at the same gas station at precisely the same moment? Could it be that we were supposed to meet?

The idea was a lot to wrap my mind around, and I had to think this through, because if I believed this—believed that our paths had crossed, then that would mean that Oliver was real and speaking for Earth.

Still, I couldn't fathom why Earth Mother would need me, of all people. What makes her believe that I could do this—that I could help her? That made no sense. I knew nothing of "Ancient Ones," the desert, or some secret it held, but...

I stopped mid-thought.

"But, what if Leo Biscolli does?" I heard myself say aloud. An icy chill ran through me. If that were true, was I ready for this?

Was I? Really?

I began walking again, slowly.

This bewildering puzzle had gotten under my skin. What was going on here? If Leo Biscolli had been put in my path—or rather,

I'd been put in his, then that would suggest that something bigger than us was at work here. I was suddenly terrified and unafraid at the same time. I understood absolutely none of this at one level. And yet, I felt wholly sure of it at another.

I decided to find Leo again. But where? Where could I look? I remembered that Miss Brunette had said that he worked somewhere, but where? Did she really know? What had Miss Brunette said? He was a what? At where?

'Think, True!' I said to myself, dangerously close to saying it out loud. It was useless though. I'd have to ask. My one hope was Cowboy Earl. But after this morning's argument with Leo, I wasn't sure how free he'd be with the information I needed. Earl had, after all, witnessed Leo's scoffing. Whatever I may have thought of this archaeologist, I had to give this another go. All I could do was try. I started walking again, picked up my pace, and headed toward the motel.

Once there, I stepped into the office to ask for a 6:30 AM wakeup call. That would give me enough time to meditate, eat breakfast, and arrive at the gas station around eight. On my way out of the lobby, a wall display caught my eye, It was lined with colorful brochures for everything from local raft trips to chuck wagon meals at a reservation casino somewhere out west. I pulled a couple from the display and closed the door behind me. When I had settled back into my room, I showered, readied for bed, and then leaned against the headboard to make my first journal entry:

> **Friday, May 13**
>
> "Good Lord, what a crazy day! There's been a bizarre detour in my plans for a vision quest. I'm in Cortez, Colorado, looking for an archaeologist named Leo Biscolli.

I was told to find him by a little old man that scared the crap out of me last night on my boulder. I still don't know how he scaled the six-foot boulder—and I don't know what to make of any of this.

I found Leo today. Every bit of it was a train wreck, but at least I know he exists. I'm hoping to talk with someone who knows him tomorrow. We'll see how that goes—it's all I know to do. I hope tomorrow is a better day.

I wish I knew more of what was going on here. On second thought, maybe it's best I don't. I'm terrified enough of what seems to be the truth. The fact that Leo is real suggests something big is going on here. What? I don't know. For future reference, Cortez is a great little town."

I set aside my journal and leafed through the brochures that I'd tossed onto the nightstand. The top one was right up my alley: The Dolores River Canyon wilderness area. It sounded like a great river to fish, especially in autumn when the aspens changed color.

The second looked interesting too. It read: "Have you ever wanted to participate in an archeological dig and live first-hand the day-to-day life of an archaeologist? You can do this at the Red Rock Archaeological Campus. The current sites under excavation are Raven Creek and Yellow Bar. All you need is a desire for learning and adventure. No experience required."

"Huh… that sounds kinda fun. Maybe next trip." I looked over a third brochure and found myself yawning, the telltale sign I was about to nod off. This was enough for one day. I slid everything onto the nightstand, turned over, and closed my eyes.

# ANASAZI VISION

My wakeup call was right on time. I eased out of bed to begin what I hoped would be a significantly better day than the one I'd put to rest last night. When it came to Cowboy Earl, I realized that I was trying to analyze a man I knew absolutely nothing about. Just how Earl would react to my asking questions about a man who clearly wanted nothing to do with me, I didn't know.

My morning meditation was glorious. I slipped into stillness easily, a delicious contrast to yesterday's mental and emotional gymnastics. The quiet was restorative and it grounded me. However, toward the end of my meditation, I began to hear Oliver's voice. At first, it was just a word, then a second, and finally a complete sentence. Was I remembering his words? Was I hearing them again? It was an odd experience. I reached for my journal and wrote exactly what I heard during my meditation. On my way out of the room, I slid all the loose, incidental stuff that I'd set on the nightstand into my purse and left.

Apparently, all of Cortez was out for Saturday morning breakfast. I waited with the cowboys and ranch hands for a table in the small, knotty-pine diner and considered today's search for Leo Biscolli. I had just one plan: talk to Earl. If that didn't pan out, I had nothing and that worried me. I needed a backup plan in case the mechanic wouldn't talk to me. Maybe Miss Brunette?

I concluded that Leo had been found once and he could be found again... somehow. I gnawed on "somehow" over a cup of coffee, then glanced at the menu and reached into my purse to grab my phone. The brochures were on top. Why had I grabbed these? They had to go.

I was just checking the weather on my phone when a waitress stepped up to my table. I read her name tag.

"Good morning, Claire," I said. "Is your special good?"

"Ray's tending the grill this morning. You'll love it."

"Great. I'll take it."

"You've got it," she said, scribbling on a notepad.

"Say, can I ask you something?"

"Shoot, Sweetie."

I knew I liked this woman already. She stopped writing, slid the tablet into the pocket of her apron, and picked up the menu.

"Have you ever heard of a Leo Biscolli?"

"Leo? Oh yes!"

"Really? Do you know where I can find him?"

"Well, you've got a pamphlet for the Campus right there," she said, pointing her ballpoint to the table. I pinched the top brochure and slid it toward me. It read, "Red Rock Archaeological Campus." Impatiently, I scanned it again. This was it, the campus that Miss Brunette had mentioned. It had been right there in front of me the whole time. How could I have missed it? There at the bottom of the brochure, tucked between the copy and contact information, was a list of the staff: Eric Ward - Director, Emma Ott, Randy Ummel, and Leonard Biscolli - Field Supervisors.

My unfriendly cards had turned. I leapt from the booth, nearly crushing my legs into the table. Claire took a step back and spun around in place, righting herself in front of me.

"Thank you, I love you," I said, excitedly. I fumbled with my wallet and managed to pass Claire a five-dollar bill and wrapped her in a hug. "For the coffee," I said, turning back to snatch the brochure from the table.

# 10

# RED ROCK

The sign at the end of the three-quarter mile driveway read: "Red Rock Archaeological Campus." 'This must be it,' I thought as I eased into the graveled parking lot. I glanced at the clock on the dash: 9:13 AM. Two patrol cars were parked in the lot. The very sight of them made me uneasy.

'What now?'

I sat in the car for a while, wondering what sort of place this was. Only when I walked through the parking lot, did I get my first real glimpse of the buildings and their surroundings. My first thought was they may be retired Army Corps barracks; resurrected, painted over, and recycled into an archaeological research campus.

There were three structures. One was a metal garage of sorts, with a massive sliding door across the face of it. It sat within a cyclone wire fence and sliding gate. Within the fenced area were half a dozen passenger vans, each outfitted with long cargo boxes on their roofs, overflowing with an assortment of ropes and gear that I assumed was archaeological equipment. All were filthy. I recognized a white one among them: "God's" van, I reminded myself.

The other two single-story buildings were joined by an enclosed breezeway. They were of equal size, but one had a dozen or more windows, whereas the other had few large ones. I'd come to learn that the second building was where the administrative offices and laboratories were housed. The building with natural light was the chow hall and sleeping quarters.

The grounds were not large, but they were immaculate and the landscape showed that trained talent had done it. The age of the buildings and the landscape didn't match, however. Young maple trees were dwarfed beside the Roosevelt New Deal-era structure, and a vibrant border of spring flowers spilled onto the broad walkway leading to large brown metal double doors. A sprinkler was running, adding a glistening sheen to the scene.

The entire campus was perched on an impressive mountainous peninsula that jutted into a canyon, seemingly dropping off into the abyss. It was an isolated world of pristine beauty, rising several hundred feet above the irregular land masses of the plateau country that it overlooked. Somewhere, along the thirty-five-minute drive to the campus from Cortez, a subtle transition of vegetation zones had occurred. The Center sat on a stair-step peninsula, between the Rocky Mountains and the broad desert floor. In one direction was an alpine world dotted with an occasional white-capped mountain and, in the other, a vast expanse of indistinguishable colorful mesas and plateaus, with roads winding in all directions around them. I was awestruck at the sheer magnitude of this place—an expansive property bridging two seemingly different worlds.

No one seemed to mind that I was walking the grounds. People of all ages were meandering around the campus. I entered the building with few windows, through the heavy double doors. The interior was a simple floor plan. A central lobby, housing a waiting area with display cases filled with artifacts, photographs, and maps.

The focal point, however, of the large sitting room was a scale model of the archeological sites currently under excavation.

It was an interesting room and I hoped to return to it after I spoke with Leo Biscolli. The campus was an active place. People moved about the network of long hallways, entering and leaving doors in the corridors that branched off of the lobby in all directions from the main entrance. Their voices echoed in the corridors.

"Good morning, have you been helped?"

"No. No, not yet," I said, turning toward the voice. The young dark-skinned woman with long black curls was seated behind an ornately carved wood desk that looked out of place in a building constructed with so much metal. A green, bell-shaped lamp on the desk lit her soft features.

"I'm looking for Leo Biscolli."

"Well, I'm sure he's around here somewhere. I can check if you'd like. You can wait here, or maybe you would prefer to wait in our library. Either way, he'll find you."

"A library? Oh, thanks. I'll wait there."

"All right then," she replied, with a smile.

The library was the first door adjacent to the lobby. It was a large open room with a massive window on the facing wall. I remembered seeing the window from outside. Half a dozen ancient-looking metal light fixtures hung from the high ceiling, casting a glow over the neatly arranged rows of shelves that filled most of the space. At the center stood an enormous wooden table, perhaps the largest I had ever seen in a library. Beneath the large window was a well-worn brown plaid sofa. Two people sat on it, reading in the natural light.

I poured over book titles as I waited and three caught my eye. I pulled one from the shelf and began to leaf through it. Soon, I heard the sound of the library door opening and shut. I wedged my finger into the book I was holding. When I looked up, I could see from Leo's sour expression, that he instantly recognized me as the "damn tourist" from the gas station yesterday.

From fifteen feet away, we eyed one another as I weighed my options. It was the first opportunity I'd had to take a close look at him. Actually, he didn't look so terrifying surrounded by books. But, the man was definitely built to fill his boots.

I had worked alongside enough men in not just one, but two, male-dominated fields: the military and bodybuilding, to recognize a "man's man." He's the one that sets the mood, the pace, the standard. When he shows up, the work day starts. He's his own man—doesn't need approval or validation from anyone; not so good with rules and usually too smart and self-reliant for his own good. He's an idea man, a self-starter, and not one to back down—always in control of his time, who gets to know him, and how close they get. He's not an Alpha male. He's a Sigma—the rarest of the rare. And I was looking at one.

Leo Biscolli stood tall, his wide shoulders and thick arms contrasting with a trim waist. His thighs, honed to perfection from months of traversing the rugged terrain of the high desert, suggested a life of rigorous activity. I had to admit, he had a magnificent physique. He was a good-looking blonde, muscular, and… intoxicated. That's right: it was only nine-thirty in the morning, and Leo lumbered into the library, clearly under the influence. Who was this guy?

The physique may have been impressive, but that's where it stopped. He was a sorry sight standing there: untrained blonde hair, face unshaven, wearing stringy cut-offs and a wrinkled blue tee shirt that read, "The Seven Habits of Highly Defective People." For all I knew, the guy had just rolled out of bed and started sucking on Jack Daniels.

We stared at each other a long time; long enough that the two young people on the sofa excused themselves from the room. I spoke first.

"Biscolli. You're Italian?"

"Hardly. Adopted, you know…"

"Oh yeah, right. Well, my name is True. True North. I think we got off to a bad start," I said, extending my hand to the man.

"Uh-huh," he replied with passing interest, offering me a half-assed handshake. I could smell his breath.

"You are Leo. Leo Biscolli, right?"

Yeah," he said, cautiously. It appeared the alcohol had only moderately impaired him. The overt unfriendliness, however, was a choice. Whatever his problem was, he wasn't making this easy.

"Well, uh… can we sit?"

"Depends…"

This was going nowhere fast, In fact, this whole thing was wearing my patience dangerously thin. It shouldn't take this much work to talk with the man. I was this close to getting mad.

"Is something going on here? I mean, there are two patrol cars in the parking lot, and excuse me for saying so, but you're acting pretty sketchy for someone who's supposed to be in charge here."

Am I now?" he answered, cooly.

I was done measuring my words. "Look, I don't know what's going on here at your little campus, I was just told to find you. If you're running from something—gambling debt or God knows what, that's your business, but I don't have anything to do with that. I just came here to talk. That's all."

"My turn," Leo interrupted, finally turning his full attention on me. "Mind if I ask one question? Who sent you here?"

"Well, that's why I'm hoping we can sit down. See, I'm only a little less confused than you are, right now. So humor me, please. Can we sit?"

"All right," Leo replied.

It was a start. We took a seat on the sofa. Up close, he wasn't as drunk as he'd first appeared.

"Seriously. Do you treat all your guests this way? Look, I don't know why the boulder wants you to help. Heck, what am I saying? I don't even know why it wants me to help," I said.

"What are you talking about?" he asked, shaking his head.

"Well, this is going to sound a little screwy, I know. But bear with me, please. I'm still trying to believe this myself."

"Yeah, go on…"

"I'm from Portland, Oregon. My mom just passed, and I came here for a vision quest. You know, some time alone in nature, looking for answers."

"All right…"

'Good, we're getting somewhere here,' I thought.

"Well, I was just going about my quest, when I got this dream. At least, I thought it was a dream. Only now, I'm not so sure—the little man seemed so real. Oh, I don't know! Anyway, he said… just don't think I'm nuts, okay?"

"Yeah, sure… go on," he said.

"Well, see, the boulder I was sleeping on became wet. My sleeping bag and clothes became soaked through, and you know it hasn't rained. I can show you my sleeping bag if you want… it's probably still wet. Anyway, he told me that the boulder was crying and that it wanted him to speak for it; I mean, speak to me."

"Somebody told you this?" he asked.

"Yeah, the little man. Oliver was his name."

"Uh-huh…"

"He said something about the desert at Four Corners, that it held a power capable of helping the planet—to help bring it into balance. There was something else too. He said the secret was with the Ancient Ones, and that I should find you. So, Leo, that's why I'm here. Make any sense to you?" I asked.

"Not really. Then, you're not with Collier? You're not tailing me? I wouldn't put it past him to use some babe."

"Collier? No! Who's that? Not one of your friends, I take it. And please don't call me a 'babe.'"

"No. No, he's not. And, sorry, I…"

A man rushed into the library calling, "Biscolli," loudly as he passed through the spring-loaded door. When he noticed us on the sofa, he retracted like a pistol accidentally cocked, and came to an abrupt stop. He wobbled a bit, then quickly redeemed himself by adding, "Oh, sorry! Ah, Biscolli, got a minute? The officers want to see you again before they take off."

The anxious man looked to be in his fifties. His heightened state of anxiety only slightly outweighed his level of intoxication. He was more liquored up than Leo. Though, it appeared that he had at least taken the time to shave. He was working hard at gaining his composure.

"Sure," Leo called to him over his shoulder. "Be right back. Are you okay here?" he asked me.

"Yeah, go ahead."

His voice sounded almost sincere. As the two passed through the door, I heard the anxious man ask Leo, "Who's that?" Admittedly,

I strained to hear Leo's reply, but his answer came on the other side of the door.

I was having a hard time figuring out Leo. I wasn't sure I liked him, but his last words to me had been kind, so I made up my mind to at least try and cut him some slack. I needed him, or at least, Earth Mother did. Besides, my brain was riddled with questions, and there was so much I wanted to ask him.

Within minutes of Leo's departure, I'd located the "Ancient Civilizations" section of the library. I wasn't sure what I was looking for. At first, I just scanned the neat rows of books, reading titles and flipping through an occasional one that caught my eye. I selected one book, then another, and another. Before long, I was removing books from the shelves, stacking them in my arm, and transferring them onto the enormous table in the center of the room. Once I had a decent stack of books, I dove into them and my world turned into flying words. I went from chapter to chapter, reading under the old light fixture. An hour slipped by unnoticed. I took a break and asked where I might get a cup of strong coffee. I was directed to the chow hall, where I poured myself a cup, and returned to my reading.

Had I not shut out everything alive, I might have heard Leo enter the room. But he wasn't in my world, which is why I suppose he felt that he had to bring me into his, any way he could. He chose to do it by clearing his throat.

"What the…? I said, jumping with a start.

"Sorry, there was no easy way of doing that. What's got your interest?" He appeared far more sober.

"Oh, this," I said, slapping the book closed and showing him the cover.

"Hum, Anasazi: Ancient People of the Rocks. I know it."

I showed him two others, held open by the weight of the first. "Here, take this for a second," I said, handing Leo the book in my hand. I reached across the pile of books strewn on the table for another. When I glanced up, it was the first time that I'd seen interest on his face, and his words soon confirmed it.

"I've never seen a tourist use this library before, and here you are, devouring it whole. What gives?"

"Well, I can't very well discover some Anasazi secret if I know nothing about them," I said.

"Wait, hold on. What do you mean, some Anasazi secret?"

"From what I've read, they're the Ancient Ones, and were extraordinary people."

"You're right about that," he replied.

"I just wish I knew exactly what it is I'm looking for…"

"What's that?" Leo asked.

"Well, I'm not sure," I sighed. "But I've got a hunch I'll know it when I see it. Have you ever had that feeling?"

"Of course, I'm a scientist. I live by facts but run with my hunches all the time."

"Yeah, I guess so," I said, studying Leo's expression. He was a handsome man, clear blue eyes behind the smudged glasses he'd put on—eyes that told me he was in trouble. Unlike earlier, this was a new trouble, and I wondered if somehow he saw me connected to it. I reached out and took the book from his hand. Leo took a seat across the table from me.

"Say, Leo…"

"Biscolli, please." He interrupted.

"Biscolli," I said, nodding. "I'm not keeping you from something, am I? I understand you're a field supervisor. I suppose you're in high demand around here."

"Ha, that's a good one!" Biscolli laughed. His face then turned suddenly serious and he hid it from me. I'd struck an open nerve. "We have several excellent people here. Excellent." He said, almost to himself. "No, you're not keeping me from anything." His voice sounded somber. "I'm free for about another hour, anyway. What do you know of Four Corners?" he asked.

Watching his face had been difficult. I was curious where my question had taken him. Did it have something to do with the man who'd burst into the room or the patrol cars? I decided rather than jump the track to pursue it with a man I knew nothing about, I answered his question.

"Nothing, other than a couple of fishing spots and a few ruins."

We were face-to-face. His expression had quietly softened to a faint smile. Whatever his dragon was, it had gone back into its cave. I was running out of reasons to dislike him. We sat in silence for a long minute. I noticed he'd glanced between me and the books strewn across the table, twice. I just eyed him. Biscolli then leaned back in his chair and his smile broadened. It instantly infected me. What was up? This wasn't the alcohol raising a smile—traces of that were gone. I looked at him, curiously.

"What…?" I finally asked, confused.

He waited, and I finally caught up to the idea that the irritation between us had waned, and cleared a space for something more congenial to exist. I returned his smile.

"You mentioned some things earlier," he said, leaning forward. "And I have to admit, I wasn't paying attention. Could you repeat…?"

"Well, I'm glad you don't think I'm crazy," I interrupted.

"I didn't say that!" Biscolli replied, then let out an enormous laugh. It pulled me in, and our laughter filled the library. It was pretty funny. I had, after all, felt nuts since Oliver's visit. The spontaneous outburst, gratefully, diffused the mishmash of emotions I'd wrestled with since leaving my boulder. It felt wonderful to laugh. Eventually, we quieted down, and I regained composure, wiping the tears from my eyes. I then tried to recall everything Oliver had told me without access to the journal I'd written it in.

The archaeologist listened as I shared what I remembered of Oliver's visit. When I'd finished, Biscolli searched my face for a trace of fiction, then leaned across the table and whispered, "There's something you should know."

# 11

## TWO INFANTS

I stood outside the library door, gazing down the long corridor. Natural light from a double glass door at the end of the hall cast a soft glow on the polished gray floor tiles that ran its length. The soft-spoken woman who had greeted me earlier was working at her desk. The lamp beside her was lit, and as she moved, it raised a luminous glow on her ebony skin. I marveled how the lamp did its trick with her skin, and my eyes followed her arms as she worked. Like clockwork, the attractive woman would brush her long, thick curls from her face, and we would exchange polite smiles. She must be from Cortez, I mused.

Leo Biscolli and I had come a long way this morning. Though there were still plenty of potholes between us, I was encouraged. I'd seen attention on his face and it'd given me a needed boost. Then, just as he appeared willing to share some important information, he suddenly excused himself and left the library. Where he disappeared to, I had no clue. All he said on his way out the door, was to wait in the hallway. His abrupt exit was a disappointment, but he smiled on his way out the door, and that's what I was hanging on to.

Waiting for someone I didn't know or trust, only fueled my anxiety. Fifteen minutes passed, and my faith was nearly spent when a door opened midway along the corridor, and Leo stepped from it, very excited about something. His muscular silhouette cast a long shadow over the waxed floor. Upon spotting me, he waved maniacally, making a spectacle of himself. Two girls filing past the door, covered their mouths to giggle. It didn't faze him.

Leo led me through the doorway and into a classroom. It was long and rectangular, lit by a neat row of uncovered windows that ran the length of the wall facing me. Laboratory equipment had been situated on a large table at the head of the room. Behind it were two chalkboards. Five long tables forming a U-shape filled the better part of the sunny room.

Scattered over the tables were pottery shards, paper sacks, grease pencils, and shoeboxes. Shelves that had been crammed with plastic dish tubs, baskets, and hundreds of lunch-size paper sacks, each marked with identifying numbers. Under the wall of windows sat a 4x4-foot sieve made of two-by-fours, alongside an eight-foot-long trough. Pottery shards were strewn across the expansive screen of the sieve, while a portable container beneath it held dirt.

Sunlight filtering through dingy windows lit the air and illuminated fine dust particles floating on it. A thin film of dust covered everything. Images of high school biology lab flashed through my head. I looked around to find Leo. He was at the instructor's table, pulling on white cloth gloves.

"I thought you'd left me for dead," I said.

"Hardly," Leo replied. "It took some time to track these down and sign them out of inventory. Check this out..."

The instructor's table sat on a platform that elevated it above the classroom floor by several inches. I stepped onto it and stood beside him, then glanced to see what had his interest. At first, I couldn't figure out what it was, but then it occurred to me that I was looking at a tiny infant skeleton, wrapped in decayed cloth.

"Oh, wow," I said, staring at the little bundle carefully packed in a wooden crate. "This is amazing."

"Isn't it fascinating?" Leo said, gently touching a tiny, darkened skull fused to the decomposed fabric. "This was recovered from our Raven Creek site. It's over 700 years old, and the reason the cops were here."

"What?"

"Hold your horses and let me explain," he said, pulling up two stools and tapping his hand on the one intended for me. "The Anasazi typically buried their deceased in plots located southwest of their villages. Long before we remove the first trowel of dirt from an archaeological dig, we've done a thorough job locating potential burial sites."

I listened.

"Look at this," he said, unrolling a length of drafting paper with worn and dirty edges. "A colleague drew this sketch after seismic readings were done on the Raven Creek site. We've been excavating that particular site for nine-and-a-half years now. Our digs have been restricted to here, here, and here," he explained, tapping on the drawing.

"That's some dig," I said, looking at the drawing.

"Now, here's where it gets tricky." Leo turned and looked at me. "The death of a young child was considered a private loss rather than a communal one, so the Anasazi buried very young children under the dirt floors of their private dwellings. Once a child became of age—and was a participating community member, any untimely death would have resulted in burial at a communal site."

"I see," I said, nodding my head.

"We never know where we might unearth an infant such as this one. Our protocol is, if we do find human remains, we fill in the area, flag it, and leave it undisturbed."

I nodded my head.

"A treaty has been made with the local Ute tribe, protecting human remains in this corner of the southwest, but that's not why we comply. It's a matter of respect. These are the remains of their ancestors," Leo said, then glanced around, as if someone might be listening.

"This child was unearthed by Dan Collier and his boys; artifact thieves the local authorities have been trying to apprehend for decades. Their methods for securing artifacts, which they then sell to dealers, involve heavy equipment and helicopters. No one doubts Collier is behind the latest rash of looting but, to put him away, he has to be caught in the act."

"I had no idea," I said.

"Most people don't realize the problem. Increased interest in Native Americans and their artifacts has also increased the demand for them, especially ancient ones. With demand high, Collier has upped his game. The bastard's been in business for thirty years. He was caught once, convicted, and served five years. He claims he's clean, but we all recognize Collier's work."

"So, let me see if I understand. Are you saying…?"

"We didn't dig up this baby," Leo interrupted. "Collier did! But that's not the worst of it. See, he sure as hell knows he can't be caught with human remains, so when his men unearthed this infant with their backhoe, Collier had his men toss her."

"What? Who would do such a thing?"

"Collier, I'm telling you. Besides, I have proof."

"Proof? What kind of proof?"

"Later. That's another story." Leo studied my face then continued. "The reason I wanted you to see the remains, True, is because of this!"

Leo slid over another wooden crate.

"This was recovered from a Mogollon site under excavation in Chihuahua, Mexico. It's on loan to us, but I wanted you to see it. It may help you find what you're looking for. Oh, and Mogollon is pronounced, 'mogge-yon'," Leo added. "I thought I'd help you pronounce that one. Most people get it wrong."

I watched with intense curiosity, as he lifted the lid and painstakingly unwrapped something inside with his gloved fingers. It was another infant, swaddled in a swatch of extremely damaged material. It was exquisite. The way its tiny body had been prepared and wrapped, it looked remarkably similar to the first infant.

"Leo?" I questioned. "You say this was found in Mexico? Why, this infant looks like… It's practically identical to…"

"Exactly!" he said, excitedly. "There's plenty of speculation among archaeologists about a link between the Mogollon and the Anasazi… well, a few of us suspect it, anyway. But, we had no solid proof actually linking the two. Fortunately, this little one was still in our possession when Collier chewed up our dig. Side by side, they support our… well, my theory. You can't miss it, just look at the two of them!"

"Fascinating," I said, marveling at the infants.

"Rarely do we get an opportunity like this. You understand the Anasazi remains shouldn't be here. We never remove remains from a site," he continued.

"Of course."

"These, however, are being held as evidence against Collier. The Ute tribe is understandably upset that we are retaining the infant, but what can we do? If we nail this creep, perhaps this sort of thing will taper off—at least for a while. It'll be better for their people in the long run, but they don't see it that way."

"So, what are you telling me?"

"My bet is, the Mogollon and Anasazi are cousins of the same culture. True, I swear it's an archaeologist's curse," Leo continued. "We depend on our hunches to push the envelope of our understanding but refuse to believe any part of it until there is imperial evidence to support what we've instinctively known all along. We live in a strange box we just can't seem to climb out of. It's an occupational hazard, I suppose."

"I can relate to that," I said.

Leo pulled a map from one of the dusty shelves, unfolded it, and pressed out the creases with his gloved hands.

"Look here," he said, tapping his finger on it. "What we know for certain is that two thousand years ago, primitive hunters and gatherers inhabited the Southwest. Gradually, they transitioned from hunting and gathering to farming, and bands of these people began settling the canyon valleys and mesa tops to farm. Their rough pit houses gave way to beautifully crafted pueblos of stone, clay mortar, and adobe."

"Yes, I've visited some ruins. They're amazing," I said.

"We're not talking about a simple civilization here. The Anasazi designed ingenious dams and culverts to divert rainwater to their crops. They built a massive road system, found a way to communicate over vast distances, and mastered the art of pottery. These beautiful pieces are the artifacts Collier is digging for."

"I see…"

"The decision to settle the high mesas and cliff sides was no accident. They determined that the mesas gave them several more inches of rainfall each year, extending their growing season, and the south-facing walls captured warmth, and gave them year-round shelter."

"So, that's why they went to the mesas?"

"Yes, the mesas could be 2,000 feet above the desert floor. Their settlements spread, and by 1100 AD, they were building pueblo apartments, hundreds of rooms in size. Chaco Canyon has over 600 structures, some reaching three stories high," Leo said, looking at me. "There was a surge of construction between 950 and 1100 AD. That was when most of Chaco was built, as well as the road system I just mentioned. These roads radiated outward some 30,000 square miles from Chaco—30,000, True. To give you some perspective, that's the size of Scotland!"

He paused and let me catch up. Making sure that I was following what he was teaching me.

"Now, this may be important in your search… and why I'm going into detail about Chaco Canyon. Chaco was a hub; the trade center and economic stronghold for the Ancestral Puebloans—basically, their version of what London is to the UK. Pueblo Bonito was the heart of the Chacoan complex, home to 7,000 people at its peak of occupation. These are your 'Ancient Ones,'" Leo said.

I was following what the archaeologist was saying, but it didn't take a rocket scientist to figure out these people were dead, and without a written record to impart their knowledge, how would I find the secret Earth Mother said they had?

"I have a question," I said.

"Sure, shoot."

"So, if the mecca of the Anasazi was Chaco, and they left no written record, where do I begin to uncover their secret in the desert?"

"You keep talking about a secret. I don't know what you think you're looking for, but you may be disappointed," he said, studying my face. "I believe the extent of the Anasazi's technical, medical, agricultural, and astrological advances suggests they had many 'secrets,' if that is what you want to call them. Hell, their architectural accomplishments alone set them apart as one of the most advanced civilizations to have lived on the planet."

"Yes, but we already know all these things—they're documented," I said. "Oliver was emphatic that there was something there, hidden from plain sight; something protected by the desert. If I remember correctly, his very words were: 'The Ancient Ones hold a secret, as does the land. Learn this secret and you will unlock a floodgate that will renew the world, restoring it anew.'" I paused and tried to recall the rest of his message off the top of my head. Nothing. I looked to Leo for some direction or guidance.

"Well, I don't know what to tell you, True. I thought this might help," Leo said, shaking his head. "Why, again, are you doing this?"

I ran my fingers through my hair and sighed. It was a legitimate question. Did I have an honest answer? Did I?

"Leo," I said, looking directly at him. "I know we just met, and you have no reason to trust me, but, I just have to say…," I then paused, closed my eyes, and brought my attention to my heart, where I hoped the truth of my answer lived. I knew the archaeologist was looking at me—waiting and probably wondering what the hell I was doing. When I felt centered and calm, I opened my eyes and continued.

"I came to the desert thinking that I was going to get some direction for my life. Just something simple, you know, like where to live when I pack up my stuff at my mom's."

I paused again, feeling tears starting to form and my heart now taking over this conversation. I decided to go with it. Leo had walked away once. He could do it again—but, at least I would have spoken my truth. I could live with that, so I continued.

"I wasn't expecting to have a grand vision. Not like this, anyway. Leo, there was a little man. He was real. He spoke for the earth. He delivered her message. She asked for our help, and the answer is somewhere out here, in this desert."

I could feel the first tear roll down my cheek. I wiped it away with my hand, hoping Leo wouldn't get up and walk out. Could he handle a woman crying?

"I have no idea why Oliver wants me to help," I said. "I'm nobody. I have no idea what I can do. I'm just one person. All this feels huge, and honestly, it scares me. But, Oliver was speaking for Earth Mother... and I do love her." I wiped away another tear. "I don't know anything about this desert other than what I've read and you've told me. I guess that's why I need you," I confessed.

I turned away. I just couldn't meet his eyes. I was confused. I felt pulled to Four Corners, to him, to this ancient culture, but it was all a big mystery to me.

"I'm here because I didn't say 'yes' to Oliver. Some inner part of me said it. I know I'm supposed to do this. I can't tell you why or how. I just know that I have to."

I turned toward Leo again.

"There's something here—something vitally important. Oliver said there's a power here—some key for Earth and all of us." I paused and wiped a tear from my cheek. "Leo, advanced civilizations were wiped off the earth when they upset her balance... and we're headed that way—but we still have time." I dabbed my eyes with the back of my hand.

"I don't know what the Ancient Ones have to do with bringing Earth into balance—or how that's supposed to keep us from making the same mistakes other civilizations did. Oliver just said the secret was here and it was being protected. This is big, Leo—and apparently, I'm supposed to do this with you. That's why I'm here."

Leo dug a handkerchief out of his back pocket and handed it to me. The thoughtful gesture made me laugh. This man was an enigma: a mop of bed hair, a wrinkled shirt, recently intoxicated—and the man had a clean handkerchief!

"Thank you," I said and wiped my eyes.

Leo stared at me for what felt like an eternity before he finally spoke. I was ready for whatever way this would go. I now knew in my bones that I was going to do this thing, one way or another.

"I don't know what planet you dropped in from..." Leo said, finally, and paused studying my face.

I let his words sink in.

So, this was his answer. I stood, ready to turn and walk away. He reached for my forearm.

"...but, I'm in, True. I'm in. You're some woman, and I respect you. I can see this is important to you." Leo withdrew his hand but continued to look up at me. "It's no secret around here that the Anasazi are, well... my life. This sounds significant. If it involves the Anasazi, then it involves me. I've always suspected there's more to these people than we know," he said.

I smiled, relieved, and equally frightened that the archaeologist believed me.

"Tell you what," Leo said, brightly. "Are you hungry? We can talk over breakfast. I could use some. How about you?"

Since I had flown out of the cafe that morning with nothing more than coffee in my stomach and had just poured out my heart, breakfast sounded like a wonderful idea.

I composed myself and handed back the handkerchief. Leo smiled. He then replaced the lids of the wooden boxes, removed his gloves, carefully placed one box on my waiting arms, and picked up the other. We then exited the classroom, and he walked us to a secured area. He let himself in and spoke with someone who inspected the box he was holding. Leo then returned to me, retrieved the box I was carrying, and repeated the process. When the bald man with glasses was satisfied, Leo rejoined me and led the way again.

I tried to keep pace with Leo, I wondered if this was his natural stride, or one that took over when he was excited—or agitated. He eventually reduced his stride, and I was glad for it. A moment later, he turned to me.

"I take it, you've just had your world rocked."

That was an understatement. In truth, none of this had truly sunk in as actually happening yet. I was simply trying to hang on and keep up. I found humor in the thought: Indeed, not only was I trying to keep up with this man's stride, physically, but academically.

"That's an understatement," I said, repeating my thought aloud.

Leo smiled. There was a healthy trace of understanding in it. He led us along several corridors, and eventually through a set of double doors I recognized. We'd entered the Chow Hall. It was cafeteria style. Leo pulled a tray and ordered two breakfast burritos, hash browns, orange juice, and black coffee. I ordered scrambled eggs with feta, avocado, and salsa on the side, sourdough toast, and a coffee with cream. Once seated with our trays, Leo looked across the table at me.

"You okay? Want to continue?" he asked.

I nodded, and at that, Leo returned to his tutelage.

"Okay. So, where was I...?

"Chaco..." I said, spooning salsa onto my eggs.

"Right... Well, not all farmers remained in the mesas and valleys. Some moved onto the cliff walls themselves, building pueblos into the cliff. Villages, like those at Mesa Verde, could only be accessed by a series of ladders, a maze of trails, or scaling steep rock. Now, remember, these cliffs are seven to eight thousand feet in elevation. These people were human mountain goats, all right."

I smiled, imagining the lung capacity of a human mountain goat.

"These cliff villages lasted only two centuries. By 1300 AD the caverns were abandoned," Leo said, then took a bite of his breakfast burrito.

"I read about that. What's your personal opinion on why they abandoned their homes?" I asked.

"Well, everything we've dug up suggests a decade-long drought drove them south. Without rainfall, they had no food. They were starving. That's usually the way it goes, even today. Natural disasters force people from their homes and communities." Leo sipped his coffee. "They weren't so different from us, you know. They had families to feed and kids to raise. In their case, there were generations of families living together." Leo stopped talking and ate his first breakfast burrito, occasionally glancing up between bites to scan the room or glance my way.

"Then, they didn't just vanish?" I asked.

"Vanish? You mean like spacemen picked them up? That kind of vanished?" Leo asked, his coffee cup suspended between the table and his mouth.

"Well, no. Not exactly. I read they, well... somehow, vanished."

"It'd be closer to the truth to say they abandoned their land. Most of their occupied settlements were left within five to fifteen years," Leo said, then sipped his coffee.

"We need to put this in context," he added. "Our idea of sudden is far different than the Ancestral Puebloans. We live in a world of satellites, AI, and self-driving cars. It's all relative. Five to fifteen years could be considered sudden when you've occupied a land for a thousand years—the United States is what? 250 years old? Just a fraction of the time they lived here."

"Yeah, I get that," I said.

"The Ancestral Puebloans had survived dozens of droughts through the centuries. Their dry-farming agricultural techniques—which I'll explain later, were among the most efficient farming methods in history. But this mega-drought, as we call it, was preceded by years of poor harvests that forced people into starvation. End result? They fled to feed themselves."

"So what's the big mystery?" I asked, buttering my toast.

"Ah," Leo said, his eyes widening. "What I just told you is the theory we archaeologists have agreed upon. It's what we call our 'History Book Version.'"

"So, there is more? I take it you don't buy that theory. What do you think happened?"

"Now, you're getting ahead of yourself, True. Let's just stick with what we know for the moment, shall we? Let's back up. We talked about Chaco, and it being the mega-center for the Anasazi. Now, we're talking about cliff-dwellers. There's a spectrum of Ancestral Puebloans. These people occupied Four Corners for a thousand years. Just like us, clans had different patterns, values; even temperaments, depending on where, when, and how they lived. The cliff dwellers only occupied their homes for about two hundred years." Leo ate a bite of hash browns.

"These cliff dwellings, however, are what led us to discover this ancient culture. You might know this story, so stop me if you do." Leo said, then continued. "The ruins sat for six hundred years until a rancher, looking for stray cattle, stumbled upon a site now known as Cliff Palace, at Mesa Verde."

"I've been there," I said, excitedly.

"Yes, they're marvelous," Leo said, nodding. "So, here's where we start to connect the dots. In 1887, a man named Carl Lumholtz formed an expedition to map the ancient sites. During that eight-year expedition, he not only found villages throughout Four Corners—with their various structures, including ollas, the Anasazi used as granaries—but, he also discovered descendants of the Anasazi."

Leo looked up from his hash browns and made sure I was listening. I set down my fork and focused on him.

"Descendants?" I queried.

"That's right, descendants," Leo confirmed, grinning. "I thought you'd be interested in that."

"Well, that's a place to start. Who were they?"

"Hold on a minute. So, this search took Lumholtz throughout Arizona, and south, to the Sierra Madres of Mexico. When his expedition descended into Chihuahua, Mexico, he was astonished to find similar ollas—they looked like bulging pillars built into the cliffs of the Madres."

"Yes, go on," I said, anxiously hoping he would get to his point about descendants.

"By all appearances, he'd found the Anasazi. Differences in craftsmanship were attributed to the terrain, of course… You still tracking?"

"Yes." I nodded.

"We've since learned that the structures Lumholtz discovered in northern Mexico, weren't Anasazi, but belonged to a Pre-Columbian sister-civilization, named the Mogollon."

Leo set his elbows on the table and leaned towards me.

"True, the infant you were looking at earlier was found in the ruins of a mountain site in northern Chihuahua, Mexico, 150 miles from the U.S.-Mexican border. As you saw, it's identical to the Anasazi infant that Collier unearthed at Raven Creek."

I studied Leo's face, trying to put together pieces of the puzzle he laid out before me.

"In my opinion, the similarities between the two infants seriously narrow the gap between the Anasazi and Mogollon. If you're looking for the Ancient Ones, I'd start with the Anasazi-Mogollon connection… or with their descendants. That'd be the Hopi and Ute."

My mind raced at the possibilities, trying to organize the information Leo had shared. Had he just given me my first solid lead? I looked at him and smiled. He was no longer the smart-mouthed jerk in the dingy van I'd met yesterday. He was a highly educated archaeologist. Clearly, he respected the Anasazi culture.

"Thanks. I sincerely appreciate your time… and the lead."

"No problem," Leo replied, then went on to explain the history of the Anasazi, which he frequently referred to as "Ancestral Puebloans." I followed his narratives closely, so as not to be left behind. At times, I'd get lost in his descriptions or stories, so he'd back up and cover the material again until we were both satisfied I understood their overall significance.

It was an epic bit of instruction. By all rights, he was a fine teacher. Eventually, Leo stood from the bench and cleared his breakfast tray from the table.

"So, you're saying those who fled Four Corners ended up in Mexico?" I asked, clearing my own place.

"Yes, I believe some did," Leo agreed, walking toward a row of trash bins and a dishtub containing soapy water.

"Leo?"

"Biscolli, please. Everyone calls me Biscolli."

"Okay. Biscolli. Thank you for believing me. This has all been a bit much," I said.

"I'm sure it's been beyond weird," he said, "But, you've got this, True." I hoped he was right.

**Saturday, May 14**

"Whew, what a day! I've spent most of today with Leo Biscolli at Red Rock Archaeological Campus outside Cortez. He believes me—much to my relief and is willing to help. Meeting him (again) was not as disastrous as I thought it would be, and he's not the jerk I thought he was either. However, something is going on here at the campus. The police were here when I arrived, and the director was on edge. Something is definitely up… both he and Biscolli were drunk this morning. The staff here warmed up to me after Biscolli's introduction.

All in all, things are going well. The Campus has a lot of resources, and Biscolli's knowledge and insight is tremendously helpful. I'm largely depending on him—he's an expert. He thinks I should track down a sister-civilization of the Anasazi that he called the Mogollon, or their descendants. I think it's a good place to start. I've been invited to stay through the weekend and do research here.

I called Lidija and Linda to let them know I'm at the RAC for now. Linda told me Mama's will had been read and the house had been left to me. I asked her how she felt about that, and she said she was good—she and Dan inherited the property in Montana.

Also, I recorded the vision in its entirety, so as not to have it distorted by my research or imagination. Yep, I just called it a vision. I guess maybe that's what it was—a vision. I'm still wrapping my head around all of this, but I'm leaning in. It's all I know to do."

# 12

## RAVEN CREEK

My first childhood memory is of crawling up the back steps of our ranch home in Powder, Montana. I am not sure what age I was, but was young enough to be on my hands and knees. I remember trying to navigate the steps, and being frustrated that the dress I was wearing kept getting caught under my knees. Imagine that? My first memory is of feeling frustrated.

    Without knowing what Earth Mother needed from me, I was fishing without a line, and that frustrated me. The Anasazi story was one told in bits and pieces. Unlike other advanced civilizations, they kept no written record, other than great sketches etched into rock over hundreds of walls throughout Four Corners. What the sketches reveal of the lives, beliefs, hopes, and dreams of the Anasazi, and their mysterious departure, has been lifted from the walls and carried off by the wind.

    In truth, no one could agree on what drove them from their homes. Was it drought? Infighting? Disease? Enemies? Perhaps their numbers had grown beyond what the land could sustain, and they simply moved on. But to where? And why total evacuation?

Biscolli had referred to the drought theory as their, "History Book" explanation. His tone, however, suggested that there was more to the story. But what?

He'd said that archaeologists painstakingly sift through the remnants of the pueblos asking these very questions. They probe for years—decades even, in hope of a breakthrough. I didn't have years. Oliver's message sounded urgent.

I spent the rest of the weekend learning more about the Mogollon, reviewing my notes, and trying to decipher Oliver's message. Except for an occasional visitor, the library was mine. Biscolli had been right about the library. Not even the students used it. He came by occasionally and checked on me, patiently answering my evolving questions.

Something Oliver had said kept returning to me, so I decided I'd get Biscolli's take on it the next time I saw him. When he stepped into the library around 9 AM on Sunday, I seized the opportunity.

"Can I run something by you?" I asked.

"Of course," Biscolli replied and pulled up a chair.

"Oliver said that man has discounted this desert as worthless miles to cross, blind to the power it holds. He said 'this' desert, so I'm assuming he's referring to Four Corners. Do you have an idea what power he's talking about?"

"Well, there's sun, wind, and water power."

"Yes," I replied. "But that seems obvious. He said man's blindness has protected it. Blindness would indicate that it's not obvious."

"Yes, I see what you're saying."

"Oliver said a secret lives here; beneath this desert. Beneath it, Biscolli."

I searched his face. He appeared as perplexed as I was.

"There is something here, protected by the land itself; something discounted by people because they see the desert as worthless miles to cross. That's what I get from all this. What about you?"

"That's what I get as well," Biscolli said. "I don't think your Oliver is trying to make a riddle out of this. It seems straightforward enough. I can tell you that we've unearthed many precious things in the desert. Like I said earlier, it appears to me that what we're looking for is either with the Ancient Ones themselves or with their descendants. Let me tinker on this for a while, okay?" he asked, then stood. "Anything else?"

"No, not now. Thanks, Biscolli," I said, sincerely.

"You bet. We'll get to the bottom of this," he added, squeezed my shoulder, and excused himself.

The supportive gesture was thoughtful, but it wasn't reassuring. I was no closer to unraveling Oliver's message—it just didn't make sense. Biscolli was right, though. Oliver wouldn't have masked the answer in a riddle. He had given me information. I just needed to know how to use it.

I leaned back in my chair, massaged my temples, and then closed my eyes. What was Earth Mother trying to tell me? If she could only talk, I mused and then giggled—silly girl, that's what she had done.

The humor helped lift my spirit, still, I needed something tangible if I was going to do this thing for her. I decided it was time for some fresh air and a change of scenery, so I exited the building and strolled the grounds. They were quite lovely. The late-spring flowers cascaded onto the walkway and the shrubbery showed signs of being recently trimmed.

I discovered an arbor. The talent that had designed this landscape clearly knew what they were doing. A bench was situated beneath the arbor, so I took the opportunity to sit under the vines that had been trained to climb it.

The high desert air was fresh and carried a delightful hint of juniper. As I sat, I considered all that I'd been able to glean about this remarkable civilization. What had begun as a naïve fascination with the ruins at Grand Gulch, had grown into a deep respect for these people.

I closed my eyes, quieted myself, and breathed the desert air. The cool morning was glorious. Fresh. Clean. I reminded myself how quickly I can get caught up in the details of life and forget the big picture—the larger, slower clock, moving life forward.

I allowed Oliver, library books, and Biscolli to drain from my mind. I drew in a deep breath, held it a moment, and returned it to the desert.

"Earth Mother," I said. "You've got my attention. I know you have something to say. I want to listen. I'm trying to listen, but I'm confused. I know you are with me—I do. I just need to know where you want me to go, who you want me to talk to, and what you want me to find. I will listen the best I can. Please help me."

It was a simple prayer. I liked the concept of simple right now. I stood, placed my palms on the trunk of a tree, and thanked Earth Mother for listening and for bringing me to the RAC.

I wandered the grounds and then made my way through the heavy double-door entrance, leisurely strolling the corridors and occasionally glancing into a classroom window. I passed about a dozen people. I recognized no one and assumed that they were students. I rounded a final corridor, walked to the library, and entered. The huge table was a sight: books and papers were strewn everywhere. Standing at a distance from it, I became aware of just how tiny and focused my world had become. Life, right now, was this table. I walked to the massive window, gazed out, and considered the promise I'd just made to Earth Mother.

At about 11 AM, Biscolli passed through the library door. I looked up from my reading, surprised to see him again so soon.

"I've decided to go to Mexico," I announced. "A trip to Mogollon sites will give me the opportunity to..."

He quietly walked past me and sank onto the sofa, turning his attention toward the window. This visit had nothing to do with me.

I watched the man at a distance, not knowing if "asking" would be considered a violation of his privacy. I counted three heavy sighs and took that as permission to approach. In the ten steps it took to reach Biscolli, I concluded that I didn't know a thing about this man. I searched my own life for something that might help at this moment, but without knowing what was troubling him, I simply pulled up a chair.

"Got time for a story?" Biscolli asked, still looking out the window. He continued without acknowledging me. "On a hill overlooking the Little Colorado River are the ruins of a prehistoric city, abandoned about seven hundred years ago. They're named Raven Creek." He said, then paused.

"The first Anasazi sites were found in the late 1800s and that led to an interest in their artifacts. In the 1890s, a wave of looters hit the ruins, desecrating burial sites and removing thousands of pottery vessels, which they sold to dealers. The skeletal remains were sold to Mexican witches, who ground them into potions. Pathetic," he said, shaking his head.

"Anyway, once the looters were satisfied with their haul, the land sat dormant until a second wave of looters struck eighty years later. This time, they came in with heavy equipment so they could quickly unearth the grounds. Collier and his men would move into an area at night and rape the grounds in a matter of hours. Their diesel-powered scoops chewed up centuries of scientific information. He didn't care what valuable historical information he destroyed in the process, or that ancestral burial sites were disturbed, as long as he got his relics. Collier has been at this for a long time.

"Collier? Is that the same...? You once asked if I was with Collier. Did you think...?"

"Please, can I continue?" Biscolli asked, turning to face me for the first time. His eyes were red and full of disappointment. I am embarrassed to say it, but I examined him for traces of alcohol. There was none. I silenced my questions and just listened.

"It seemed nothing could protect remote sites. Rangers were given jurisdiction, but a single ranger's territory could cover hundreds of miles. Archaeological protection acts were passed, but they were nearly impossible to enforce due to understaffing. All the while, interest in Native Americans was increasing, and so was the looting."

Biscolli pivoted towards me.

"The owners of the land where Raven Creek sits contacted universities in an attempt to have the site properly excavated, researched, and preserved. No one wanted to take on the project. Finally, a group of archaeologists formed Red Rock Archaeological Campus—the RAC, with the sole purpose of preserving the ruins and curating the material found there—and, at a second site called Yellow Bar."

"Were you one of the founding group?" I asked.

"No, I was in graduate school then. I came along four years later. Anyway, the founding group decided that rather than rely on government grants to fund its research, they would develop a program that encouraged anyone with an interest in archaeology to participate in its ongoing excavations and curation. Thus, the campus was established."

"I read about that in one of your brochures. I think it's a great idea."

"Yes, it's pretty novel, all right. Well, the program soon caught on, and now students and volunteers come from all over the world to participate in our projects. We have eight full-time staff, twenty or so archaeological students, and a dozen volunteers at any given time. I guess you could say the rest is history," Biscolli said, grinning at his own joke.

"That's a nice story, but I still don't understand the problem."

"Remember when we were in the classroom and I told you I had proof Collier dug up the infant at Raven Creek?"

"Yes."

"Well, the night he and his boys were out there, I got it on video."

"You did? That's wonderful! That means you'll probably get a conviction, just like you'd hoped," I said.

"Yeah, there's a good chance it could help."

"So, what's the problem?"

"Well, they saw me, roughed me up, and have been threatening me ever since."

"What do you mean, threatening you?" I asked, watching his face carefully.

"Funny, that's the same thing my boss, Eric, asked when I told him. When you showed up here yesterday, Eric had just watched the video. Man, he was pissed!"

"Why? I'd think he'd be happy you caught them," I said.

"Oh yeah, he was real happy, all right. Just thrilled. Especially when he heard about the death threats."

"Jesus! You didn't say anything about death threats."

"What other kinds of threats are there? These guys know their necks are in the noose. Eric went off like a pistol. He said I'd put all our lives at risk, which, I suppose is true. Then, he told me that he had no choice but to abort the Raven Creek site, and move everyone to Yellow Bar during the investigation. That could take months—or years. Raven Creek is chewed up, and now, it's been taped off by the cops."

Biscolli lowered his head into his hands.

"I botched the whole project—nine years worth of digging, down the drain. That's when Eric and I brought out the booze. The cops came out later that morning to take a statement, and then you, my friend, walked through the door. So, how's your day?" he asked, trailing off.

"I had no idea, Biscolli. I'm really sorry."

"Yeah, me too... me too. Only the field supers were told right away. Eric told the rest of the staff about an hour ago. I was ready to take their punches, and what do they do? Hell, the staff have been coming to me to console them since we adjourned. Get that!" he sighed. "Our students will find out tomorrow that they're all being reassigned to Yellow Bar or transferred back to school."

"What are you going to do?" I asked.

"Oh, that's the other thing. Eric insists I take 'mandatory time off.' Apparently, with the threats out there, everyone on staff is in danger. He wants me out of here pronto, until Collier is either caught or the threats stop."

"So that's what was going on at the gas station? You thought I was with Collier? Seriously?" I asked, searching his face.

"Well, you could have been. I wouldn't put it past the creep. Better to err on the side of caution than to wind up dead because you heard too much and squealed."

# 13

# LEAVING CAMPUS

I was spending my nights in a nine-bunk dorm room for campus volunteers at Red Rock. It reminded me of a youth hostel: pillow, sheets, a folded blanket at the head of the mattress, and a set of towels at the foot. Six women slept in our bay and we shared a common restroom. The men were down another hall.

I spoke to some of the volunteers in passing. A couple in their sixties were visiting from Brazil. They'd traveled extensively throughout South, Central, and North America, but had never heard of Powder, Montana. Rebecca and Karen were from the grapefruit country of southern Texas and swore that I was Jane Seymour's look-alike. I thought it was kind of them to say so. Finally, a young fellow, who went by the name Rustin' Root, was visiting from Kansas. I never did get the story behind his name.

The staff had their own quarters, as did the resident students. Early Monday morning, a young man who introduced himself as a student was manning the reception desk. Not long thereafter, when I had assumed my customary seat at the library table, he entered carrying a tray with a pot of coffee, cream, and one cup. I smiled and thanked him for his kindness. He said to thank Mr. Biscolli.

I sipped hot coffee and studied the itinerary I'd printed out. I had purchased a ticket to Chihuahua, Mexico from the La Plata County

Airport in Durango, Colorado, forty-five miles east of Cortez. I would fly out the day after tomorrow at 8 AM.

I had a mound of questions for Biscolli about the Mogollon before I left, so I was happy to see him when he stopped by the library. He seemed glad to see me as well, though, when I mentioned I'd decided to go to Mexico, he didn't seem as pleased as I would've expected. He nodded and looked interested enough, but he didn't smile. Something was very different about him. He continued to the sofa and took a seat.

"How'd things go with Eric?" I asked.

"Not well," Biscolli answered. "I thought I was doing the right thing, but it appears all I've done is cause a lot of damage."

"I'm sorry," I said, studying his face. "I can see archaeology is your life and the people here are a second family."

"Yeah, well…" he said, then turned and looked away.

He seemed reluctant to share, and I didn't know enough about him to determine if he wanted to talk about it or not. On the one hand, Biscolli was easy to read: he wore his troubles like a heavy crown. On the other hand, he guarded both his emotions and his words. I rose from my chair, approached him, and returned the thoughtful gesture he'd extended to me earlier, placing my hand on his shoulder. He released some of the tension held there and nodded.

"Thanks. So, what's this about you going to Mexico?"

"Well, I have to start somewhere," I said. "My nose in a book has done about as much good as it's going to do."

I took a seat on the sofa and tried to catch his eyes. I knew Biscolli had the time to go to Mexico, but I wasn't sure it was my place to ask him to step any further into this new world of mine than he already had.

"It feels like the right thing to do based on what I've learned and what you've told me," I said. "I can probably figure this out on my own, but if you'd consider coming with me, I'd appreciate it." I waited for a response, but he gave none. So, I proceeded with caution. "Think about it," I said. "I have a flight out of Durango the day after tomorrow. That's as far as I've gone with my plans."

In the end, Biscolli decided to go to Mexico. He knew people—his cohorts—real diggers with extensive knowledge of the Mogollon who were currently excavating a site. He knew the Chihuahua area and he spoke fluid Spanish. This could be good.

After clearing out my motel room and a craze of calls, details, and packing, we loaded my rental car at 5:30 AM and headed for Durango to catch our flight. Based on the itinerary, we'd arrive in Chihuahua City, Chihuahua, Mexico at 3:05 PM, with plenty of time to check into the hotel and clean up before meeting Biscolli's colleagues. Not knowing how much time would be required in Mexico, we'd purchased one-way tickets.

There seemed to be genuine enthusiasm on Biscolli's part for getting involved. He'd arranged for hotel accommodations, ground transportation, and had contacted his cohorts.

"I'm glad you decided to come along," I said, as Biscolli drove us east, towards the highway. "I feel better having you with me."

"Well, you didn't think I was actually going to turn you loose down there alone, did you?" he replied, without taking his eyes off the road.

A smile drained from my face. What was that supposed to mean? Was he genuinely concerned about my welfare or did he think I couldn't take care of myself? To say that I knew him well enough to merely discount the comment as a joke, would be a lie. Not only had I been the brunt of his cruelty at the gas station, but I'd also witnessed him fillet Cowboy Earl on the spot. He could be kind, but he also had a mean streak, and it wasn't clear what triggered it.

It was an awkward moment—a pause made even quieter by the desert that engulfed us. I felt insecure for the first time in days. A chuckle from him would've helped me to know that his comment was a joke, but he hadn't even grinned. Was I still a "damn tourist?" I'd felt we'd covered a lot of ground over the weekend and built mutual respect. Was I wrong? I needed to know where I stood.

"That's an odd thing to say. You think I can't handle myself down there?"

Biscolli was perfectly still, his eyes on the road, driving over the speed limit. He closed his eyes momentarily, then shook his head.

"Good God, woman," he said, shaking his head again. "What's with you women and this, 'gotta do it myself, macho crap.' I thought you were different. No, that's not it! In fact, you're way off base."

He glanced at me.

"For the record, I'm more than confident you can handle yourself. My point is, you'll get a lot further if I'm with you—but then, you already know that. Besides, I've made some calls. I can get you to places you might not think of or be welcome at. I told you I was 'in.' That's why I'm here. Don't you trust me or my word?"

I met his eyes. Of course, he was right. He'd made it clear he was committed, and honestly, that was the reason I felt confident this trip would produce answers.

"Well, this is embarrassing," I admitted. "I'm sorry Biscolli, I misspoke…"

"Don't worry about it," he replied before I'd finished apologizing.

I continued to look at Biscolli for a long second, studying his profile. In the little we'd actually interacted, one thing had become evident about this man: he didn't mince words. There was no reason not to trust him.

"What?" Biscolli asked, turning toward me. "Are we good?"

"Yes, we're good," I answered.

"You do realize you're staring."

I laughed. "Yes, I do that sometimes. Sorry, it's a trainer's habit. You've got quite the physique."

"Trainer?"

"Yes. U.S. Army fitness trainer."

"No way! You, military? I didn't see that one coming. Don't get me wrong… sure, you're fit, but you don't exactly look like you could boss soldiers around. I mean, you're beautiful. Ah… and intelligent," he quickly added.

"Fourteen years."

"Wow, you're a veteran. Impressive."

"Yeah, but that was a lifetime ago," I added.

"So, you gave orders to soldiers?"

"It'd be closer to say that I got them in shape so they'd pass their fitness tests, but, yes."

"Huh… that's cool. Well, digging is all I know. Once I decided on digging, I gave my heart to it. There wasn't much before that—nothing to anchor me anyway." He gave me a brief glance. "Look, I just want to get this out of the way. I know what women wonder. No, there hasn't been a woman. Women, yes, but never a woman.

Digging is all I know." He paused. "How about you, True? What are you devoted to? Something must be in Portland."

I thought about his question for a second, then met his gaze.

"I'm not so sure about Portland anymore," I answered. "Most of what I do… or did, anyway, can be done online."

"What's that?"

"Well, I led a mastermind group and created websites. My true passion, though, is bringing women together for personal development and growth. I love that."

"And, someone?"

I eyed Biscolli and nodded my head. "Yes, four children. No man."

"Wow, mom of four. You're full of surprises."

I let out a little chuckle.

"Not really. One girl, three boys," I said. "They're great kids. Young adults now… we're close. You? Family? Siblings?"

"A sister. That's it for me. Suzi's in Thailand… Chiang Mai. So not many lunch dates with her."

I nodded.

"That's got to be hard. I'm just getting used to having no parents on the planet."

"Yeah, losing them was rough. Truth is, Suzi kinda pulled way after our folks died." Biscolli turned towards me. "Appreciate the family you've got, True."

I studied his face and nodded. At that, we drifted into silence. I leaned my head back, turned toward the window, and watched the desert pass by—alive with spring color. After several minutes, Biscolli broke the silence by saying something that sounded more like an answer to a question.

"I got through my first improv. It went okay."

"Wait. You do improv? Really? That's cool."

"Yeah, it was open mic night. Randy—another super—and I decided to go for it. We'd goofed around a bit on campus… just for students. First ever on stage though. A little unnerving, but adrenaline kicked in and we managed to pull it off. That was the week before Collier chewed up Raven Creek."

"That must've been fun."

"It was." Biscolli then paused. "Tell me something about you I don't know. Surprise me."

That could be anything from my life. The man didn't know me at all. Of all the things I could have said, whether it be dangerous, adventurous, intelligent, playful, or clever, I said, "I love Chiang Mai. I could live there in a heartbeat."

"Interesting. Do you travel much?"

"Yes, all the time. Or, at least, I did."

Biscolli looked at me.

"Hey, True, we're friends, right?"

"Yes, I suppose so."

"Friends make observations, right?"

"Yes, I suppose so," I answered, wondering where he was going with his comment.

"Just an observation, but everything you shared just now is something you 'used' to do. Tell me something about this True—the one sitting next to me."

Huh… that's interesting. Was that true?' I thought for a moment. He had said to surprise him, so I decided to go for it. I turned towards Biscolli.

"Okay. Do you know what a 'masculine container' is?"

"No."

"All right. I'll tell you a little secret about women—about me. I got defensive when I thought you believed I couldn't take care of myself because I know I'm smart and capable. We women run businesses, raise babies, and chase after our dreams. When we figure out what we want, we're unstoppable and know how to get stuff done. But here's the deal, when there's no one to hand off the baton to—or balance out all that masculine 'doing' energy, we can get stuck in that mode. We may look very feminine, but our energy is masculine—action, results, logistics, get it done."

"Yeah, I know women like that."

"I'm sure you do. I unintentionally fell into that. See, I always had an independent streak, which is beautiful, but when my husband died, I took on all the logistics and details—the finances and investing, home repairs and car maintenance, yard upkeep, moving heavy furniture and travel arrangements, I lost a part of me I love."

"What's that?"

"My softness. My playfulness. It's hard to be playful and affectionate, receptive, or creative when you're trying to get stuff done. For me, it's when someone else is in their masculine energy that I can drop mine and access all those yummy softer parts of myself. A masculine container is actively creating a space for a woman to do that."

"Interesting. So, your soft side comes out when there's a man around?"

"Not necessarily. Rather than gender, it has more to do with being in your head or heart. Remember when you came into the library Saturday morning and recognized me? We were both in our masculine energy. We were operating from our heads. When you told me about Raven Creek, and how shutting it down would affect your friends, that was you coming from your heart—feeling and expressing."

"I see what you're saying. So it has more to do with someone's intention and motivation."

"Sort of. We shift between masculine and feminine energy all the time—like this hybrid car shifts from electric to gas—it's seamless. A man doesn't diminish his masculinity just because he expresses attributes deemed 'feminine,' and vice versa. In fact, it balances it," I said, glancing towards Biscolli.

"I'm listening," he said, his eyes on the road.

"Okay, so here's another secret about women—one that most guys have all wrong," I said. "A 'high value' man isn't the one with the cash, the position, or power; he's the one who offers a steady, supportive presence in a woman's life. The one who can be present and operate from his heart space in a world pumping out fear and scarcity. That's high value."

"Interesting."

"See, women feel safe with a man like that. He's the kind of provider she actually wants—the provider her nervous system needs. He can provide an emotional haven for her and their family because he has it within himself. And that has nothing to do with slinging a hammer or being CEO."

"Hum… this is an interesting conversation," Biscolli said, then turned towards me. "Look, we men aren't complicated. Basically, what you see is what you get. We fix things and solve problems, and what you're saying is that if we do it with heart, we're considered high value."

"Yes."

"Go figure. So, here's a secret about men for you. We need to be needed. With all you smart, capable women out there, tell me True, what the heck do you need us for?"

"I love this," I said. "And this comes up all the time in my women's circles because a lot of women's partners say that very thing: 'I feel like you don't need me.'"

"Yeah," Biscolli agreed. "We need to feel useful—like we make a difference."

"I'll bet being useful, especially to a woman, brings satisfaction—even joy. Happy wife, happy life, right?"

"Exactly. Though, I wouldn't know. Sounds like a hornet's nest to me."

I laughed.

"I think we're on common ground here, though. See, we're wired to believe that providing for a woman means financially. It's one way, for sure. But a lot of women make their own money and still need something that no amount of cash can give them. If a man can provide a masculine container for a woman, he'll have her heart, respect, and devotion."

"So, what's this container again?"

"It's being a steady presence for a woman. It's providing a sense of safety and support for her—a landing place where she feels secure—where she can be herself and feel seen and heard. It's a safe place—her safe place, to exhale, because you 'get her,' and you do what you can to create a space where she can thrive."

"That sounds great in theory, but anytime I tried to be there, I got pushback… like it wasn't right—wasn't enough. Digging is far less complicated. I think I'd just as soon dig as try to figure out a woman."

I laughed again.

"Women are tired. I know, I am. We're tired of doing it all on our own. Just because we can, doesn't mean we want the weight on our shoulders—not all the time. We want a break. We want to drop our masculine energy and just be. Being is feminine. It's where we get to embody all our yumminess."

Biscolli merged us onto Highway 160. He then set the cruise control and balanced his attention between our conversation and the road. I took a sip from my water bottle and looked out the passenger's window.

"Thanks for taking care of hotel arrangements and ground transportation in Chihuahua," I said. "I really appreciate it. That's the kind of stuff I've had to do for years. You have no idea how good it feels to have someone else do it. Thank you."

"You're welcome... I guess," Biscolli replied, then glanced my way. "Yeah, you're welcome... my pleasure."

I capped my water bottle and put it in the cupholder.

"You're all right, True. I've never heard a woman communicate the way you do—I mean, I never knew what I could give a woman, so I've steered clear. Now, at least, I have an idea where to start. Thanks," he said.

"You're welcome. Thanks for listening. You're the first man I've shared any of this with. You're all right yourself, Biscolli."

During the remaining miles to Durango, I read aloud a sports page Biscolli had brought with him: six weeks into the season, the Rays were eight games behind the Yankees and four behind the Orioles, but it was anyone's guess what the season would bring. We arrived at the airport in time to eat breakfast before passing through security and locating our flight.

Our itinerary was nothing complicated. Three flights: a commuter plane to Phoenix. A three-hour flight to Houston, and a commuter plane into Chihuahua. We were told that customs and security should take fifty minutes to clear.

Our plane to Phoenix was waiting on the tarmac. Biscolli insisted on the window seat but fell asleep immediately. I read the novel I'd begun at White's motel as he slept against the vibrating window. We made our transfers without a hitch and caught the final leg of our trip.

It was a long, noisy ninety minutes. Finally, the pitch of the engines changed, and I looked beyond Biscolli's head, out the window. We were descending. Within moments, the clouds parted and land became visible. It was another world.

Below appeared a dizzy network of small streams and tributaries spiraled in all directions. Amongst the lush green terrain, were broken meadows of farmlands and pastures. Quiet valleys were lost to irregular land that crept upward to the Sierra Madres, which looked like a school of humpback whales against the blue sky.

Then, the city of Chihuahua appeared. It was a sprawling metropolitan area. I studied the landscape and tried to imagine where the million people this city housed might live. Biscolli finally stirred.

"Oh, True," he said, leaning towards me. "Brush up on your Spanish, even if it's just to say "hola," "disculpe," or "gracias" to the locals. Otherwise, they'll think you're a snobby American tourist and won't talk to you."

I nodded and glanced at my watch. It was 3:45 PM local time. A vehicle was waiting for us.

# 14

## CHIHUAHUA

Biscolli's idea of transportation was a World War II Mongoose—the U.S. military's five-ton, six-wheel drive answer to a pickup truck. The 1940's vintage heap of steel had its original drab green paint, though scraped and scabbed from thousands of tree branches. It was outfitted with a winch mounted to the front bumper and waist-high hard rubber tires. I stared at the rattrap and wondered what I had gotten myself into.

He couldn't be serious.

"I called ahead and let my colleagues know we were flying in. They're expecting us tonight for chow," Biscolli said, as he walked toward the driver's side. "They offered to let us stay in the off-site field house, but I assumed you'd want a clean room, so I arranged for a hotel."

He climbed in.

"I'm sure you know this, True, world traveler that you are and all, but steer clear of the water. I've arranged for bottled water at the hotel. The door's open," Biscolli said.

The man may have been a heck of an archaeologist, but he wasn't much of a gentleman. I heaved my bags three feet up into the cab and climbed in. Perhaps he knew how loud the engine would be, or maybe he just wanted to share all the details before he forgot them.

Either way, I was lucky that Biscolli had shared the information before he pushed a red button that turned on the engine. Once it started, everything said afterward was pure pantomime.

Smoke billowed from an exhaust pipe located behind the passenger door, collecting in a dark cloud over the cab of the truck. I pulled my tee shirt over my mouth and glowered at him. After a few attempts, Biscolli discovered the right combination of gear shifting and clutch, and we thundered down the road separating the airport from the cosmopolitan city of Chihuahua, swerving extra wide to miss hitting cars and the occasional pedestrian, both concealed by the enormous front end.

Chihuahua was the capital of a state by the same name, and with its diverse resources, was a hub for mining, lumber, and cattle. From the road we could see some low hills and, of course, the Madres, but for the most part, the land was flat with cottonwood, oak trees, and low brush.

Biscolli pointed out a silver mining operation against the rugged gray mountains. We passed a brewery and a wood molding plant. As we rolled into town, I admired a couple of historic buildings: a large museum and a lavishly decorated stone cathedral. Several blocks beyond a large grassy plaza, crowded with beautiful hotels and restaurants, we thundered past the state capital building and government palace. Downtown was busy with activity: cars veering in all directions and pedestrians scurrying out of their way.

We continued through town, bouncing along in the Mongoose. The streets eventually narrowed and we passed a school, a church, and a lumberyard. Most buildings in this section of the city were either pink adobe or weathered lumber. Sidewalk cafés and bars dotted the sidewalks. Biscolli slowed the rig and steered it into a paved lot across from a single-story, clay-roofed hotel. We pulled our bags from the cab. I was deaf.

The Mexican air was hot and suffocating. A storm had moved inland the previous night, dropping two inches of rain. The mosquitoes were thick and attacked my exposed skin immediately. Biscolli swatted a few, but the locals appeared immune to the pests. I fished through my backpack for insect repellent, but within minutes, my skin looked like someone had beaten it repeatedly with a switch.

"Ugh, I can't wait to get to the room," I said to myself.

Chihuahua was pleasant enough, but the mosquitoes were intolerable. I was sure that I would be covered in clothing and slathered in insect repellent every moment of my time here.

The hotel was an old adobe building with hand-painted tile floors, ceiling fans, and colorful woven curtains covering the lobby windows. We passed through a black wrought-iron gate and picked up our key from a man with a broad smile and lightning-fast Spanish. I was instantly worried that I might have to resort to pointing and fumbling my way around Chihuahua.

My room was refreshingly cool and free of flying insects. There was no sign of creeping ones either, but I decided that it was too early to deem the room bug-free. I would save that declaration until tonight after the lights were out. I heard a knock at the door. It was Biscolli.

"How's your room? Will this work for you?" he asked, as I welcomed him in.

I panned my room and could see no bathroom. When I asked Biscolli about it, he explained that the stream of Spanish at the front desk was to inform us that hotel guests shared a common restroom down the hall. I shook my head at him, wondering what else he had neglected to mention from that conversation.

I walked to one of the windows. From it, I could see a couple of buildings along the street. Beyond them was a fence and an orchard. On a distant hill, sheep were grazing. I walked to another window. From there, the Sierra Madres could be seen. Somewhere among them were the Mogollon cliff dwellings. According to Biscolli, the Sierra Madre Occidental had many archaeological cave sites similar to the one we would visit. Most had not been excavated and many were still undiscovered. The site we wanted was a thirty-mile trip up the steep canyon and could take over an hour to reach in the six-wheel-drive Mongoose. Biscolli joined me at the window.

"Do you need to rest or would you like to drive up to the site?" he asked. "It's a bit of a drive, so we'll need to stay the night. If you're up for it, grab what you'll need."

I turned from the window and looked at my luggage.

"Give me a few moments," I said, then asked, "Do you happen to have anything with you that I can put on these bug bites? The mosquitoes are thick."

"Yes, actually. And, I have earplugs for you. I forgot to give you a set before we left the airport. It's kind of a noisy ride. But, I guess you noticed that.

"What'd you say?" I said, cupping my hand to my ear." At that, we both laughed. "Yeah, Biscolli, that's some ride."

"We'll need it… you'll see. And you'll be glad we have it once we head up the hill. So I take it, that's a yes? You want to see the site?"

"Sure, let's check it out."

Biscolli grinned. "Oh, and True, how's your stamina? These diggers are in shape. Two of them are pushing sixty, and they can run the seat off of me. They eat next to nothing and go like a bat out of hell over the cliffs and crags. They'll put in a day's work that would tax most athletes. It's the elevation, you know. They live at 6,200 feet and work two thousand above that," he said, then walked toward the door. He paused with his hand on the doorknob and turned to look over his shoulder at me.

"Here you'll need to push a lot of oxygen, and not much trains you for that, especially if you live in Oregon. Portland is what, close to sea level? If we're lucky, they'll be done for the day and back at the field house."

I was only mildly worried. I would save my big worry until after I had seen these two-legged mountain goats in action. I walked to my luggage. Unpacking could wait. I retrieved what I would need for an overnight stay, pulled on a long-sleeve shirt, and then slathered what it didn't cover with insect repellent.

The road to the digger's field house was roughly mid-way up a rugged canyon. From there, it was another seventeen miles to the dig site. We climbed into the Mongoose and Biscolli slipped it into gear. I gave myself over to the rolling rattrap, and let my body roll along with the uneven terrain. It was a rough, bone-jarring ride uphill, and an occasional rock that Biscolli overlooked, jostled me. Still, as we climbed, so did my spirits. I was thrilled to be here.

The dig crew was waiting for us at their modest field house—which served not only as headquarters but also as living quarters for the diggers. They were already showered from the day's dig and preparing dinner. The field house was a rough-looking lumber home they called 'Casa de Madre'. I met Sesha, Miguel, André, Laura, Russell, and Kathi. I estimated the diggers ranged in age between twenty-five and sixty. Kathi and André got my vote for senior mountain goats.

# ANASAZI VISION

We were welcomed into their makeshift home with open arms. Sesha put a cold drink in our hands and led us from room to room showing off their ingenuity and sharing stories about their work. The place was pretty much a six-room shack, stacked to the rafters with personal belongings, mountains of books, and boxes of artifacts, but it was clean enough and organized.

These rugged people lived with the rocks and history they loved. It was their life's work and I could see that they wore it, ate it, and drank it every day. I liked them immediately. They were a happy lot, though by worldly standards, their life was simple and boring. They were overjoyed we were there. I attributed their exuberance to the fact that we walked on two legs and spoke English, but, I later learned that we had brought cold beer.

The site the crew worked on was called Cueva de la Vasija, or Cave of the Vessel. It had been under excavation since 1986 and was situated at an elevation of 8,400 feet in the Sierra Madres, in the state of Chihuahua, Mexico. I was told that this crew was the seventh generation of diggers to work on the project, each here for a stay of months or years. At twenty-six months, Laura had called this place home the longest, though this was André's second go-round. His first stretch had lasted three years. He had hoped to stay at least that long, this time.

I learned that the dig site was embedded in a cavern tucked among the jagged crests, V-shaped gorges, and waterless streambeds of the Madres. I was promised that I could examine the ruins in the morning, but tonight was set aside for food, fun, and a lively reunion of colleagues.

Following a short night's sleep, Biscolli and I made the bumpy trip to the digger's base camp, further up the steep terrain. The sights were still new and I enjoyed the trip, but knew that after many days on the sad road, my mind would change. I would learn that base camp minimized the need to drive to the field house, where the diggers lived. It was at base camp, that the crew stored equipment used at the dig site, rested, and prepared most meals.

The crew was already at base camp when we arrived. We were greeted at the back door by the smell of freshly brewed coffee. Kathi offered me a cup, along with scrambled eggs and toast as we passed through the kitchen. I settled into an overstuffed chair in the common area, while the others buzzed around me in an organized frenzy. Their voices rose and fell with the tasks that they performed.

They were laughing as they filed out the back door. I assumed that their departure was a signal that it was time to leave, so I set down my plate and coffee cup and hurried outside. Biscolli motioned for me to climb into the Mongoose as he finished a conversation with Russell. Soon, we were behind the crew's rig. Biscolli liked to keep his foot on the pedal, but after choking on their dust for a mile, he backed off. I was glad to see that some common sense sat in the seat next to me. I had, after all, relinquished my safety over to him.

I looked out the window, and for several sweet moments, I imagined that I was a young girl again, embarking on some dangerous adventure in a land of magic and mystery. The foreign panorama transported me back in time to a creek that my brother and I would often wander to on our walk home from school. It was there, that our imaginations ran wild, and we would become sea captains, pirates, treasure hunters, or private investigators, following "clues" we had found along the creek bank. We would climb trees, scale logs, and tromp through the creek looking for frogs and crawdads. The memory raised a happy smile on my face.

I refocused my attention, and was drawn like a magnet to the spectacular mountain scenery surrounding us: the massive cliffs, deep canyons, and magnificent rock formations. My excitement steadily grew. Biscolli ground the gears and swore at the stiff steering wheel as we negotiated the rutty surface, which was becoming less of a road and more of a trail as we climbed. It was 6:30 AM and he was perspiring.

I turned back to the window. On the face of an adjacent hill, I spotted a rooster tail of dust. It was the digger's rig. Before them was a thin line of road, cut into the rugged mountainside. Biscolli bounced us over a couple of fallen rocks and I hit my head on the ceiling.

"Sorry," he called, jerking on the steering wheel.

We followed the steep, narrowing strip of land around a couple more bends, and it trailed off into a dirt path. We had climbed very high. I peered over the edge of the sheer cliff, and my heart leaped into my throat. I grabbed for the door rest but remembered that there was none, just a metal door and a handle. I wanted to be nowhere near the handle, so I gripped my seat instead. Biscolli took the advancing turns confidently; still, it didn't take an Einstein to see that there was no room to turn around safely, should we have to. Riding so close to the cliff face, it took all my effort to quiet my fear.

I didn't dare look at Biscolli, for fear he would take his eyes off the path to acknowledge me. Forty minutes into the ascent, we came to an abrupt stop. I said a quick "Hail Mary," and made sure my breakfast wasn't on the floorboard.

The diggers were already out of their rig and sipping on jugs of water. Russell walked up to the passenger window, grinned through it to Biscolli, and winked. "How'd you do, True?" he asked. I gave him the answer that I had memorized for speechless occasions such as this.

"Huh?"

Russell stepped aside and I slid out of the Mongoose. I stepped behind the rig for a moment to calm my nerves, then joined the others. With my heart safely back in my chest, I followed the gaze of the seven diggers. There, before us, was the most astonishing piece of life-sized artwork. In the craggy gray rock, towering overhead, was a cavern punched into the face of an enormous cliff. It provided natural cover for a crude village made of flat rocks and held together with mud mortar. I stood there immovable in its commanding presence.

"I needn't remind you of what a rattler sounds like," Russell called out. "It can't be mistaken for anything else. Most of my friends have been bitten by rattlers… some are dead."

The announcement snapped me back from the cliffside trance that I was in. All seven diggers were laughing, and since they were looking my way, I could see the joke had been a big score. I wondered if they cared that I had nearly soiled my pants. It appeared not. They were busy giving each other "high-fives." Russell, in his compassion—or guilt, walked over and slapped his hand on my back.

"All in good fun, True," he said.

André joined us, patting his hand on my back.

"Say, Biscolli mentioned you're doing some research on the Mogollon. Mind if I ask what you know?"

I looked over my shoulder at the close-knit group, making sure this wasn't another one of their gags. They had forgotten me.

"That's easy. Nothing other than a brief sketch Biscolli gave me of his theory."

"Oh yeah, right… Biscolli's theory. You and I can talk about that later."

I was happy that I would have an opportunity to talk to one of the archeologists about the Anasazi-Mogollon connection, and it raised my hope that we were on track.

"Biscolli is a good man and a hell of an archaeologist," André said. "…but God only knows what goes on in that goofy head of his. I'll talk to him later. Anyway, True, are you ready to climb?" he asked, pointing to a distant ladder.

I wasn't sure what to make of his comment about Biscolli. Banter between friends I suppose.

"Yeah, sure," I answered.

André led me along a worn trail to the base of the cliff.

"After a century of investigation, we've learned a tremendous amount about these people but, all in all, I'd say only about four percent of Mogollon sites have been excavated," André called over his shoulder as we walked. "Now, you'll notice when we get up there that this alcove doesn't have any petroglyphs. Many do, but not here," he continued. "The Mogollon people would chip a series of cryptic images, often radiating out from a central point; in sort of a spiral. We've come to believe the spiral has something to do with the solstice, which is a way of marking time. They kept no written records, you know."

"Just like the Anasazi…" I said. André nodded.

The cavern containing the ruins was roughly fifteen feet directly above us. André stopped at a ladder and then scaled it like a cheetah. Seven diggers, and I had to choose a gladiator to climb with.

He smiled at me from the top and waved me up. The long ladder, made from narrow, honed pine logs, had closely spaced rungs tied with leather reinforcements to the main shaft. I ascended it carefully—it was narrow but stable. Midway up, I peeked over my shoulder to take in the surroundings. The road we had come in on was little more than a steep, narrow track. The crew was beneath us, unpacking their rig, but Biscolli had stopped to watch me. He raised his hand in the air and flashed a spirited thumbs-up. I smiled and scaled the remaining rungs.

Once sure-footed on top, André escorted me into the cavity of the rock. My first reaction to the cave was a certainty that I had entered something indelibly ancient, and it brought back memories of Grand Gulch, only this was on a much grander scale. I had poured over pictures of such large caverns in Biscolli's library, but to actually be here, inside one, was thrilling. 'Who had lived in here?' I wondered.

Common doors joined one room to the next. My imagination raced to recreate the people who may have lived here. I envisioned strikingly beautiful people, with their silken black hair, mahogany-colored skin, and magnificent physiques. There was no way to know how many people had shared these rooms.

It was cool inside the large, open cavern. The jagged eighteen-foot-high ceiling of the alcove extended several feet beyond the lip of the floor, scorched with soot. It gradually receded toward the back of the cave. Numerous structures, in varying states of deterioration, stood within the alcove, constructed from linear granite rocks. As I stepped, powdery dirt floated up from the ground.

"Incredible, huh?" André said. "It's typical of many archaeological cave sites spread across the Sierra Madre Occidental."

"This is amazing," I said, taking it all in.

"The Mogollon flourished here in northern Mexico, around 1300 AD. Evidence of their trade routes extended to the Pacific Ocean, the Gulf of Mexico, and other cultural centers up north, such as Mesa Verde in Colorado and Chaco Canyon in New Mexico. We're talking about some extensive mobility and technology. Remember, this was five hundred years before America was discovered."

"Yeah, Biscolli explained that Chaco was an economic hub for the Anasazi."

"That and more," André added. "There are forty houses here. They're called, cuarenta casas. Go ahead, look around."

I wandered in and out of the rooms, running my eyes over the rough mortared walls, until I came to the clearing where we had entered into the alcove. From the enormous belly of the cave, I looked at the forested land that stretched before me. I felt that I was on top of the world, overlooking a gentle river flowing in the valley floor hundreds of feet below us. The Mongoose had climbed a steep grade, creeping up from the dusty desert valley floor of oak and pine to this rugged Chihuahuan perch, tucked in a pristine setting of lush alpine forests and ancient granite that extended as far as I could see. The world was silent. It was breathtakingly beautiful! I brought one hand to my heart, became silent, and took it all in.

"Sometimes, I forget to look," André said, adjusting the wide brim of his canvas sunhat as he took in the long valley. The digger's rugged face, toughened by a long courtship with the sun, studied the ravine. I wondered what he saw. Was he seeing the valley through the eyes of a scientist or a poet?

"It's called Cueva Valley. Chihuahua has the most forested land in all of Mexico," he said, taking a seat in the dirt. "From 2007 to 2012, I was involved in a dig at Rattler's Bend in Arizona. All said and done, the dig lasted twenty-seven years and was the last major Mogollon dig in the southwest." He paused and took a sip from his Camelback. "We uncovered a 460-room pueblo that housed perhaps 575 people, between 1275 and 1400 AD. It was an intriguing site. When we finished the dig in 2012, it was backfilled to protect it."

I took a seat and looked into the long valley while running a finger through the dirt, leaving an inch furrow in the gray powder. André turned toward me.

"Are you and Biscolli an item?" he asked.

I turned to meet his gaze, stunned. "No, not at all," I replied.

"Just wondering," he said. "In all the years I've known Biscolli, he's never brought a woman with him to a dig, even on his own turf. He has to care if he brought you all the way down here."

"No… no, he's helping me," I said, then, regarding my answer, promptly corrected myself. "At this point, we're kind of in this together."

"Oh, okay. Well, it's obvious he cares. I wasn't sure if it was just the dig, or…"

Obvious he cares? He couldn't be serious.

André's voice trailed off, then he quickly recovered. "This is my second stretch at this site," he said, then took another sip of water. "When I arrived here the first time, back in 2013, I recognized that the brown potshards we were finding were identical to the ones we had found at Rattler's Bend, 300 miles northwest of there." He turned to me. "There was no doubt in my mind that there was a link between the northern Mogollon and those here. As far as what that link was, well, that's where the speculation begins. We believe there was a Mexican branch of the ancient Mogollon who once lived in the North American southwest."

"Wait a minute, you lost me. Are we talking about the Mogollon or Anasazi here?"

"The Mogollon thrived in Arizona, New Mexico, and Mexico, much like the Anasazi did."

"Then what does this have to do with the Anasazi?"

"Oh, I see where you're headed. Biscolli has been talking to you. Just hold on and let me explain," André said.

"The homes in this recess were built some 650 years ago. Look up, True. See the soot on the ceiling of this alcove? It's over six hundred years old."

"Wow!" I said, staring at the charcoal canopy above me."

"All across the southwestern United States, similar rock-and-mud cliff dwellings can be found. Come on, get up for a minute. Let's take a look at something."

André led me around the dwellings to a bizarre, bulb-shaped structure standing in the center of the cave. It looked like a twelve-foot-high mud onion, about seven feet in diameter. I ran my hand over the rough mortar and looked through one of the three tiny holes in its thick wall. It was hollow. I looked up and saw that it tapered to a small, open roof a few feet below the cave ceiling.

"It's called an Olla," André said. "It was used by the Mogollon as a granary. If you look closely, you can see a rope embedded in the mud to form the walls. Pretty ingenious, huh? Those holes weren't there originally. Eons of wind, plus a little help from rodents and vandals, put them there."

"Vandals? All the way up here?" I asked, startled.

"You'd be surprised," André replied, shaking his head.

"This cave was first discovered by Carl Lumholtz in 1891. He recognized this mud structure as an olla, although its size and shape certainly looked nothing like the corn granaries he'd encountered in Four Corners. The Anasazi tended to build small, neatly mortared cubicles with slab doors. I assume Biscolli took you to see the one at Raven Creek."

"No, but this is sounding familiar. Biscolli told me about Lumholtz and these Ollas, still, I never imagined I'd see one up close," I said.

"Hum... well this olla isn't Anasazi. It belongs to the Mogollon," André said.

"So, what is the connection between the two cultures?" I asked.

We sat in the dirt again.

"I'm sorry to have to be the one to tell you, but Biscolli's fishing here. He's reading far more into this than there actually is. I think he wants there to be a tight connection between the cultures, so he looks for anything that will support his hunch. He's done this before. He's a smart man and his hunches have been right, but this time he's barking up the wrong tree."

"What? Could this be true?" I asked myself, taking in André's words.

"What about the infants? Did he tell you about the two infants?" I asked.

"First of all," he said, turning to look directly at me. "Had Biscolli really examined the two infant skulls, he would have found that the Mogollon one—the one we call, 'Baby Lilly,' has a slight skull deformation from the flat cradleboard that the Mogollon carried their infants on. Maybe the infant was too young for it to be discernible, but believe me, you can't miss it in the adult skulls. The Anasazi didn't carry their infants this way, and their adult skulls confirm this. For whatever reason, there are some things Biscolli consistently overlooks, things that separate the two cultures—in spite of what he believes," André said.

I listened carefully, trying to make sense of what André was saying.

"The Mogollon and Anasazi are two separate cultures. The Mogollon people lived in the mountains and were far more nomadic than the settled Anasazi. They never fully adopted full-fledged agriculture or sedentary life," André said, then adjusted his hat.

"The Mogollon diet included meat, especially deer, rabbits, squirrels, and even fish—when they could find them. Yes, the Mogollon grew and stored corn, but unlike the Anasazi, who were highly dependent on their corn crop and developed an integrated irrigation system, the Mogollon had other food sources and didn't irrigate. There was also a third culture called the Hohokam during the same time period. A smaller total population. They lived in the area that's now Phoenix—but we won't get into that."

This wasn't sounding good. I had gotten the impression from Biscolli that the Mogollon and Anasazi cultures were basically the same—and were the Ancient Ones that Oliver had said we were to look for. If they were separate cultures, were we still on track, or were we wasting our time here? André paused, studied my face, and then continued.

"Just because both cultures resided in cliff dwellings, doesn't mean they were joined at the hip. The Mogollon tended to build in deep, dark caves with large overhangs, not far off the ground, like this one. Whereas, the Anasazi perched themselves on high, nearly inaccessible cliff ledges. Their lives were very different—and it wasn't due to terrain. They were different cultures," André said again, matter-of-factly.

This was hard to hear, and my questions for Biscolli mounted with each successive revelation.

"There are other things he's overlooking, as well. Blatantly obvious things. The Mogollon burial position was flat, on their backs. The Anasazi, on the other hand, always buried their people in the fetal position.

"Oh..." I said, finally speaking, my mind swirling with confusion. Trouble—big trouble—began brewing within me.

"For whatever reason, Biscolli's got it in his goofy head that he knows more than the rest of us. But then, what do we know? We just dig up the Mogollon every day," André said, then took a long drink from his Camelback.

My "big trouble" gave way to fear, and I was suddenly terrified. What was I doing in Mexico? I was sitting in Mogollon ruins in the middle of nowhere, mosquito-bitten, and having a conversation with an archaeologist who was telling me that my supposed Anasazi expert was living in some fantasy world. I didn't have time for this.

There had been an urgency to Oliver's message. It wasn't an impending disaster, but it was a call from Earth Mother for us to get our act together. She was done warning us through severe weather. Now, she was speaking. Her requirement was that her balance be restored. Advanced civilizations from the past had been wiped out when her balance had been disturbed. People needed to know that she had spoken—and they needed whatever it was that we were searching for that would help us restore and maintain her balance… and our own.

I felt more alone than ever. Like some naïve schoolgirl, I had relied on Biscolli to steer me toward the truth. I had done my own research, of course, but under his guidance. Up to this moment, I believed that Oliver had led me to him for his knowledge and expertise. And now, I wasn't so sure. We were on the cliffs of Mexico, and no closer to what we were looking for.

Was Biscolli that much of an egomaniac, that he had to be right? Would he put his own theory before the business of tracking down the secret?

Had he flat-out lied to me?

What kind of person would do that?

Or, could it be that he actually did know a secret about the Anasazi that he didn't want me to discover?

What were we doing here?

Had he led me to Mexico to throw me off?

Really? No, that couldn't be. Could it?

Was he simply a buffoon? Or was I the buffoon for believing him?

My trust waned in an instant. I felt betrayed by the one person that I had shared Oliver's words with in their entirety—the person who was supposed to be helping me. It was a long moment of despair. I stared into the valley in disbelief, on the verge of tears, not knowing what to do next. I couldn't cry, not in front of André. What I actually felt like doing was rolling Biscolli over the cliff, to where my heart had already tumbled—the bottom of Cueva Valley.

'Who was this guy?' I wasn't sure anymore. I didn't want to believe that he had purposefully lied to me. I had many questions—questions that deserved answers. Questions that he was going to answer. I certainly didn't know the man, but thought that I knew

Biscolli well enough that he wouldn't lie. I had trusted him. It was clear now that I didn't know the man at all.

The senior gladiator pushed himself upright, unaware of the anxiety and temper growing within me.

"It is beautiful, isn't it?" he volunteered. "Imagine living with views like this your entire life." He started to turn away, then paused, as if recalling something. "I came up here once, years ago, when I first arrived. It was one of those unbelievable moonless nights. The sheer number of stars astounded me… so close that I could reach out and pull any one of them down. Just as I was feeling like a meaningless speck among the cosmos, I had a magical experience," he continued, speaking as if I wasn't there beside him. "The Old Ones, they knew God, and they understood the stars. I'm sure of it." André smiled. "What made me remember that?" he mused. "I haven't thought of that night in years. True, you've got a strange influence on people."

He stood and dusted the dirt from his shorts. "Well, I'd better get to work. Hey, find me before we pull out for the day. I'd like you to see the remains of a twelve-foot check dam, built across rivulets to shore up the terraces for planting milpa—that's corn," he said, smiling again. "If you want to talk some more, I'll be on the mesa. In fact, you might just want to come up there anyway. We uncovered some basins yesterday that you might like to take a look at."

I heard his narrative about the stars, or God, or something, but I never got the point of his story. I was lost in the blow my trust had just taken. I managed a strained smile, but was speechless—a jumble of emotions: dazed, confused, frustrated… and pissed. I pulled myself to my feet and stepped precariously close to the edge of the cliff. It was fifteen feet to the ground beneath where the rigs were parked, and beyond that narrow outcropping, likely a six hundred foot drop to a deep plateau. The lush valley seemed so still, and the Madres were perfectly at peace. Nothing external had changed, but my inner world was under assault. I was a mess.

Alone, I stood there and tried to come up with one good reason why I should be in this alcove. Of all places on the planet that I could be, why was I here? Why? This trip now felt like a stupid waste of time. Was Biscolli so bent on proving a theory that he would put his agenda before anything else? I was trying to keep my thoughts from spinning out of control, but one thing was clear, that so-called expert archaeologist had some explaining to do.

I felt hot. This was taxing my nervous system. I knew I needed to blow off some steam. Perhaps, heaving Biscolli over this cliff would do the trick. Ha… I felt better already.

My cage had been rattled, and despite the fact that Biscolli was just above me on the mesa, I knew I couldn't talk to him—not now, not here. This "talk" of ours would have to wait until we were alone. It couldn't happen in the Mongoose, so it would have to be at the hotel. Damn, it felt like an eternity stood between me and any sort of resolution.

In the meantime, I knew that I had to calm myself down; I had to regulate my nervous system. My body shouldn't have to pay the price for this guy's archaeological fantasy. I closed my eyes and shook my head. "I trusted him completely," I repeated to myself. 'Ugh…'

I sat down, close to the lip of the cave, and dangled my feet over the edge of the cliff. I knew I wasn't in my right mind, but it felt so good to be defiant—even if it was to my own fears. In a way, "giving it" to my fears substituted for "giving it" to Biscolli. At least, for the time being. Soon enough, though, reason crept back in, and I scooted myself just far enough from the edge so my legs no longer hung over the abyss. No need to flirt with danger that closely.

I laid down. I knew I was lying in the powdery dirt. I knew I would be covered from head to toe with it. And I knew that I didn't care. The fact is, right now, I didn't care about much of anything. It could all go to hell—all of it, for that matter. I didn't need any of this! I was done!

I glanced up to the rugged, stony outcropping that extended beyond the cave, and a curious V-shaped notch in the ceiling caught my attention. Had it not appeared so out of place, I might have passed it off as a mere chip in the rock, but it looked odd, almost chiseled into the long protective overhang that jutted several feet beyond the cave floor.

I rose to my feet, circled beneath it, as best I could, observing the notch—or whatever it was, from every conceivable angle. I came to the cliff edge again. A couple of loose rocks gave way this time, bounced once near the vehicles, and rolled to oblivion.

I couldn't bear to look down, so I looked up. It was manmade. I was sure of it. If someone had notched it into the rock, they would have had to be Spiderman. It was at least two yards beyond the drop-off. The thought itself made me queasy. Perhaps André could make heads or tails of it. I would ask.

It was nearly one o'clock when Sesha, André, and Laura passed through the alcove on their way down to the rig to grab a cooler packed with sandwiches, potato chips, and Hostess fruit pies. I had dozed off in the shade but stirred when I heard their voices.

Apparently, the archaeologists knew nothing of the notch, which astounded me. Sesha, upon hearing of it, cried out. The fact that she was smiling, eased my mind considerably; because, at first, her gapping mouth and big eyes scared me.

When the weight of the news registered with the other two archaeologists, they piped in, reached for one another, and began jumping. There was nowhere for me to go, so the three drew me into their celebration. It was impossible to believe that none of them had seen it there before. Laura dropped out of the would-be celebratory dance and raced to the mesa to tell the others.

"True, you've found a solstice site notch!" Sesha exclaimed, trembling. "I can't believe we never saw it. All the signs are here: the north-facing alcove, an eastern canyon rim, and the extended roof rock. How did you see it?" she asked, and then gave each of us another hug, squealing. "What a find!"

Somewhere amidst all the hugging and cheering, she must have remembered my question about it being there and answered. Her voice was scratchy from the screaming and had risen an octave or two.

"André, would you like to explain it or should I?" she asked.

He nodded for her to continue. I can't say I was looking forward to her strained voice.

"Well," she began, pausing to catch her breath. "Ancient people watched the stars. They depended on the night sky as a crude, but reasonably accurate calendar for their crop planting, ceremonies, healings, and seasonal travel or migrations."

"The Mogollon would have lived here during the summer solstice, and have watched for gradual changes in the northern sky," she said, excitedly. "Cliff-villages such as this one, with north-facing overhangs, were known to provide particularly excellent

# ANASAZI VISION

reads, because a notch could be chiseled out of the overhanging dome, permitting a sky watcher to track Earth's movement."

"Amazing. So how did they use the notch?" I asked, curious.

The sound of her own voice must have relaxed Sesha because she slowed considerably and took on the tone of a scientist.

"Well, True, if you were to position yourself... about here, on a starlit night, and look up," she said, moving to stand directly in alignment with the notch. "Polaris would be visible right about there," she said, pointing through the nick.

"If you'll remember, Polaris is most often called the North Star—or the Axis of the Universe, because it appears as the one fixed point in the sky around which the heavens seem to turn from our earthly perspective."

"That's wild!" I said, examining the notch overhead.

"As you know, the earth rotates around the sun," André said. "The Mogollon who lived here between 1300 and 1450 AD, understood the movements of the heavens. When they occupied this vestige, a 'Sky Watcher' would sit right about where you're standing and look through the notch to observe star constellation changes in relation to Polaris. That's how they calculated time. This was their seasonal calendar." André pointed along the roofline of the alcove. "Relatively, few cliff villages have all the natural elements required to create a site line," he added. "Usually, alcoves are too vertical or they sit at the wrong angle to position a notch. That's why it's such a big deal, that Cueva de la Vasija has one. It's literally beyond me how we could have missed it. Diggers have been excavating this site for years. Naturally, we look for one, but True, you're the one who found it. Congratulations!" André said.

"I can't wait for the others to take a look. They'll be so excited," Sesha said.

I was the woman of the hour, but since, "How did you...?" can be asked only so many times, the honor soon faded, and I became invisible again—unimportant to Cueva de la Vasija and the canyon walls there.

The rest of the diggers' afternoon was spent carrying ladders and equipment into the cave and taking physical measurements. From these, calculations would be made to project which sights might be visible from the notch. An evening sight-reading would be conducted after the numbers had been crunched, perhaps in a couple of days.

It was dangerous work. Patience and accuracy accompanied every movement the professionals made. No one wanted my opinion, so I steadied the ladder and turned my attention to Oliver and his words that'd started this whole affair. I found that I could pull the vision from my memory with amazing clarity now. I recalled every detail and remembered every word spoken. Had I missed something that Oliver had said that would account for us being in Mexico? I ran through every possibility, but none of them made sense. I petitioned the heavens for help.

The crew called it a "wrap" at six o'clock. It had been a long, arduous day. Even the mountain goats were tired. Granted, their afternoon had been spent scaling rock while mine involved steadying a ladder, but close enough. The decision was made that Biscolli and I would head back to Chihuahua this evening. I was relieved. I needed answers from this guy.

**Thursday, May 19**

"So, Biscolli and I are in Chihuahua, Mexico. It is a wild, pristine, and wonderful place, much greener than I ever imagined. At times, this all seems like a dream—honestly, sometimes I wish it was a dream. Today, the diggers took us to a set of ruins under excavation called Cueva de la Vasija. It was inspiring and the view from them is breathtaking. I discovered a notch in the rock overhang. They called it a site-notch. Supposedly, it was used in ancient times to determine the placement of the Earth in relation to the sun and other celestial bodies. This sounds odd, but since I've been here, things have felt familiar—things I can't explain, like the notch or the energy boost I felt when I faced north. Odd. It makes no sense to me. We're back at our hotel and I'm glad about it. I need sleep, and need to talk to Biscolli!

So, here's the deal—André (one of the diggers here) says Biscolli's theory of the Mogollon-Anasazi connection is a total wash. Biscolli doesn't know what's up yet, but he knows I'm upset and want to talk. I'm writing this while I'm waiting for him. I don't know if I trust this guy anymore. I think he's hiding something. He has a lot of explaining to do. I'll write details when I get some answers."

# 15

# SPIRIT EYES

Anything between two people living out of suitcases is hard-pressed to remain a secret for long. There had been only necessary conversation between us since Biscolli had pulled into the hotel, parked the Mongoose, and shut off the cacophonous engine. I was upset, that much was clear, but just how upset, even I wasn't certain. I wanted to blame this guy for his ego-centered, conjured-up theory, for the ringing in my ears, for my irritation, and for my hundreds of mosquito bites. Telling him off was like a bad itch, just aching to be scratched. I didn't want to be upset, but I needed to know what was going on. Was I being taken on a ride?

As we walked towards our rooms, I told Biscolli we needed to talk. He gave me a thumbs-up. I then showered and managed to calm myself down. Perhaps, Biscolli had a good reason for what he'd done. Perhaps, he'd made a blundering error. Could I forgive him for misleading my research—for misleading me? Is that what he'd done, or had he flat-out lied? I was spinning again, and that served no purpose. Ultimately, I concluded that it wasn't so much my questions, but his answers, that I should be concerned with. I needed information. We'd proceed from there.

Twenty minutes passed and there was a knock on my door. I let Biscolli in and sat on a chair. He sat on the edge of the bed. I waited a moment. I couldn't open my mouth. Not yet, I could still say something I'd regret.

"Is something on your mind?" Biscolli asked, looking up from a yoga magazine I'd tossed onto my bed.

The questioning then began: No, he wasn't lying to me. No, he wasn't trying to throw me off track. "How ridiculous," was his exact comment. No, he wasn't hiding some Anasazi secret—there was nothing to hide. The questions continued: Yes, his theory was a stretch, but it still had merit—the Mogollon were Ancient Ones, after all. Yes, he was serious about helping me find a secret somewhere in the desert. Yes, he was through with this idiotic interrogation. He was starved and wanted a beer. Biscolli stood and barged from my room. He caught the closing door on his way out with his boot and glared at me.

"This is the second time you've not trusted me, my commitment, or my word. This is getting old." He turned and the door slapped closed behind him.

I had a hard time sleeping that night. I was confused and lost for answers. At daybreak, I could hear Biscolli next door. He'd begun some ludicrous, noisy process of blowing his nose. I wanted to pulverize him. I threw back the covers and got up. I hated waking up tired, and today I was not only tired, I was still agitated—and far from wanting to be near Leonard Biscolli.

I wet my face and looked in the mirror, then heaved a big sigh. The truth was, I didn't want to be in my own company. I attempted to meditate, but nothing quieted the dragon that morning. I didn't want to be irritable. This was far from my normal mood, and that was irritating me too. Something more was going on here that wasn't ready to reveal itself to me. I picked up the novel again and leaned against the headboard to begin Chapter 23. An hour into the morning, there was a knock on my door. I opened it just enough to see it was Biscolli.

"Are you ready to go to the site?"

My sour face and bedclothes should have been enough of an answer, but no, he needed to hear it.

"No, Leo, I've decided to stay back today," I said. My answer came as no surprise. He informed me that he planned on staying overnight at the field house with the other diggers and returning tomorrow evening. We could make plans to head back to the States then. I agreed that was a good idea.

I closed the door, glad to be rid of the man for two days. He'd done nothing wrong, per se, and though I intellectually understood that, I was still not happy we were in Mexico and no closer to what we were looking for.

Around nine o'clock, I stopped by the hotel kitchen, hoping to find the cook I'd befriended. José and I chatted briefly while he fried some eggs with green chilis for me, served with salsa and fresh tortillas.

After a quiet breakfast in the hotel kitchen, I took my coffee onto the veranda, which overlooked a shady courtyard. The morning air was pleasantly cool and perfumed by the combined fragrances of climbing roses and Mexican honeysuckle. Bougainvillea blossoms cascaded from the veranda walls. Gratefully, the mosquitoes had fled with the warmer, dryer air. I noted my mood had lifted considerably, and was glad for it.

I took a seat in the small flower garden and sipped my coffee. Shortly thereafter, I heard a stream of Spanish behind me and turned to find a couple that looked to be in their mid-sixties, strolling along the veranda walkway. Each carried a cup of steaming coffee. The man withdrew a chair for the gray-haired woman, and they continued their conversation at a small table across from me.

My Spanish is limited at best. It hadn't deterred my travels, but was a nuisance when I truly wanted to communicate. Even with immersion and practice, the language never seemed to stick. I could surmise what was being said, but, admittedly, my responses were limited to a few words I'd polished over time, and I relied on them far too much. It was noticeable.

As the couple spoke, I couldn't help but notice the woman's regular glances my way. Her companion turned once and gave me a curious look, then returned to their conversation.

She was an astonishing-looking woman who knew how to bring out the beauty of her dark features. The purple blouse she wore raised a radiant glow on her light mahogany-colored skin, and a shawl she wore over her shoulders, glistened as she moved in the morning light. She was a large-breasted woman; a bit heavy, but her face easily forgave whatever softened her body. An air of femininity graced her every move. For several minutes, we continued to exchange glances—hers were deep and piercing.

I sipped my coffee and contemplated what needed to be done for us to return to the States. Biscolli would return from the field house tomorrow evening. Perhaps we could leave as soon as Saturday.

'Two glorious days without Biscolli,' I thought, swirling what remained of my coffee. I sighed, sipped the last drop, and watched the woman speak with the man. I stood, placed the cup on a nearby table, left a tip, and turned to leave.

"Señora, quédase un momento, por favor (Stay a moment, please)," the woman said, extending her hand and touching my forearm as I passed.

"I beg your pardon?"

"Quédase un momento, por favor (Stay a moment, please)," the woman repeated, raising her deep brown eyes to mine. She smiled, then turned to the man she was with. "Juan excúsame, este es la señora. Voy á hablarla (Juan, excuse me, this is the lady. I'm going to talk to her)," she said to him.

Her Spanish was slow and soft, as unhurried as she was, and though I could comprehend very little, it was beautiful to listen to. Her companion looked up and greeted me with a warm smile and slight nod. Still seated, she brought his hand to her lips, kissed it, then stood and wrapped her fingers around my forearm. A full skirt tied off with a sash fell below her knees. The air carried her fragrance.

"Con su permiso. Vamos andando (With your permission. Let's walk)," she said, motioning me forward, and we passed through the iron gateway and onto the street. "Habla ustéd el español (Do you speak Spanish)?" she asked.

"Un poquito (A bit)," I replied, holding my index finger and thumb slightly apart, trusting she'd understand that my Spanish was limited. She smiled.

"Ah, then we speak the Inglés," she said, patting my forearm. Her hand was soft.

"Yes, let's speak English," I agreed. "What can I do for you?"

"Ah, Señora," she laughed. "Not what you can do for me. Me llamo Ojos Espíritu. How do you say? I am Spirit Eyes. My eyes see more than most. Señora needs to be taught to see what most cannot. Please, come with Spirit Eyes, and let my eyes see for you.

Her words intrigued me.

"You're a seer?" I asked.

"La psiquica. Ah, psychic. Today these eyes are yours."

She wasn't an elderly woman by any means, but something about her seemed ancient. We strolled along a street until we came to a small pastel-green home surrounded by flowering shrubs. She invited me in. It felt right, so I decided to trust my intuition.

Our walk had given me time to think. Perhaps, Spirit Eyes could see why I was in Mexico, explain the vision, or at least, help interpret it. I hoped all this might be possible as I followed her into a small sitting room. The colorful room was dressed with uncovered windows, an orange sofa swallowed by half a dozen pillows, a wooden rocker, simple tables, and dozens of plants. She removed her shawl, and I took a seat on the sofa. I'd barely sat when she returned with a cup of tea.

"For Señora. Spirit Eyes was prepared for your visit," she said, taking a seat in the rocker. Her comment puzzled me; it felt as if she'd known I'd be on the veranda and had come to retrieve me. I wondered if that's the kind of thing psychics saw. Before I could ask her about it, she spoke.

"You have need to know great things," she said, watching me as she rocked. "Señora's heart is troubled. Tell Spirit Eyes what you wish for me to see."

I didn't know exactly how this worked, so asked if it'd be all right if she revealed what she'd seen when she'd looked at me on the veranda.

"Ah, you are alone. I see children—grown ones; cuatro niños. They no longer live with you. I see being alone is not a bad thing for you. There is a fire in your heart, though. I see grief at your Madre's death, yet still, too much fire. You come to the sacred desert, far from your forest home, bringing many sorrowful things to release, to give wings so they may pass from you. This is good. Bueno."

"Yes," I said, nodding, then set down my teacup.

"I see a compañero join you. You and the señor shall be one, as before. I see this happen soon. You are blessed with a compañero in this lifetime," she said and smiled.

Spirit Eyes could see. She'd seen my children, Mama's passing, and a companion?

'Hmmm…?' I mused for a moment over the possibility. Yet that wasn't what was weighing on me—the vision was. I had to ask.

"Spirit Eyes… ma'am, do you see anything about a little man named Oliver? A secret beneath the desert, or Earth Mother?" I asked.

Spirit Eyes closed her eyes a moment, nodded, and then opened them.

"Ojos Espíritu sees you in the sacred desert. You search for the old medicine. I see no small hombre with you. I only see you search for the medicine. This desert is the place of your second lesson. You will heal this 'big fire' in your heart."

"Second lesson?" I inquired. "Spirit Eyes, what does a second lesson mean? And what is this 'big fire' in my heart?" I asked.

"Ah," she said, nodding again. "Before your birth, you chose three life lessons you should learn this lifetime. Uno, dos, tres… tres leccions, for your soul to grow during this walk on earth," she said. "The first lesson visited you early in life. You learned to listen to Spirit and follow your spirit heart. You learned to separate 'man-speak' from 'spirit-speak.' Ah, this is very good… muy bueno."

I panned over my life and wondered if she was referring to when I determined the difference between organized religion and spirituality. I nodded.

"Ojos Espíritu sees a big fire in your heart, only this is not grief fire over your Madre's death. This is anger fire."

I immediately thought of Biscolli and our heated exchange last night.

"Yes," I said and took a deep breath. "There's a man... an archaeologist."

"Yes, I see the man—blonde, brawny. But this fire is bigger than one man. This fire you brought to the sacred desert," Spirit Eyes said, then swayed in her rocker.

I watched her gently rock as I processed her words.

"This fire?" I asked. "Can you tell me more, please?"

The rocking motion stopped and Spirit Eyes spoke slowly.

"It starts from an inability to understand your needs and fill them. This uncertainty is original source of your frustration. It grows to anger—big fire. This happened often as a child. You did not understand your needs, so agree to what you are told to do though your gut knew better. It is not your fault, you just did not know how to read and trust it."

I nodded, finding truth and recognition in her words.

"After first life lesson, you feel inner guidance in a strong way—what your gut says is right for you. You know what way to go, but when you deny it, Señora feels backed into a corner—disturbed, even angry."

"Yes, that explains a lot," I agreed.

"This frustration fans big when you agree to things that don't align with your inner knowing. This tension is the conflict inside you, and source of big fire. It flames when your goal is blocked or you not listen to your gut. Señora not trust others because she not trust herself to follow inner knowing."

Wow. I took a deep, slow, purposeful breath, and received everything Spirit Eyes had shared with me. Her inner sight addressed my frustration as a child, and the way I often felt as I made decisions for my life. I met Spirit Eye's gaze, which radiated calm, compassion, and non-judgment. I nodded.

"Señora's second lesson is in the sacred desert. This man with you brings up your big fire, so you can see it." Spirit Eyes looked directly at me. "Dear soul, no old medicine can be found with conflict in your heart. Unsettled emotions of anger, frustration, judgment, and resentment in Señora's body, not match the vibration of old medicine. Old medicine could be here, in front of you in this room, but you would not see it because you and it are at different vibrations. Sí?"

'Good Lord, could this be true?' Yes, I understood that everything was energy and it vibrated at a specific rate, but was my unresolved frustration affecting my vibratory rate—was it lowering it that much?

"When Señora match the vibration of old medicine, she will see it easy, because they now vibrating at the same rate. Like a radio dial… she can not hear the 94.5 station if she sets dial to 94.2. Sacred desert medicine does not come to you by wanting, pushing, or forcing. It comes by matching. Your emotions are vibrational frequency that reaches out to universe, and it responds in kind. Frustration energy returns more frustration experiences."

I nodded. This was making so much sense.

"Thoughts are vibrational energy too," Spirit Eyes continued. "When you have strong emotion about a thought in your head, it becomes—what do you say? Supercharged. Señora match vibration of old medicine and you will see it."

I nodded again.

"If old medicine is yours to do, you have great help—both seen and unseen, but you must trust that help is there. You cannot see old medicine or accept this help when there is big fire in your heart. The obstacle in your road is your own doing. That is why big fire must go out first. The man is here to help it burn big, so you can see this obstacle and heal it."

This was hard to hear. It was easy to blame Biscolli for everything that'd happened, but my big fire? Could my frustration be at the root of this? Had I brought this on myself? Was Biscolli merely turning up the heat, so I could heal this? I sighed. I knew it was true.

"Spirit Eyes," I said, leaning forward. "How do I heal this big fire?"

"Ah, Ojos Espíritu sees two rivers: the first river is Trust. Señora does not trust this man," she said shaking her head. "She does not trust Spirit will provide. She does not trust help be there. She do, do, do, because she does not trust."

This was even more difficult to hear, but there was truth in her words. I knew this pattern well—doing because I assumed no help or support would be there; and the bigger the challenge, task, or decision, the more alone or unsupported I felt. Spirit Eyes had her hand on the taproot of my life pattern, it was now mine to weed it out. I nodded, understanding.

"Sweet soul, I see your medicine is to roll onto your back and float the river of Trust. Flapping your arms is a waste of energy. That is not trust. Will the river hold you?"

She paused and studied me.

"Will it?" she asked.

Spirit Eyes looked into my eyes, and a gentle smile rose on her beautiful face.

"That is the lesson you must learn—that is your lesson number two." Spirit Eyes began rocking again.

This was a lot to take in, but all of it felt accurate. This had nothing to with Biscolli, with Oliver, or even the Ancient Ones, and the secret. It had everything to do with me. I took a deep breath again. Spirit Eyes was looking at me, but her gaze was not accusatory, it was kind, tender, and deeply compassionate. I felt safe and secure in her presence, and it helped me to soften and receive these insights about myself.

"Thank you," I said. "Can you tell me about the second river?"

"Sweet Señora," she said. "Remember that this is a life lesson you chose to learn. This is not supposed to be easy, but it will be thorough—or, it will return again. Round and round lessons go until they are learned," she said and then smiled. "That is the way life lessons work—they are Life lessons. Ojos Espíritu sees you do this. Señora will feel the river of Trust hold her. Always remember, sweet soul, it brings great joy to the river to support you. This is the way of the universe. Sí?"

I nodded. "Sí."

Spirit Eyes laughed. Something had humored her.

"Spirit says to just relax. This is not a chore. If Señora floats on her back in river of Trust, the second river—Acceptance, is easy. Trust breaks the need to control and brings acceptance. Remember that you see through one set of eyes. Spirit sees everything, knows everything—is everything. This is how anything becomes possible. Señora's eyes see un poquito," she said, holding her index finger and thumb slightly apart. She laughed, and I joined in, seeing the humor in her referencing my earlier gesture. I sat down my teacup, reached forward, and squeezed her hand.

"Thank you," I said. I found it interesting that this information about myself had hushed the questions I had about Oliver, the Ancient Ones, or even why I was in Chihuahua.

"Is there anything else I should know?" I asked.

She paused, narrowing her eyes as though listening to a far-off voice.

"Ojos Espíritu sees the old medicine you seek. It is mighty and can tip big scales. Powerful. Essential. This medicine path of yours also leads to your compañero." Spirit Eyes' voice then trailed off. "We will speak again. That is all Spirit Eyes sees for you today. My seeing eyes are now closed. Remember dear soul, it is important to have your sight not clouded by fear. All people are moved by two emotions—love or fear," she said. "Go your way with no fear."

Spirit Eyes slid forward, stood from her rocker, took my hand, and escorted me to the door.

"It is time that you should go, Señora. I see no more with my eyes today. You come see Ojos Espíritu again. Sí?" she said, depressing the door latch.

I wanted to thank her once more—to say something, but I felt her urging me to be on my way. Spirit Eyes smiled kindly, lifted my hand to her lips, and kissed it. As she did so, I felt a rush of incredible love surge through me. I hugged her and she bid me goodbye.

I made my way toward the hotel—just a few blocks from Spirit Eye's home and came upon a plaza where birds were flocking around an old man tossing them crumbs. The mid-morning sun had warmed the air. It was pleasantly comfortable. The humidity and mosquitoes, gratefully, were gone.

I wandered through the plaza, thinking of Spirit Eyes and our conversation. Our encounter had both touched and unraveled me. The psychic had been accurate about my children, and Mama's death, and she had seen me in the desert. She'd even seen Biscolli and my argument with him.

She had said I chose three life lessons before my birth. I remembered back to Grand Gulch, when Roger had sat with me in the cave. He had said something about life lessons too. Was that the same thing?

Spirit Eyes had seen me discern between spirituality and religion, and had said my second life lesson would be to learn trust, and it could heal my pattern of frustration—of feeling alone and my perpetual "doing." It could quiet my urge to control, and bring acceptance.

She had said that unresolved emotions were keeping my vibrational frequency low and that my frequency didn't match the secret in the sacred desert—which she called "old medicine." Would Oliver, or for that matter, Earth Mother, have asked me to find Biscolli and whatever we were looking for, if they knew my vibration was low? They must've known that I could raise it.

I walked to a park bench, sat, and watched Chihuahua pass by. A little girl darted across the plaza and ran towards the birds. They scattered and then returned to the feeding frenzy at the man's feet. A señorita chased the girl around the plaza, clasped her hand, and steered her away from the birds. The two crossed the busy street and were gone. I returned to my thoughts.

Spirit Eyes had said to roll onto my back—to float in the river of Trust and relax. That direction sounded simple enough but, in reality, could I do that? Could I let go completely and trust?

Could I?

The very thought of doing so made my chest tight. Was Earth Mother depending on me to let go so the secret that would tip "big scales" could be found? The thought stirred up anxiety and my body began to tighten. I drew in a deep breath and tried to relax my chest.

Across the plaza, the old man feeding the birds rolled up the paper sack that he'd been dipping into for crumbs and tossed it in a trash bin. He then strolled along the sidewalk and stopped when he reached me. I smiled and struggled my way through our brief exchange. I was embarrassed that I didn't have a better vocabulary. I made a commitment to try again to learn the language of these friendly people.

As he turned and departed, a disturbing sensation began to swirl within me. I couldn't name it, but it felt big—enormous, actually. I wanted to suppress it—to send it back into its cave but, having just been told by Spirit Eyes that unprocessed emotions were fueling my frustration, I chose to let the emotion be there and ride it out. This was scary territory.

I left the plaza, bought bottled water, and sipped it as I walked the final street towards the hotel. Just inside the wrought iron gate, I passed the veranda where I'd met Spirit Eyes less than two hours earlier. Beyond it was a pleasant courtyard with lush foliage and a flowing water feature. The shady adobe courtyard cooled me. It was a welcome refuge from the heat rising on the street. The hotel office and kitchen were located to the left, with the guest rooms to the right.

## ANASAZI VISION

I unlocked my door, still pondering the psychic's message. What was I supposed to do with the information now that I'd received it? I dropped everything from my hands. The disturbing sensation was rising. I sensed blackness closing in on me—a gaping emotional hole, and I wanted to be nowhere near it.

I felt feverish—no, cold. I slid off my shoes, curled up in bed, and pulled a cover over me. Was I getting sick? I laid still and heard Spirit Eyes' last words to me: "All people moved by two emotions: love or fear."

I drew my knees to my chest. I wanted to believe love steered my life, but knew frustration repeatedly hijacked love. For God's sake, my first childhood memory was of being frustrated. Had I been frustrated and afraid my entire life? Really? What kind of life was that?

I began to cry, wanting so much more for myself. Last night's argument with Biscolli played out in my mind—I'd been demanding, ugly, demeaning. 'Oh, God…'

The thought pushed me into the black hole. Shocked, I fumbled for the edge to pull myself out, struggling to keep from plummeting. But, there was nothing to grab.

With no anchors, I shot like a bullet downward—a lightning-fast free fall, whizzing past what I could only imagine were walls. In a panic, I grasped at anything to slow my velocity.

Hurling downward and immersed in darkness, images began flashing before me: a parade of arguments, conflicts, and irritations. I saw myself at odds with Life—a succession of stupid, unnecessary irritations—a flight delay, a fly rod that wouldn't collapse… not finishing my vision quest.

More images flashed: the tension and stress I brought on myself and others by distilling benign situations until all that remained were issues, unknowns, and compromises suffocating any joy existing there. This I'd done dozens of times while caring for Mama. I was the source of my grief, sadness, struggle, and conflict. Me!

It was coming fast now. I witnessed my fierce resistance to situations and decisions that adults imposed upon me as a child. I relived the stomach aches, the pouting, the tantrums—and the ensuing timeouts and spankings that addressed my willful defiance or need to be right. I then witnessed myself swing to the other extreme—do what I was told to do, and resent it.

A life of resistance, defiance, resentment, and frustration. I began to sob, feeling the impact this had made on the lives of those I said I loved. I wanted to be held, but there was no one to hold me.

I plunged even deeper.

I was the one who forced my will, who persuaded, blamed, and pouted—just as I'd done this morning when Biscolli knocked on my door. Was all this making me happier? Was this making others happier?

I plummeted deeper into the hole. Panicked, I yelled.

"Help me! Dear God, help me. I'm sorry. Help me."

That's when it happened. Like a big fish heaved from its wet home, I pitched between two worlds—straddling the life I knew, and a foreign world of trust. My reality careened in one direction and then another—pulled, tugged, and torn, mind, body, and soul, between two paradigms.

Why did things annoy me so? Why did I need things to be different than they were? Who was I to know how things should be, or how they should turn out? I had just one set of eyes. Isn't that what Spirit Eyes had said… "One set of eyes." What did I know, anyway? And yet, here I was, forcing my will on the world.

Deep remorse filled me. Spirit Eyes had been right, I didn't trust. For all my supposed smarts and talk about an abundant universe, I was a fraud. When backed into a corner and all that remained was Trust and me, I chose me. The odds seemed better. At least I knew what I was working with. Problem was, I was drained. I didn't want to live that way anymore.

A pressure grew in my chest, as though a hand was squeezing my heart. I held my chest and sobbed.

"Help me!" I pleaded. "I don't want to live like this. I want to trust something besides myself."

I must have blacked out because I don't remember what happened next. I suspect at some point I must have rolled onto my back and crossed my arms over my chest because that's the position I found myself in when I came to.

As I awoke, I had a visceral sensation of floating, not just in something, but above it as well. I just let things be, as I tried to determine where I was.

I found that I was floating further and further away from what looked to be my body, resting there. The perspective provided a beautiful view, and I could see myself drifting amongst scenery, which appeared to be a backdrop for my life. From this perspective, I felt enormous appreciation for the life I'd created.

This image of my life gave me a sense of peace and ease. I then heard a voice say, 'This is what your higher self does," and understood that it watches over my body and sees everything around me, as well as my past and events to come.

I understood my higher self serves as my guide—my all-seeing eyes, and it knows the way; lovingly watching out for me—protecting me, serving me, guiding me. Understanding this brought so much peace that I felt myself let go of trying to control. I relaxed, so the higher self could do its job of serving and guiding me.

I sensed my life was unfolding precisely in a way that served my life path, whether it looked (or felt) like that, to my thinking mind. I could rest, knowing all was well. I was safe. Anything I'd been worried about; any problems I thought I needed to solve, or answers I needed to come up with, were all known by my higher self. All I had to do was allow it. I began to feel empowered, assured I would know every answer or solution, and that every path would become visible and available at the time I would need it. I felt cradled, loved, and supported.

As I continued to lay there, sensations returned to my body and I became more and more aware of my surroundings. I pulled in a couple of full breaths and felt myself on the bed of my hotel room.

I'd lost all track of time. From where I'd just returned, time was of no importance and of little consequence. I was in complete bliss and equally exhausted. All I wanted and could do was sleep. I closed my eyes and willingly gave myself to it.

I am not sure how long I slept, but when I awoke, I felt alert, energized, and had a strong urge to be outdoors. I slipped into a sundress and soon found a fresh-air market. I meandered through the crowd, admiring the ceramics, clothing, hand-woven blankets, and every type of local produce imaginable. I noticed everything in great detail and marveled that each item seemed to have a luminous quality about it.

As I was purchasing a melon from a vendor, I thought I heard someone call my name. It seemed unlikely since I didn't know a soul other than Spirit Eyes, and Biscolli was at the site. I paid no attention. Moments later, I felt a tug on my dress and turned, surprised to find that it was André.

"Biscolli is very ill," he said. "I've taken him to the hotel."

I handed back the melon and we hurried to the hotel. When we arrived, we found Biscolli lying on his bed in a wad of disheveled sheets, his thick arms wrapped around his belly, moaning. I came closer and could see the sheets were damp with sweat. He was burning with fever. Biscolli wailed and drew his knees onto his chest.

"Biscolli," I called, struggling to get his attention.

"Son of a bitch!" he cried.

"All right," I said, "But, that doesn't help me.

André leaned in and said that Biscolli had doubled over in the alcove. They'd managed to carry him down the ladder—no easy feat.

"He held his right side and said his back hurt like hell," André added.

"Biscolli," I said, applying slight pressure over his kidneys. "Does it hurt here?"

"Son of a bitch!" he yelled, flinching. André jumped backward, putting as much distance as possible between himself and the pain.

Another gentle assessment and my probing backfired. I withdrew my hand, but not before Biscolli exploded into a rage of grabbing and punching. In the struggle to stay on my feet, I didn't feel the jolt of the first blow to my arm, only the sting that followed. I hadn't expected Biscolli would start punching, so when the second strike came, it hit me in the chest. Instantly it stung like turpentine. André leapt forward and was on Biscolli in a moment.

Apparently, the digger didn't know better than to get between a man and his pain, so he took the brunt of the next blow in his gut. André shouted something as he crumpled and fell to the floor. I threw all of my weight onto the flailing arm. André appeared out of nowhere and caught the striking arm before impact. I rolled back from the action, ran to wet a washcloth, and dropped it onto Biscolli's forehead. He quieted down like a spoiled baby.

André and I exchanged a quick sigh of relief.

"Biscolli, listen to me," I called out, raising my voice so he could hear it over his moaning. "Have you been drinking water?"

He gave no response, so I turned to André and asked if he had seen Biscolli drinking water the past two days. He said he hadn't noticed either way.

"Is he dehydrated or did he get a bug?" André asked.

"No," I answered, "I think he's trying to pass a kidney stone—maybe a couple. The pain is unbearable till it passes. He'll be all right, but I need you to get me a few things, and get a doctor. I need Burdock root, dried if you can find it, and catnip. Also, have José in the kitchen give you some virgin olive oil, molasses, and lemon juice. Go!"

André shouted over Biscolli's moaning that they had called for a doctor, but she was on an emergency. He then bolted from the room.

Biscolli rolled onto his back and flung the washcloth from his forehead.

"What the hell are you doin'? You tryin' to kill me?"

I retrieved the cloth, wet it with cold water, and reapplied it.

"Trust me, friend, we'll have you better in no time. Just lie on your right side and drink water till André gets back."

Thankfully, he offered little resistance, drank a bottle of water, and eventually slipped into a fitful sleep. André returned with everything I'd asked for. I poured lemon juice into a bottle of water and asked him to have Biscolli drink it and to keep a cool cloth on his forehead. André monitored him at arm's length.

I gathered the ingredients, ran to the hotel kitchen, and asked José if I could prepare a medicinal tea for Biscolli. Over the next twelve hours, I had Biscolli sip the tea, following it with an olive oil chaser.

André and I sat with Biscolli throughout the night, urging him to drink water, reapplying the cloth to his forehead, and reassuring him when he moaned from the pain. I envisioned his kidneys bathed in healing energy and the stones passing with as little discomfort as possible. André accompanied him to the restroom which, unfortunately, was down the hall. He said that Biscolli was passing blood. The following afternoon he passed a stone the size of a pea and half a dozen smaller ones. Gratefully, we all got some sleep after that, and by evening, Biscolli was back to his old self.

"The hell you say, I actually punched you?" Biscolli said, facing André, then laughed. "If I'd have known that, I'd have made it a good one."

"Oh, it was good, all right," André said, running his hand over his gut. "Unfortunately, you punched True too." Biscolli's face turned sober at the news.

His coloring was still a bit gray but, as pitiful as he looked, it was still an improvement over the day we'd met in the library when he was liquored up. I got a change of sheets from the señorita and a clean tee shirt for Biscolli. It read: "In my defense, I was left unsupervised." I shook my head.

"Ah man, I thought I was dying," Biscolli said, sitting up in bed. "How did you know what to do, Babe? Are you a doctor or something?"

I decided to let the "babe" comment slide this time.

"No," I said, sitting on the edge of the bed, "Just a passion for plant medicine. I thought about becoming an herbalist but decided on fitness instead. Still, knowing remedies, tinctures and such, has come in handy raising kids… and times like these."

"I guess so! Well, I'll tell you what, that tea you poured down me was some gnarly stuff, but whatever it was, it worked. Thanks, I won't forget it." Biscolli sat up and reached for my hand. "I can't believe I hit you. I'm sorry, True. I'm not that kind of man. I don't know what to say. I must have been out of my head. I would never hurt you. I'm sorry."

# 16

# VERANDA

I had taken a liking to the veranda and thought that I would begin my morning there. It'd been a long couple of days, and I was looking forward to some fresh air. On my way to the veranda, I saw José, so I stepped into the kitchen. I thanked him for his help and we nodded our way through a conversation over some dark roast café.

He refilled my cup and a small thermos and then started his morning kitchen duties. I carefully carried my café onto the veranda. It was an overcast morning and the gray backbone of the mountains concealing Cueva Valley from the rest of the world had been swallowed in thick clouds.

André stepped onto the veranda and we exchanged greetings. I invited him to get a cup from the kitchen and poured coffee from the Thermos into it. He pulled up a chair and sat next to me.

"Biscolli appears to be well, so I'll head back up the mountain today," he said, running a hand through his graying hair. "You did a great job with him. I felt so helpless, especially when we were told the doctor was on an emergency. How'd you know what to do?"

"I've taken a few classes in plant medicine, and I've passed a stone before. It's brutal."

"Well, I think we're all glad you knew what to do."

I nodded, and then we sipped coffee and watched dark, threatening clouds stack up along the hills.

"So, André, what can you tell me about Biscolli?"

"He's a piece of work, isn't he?" André said, shaking his head. "I remember being at Red Rock on the day of immunizations. Dr. Mel was pricking the crews as they came off shift. She'd taken over Biscolli's classroom, and he was having a hissy fit about using the chow hall to do their curation. One by one, his crew trailed into the chow hall, agonizing over their sore arms. Biscolli left no doubt that he thought they were all a bunch of sissies, and that real diggers didn't get shots."

André paused and took a long sip from his cup.

"After class, his crew disappeared and Biscolli went out to the van to pull some gear from it. That's when his crew surrounded him, and Dr. Mel came running out. She dropped his drawers on the spot and jabbed a huge hypodermic into his butt. Biscolli lit up like a Christmas tree," he said, laughing so hard he spilled his coffee.

"It was hard to tell from the cursing which one was winning the fight. I swear, I've never seen anything so funny in all my life," André, said, wiping his eyes.

"Oh my God," I said, laughing. "I would've loved to have seen that!" Then I added, "He's not much for rules, is he?"

"You know, it's funny," André replied, still wiping his eyes. "The guy's strict when it comes to everyone else's safety. He won't bend a single rule, but as for himself, yeah, he'll push his limits. The guy's a natural teacher. That's what makes him such a fine supervisor."

"How long has he been an archaeologist?"

"Biscolli? …Oh, maybe six years," André said, setting down his coffee cup. "I know it took him a long time to settle on digging. He used to take these wild road trips with his dad—more like explorations, the way he talks about it. Hard to imagine, but he says they'd leave Simi Valley the day school ended and hitchhike east, crossing miles of wilderness beyond Joshua Tree. Apparently, the two of them discovered dozens of undocumented caves and petroglyphs."

"Well, that's cool."

"Yeah. I guess his dad tried to steer him toward the Forest Service, but Biscolli wanted to be a firefighter. He gave his dad's way a shot, but a couple of years into college, he gave it up. Ended up driving water mules and then bulldozers, building fire lines."

"Huh…"

"I guess building fire lines wasn't enough adventure, so he traipsed off to the headwaters of the Amazon in Columbia for a year, where he volunteered with a team of entomologists to collect insects. That trip must've triggered something, because he joined a group investigating the Mayas in the Yucatan jungle, here in Mexico. That would have been about eight years ago. That's where Biscolli met Eric." André paused. "You've met Eric Voss, haven't you? He's running Red Rock now."

"Yes, we've met."

"Great guy. We lost one hell of a digger when he took that desk job." André refilled his cup, then refilled mine. I settled back in my chair and got comfortable again. André continued.

"Anyway, Biscolli was all over the Mayas. He returned stateside on fire but, within weeks, lost his family in a car wreck. He took it real hard—they were close. I guess only a sister survived."

I remembered Biscolli saying he had a sister in Chiang Mai. That must be the one who'd survived the accident.

"Biscolli was always intense, but after the crash, he turned almost robotic, driving himself to get his Master's at an insane pace. In the years I've known him, he's never slowed down, not even for a woman. I think he gave himself to digging a long time ago."

I nodded my head. "Yeah, he said something like that to me."

"Huh… Well, we're all a little like that, I guess. But Biscolli has a passion even the rest of us don't understand. That's why I wasn't surprised when I heard he went after Dan Collier single-handedly." André paused and shook his head. "You know, pulling out of the Raven Creek dig about ripped his heart out—only figures he got sick." André and I exchanged a glance. I could see that he sincerely cared about his friend. "How do you know Biscolli?" he asked.

"We met at Red Rock on Saturday."

"Saturday? And you're down here together? Wow, that's a first. I would've never guessed that… Biscolli never warms up to anyone that fast. Granted, you're an eyeful, but as long as I've known him, he's never taken interest in a woman," André said, then, almost as an afterthought, added, "What did you say to him?"

"Beats me?"

"Huh… Since you said you two weren't an item, I thought maybe you were old surfing pals or something."

"He surfs?"

"Biscolli? Hell yeah, surfs, flys, climbs… whatever. He was even into skydiving for a while. I haven't got the nerve for that kind of stuff, but he takes to it. He's a great diver, too. We did a dive together in the Caribbean two years ago. Do you dive?"

"No," I said. "You seem to know him pretty well."

"Not really. What I just told you, took me three years to learn. I still can't believe you two just met."

"Three years to learn that? Wow. I guess I shouldn't feel out of the loop then," I said.

"Trust me, you're not out of the loop. Biscolli doesn't let many people in, and he decides just how close they'll get. He cares for you, True, whether you see it or not."

"Huh. How could that be?" I wondered. He'd seen me rattled and unsure from the moment we'd met, and I'd been a brat a couple of times. I then thought back to the dozens of men that I'd worked alongside through two male-dominated careers—military and fitness. I'd encountered Sigma males before, but never anyone quite like Biscolli.

The two of us fell quiet for a moment, then I asked André about the site notch.

"Oh, glad you asked," he said. We forwarded the measurements we took to ASU, and are waiting to hear from astronomers as to what would've been visible nine hundred years ago. We're just diggers. All we can do is guess. The notch is a big deal though."

"Hum…"

"Oh, and we voted to pull an all-nighter. Yep, we're staying in the cave tonight. We can't wait to see a constellation through the notch."

"Well, that's cool."

"Truth be told, we're all a little embarrassed you found it. We still can't figure out that one. We've been all over that cave," he said, shaking his head.

"It was by accident. I just happened to be looking up. Maybe it was the angle. I don't know."

I asked André about his research, and he explained he hoped to use the information recovered from the Chihuahua dig to collaborate with others in developing sustainable communities.

"There's a growing number of people who want to simplify their lives," he said. "Communities patterned after the sustainable practices of the ancients, to encourage frugal consumption, ecological awareness, and meaningful personal growth. We'd build the communities off-grid, incorporate organic agriculture, local currencies, and exchanged-goods programs."

"That sounds wonderful."

"Yeah, families can adopt lives of simplicity, free of the burdens of city life—no commute, less work, less stress and debt—more time with one another, and nature. And time to give back," he added. "You know, live their life's work and develop meaningful personal spirituality," André said, beaming like a proud papa.

"I know people that would welcome that kind of life," I said, nodding.

"Yeah, as you can see from their sites, the ancients practiced low-impact living. I believe man is intended to live with nature—be in tune with and interact with it, and its resources—without destroying it, and one another."

"I completely agree," I said. What André was describing made me wonder if sustainable communities might be part of the ancient secret we were looking for.

"The ancients left us keys to sustainable living. They lived simple but beautiful lives of harmony and balance—connected to the earth, to the sky, and to each other. It was a gentle way to live."

As André spoke, I imagined the sustainable community he'd described.

"You're really onto something, André," I said. "I applaud you for your foresight. We need more people working toward harmony and caring for Mama Gaia."

"Thanks, True."

"Honestly, that's my motivation for coming down here," I said. "I believe the way we're living is unsustainable, and we're running out of time to turn the ship around. Profit at the price of a planet is a hell of a steep price to pay. These ancients knew something."

"Yes, we're a shortsighted lot, I'm afraid. But with enough people like us, we'll figure it out."

"Let's hope so. We should keep in touch" I suggested. "I'd like to hear more about your sustainable community." André nodded, and we sat in silence for a moment longer.

"Well, I'd better be off. I figure as long as I'm in town, I may as well pick up supplies before heading back up the mountain, and that'll take some time. It's been great, True. Sorry it had to be under these circumstances the second time around, but I'm glad we got to talk. You're easy to talk to."

André extended his hand to shake mine, and I leaned in for a hug instead. He appeared grateful for the gesture.

"I'll stop in and say goodbye to Biscolli. My bet is he won't be coming back to the dig… it's best he rests." André turned, then paused mid-step and called over his shoulder. "Get my number from Biscolli. Stay strong and take care of yourself."

"You too, André."

I tapped on Biscolli's door. I owed the man an apology—and he deserved tremendous leeway for putting up with my shenanigans.

He answered the door, looking far better than he had the night before. I was glad to see him and relieved that he appeared to be feeling better.

"Hey, may I come in?" I asked.

"Of course," he said, opening the door, and then turned to tidy up his bed so I could sit on it. He sat beside me.

"I owe you an apology, Biscolli," I said. "It was wrong of me to assume that you'd done anything malicious and to speak to you that way. You didn't deserve that. I'm really sorry." I felt tears begin to fill my eyes, but had to continue. "I haven't done right by you since we met. I've taken out my own frustration on you. I see how wrong I've been, and yet, you've managed to stick around. Why? I don't know. I want you to know I'm sincerely sorry."

The first tear ran down my cheek. Biscolli got to his feet, took one step to the chest of drawers, pulled out a handkerchief, handed it to me, and sat back down.

"You silly girl," he said, shaking his head. Then he reached his arms around me, lifted me onto his lap, and leaned me to his chest. I was crying—there was no way to stop the tears.

"You're not the only one who's sorry," Biscolli said, calmly. "I've put you through hell, dragging you all the way down here. Why you ever trusted me in the first place, is beyond me. You don't know me from Adam."

I felt him take a breath. The expansion of his large chest triggered pain in my own from the punch I'd taken. I instinctively raised a hand to it, and he put his hand over mine.

"I'm sorry about that, True. That's going to bruise. We'll put a steak on it."

I laughed, glad for the joke, then closed my eyes, grateful for reconciliation and the simple act of being held. I slid my arms around his waist and he raised a hand to my head, gently running his fingers through my hair. He then kissed my hair and gently pulled me closer.

# 17

# APPENDAGES

I left Biscolli's room and returned to mine to make some calls. I spoke with my kids and sister, then picked up my journal and leafed through the entries. Its first thirty-nine pages held the contents of my "brain dump" on the boulder, ten days ago. I thought back to when I'd left the book open—having ceremoniously given my cares to the wind, and the moments of tranquility following the mental purge.

I was grateful for the peace that had settled upon me then—for my quiet mind, and the glorious experience of lying naked on the boulder. Oh, how I loved the desert—its vast skies and painted sunsets, its fresh air and rock formations carved through eons of wind and weather.

I smiled. Two places in the Four Corners desert now had my heart: Grand Gulch and Hovenweep. Both were sacred ground to me—each for their own reasons.

I considered the great value that "getting away" had served. Would either of these experiences have been mine had I not given myself the gift of solitude? Probably not. I loved my solitude. Even moments like this, leafing through my journal and recalling my vision quest—nourished me. My vision quest seemed like it had happened months ago. So much had happened since I'd hiked in—and out of Hovenweep.

I placed my hands over my heart. How very different it felt from when I'd begun my vision quest. I smiled as I realized that today—yes today, would've been my tenth day on the boulder, had I stayed there.

I panned over the past ten days—the ceremonies I'd done, Oliver, my wet sleeping bag, and chasing God's van. I reflected on Red Rock and my time in the library, Chihuahua, and Cueva de la Vasija. I recalled the crushing blow André had delivered there, and my fight with Biscolli.

I thought of Spirit Eyes and how our brief exchange had changed an essential part of me. I thought of Biscolli and shook my head, stunned at all that'd occurred in the time I thought I'd be sitting on a rock. I began to cry. I shook my head again. That crying thing—I'd been doing a lot of that the past ten days too. The tears had needed to flow, so I'd let them. I thought of Lidija, and of how much I wanted to be with my best friend and to share all of this with her.

I called her, and we spent the next half hour catching up. My soul felt nourished by this morning's reflection and respite. My heart felt calm. I then turned on some music, leaned against the headboard, and opened my journal again, flipping through the entries. It'd been four days since my last entry. I found a pen and began writing.

**Friday, May 20**

"So, just taking a moment to exhale and gain some perspective this morning. It's been quite the ten days, that's for sure! It's funny—I thought I'd be wrapping up my vision quest today, maybe fish the San Juan for another couple of days, and head back to Oregon. Ha, far from it.

Biscolli and I are still in Chihuahua. My concerns about him were way off base. He's a good man—committed to the things he cares about. Those include: the Anasazi, digging, making sure Dan Collier is stopped, and now, apparently, me and our task.

I still have no idea why I'm in Chihuahua, other than I've met some amazing archaeologists and an incredibly beautiful human named Spirit Eyes. She's a psychic and showed me something about myself I couldn't see—she called it a Life Lesson. After seeing her, I had an experience that left me with sweet peace. I feel different.

We may be heading back to the States soon. More on that later. So, I guess that's it for now."

There was a knock on my door. It was Biscolli.

"Well, I never would have pegged you as an Old Dominion girl," he said, as I let him in.

"Oh, you heard my tunes, huh?"

"Yep," he said, reaching out and pulling me close. I slid my arms around him. Biscolli pulled me close. We kissed and held one another for a long moment. I then felt him kiss my hair. I smiled and nested my face deeper into his chest. He smelled good.

"Mmmm… you smell good," I said.

"Impressive, huh,?" Biscolli said, and then released his embrace, grinning. "What do you think of my shirt? It's one of my favorites." He took a step back and tugged the sides of the tee shirt so that I could read it—"I tried being normal once. Worst two minutes of my life," it read. I laughed so hard that I actually snorted.

"Where do you come up with this stuff?" I asked once I'd composed myself.

"What? Good, right?"

"Yeah, Biscolli, It's definitely you," I said, pulling him close again.

"You can borrow it if you'd like."

"Oh yeah. You know I'll be doing that." I said and laughed. "You're something else…"

"And you're fun to be with. I love your laugh."

"Thanks." I sighed and looked up at him. "It feels good to laugh."

"It does. Hey, you hungry?" He asked, brightly.

"Yes, I'm starved."

"I was thinking, we could get a bite and make some plans."

"That sounds great. I just need a second," I said and turned toward the closet for my sandals.

"You sure keep a neat room," Biscolli said, looking around. "Nothing like mine when I travel," he added with a grin. I grabbed my room key and he closed the door behind us.

As we walked, I relayed my experiences over the past three days—what it was like to see him ill, my encounter with Spirit Eyes and the experience that followed, and how differently it felt without angst in my body."

Biscolli pulled open the door of Rosa's Cafe, and we entered.

"I noticed there was something different about you," he said. "Don't take this wrong, but you're calmer."

I grinned.

"Yeah, I know. I feel it too."

We located a vacant table and took our seats.

"I like it," he said and handed me a breakfast menu that'd been wedged between bottles of chili sauce and a napkin holder.

Biscolli was intrigued by Spirit Eyes' suggestion that we choose life lessons. "It makes me wonder what life lessons I chose?"

"I don't know. Have you had a big hurdle to overcome, or maybe something that repeats—maybe an issue or pattern that comes up again and again?" I asked.

"Well, I've lost both of my families," he said. "I was adopted as a kid, and then, all but a sister died in a head-on accident."

"Oh, Biscolli, I'm sorry. I can't even imagine what it's like to lose your family."

"Thanks. I try not to think about it. It's odd though— that's the first thing you know about me."

"Thank you for trusting me enough to share that. You can talk to me about anything. I have a big capacity to listen."

"I'm sure you do."

We ordered breakfast and discussed plans for returning to the States. I was surprised when Biscolli said he wanted to head back up the mountain with André.

"He stopped by this morning. It seems the crew is pulling an overnighter. They want to use the site notch to determine what can be seen from it in June. Would you like to come? They've been asking about you. I know they'd like to see you again."

"Thank you. I'd love that. And I'm getting a strong nudge to see Spirit Eyes. I was hoping to see her again before we leave."

"Okay."

"When would you head up the mountain?" I asked.

"Sometime this afternoon. André is running errands now. I'll call after breakfast and check with him."

"Yes, we had coffee earlier this morning. He mentioned he'd be running errands. I'll tell you what—if I get back from Spirit Eyes' before you need to leave, I'll go with you," I said.

"Terrific."

I looked at Biscolli and smiled.

"What?"

"You're a good man, Biscolli," I said, reaching across the table to touch his hand.

"Thanks. I don't know what you see, but if you say so…"

"Well, it's true. I've known my fair share of men, and you're a good one."

Our meals arrived, and we slipped into silence. My thoughts turned to Spirit Eyes. She'd explained that I couldn't find the ancient secret with "big fire" in my heart. I concluded that—for me at least, Chihuahua had been a place to raise my vibration. Maybe we could find what we were looking for now. I closed my eyes for a moment, sincerely grateful we'd come to Mexico.

I had a deep appreciation for Spirit Eyes, and as I walked the few short blocks to her home, I hoped she'd be available to visit with me. As I approached, I saw she was in front of her home, filling a bird feeder. I called to her.

"Hola, Ojos Espíritu," I said, raising my hand.

"Ah, Señora," she said, lifting a broad smile. "You've come to visit Ojos Espíritu?"

"Sí, do you have a few moments?"

"Sí, sweet Señora. It is good to see you," she said cheerfully.

We hugged, holding our embrace for several seconds.

"Your visit makes my heart smile. Bueno. Shall we sit on the pórtico?" she asked, pointing towards her porch.

"Sí. That would be lovely."

"Would Señora enjoy some hibiscus tea?" she asked.

"Yes, good... bueno."

Spirit Eyes excused herself and passed through the screened door. I took a seat at a small table on her porch. A variety of palms and succulents had been arranged on the wooden floor, and hanging baskets of firecracker plant, trailing lantana and Christmas cactus hung from the eves. They were healthy, and I could see great care had been given to them. As I was admiring the foliage, a gray tabby cat leapt onto the porch and affectionately rubbed against my bare legs. I bent over to pet it.

Spirit Eyes appeared at the door. I stood and opened it for her. She was carrying a tray with a teapot, cups, and spoons, a dish of honey, a plate of apple slices and figs, and a single orchid blossom floated in a shallow dish of water.

"Hermoso... hermoso. Muchas gracias," I said, admiring the care and attention she'd given to the presentation. "I adore orchids. Beautiful."

"I have been hoping for your visit. It has been several days."

"Yes, the archaeologist fell ill—kidney stones. He's better now, but needed my care," I said and poured tea into both of our cups.

"Ah, you know the earth medicine way. Sí?"

"Sí," I said and smiled.

"Señora is a smart woman. You trust plant wisdom. Ojos Espíritu's own grandmama was a medicine woman. She taught me many things. She is gone now, but earth medicine is one of my cuatro apéndices. Ah, how you say... four appendages?"

"I'm not sure I understand."

"Ah, cuatro apéndices. Sí.? Uno, dose, tres, cuatro," she said, pointing to her arms and legs.

I nodded, though still confused.

"My first appendage is intuition. The second appendage is sovereignty. The third is creation, and forth, earth wisdom."

"Oh, I see," I said, nodding. "That's interesting. Can you tell me about that?" I asked, curious what those four things meant to her.

"Sí." Spirit Eyes reached for her tea, sipped, and studied my face. I wondered what she was looking for. Was she testing my sincerity?

"Spirit Eyes?" I inquired.

"Señora, my seeing eyes are open. Ojos Espíritu is seeing... listening to your soul."

"You can see and hear my soul?" I asked.

"It is a privilege. I see you have calmed your 'big fire.'"

Her words stirred my heart.

"You see that?" I asked.

"Sí. Es hermoso. Hermoso," Spirit Eyes said, her eyes full of understanding. "Señora did not wait for the sacred desert to learn Life Lesson dos," Spirit Eyes added, grinning.

"No, I suppose not. Thank you. It feels very different living in my body now. I never realized how much anxiety I was holding."

Spirit Eyes nodded. "Muy bueno, sweet Señora. She took another sip from her cup. "Ojos Espíritu will talk about appendices. Sí?"

"Yes, please. I'd love that," I replied and reached for a fig.

"My first appendage is intuition," she said, raising her right foot from the floor. "Ojos Espíritu can use Señora as her example. People may tell you they know what is best for you. Sometimes they may have that wisdom, but it is more powerful for you to know from your soul what to do," she said, looking at me.

"Searching others for knowledge makes you susceptible to misinterpret their words. Everyone has inner eyes to see the truth, but not everyone knows how to use their sight. This is what Ojos Espíritu will show you. Sí?"

"Yes, please."

"It is important you know that truth comes from one source. Many teachers may show you, guide you, and remind you of the truth. This can be a first step, but always, your greatest reminder is your own soul. What is true for your soul comes not in your mind, but in your belly. Señora sidesteps the mind to get to her truth. Si? The belly says 'Ah' or 'Na.' This is your truth. Would you like to try now?"

"Yes, I'd like that. What should I do?" I asked.

"Do you have a question or a choice to make?"

The first thing that came to my mind was returning to Four Corners.

"Does Señora have it?"

"Yes," I said.

"Ask the question, 'Does this feel right for me?' and then feel the answer 'Ah' or 'Na' in your belly."

"Okay."

I silently asked, "I need to return to the States as soon as possible. Does this feel right for me?," and then listened with my gut for an 'Ah' or 'Na' answer. I got a 'Na,' which surprised me.

"So, may I share what just happened?" I asked.

"Sí."

"I asked if I should return to the States as soon as possible, and felt a 'Na' answer in my gut. But that doesn't make sense, because

I know the archaeologist and I need to return." I went on to share my vision and the task we'd been given by Earth Mother—the reason Biscolli and I needed to return.

"Ah, Señora moved from her belly to her head and speaks many words from there. Your answer is in your belly. Maybe, this is the first time you've trusted since your 'big fire' release? Does Señora trust? This is her soul truth—not her logic-mind talk," Spirit Eyes said.

"I don't understand," I confessed.

"Ah, we are not born without help to make decisions; big and small. There are two rivers of intuition—knowing, which is the soul's perspective... some say this is the higher self because the soul sees everything. This is possible because the soul is part of all that is."

Spirit Eyes took a sip of her tea, then continued.

"This is where Señora's 'Ah' and 'Na' come from—from the soul. The second river of intuition is spirit guides and angels, here to assist Señora for her whole life. They are unseen helpers on the other side, to keep Señora from great harm, and to lead her to answers and synchronicities, like our meeting at the hotel. The two rivers of intuition are different, but both are Señora's to listen to. Sí?"

"Yes, I think so. You're saying that I can pay attention to my soul and its higher perspective and that I have angels and guides who keep me alive and guide me. Yes?"

"Si. Señora understands," Spirit Eyes said, nodding. I decided to tell her about my experience of floating in—and above—the River of Trust, describing how I floated above my body and observed the scenery of my life.

"I was seeing everything, including myself, from my higher self—my soul's perspective. It was incredible... and so peaceful. I knew then that it sees, knows, and has access to everything because it's one with its source."

"Bueno. Felicidades Señora! One thing to remember is you do not *have* a soul, you *are* soul. This is what sees all. You are the soul in a body for this lifetime. Muy bueno!"

I reached for her hand and smiled.

"I just can't imagine why we'd need to stay here, though, if the secret is in Four Corners," I said. "It just doesn't make sense."

"Maybe Señora needs something in Chihuahua? Maybe she is here to learn something? Maybe the archaeologist man needs something here?" She said as she studied my face. "This is where trust comes in, dear Señora. It is easy for the mind to talk you out of your intuition. It happens all the time to people. This is why intuition is Ojos Espíritu's first appendage. It is an important leg to stand on. Sí,?" she said and laughed.

"Señora's body has great wisdom. It gets easier. You are used to trusting yourself—depending on your mind for choices. When you ask now, use patience and listen to your belly. Remember, you have only one set of eyes, but the soul is part of all there is. It takes in all information and knows what is best. This is Señora's trust."

"All right, I can do that," I said, nodding.

The tabby cat leapt onto my lap, and I began petting it as I contemplated our conversation.

"Ah, el gato, Mateo," Spirit Eyes said, grinning at the cat. "Chico guapo."

"Hola Mateo," I said, petting the male kitty. "You're a handsome boy."

Spirit Eyes smiled, emptied the teapot into our cups, and motioned toward the apples. I acknowledged and continued to pet Mateo as Spirit Eyes sipped her tea.

"Enough for now, or would you have Ojos Espíritu share another apéndice?" she asked.

Her question raised a broad smile on my face.

"Yes. I'm learning a lot. Please, I'd love to hear about your second appendage."

"Sí. Dos apéndice es sovereignty," Spirit Eyes said, then raised her right arm. "For its life, a tree sends deep roots into Earth Mother. When a storm comes and pushes high winds against the tree, it remains still. The trunk does not move, for it is rooted. If I deeply root myself, I will not be tossed around by outside forces. Ojos Espíritu is her own boss—my own authority. I am my own power. This power that we are born with, not something given to outside forces or people."

I nodded. This appendage sounded important and I looked forward to what she had to say about it.

"People are happy to take my power of choice, and tell Ojos Espíritu what to believe, what to do, and what to buy."

"Yes, I think that's true for everyone, but it's escalated with social media and influencers."

"Sí, es verdad," Spirit Eyes said, nodding. "For Ojos Espíritu to live in her sovereignty, I first needed to know myself—who I am and what I am not. These are the roots I send deep into Earth Mother. I then know my truth and no one can take that from me."

"Yes, I see. That's powerful. How old were you when you knew yourself?"

"Ojos Espíritu was seventeen. My psíquico eyes opened at eleven years old, but I did not trust these eyes. Tenía miedo… I was afraid. I tried to deny these eyes, but they are my gift. I tried to force them closed, but they wanted to be open. At seventeen, I said, 'Let my inner eyes be open,' and this is my Life Path. Many gifts have come to me because I had courage and let these eyes see the inner realm—beyond the veil to the other side. This is my truth. It is my sovereign choice to live this truth. Sí?"

"That's beautiful Spirit Eyes. I know you've blessed me with your gift. Thank you. You're an amazing woman and I'm grateful we met."

"These eyes found you," she said. "They led me to you. It fills my heart with happiness too, sweet Señora," Spirit Eyes said, then smiled.

"It is one thing to believe what others believe, but these are shallow roots," she continued. "That is not self-knowing. That is leaning on others, and they can go this way and that way," she said, waving her hands. "That is not sovereignty."

"I think most of us do that when we're young. I replied. We try to fit in—go along. We want friends."

"Sí. The trouble is, they don't take the time to know what is true for them, so they depend on others. This is not their truth, and they can live their whole life that way."

"Yes, I can totally relate. My first Life Lesson was sorting through the dogma I'd been raised with. I just had to know if it was my truth or something I'd just adopted."

"Sí. It is a brave thing to discover yourself; to go your own way—to lead your own path. It is important we first know ourselves and then speak that truth. This is ours to do. It is our birthright. And this, too, is how others come to trust us and we trust them. Each of us, with deep roots, knowing ourselves. We can trust this. This is sovereignty."

I loved her description of sovereignty. Spirit Eyes had a way of making things clear, despite her broken English. I adored this woman.

We sipped the last of our tea and nibbled on apple slices. It felt wonderful sitting with my new friend, and I appreciated our conversation. These were the types of discussions I enjoyed—stimulating and meaningful. They nourished me and made me think, contemplate, and seek my own answers from within—my sovereignty. My grandma had been the source of these conversations for the first thirty-two years of my life. She'd been gone eleven years now, and I missed her terribly.

All my life I'd sought to understand the world, myself, and my place within it. I could see that deeply knowing myself and grounding those roots of understanding into Earth Mother might strengthen my ability to say 'Yes' to the things I resonated with, and 'No' to those I didn't. That alone would save most of my incidental decision-making.

"Thank you for sharing your second appendage. I'm learning so much. I deeply appreciate you," I said.

I glanced at my watch. It was nearly 12:30 PM.

"Do you need to go?" Spirit Eyes asked.

I thought of Biscolli and Cueva de la Vasija. Did I want to go to the mountain and spend the night in the alcove—to be with Biscolli and his cohorts, observing the sky? Is that what I wanted? I wasn't sure. It would be a once-in-a-lifetime opportunity, and yet, I was enjoying my time with Spirit Eyes. I concluded I'd ask my gut. I could see the practical application of the intuition practice already.

"I'm not sure yet. I'll check," I said and winked at Spirit Eyes. I could see she understood.

"We will clear the table and you decide," she said.

I lifted Mateo from my lap and set him on the floor, then helped Spirit Eyes load the tray. She opened the screened door for me and I carried the tray to her kitchen.

It was the first I'd seen of Spirit Eyes' kitchen. It was lovely—long and narrow, much like my grandmother's kitchen in Montana, but unlike hers, this one was bright and colorful—lit by a skylight and two uncovered windows. It was equipped with turquoise appliances and decorated with lively artwork and a dozen terra-cotta pots overflowing with foliage. Spirit Eyes gently stroked the leaf of one as she passed it. I set the tray on a butcherboard countertop.

"Your plants are beautiful," I said, admiring one that was in bloom.

"Gracias. Does Señora raise live things too?"

"Oh yes, and it seems friends know I love orchids. I have a dozen of them now," I answered, grinning.

"Ah, then you sing to live things as well."

"Sing?" I asked. "I talk to my orchids, but I've never thought to sing to them. Is that what you do?"

"Si. Does Señora feel good when she receives attention and a song?"

"Well, that kinda depends…" I replied and winked again. Spirit Eyes chuckled.

"Perhaps if a beau sang, It would lift your heart?"

"Si."

"I sing to my plant family as I chop, stir, or rinse dishes. I feel happy too. The creative force of Great Spirit is found in all life, enlivening them," she said, with a smile.

"I will give you a quiet moment now to decide if you must go. You are free to use the sitting room. I will rinse our dishes."

I excused myself and sat on the orange sofa. I quieted myself and silently asked, "I will accompany Biscolli to Cueva de la Vasija for the all-night site-notch research." Then added, "Do I have the energy for this? Does this feel right for me?"

I remained still, letting go of any idea about what I should or shouldn't do based on other's expectations or wishes. I simply relaxed and listened. I got a "Na."

I sat a moment longer and thanked my belly for its wisdom, and promised I'd come to it often. I messaged Biscolli with my decision, then became aware of Spirit Eyes in the kitchen and listened. She was singing a simple tune. I stepped into the kitchen.

"May I help?"

"Dishes are done. It is easy work. What have you decided?" she asked.

"It looks like you've got me a little longer. I've decided not to go to the mountain."

"Bueno. Juan is away for our afternoon. His sister is recovering from a hip operation, and he goes to assist her on some days."

"Perhaps we can walk to the plaza?" I suggested.

"Excelente."

When we'd passed from her yard and reached the street, Spirit Eyes wrapped her soft fingers around my forearm and we strolled towards the plaza.

"Spirit Eyes, may I ask you something?"

"Por supuesto," she answered, nodding.

"There's something I've been meaning to ask you. I'm curious about the soul companion you saw the other day."

"Ah, Ojos Espiritu has been waiting for Señora to ask," she said, then laughed. "Imagine that souls are like Eternal Tree, alive for all time. Everything created by Great Spirit is soul—each thing vibrates. Si?" she said, patting my forearm.

"Now imagine this, Eternal Tree is made of rocks, plants, animals, and man. Each has a place on the Eternal Tree, having no particular gender. Let us say man makes up branches of the tree. The many branches all share a common life source. Si?"

"Si," I replied.

"On the branches are twigs with many clumps of leaves. There is this clump and that clump, many thousands of clumps. One clump is Señora's soul family—those souls you pass through lifetimes with, experiencing them, perhaps, as a brother or a child, a friend, a madre, padre, or as a boss or beau. Si?"

"I don't know about all that. I'm a little skeptical about reincarnation," I admitted.

"Ah, one belief is as good as any other if it harms no being—that is one's sovereignty." Spirit Eyes nodded, then continued. "Through each lifetime, Señora gains experience. In one, her soul chooses to be a woman and lose a child to know sorrow. In another, chooses to be a warrior and experience bravery. In yet another, chooses to be an alcoholic and know addiction. Finally, after many lifetimes, Señora experiences all things possible, and realizes she is none of the actions, emotions, or people of those lifetimes, but is soul."

"And my soul companion?"

"Ah, sol compañero, closest leaf to Señora on twig. You are two separate souls, but always play a big role in each other's lives. Often a source of Life Lessons. Not always smooth going—depends on what experience you choose for a lifetime. It is not true that a sol compañero is half of your soul. That is not possible. Intuition speaks loudly when a compañero is nearby. This is soon to happen for you, sweet soul."

"So, he's real? How will I know when I meet him?"

"Does Señora know when she has been brushed with the wind? There will be no mistake. Both Señor and Señora will know."

"So, I just wait?" I asked.

"No anticipation. That is not good for your heart. You look into these eyes... look into those eyes. Nada, nada, nada. There is a journey for you to take now, and archaeologist man is good for your soul. You are good for his soul. That is the way it works. Señora and archaeologist close leaves, here for one another."

I thought of Biscolli. I was attracted to him. Honestly, I'd even wondered if he might be the companion Spirit Eyes had seen. But now, if he wasn't my guy—and I knew it, would it be a lie to lead him on?

"Ojos Espiritu sees your worry," she said, pausing our walk to turn and look at me. "It's unnecessary. Continue your life... fall in love even. Have this experience if you get a firm 'Ya.' When you get, 'Na,' it is time to move on—and this is for both your soul's growth. Remember, nothing happens by accident. You and archaeologist man have much to share. No impaciencia. When you are not looking for sol compañero, he arrives." Spirit Eyes said, then began to stroll again.

I let her words sink in. They buoyed my spirit but also challenged long-held beliefs I'd assumed to be true. The thought that my soul had lived before—perhaps as an African slave, or woman in the jungles of Brazil, or prisoner in a concentration camp, tested me. Did we return again and again for experiences and Life Lessons through interacting with our soul family—our closest leaves on the Eternal Tree? Was that what she'd suggested? If that were the case, just how experienced was my soul? Did that mean I'd chosen to experience grief, trust, and find a secret in the desert this lifetime? Really? Just how much of my life was random, and how much of it was a series of synchronicities, designed for me to have the experiences and opportunities I needed?

I began to suspect there was a lot more going on behind the scenes than I'd ever been aware of. Is this what my angels and guides were doing—setting up situations? I wondered.

Spirit Eyes broke my string of inward questions with her soft voice.

"Lifetimes like deep sleep. When Señora sleeps, she dreams. The dream is real, though forgotten when she wakes. Just because she is awake now does not make the dream less real, only forgotten. Lifetimes are in our deep memory," she said, pressing her dark finger into my temple.

"Soul remembers all experiences. It never dies. When Señora's consciousness sleeps, the memory of all lives can be found and remembered."

"You mean I might be able to remember another lifetime and my experiences in it? How?"

"Señora is too eager. It is not necessary to remember the past. Live this lifetime—this is the one that matters. There are reasons why we forget."

"But it is possible?" I asked.

"Si. Hipnotismo gently guides consciousness to sleep, yet soul memory stays wide awake. That is how Señora remembers previous lifetimes."

"How do you do it? I mean, I've never been hypnotized. Can you hypnotize me?" I asked.

"My gift is eyes," Spirit Eyes said, patiently. "La psiquica, Señora, no hipnotismo."

We turned a final corner and entered the plaza. Vendors had filled the space with their booths. Spirit Eyes and I glanced at one another. The plaza was alive with people eyeing goods, examining produce, and making exchanges. We strolled the perimeter, and I took the opportunity to check my phone for messages.

There was a long text from Biscolli, explaining that the crew had made additional plans, and he'd be staying on the mountain for another day. He was sorry that I hadn't come along—especially now—and hoped I wouldn't be too disappointed or bored in Chihuahua. I frowned. I hadn't expected the delay. Biscolli knew as well as I did that we needed to return to the States.

"Hum… that's interesting," I said. "I wonder what that's all about?"

"Señora?"

"It's a message from Biscolli… the archaeologist. He's staying an extra day at the mountain."

"I hope all is fine."

"Yes, I'm sure it is. I just have another day in Chihuahua now, that's all."

Spirit Eyes nodded, and we entered the open-air market. She recognized a vendor selling honey, honeycomb, and bee pollen, and introduced me. I listened as they chatted in Spanish. We stopped at a produce stand, where Spirit Eyes purchased a few vegetables, and then I paused at a flower vendor to purchase a bouquet for her.

"Spirit Eyes?" I inquired as we were strolling back to her home. "You seem to just take all this in stride. Have you always believed in Eternal Trees, intuition, Life Lessons, singing to plants, and reincarnation? How do you know these things?"

"Ah, Ojos Espiritu keeps the ancient truth of Spirit Clan in her heart. My people came from the Wide Canyon where Great Spirit breathed Truth into our Fathers. Truth spoken long ago by our Fathers was lived every day, spoken every day, and celebrated through dance, thanksgiving, and ceremony. Truth passed from father to child in the pure language."

"That sounds like a beautiful linage," I said as we crossed a street. Spirit Eyes' presence was peaceful. She patted her dark hand on my forearm and we walked in silence to her home.

Spirit Eyes invited me in, and I followed her to the kitchen, where she placed her produce into a colander. She pulled a green vase from a low cupboard, filled it with water, and placed the flowers in it. I then looked on as she verbally welcomed the flowers to her home.

"Does Señora have time to join me for tea?"

I nodded, and we made tea and created a platter of fruit and cheese.

"Juan returns from his sister's casa en dos horas (two hours). I begin supper preparations in uno horas. You can stay for supper now that your friend is at the mountain. Si?"

I certainly wasn't expecting an invitation, but I accepted, glad for the opportunity not to eat at Rosa's and, instead, spend time with Juan and Spirit Eyes.

I placed the tray of tea and snacks on the patio table, withdrew a chair for Spirit Eyes, and took my seat. Spirit Eyes poured our tea and told me about the two remaining appendages of her life.

She explained that her third appendage was creation, and said that as "parts of Great Spirit," we had a creative spark within us and we are designed to create.

"Señora is one with the power that created her, and this power allows her to create her own reality."

She went on to explain that we are always creating, whether we realize it or not.

"There is talk of a law called the law of attraction," she said. "That is half the law of creation. The other half is the law of vibration. Remember the day we met?" she asked. "I explained Señora would not find old medicine in the sacred desert until she vibrate at its frequency?"

"Yes, I remember that well."

"So, to bring a thing into your life there is a simple way. I say simple, not easy. The simple way is to know the outcome you want. When Señora sits at Rosa's, she doesn't just sit there and wait for the server to put anything in front of her. The server asks for her order. Señora searches the menu and decides. Sí?"

I smiled, grateful for the simple analogy.

"Same with life. First, know the outcome. Next, Señora be grateful in her heart. People get this all wrong. A grateful heart comes first, not when the food arrives. Be grateful that you are sitting in the restaurant. Be grateful you are dry, have a chair to sit in, and are hungry. A grateful heart is a frequency that sends out a vibration you are grateful for what you already have. The universe responds to this. It's like a flashlight shining to the other side.

I nodded.

"Next, imagine—see and taste the food the server will bring. Then, you trust that the server will bring the platter of food. At Rosa's, when you order, does Señora worry the food won't come? Does she go to the kitchen to check on the cook? Does she call the server to the table again and again? No, she's confident the cook has the ingredients and knows how to combine them. Señora relaxes at the table, having a conversation with Ojos Espíritu," she said, laughing. I laughed and spilled my tea.

"This is creation. It's the great power that Great Spirit gave to all its parts. Señora can create with intent or willy-nilly. It is an important power. This is why creation Ojos Espíritu's tres apéndice."

"Wow, I've never heard it put like that. We create because we're built to create. Man, have I been unconscious? I think back to all the stuff I just let happen in my life. I took things as they came. Life was a conveyor belt, especially as a young mother. I was always too busy and too tired to think I had any say in how my day was going. I was just holding on, flying by the seat of my pants, and praying."

Spirit Eyes laughed.

"I was a young mother too, once. It is a practice. Creation happens... we do it every momento. But it cannot happen consciously without practice. It's a good thing to practice. Si?"

"Absolutely. I hope I can remember this."

We were quiet for a moment. I placed a slice of cheese between apple slices and enjoyed the medley in my mouth.

"So, what is your fourth appendage? I can hardly wait to hear this one."

"Ah, Ojos Espíritu's final apéndice is plant wisdom. This apéndice was handed down to Ojos Espíritu, generation after generation, from the fathers of long ago. Ojos Espíritu's own grandmother was a medicine woman. She taught me many things. My people of the great canyon learned from the land they lived on. They learned to listen to Earth Mother and to understand her ways of listening, learning, healing, and walking with all life. I am happy that Earth Mother spoke to you. I can feel her medicine in you." Spirit Eyes looked at me, smiled, and nodded.

"To commune with live things raises sensitivity. Señora's fingers feel more. Her ears and eyes hear and see beyond human sight and hearing. This is the way of plant wisdom—to hear and interpret what is needed. We sing, we feel, we heal, with Earth Mother. I learned to listen early in life. It makes Ojos Espiritu's heart happy to share sacred things close to it with Señora. I think maybe you found me at the hotel. Si?"

Mateo leapt onto the porch. Spirit Eyes acknowledged him, then gazed beyond the eves of the porch towards the horizon. She then stood and reached to collect our cups.

"Our hour has passed, sweet soul. We will begin preparations for our supper."

I helped Spirit Eyes clear the table and we prepared a meal of lamb stew, cornbread, and roasted vegetables. I learned from Juan that he'd taught at the university and they had a daughter who lived in the States, in Taos, New Mexico. As we spoke, it became apparent to me that, despite all the hours Spirit Eyes and I had spent visiting, we knew very little of one another's lives. And yet, I felt as though I knew this woman deeply.

"Señora, it has been a lovely day. Thank you for coming to visit Ojos Espiritu. You have made my heart very happy... muy feliz. Mi casa es tu casa. Gracias for sharing your visión with me. Buen día."

"Gracias. You've given me much to take into my heart and contemplate. You have filled my heart well," I said, and we hugged goodbye.

As I neared Rosa's, I recalled Spirit Eyes' analogy of creation and smiled. I then faced the door of the café, an idea forming. I remembered seeing a bulletin board near the restrooms and wondered if, by chance, a hypnotist may have tacked a flyer there. It was worth a shot.

To my delight, three "therapists" had tacked business cards to the board, and one actually mentioned something called "hypnotherapy." However, it was a bright green card that caught my attention. It read: Lolita K. Dausz, M.A., Therapy, Family Therapy, and Personal Growth. There was nothing special about the card, and it didn't mention hypnotherapy, but that was the one I slid into my pocket.

When I arrived to my room, I pulled out the card and, to my disappointment, saw that the therapist was not in Chihuahua, but someplace called El Sueco. I frowned. Where the heck was El Sueco?

I questioned my supposed luck. Perhaps I should've checked with my belly before grabbing the card. I pulled up El Sueco on my phone. It was ninety minutes away. Did I really want to do this? It'd mean I'd have to drive the rat trap not just across town, but for ninety minutes—twice.

I picked up the card again. Nothing on it mentioned hypnotherapy. I wondered what "personal growth" meant. That didn't sound like reincarnation, past lifetimes, or soul's perspective to me.

I decided to do a belly check.

"I make an appointment with Lolita Dausz for a session." Then added, "Do I have the energy for this? Does this feel right for me?"

I remained still, letting go of any idea about what I should or shouldn't do. I got a "Ya." I have to admit, I was excited. I called the number on the card. I was a bundle of nerves.

"Hello," a bright voice said on the other end.

"Hello, is this Lolita K. Dausz, M.A.?" I asked.

"Yes. How can I help you?"

"Well, I'm looking at your business card. It reads: Individual Therapy, Family Therapy, and Personal Growth. Might you be a hypnotist?"

"Ah, you mean hypnotherapist. Yes, I do hypnotherapy. What are you interested in?"

"I'm not exactly sure. A friend mentioned that past life could be remembered with the help of a hypnotist… I mean hypnotherapist. Is that something you do?"

"Yes."

I was excited and couldn't understand why. Who would've guessed I'd want to be hypnotized… or whatever it is hypnotherapists do. I just had to know if reincarnation was real.

Lolita said she was available to see me tomorrow. I made an appointment and pulled up her address in El Sueco on my phone for directions. I couldn't believe I was doing this.

**Sunday, May 22**

"I have noted nothing in this journal for several days. So much has happened that I hardly know where to begin. Biscolli turned up ill with kidney stones. He's well now and has gone with the other diggers to the cave for a night reading. That means… yes, we're still in Chihuahua!

I've met a wonderful woman named Spirit Eyes. She is, without a doubt, the most wise and spiritual person I've ever met. She's completely at peace with herself and her beliefs. She refers to me as Señora. I've become rather accustomed to the sound of it now, and have to admit that it'd sound awkward to hear her call me anything else now.

Our two chats have been beautiful. It'd be impossible for me to write everything Spirit Eyes has shared, but I feel …well, enlightened. What she's shared comes closer to answering questions I have all my life than anything else. I suspect she's shared the tip of the iceberg, though. I don't know her ethnic heritage, but she's not Mexican. She says her people came from a wide canyon. Does she mean the Grand Canyon?

I've made an appointment with a therapist. She does something called hypnotherapy. All I want is to know if reincarnation is real. We'll see."

# 18

# LOLITA

A session with the hypnotherapist was set for Monday afternoon. I borrowed the Mongoose and drove to El Sueco, a small town ninety minutes southeast of Chihuahua, near the banks of the Rio Torreno River. Lolita was staying with a Mexican family in the village. Irrigated green fields of corn, grapes, cotton, and peanuts, insulated the town, and everything visible appeared forty years old, as if time had forgotten this place.

I climbed from the Mongoose and slammed the heavy door. There was no way to lock the truck, not that it mattered. This was a Mexican village, not East LA. At the airport, Biscolli had been given one key—not to turn over the engine, but to unlock a heavy chain welded to the cab's steel floor. To secure the monster, the chain was fed through the steering wheel so no one could drive it off. I was glad for the ride, but as I looked at it parked in the partial shade of an oak tree, I couldn't help but imagine what a glorious sight it would be to watch the thing burn. The air I stepped into was hotter than blazes. Maybe the thing would instantly combust, I mused.

The address on the business card matched the numbers on a modest stucco house, painted pastel green. A garden of rock and cactus led up to the home, with several cacti I couldn't identify were in bloom. Out of the corner of my eye, I saw a lizard dart across the caked dirt.

The front door was wide open, and from the cracked cement walkway, I could see through the aluminum screen door into the living room. Standing there, I could make out a bookcase haphazardly stuffed with paperbacks and periodicals, and an overstuffed chair against a far wall.

I knocked on the metal door. It raised a hollow rattle and brought a girl about five years old to the door. I knelt and introduced myself. She ran away. I rattled the door again and a Mexican woman with a toddler balanced on her left hip greeted me. Her Spanish was the fastest I'd heard in my short four days in Mexico. I couldn't follow a word of it, but she smiled, swung open the screened door, and waved me toward a couch in the living room. The little girl who had run from the door now stood behind the woman, clutching a handful of her mother's skirt.

I took a seat under a ceiling fan and wondered why the family wasn't in this room to take advantage of the circulating air. It was warm, but the breeze lifted the edge off the stagnant heat. As I waited for my sweat to dry, I reviewed the titles of the paperbacks on the unleveled shelves—none of which I recognized, even if printed in English.

A flush of anxiety returned, gradually rising like a fever. Nearly all the excitement I'd felt since Lolita had set our appointment was now overshadowed by anxiety. I unfolded what was left of the business card. Its green die had bled onto my sweaty hand. For the hundredth time, I read it: Lolita K. Dausz, M.A., Individual Therapy, Family Therapy, and Personal Growth.

The therapist was running a good ten minutes late for our appointment. When she finally entered the living room, there wasn't much to her. Up to this moment, I'd relied on my imagination to fill in the gaps about what this afternoon might hold—including what the therapist herself might look like.

The woman was small and thin, with high cheekbones. Her complexion was the fairest I'd seen since arriving in Mexico. Youth had left her, but not without gifting her the freckles of her girlhood. Her strawberry blonde hair was short and full of curls. My first impulse was to feed her. She carried herself with ease and grace, yet I sensed she was overworked, even in this sleepy village.

I learned she was in El Sueco doing humanitarian work. What humanitarian therapists did in Chihuahua was a mystery to me. Was she counseling? I'd read somewhere that most therapists hit burnout after five years on the job—less than it took to get their credentials. I wondered how much sand Lolita had left in her hourglass. We'd spoken at length on the phone and she impressed me as being very thorough. She knew what I wanted, and why.

The therapist extended her hand and I shook it. At a distance, the woman may have appeared weak, but her handshake cleared up that matter.

Lolita smiled and graciously welcomed me into the next room. She explained hypnosis can be an extremely successful method for uncovering the origin of fears and phobias or discovering the source of chronic pain.

She went on to explain that hypnosis could be used to address behavior or pain, as well as addictions and unhealthy relationships, including those related to food, alcohol, chemicals, or interpersonal dynamics. She was careful to mention that these issues could stem from suppressed experiences of a past lifetime—particularly if that lifetime had ended abruptly, leaving unresolved matters. Lolita emphasized that those who come to her with a clear purpose often experience the most success.

Her comment made me wonder if there was an incident behind my fear of heights and falling. I shared this with Lolita and also mentioned I'd had chronic neck pain for years. Our brief chat eased the tension I'd had in the living room. She then had me sit in a recliner, facing her, and Lolita sat in a chair.

I was instructed to close my eyes. Over the next few moments, Lolita's soothing voice led me further and further away from the noise in my head. I soon felt as though I were traveling through a passageway. Lolita referred to this as my third eye. My mind became still and my senses heightened—just as they had following my brain dump on my boulder. I became particularly aware of sound and motion, and I sensed Lolita's presence without needing to see her.

"Three, two, one…" Lolita said softly, finishing her hypnotic instructions to me. "Just take a moment for the picture to come into focus," she said. "Notice if it is light or dark if you're indoors or out."

I sat very still.

"What do you know so far," she asked. "What's the feeling?" My head began to move from side to side.

"What's the picture?" Lolita inquired. I remained quiet for a long minute and then said, "There are tall trees and a fountain. A courtyard."

"Lovely," Lolita remarked. "Be patient with yourself as you enter another time and place. You don't always know immediately what's up. It's like a mystery. You find clues and pieces, and then it all begins to make sense. Anything else in this picture?" Lolita asked. "Anything to your left or right? Do you sense yourself in a body as you look down? You can look down." Following the expression on my face, Lolita asked, "What's happening?"

"I'm scared to look down," I replied.

"Scared to look down?" Lolita repeated.

"What's scary about looking down?"

"I'm going to fall."

"Oh," she said. "Back up a bit. Find something to hold on to. Is that better?"

"Yes," I said, calming down.

"Let's stay curious about what that was. Are you near the edge of something?"

"Yes."

"What were you near?"

"A balcony."

"Oh. Perhaps we could move inside," she said. "Rather than looking far down, let's just look at your feet; your hands," Lolita suggested.

"There are velvet shoes," I said, curiously.

"Oh? What color?"

"Purple."

"And are you a man or woman, a boy or girl?"

"I'm a girl."

"Are you as frightened as you look?" Lolita asked, becoming concerned over the expression growing on my face. What's happening?"

"I'm hiding from someone."

"Oh. Are you trying to get away from them?

I nodded my head.

"Do you know who it is? What's going on?"

"Someone is chasing me."

"Go on. What is happening now?" Lolita asked.

"I'm hiding behind a curtain."

"Are you hearing anything?"

"There are voices coming up the stairs," I said, beginning to tremble.

"You can hear them coming?" Lolita asked.

"Yes."

"I'm so sorry. Breathe," Lolita reminded me. "If you prefer, you can step outside of this body and watch from the ceiling. Be an observer." Seconds passed. "She is so frightened," Lolita observed, viewing my expression.

"Were you able to do that, become an observer?" I nodded in response. "Let's move very quickly through the next few minutes, just observing. What happens?"

"She's hiding." I began to sob.

"Breathe," she reminded me.

"I see the stone," I said, trying to catch my breath. "Stone walls outside, and an iron rail. I'm bent over on it, on my back."

"Oh," Lolita sighed. "And the people?"

"There are two of them."

"What do they want?"

"They want me to tell them something."

"What is it they want you to tell them? Do you have the information they want?" I nodded. "Oh, I see. What happens next?"

I then described refusing to tell them where my father was, being pushed off the balcony, falling to the ground, and my final thoughts before dying. I went on to describe my clothing in detail—the layers of skirts, my light brown hair... long and braided, and the blood I observed coming from my ear.

"I am sixteen," I added.

"Okay. Thank you. Let's call on your spiritual helper now to help remove the trauma—any pain... her fear."

"Being chased," I added. "Being cornered on the balcony. Trying to hide. Not wanting to be found."

"Ah. That's a familiar feeling?" I nodded. "Okay. So now we know where it came from. You can let it go. She's okay. The soul survives." I began to weep.

"Does she need to cry?" Lolita asked. After a long silence, the therapist added, "She can rest. I do have a couple of questions. Can we look back into that lifetime to see her father? See what her father is like. Why she is so loyal to him."

The lines on my face softened to a smile.

"You can feel his love when he looks at you?" I nodded. "The soul that's in your father, do you recognize it as someone you know in your lifetime as True?"

I shook my head, puzzled. "How will I know?"

"Feel the soul."

"I can't see my father," I responded.

"Okay. Let's go back to an earlier time when you were younger—when were with your father," Lolita suggested.

"My mother is there," I said, smiling.

I went on to describe being three years old and on a picnic in a grassy field with my parents. I described the woods on three sides of us and the castle just over the knoll. I was running in the in the grass, playing.

I then began to pant, rolling my head from side to side against the back of the recliner. I drew my knees to my chest. Lolita asked me to describe what was happening, and I told her that a man on a horse rode out of the woods, drew his sword, and plunged it into my mother. I sobbed as the scene played out before me.

"We were just having a picnic," I cried. Suddenly, I stopped crying and began to rock ever so gently.

"How did you do that?" Lolita asked, amazed at the sudden transformation.

"My daddy picked me up."

"Okay. Is he holding you close?" I nodded. "Good," Lolita said calmly as I continued to rock. "You'll be all right. Can you tell me what happened? Does your daddy explain?"

"He's just rocking me."

"Oh, and you're three?"

A startled look came to my face. "Cedar is my mother!" I exclaimed, surprised.

"Cedar?" Lolita inquired. "You know your mother as Cedar in Trues's lifetime?" I nodded, smiling. "And who might Cedar be in your True lifetime?"

"My daughter."

"Oh. Thank you. Let's move forward many years now… maybe twelve. It's been a long recovery. As you look back, what have you learned about why your mother was killed? Did you learn why? What's your understanding?"

"To get to my father," I answered. "They wanted to break him. He's important. They want him—they all want him,"

"Whoa. Who are 'they'?" Lolita asked, and I went on to describe the coat of arms of the country we were at war with most of my life.

"My father talks with a lot of people. He makes decisions for the country," I said and described his office on the second floor of the castle—its musty-smelling rugs and heavy curtains.

"What would be your language?" Lolita asked.

"French."

"Ah, and please translate your name into English."

"Jessica."

"Okay. Thank you. Jessica, what is the year?"

"8… 802? I think."

"So just before you were killed, it sounds like your father was away or in hiding. Were the men who came into your house looking for him?"

"Yes. Their horses are outside. I am hiding from them."

"So much tragedy in your short life. All right. Let's move forward or backward to a happy time," Lolita suggested." I smiled and described taking violin lessons at age twelve, and then beamed as I described being in the kitchen with our cook when I was a girl.

"What is your cook like?" Lolita asked.

"She tells stories. She makes little things for me. I sit there and listen to her stories. Sometimes, she brings her child, and I play with her."

"Good smells here in the kitchen?" Lolita asked joyfully. I smiled.

"She makes a lot of things for me."

"Oh? Like what?"

I went on to describe the dolls and sachets our cook gave me and how I would sit and play with her little girl by the open fire.

"Cha, Cha… Chatty," I said, beaming.

"That's a name or that's a description of her?" Lolita asked, chuckling with delight.

"That's what they call her," I said, affectionately.

"Chatty," Lolita repeated. "Thank you. These two, Chatty and her mother the cook, are they familiar souls to you in your lifetime as True?"

"Yes. Linda, my sister, is the cook," I said, with a smile. And then, as if all of heaven had wrapped its arms around me, I was bathed in inexplicable joy.

"Oh," I said, with delight on my face, "My mother is the little girl."

"Sweet," Lolita said.

"Oh," I said, crying softly. "I love her so much. I want one just like her."

"You want a little Chatty?" Lolita asked, laughing in delight. "What a wonderful spiritual family you have." After a few moments, Lolita inquired, "What does Jessica believe about death?"

"She didn't fear dying for her father. She wanted to be strong for him. She knew that they couldn't kill him—that they couldn't kill her, either. Her father taught her that."

"Oh. A remarkable young woman, isn't she?"

"Yes. She loved," I said.

"She loved," Lolita confirmed.

After a moment, Lolita said, "It appears the injury in that lifetime affected your energy. Let's bring in your angelic team to straighten out the energy."

I sat calmly in the recliner, listening to her words. Before long, I felt the area between my eyes seem to open, and a bright light began to appear—it was my third eye. I felt wonderful, as though I was lying on a cloud, and my mind could transmit or absorb anything.

"Just let the fear, the trauma, and the pain drain out," Lolita said. "Very good."

For a few seconds, I remained in that blissful state. "What are you noticing? Lolita asked. "Are you sensing a color or sensation coming through your body?"

I searched for the place where I'd felt the light and noticed that it was gone, and my third eye was closing. My first thought was to try and pull it back—to experience it again. This didn't happen. I felt myself becoming more and more aware of the sounds in the room: the ticking wall clock and the gurgling fish tank. I batted my eyes and opened them.

Lolita smiled. "Hello, True. Welcome back. How do you feel?"

"Fine," I replied.

"You did really well," Lolita said and motioned to a bottle of water on a table beside the recliner. I took a sip.

"Just a couple of little things. You may notice over the next day or two that your body may begin to cleanse itself. Don't be alarmed if you experience diarrhea, frequent urination, or even vomiting. It's all natural. It's your body's way of releasing trauma and beginning the healing process."

Lolita had me continue to sip water and sit in the recliner for a few more moments, just to ensure that I was firmly back in this world. She walked me to the front door. Before I left, I asked if she might have time to see me once more. We agreed to meet the next day, provided I was feeling up to it. I felt a knot well up in my throat and reached for her hand.

"Thank you, Lolita. Thank you."

I stopped at the door of the Mongoose. There was much to contemplate. Maybe I could go someplace where I could think. I drove the truck with no particular destination in mind and found myself on a road that ran parallel to the river. I pulled over at a wide spot. As far as I could tell, I was alone, so I closed my eyes.

The peace I'd felt while in the bright light lingered. It was lovely. Though I didn't understand all that had occurred during the session, I knew that what I'd experienced was real. Any skepticism I'd had about reincarnation vanished. Not through some book or empirical evidence, but through my own simple experience.

I laid my head back in the seat. I was living one of "those" moments—you know the ones, when your perspective completely shifts. Mine happened within an hour, in a hot room in El Sueco, Mexico. I knew I'd never look at myself or life the same. My urgency to get everything done in this one life evaporated. My impatience with my weaknesses lost its grip.

I sat and watched the sky through the bug-spattered windshield of the Mongoose. The tall oak trees framed a brilliant azure sky, now shimmering with golden light cast by the sun as it cut through clouds.

In the distance came a rumble. I glanced over my shoulder to find a huge thunderhead suspended over the valley. The stifling heat had worked its magic with the clouds. When the lighting came, I sensed a subtle shift in the energy. The lightning lasted only six or seven minutes, and the sun left with it, sinking deeper into the horizon. As the sun passed, the sky's energy field shifted again, this time welcoming evening.

I smiled, grateful for the day, then pushed the red "engine" button on the dash of the oversized, rattling piece of metal and drove to the hotel.

I called my daughter, Cedar, and shared with her all that'd happened since she'd attended her grandma's funeral. Even she found it hard to believe and kept repeating, "Mom is this really you?" I asked her to call her brothers and let them know I was doing well and would call them in a day or two. Cedar had always been light years ahead of me when it came to spiritual matters. She was asking questions at twelve that'd never crossed my mind until I was twice her age. Perhaps she was one of the more experienced souls Spirit Eyes had told me about.

I had no appetite, which, as it turned out, was a good thing. As Lolita had suspected, my evening was quite interesting. Biscolli was at the field house, and I was glad for it.

# 19

## CHACO CANYON

I returned to Lolita's the following day and during our brief chat before my session, I revealed to her that Spirit Eyes had seen a soul companion, and I hoped to learn more about that. She agreed and brought me to a hypnotic state of consciousness.

"Three, two, one," Lolita said. "Just take a moment for the picture to develop. Notice if it is light or dark. If you're indoors or out. What do you know so far," she asked. "What's the feeling?"

A huge smile lit up my face.

"Oh, what are you noticing?"

"Whee…" I squealed, excitedly.

Lolita laughed.

"Sammy," I said, playfully.

"Sammy?"

"He's in the wagon. We're in the wagon."

"Where are you headed?"

"Down the street, on the sidewalk."

"In a wagon?" Lolita asked, curiously.

"Yes," I answered, laughing.

"Oh, you're little?"

"Three."

"Ah, three," Lolita repeated.

"He's pushing it now. I'm screaming," I said, louder. "Ohhh," I squealed. My mouth opened wide, and then, I began to giggle, louder and louder.

"He's pushing you in the wagon?" Lolita asked, chuckling with delight. I giggled. "You're three, and how old is he?"

"Ah, five," I said, then I shook my head. "No, four, almost five. But he tells everybody he is five."

"And, are you a boy or a girl?"

"I'm a girl. I see white fences go by really fast when he pushes. There's cracks in the sidewalk, tree roots."

"Friends or siblings? Relatives?" Lolita asked. I squinted my forehead, puzzled, searching for an answer.

"I don't know," I said. "He's always here—always at our house. I don't know."

"It doesn't matter. What's the feeling?"

For several playful moments, I described us eating cookies, and then my body tensed and fear filled my face.

"What just happened?" Lolita urged. I let out a cry and began to sob. Tears ran down my face and fell onto a thin lap blanket Lolita had placed there. I pulled my knees to my chest and curled into a ball.

"What's happening?" Lolita urged, again.

"No!" I cried for several minutes, eventually calming enough to speak. "She's hit by a truck," I said, reaching towards my legs—feeling for them.

"Your legs?" Lolita inquired.

"Yes."

"Move quickly through it, Sweetie. Remember, you can lift out of that body," Lolita instructed. She guided me through the next few moments and asked for my angelic team to assist. I sat calmly in the recliner, listening to her words. Before long, I felt the space between my eyes open, and a bright white light began to appear. It was my "Third Eye" again. This time, I saw three golden rings appear, one immediately after the other, until they superimposed, one upon the other. As each passed through my Third Eye, I felt more of the leg pain depart. The hoop they formed was filled with Light. I felt wonderful, peaceful—at rest.

"There you go," Lolita said, tenderly.

I remained in that joyful state for a few moments. Lolita followed the expressions on my face closely. After another minute, she asked, "What did Sammy call you?"

"Patty." I went on to say that Sammy and I lived next door to one another in Waterloo, Iowa, and I'd been struck by a milk truck in 1927.

"Thank you, Patty," Lolita said. "And your pal, Sammy, do you know him in your present lifetime as True?"

I searched. He felt so familiar and yet, there was no one I could recognize as his soul in my life.

"No one? Okay. Does Patty need any other help?" Lolita asked.

"My parents. I'm sorry."

"Sorry to leave them?"

"They hurt so much."

"What would she like to say to them?"

I cried.

"I feel sorry for them. They hurt for a long time. I come to see them."

"Do you? That must be a comfort to them."

My face suddenly perked up.

"Biscolli is my daddy," I said, shocked.

"Biscolli?" Lolita repeated. "Do you know your mother?"

"She's Lidija," I said smiling. "She's sweet," I said, feeling my mother's soul.

"You've had some lovely mothers in the lifetimes we've remembered the past two days," Lolita remarked softly.

"Um," I smiled. "I was their only girl, their only child."

"It's very hard to lose a child, but not so hard when you remember that there is no death for the soul."

"My father knew that, but not my mother. It broke his heart watching her suffer; trying to tell her."

"Oh? He was not able to comfort her?"

"They both suffered, but for different reasons."

"So you can ask for your angelic help to comfort them and bring healing to them as well. Is that something you would like to do for them, send them a message that you're all right and give them comfort?" I sat quietly, feeling their souls. "What would you tell your parents? Your mother, who didn't understand?"

"Mommy," I said, "Don't lose hope. I'm alive. We come back. We'll be together again. Our bodies are nothing. We are not our bodies. We live."

"Are you ready to leave Patty?" I nodded my head. "Okay. Let's move through lifetimes to see if we can find the soul you knew as Sammy in another lifetime. Move through them, and be patient. Take your time and feel the souls."

My head began to rock. "What's the picture?" Lolita inquired. I remained quiet for moments.

"There is a small stone altar, sage, crystals, sacred herbs," I said, then moved my head as if following something. "And cedar smoke," I added.

"Um," Lolita remarked. "Just look around. Anything else in this picture?" Lolita asked. "Anything to the left or right? Do you sense yourself in a body as you look?"

"I see my teacher."

"Oh, and are you a boy or a girl?"

"I am a boy. I am eight," I replied, proudly.

"Tell me about your teacher."

"He's smart, wise. I think he is very old. I'm real squirmy," I added.

"You're eight," Lolita chuckles in delight at the simple answer. "That's what boys do when they're eight. How does your teacher handle your squirminess?"

"He disciplines me. Then I see him chuckle," I said, smiling.

"Are you his only pupil?" Lolita asked. "Is he a tutor, or is it a classroom situation?" I answered that I was his only pupil. "Does your teacher go by a name?"

"Grandfather Maa-pu. He is old."

"Do you know Grandfather Maa-pu as your blood relative? Is that why you call him that or is that his name?"

"He is my blood grandfather."

"Ah. Thank you. And your name?"

"Ya-naa. I'm called Ya-naa."

"Ya-naa," Lolita repeated. "And you learn from your grandfather?

"I try," I said, smiling.

Lolita laughed.

"What's the feeling now?" she asked.

"I'm trying to make him think I am not learning, that I am not listening. But... I am," I said, grinning. "I like to fool him, and he fools me back. We play, but we don't 'play.' We play with our minds."

"He sees the brightness in you?" I nodded. "And what does your Grandfather teach you?"

"Old medicine—old as the stars. He teaches me the Star Ways healing and how to read the heavens through our site-notch. He shows me the crystals, we study the planets, and he teaches me the power of herbs. He has something around his neck."

"Your teacher?" I nodded in agreement. "This thing around your teacher's neck, what do you call it?"

"Medicine pouch. We all wear them, but his is special. He is our Medicine Man. He knows the medicine and heals us."

"Who does he heal? Who are your people?" Lolita asked, curiously.

"Saa-nu-ya," I answered.

"Please, say your name as we would say it today."

"Anasazi."

"Oh, this is old," she said, leaning back into her chair. "And where is the place you call home?"

"Chaco. I live in Chaco with my family."

"Who is in your family as Ya-naa?" Lolita asked. "Papa, called Quaa-ya; Mama, called Mu-waa; my sisters, called Naa-yu-na and Qu-nu-na; my brother, called Say-nu; and Grandfather Maa-pu. I have one grandfather, no grandmothers."

"And you are learning?" I told her yes. "How long does Grandfather remain your teacher? For how many years?" I told her until age fourteen.

"Let's move to age fourteen," Lolita suggested. A grin comes across my face.

"I'm handsome," I said, smiling. "I think girls like me, but I don't know." Lolita chuckled, amused. I joined her. "I have dark hair. It's straight on my back. New cloth sandals. I wear a woven cloth, tied here," I said, taking my hands to my hip and moving them as if tying something. I then described the new medicine pouch my grandfather gave me at a ceremony held in our Kiva. I tell her that I am about to speak before my people.

"You're going to speak?" asked Lolita. "What are you going to speak about?"

"Medicine," I said with confidence.

"And what do you know about medicine?"

"Our medicine comes from the sky. Sky Way medicine aligns all vibrations. Grandfather taught me well. He's over there," I said pointing to my right. "His arms are folded and he's looking at me."

"Have you memorized a speech or do you speak from…"

"Part of it. I will be Medicine Man for my clan."

"Anything else you remember about this day?"

"My parents are proud of me. It's been a while since I've seen them." I was quiet for a moment, then grinned. "There are girls here, but outside the Kiva. I want to see if one of them would try and catch my eye." Lolita laughed with delight. I laughed as well.

"And does one?" she asked. I answered yes, and described the girl.

"She's pretty. She smiles at me and I feel good," I said, beaming.

"What is her name?"

"Nee-yaa-nu," I said, affectionately.

"And what year is it when you meet Nee-yaa-nu?"

"1149," I said.

"Thank you. Let's move forward to the next significant event in Ya-naa's life."

I flung my head from side to side, my face filling with terror. I began to pant.

"What's happening," Lolita urged. "What has frightened you?"

I cried uncontrollably, drawing my knees up and curling myself into a tight ball in the recliner. It was several minutes before I could speak.

"Breathe," Lolita reminded me.

"They have brought her to me."

"Who did they bring to you? What's going on?"

I began to sob again.

"It's Nee-yaa-nu."

"Go on. What happens next?" Lolita urged.

"I'm trying to save her. She is bleeding and I cannot stop it," I said, trembling, and then sobbed as the scene played out before me: Nee-yaa-nu, covered in blood, the deep gash on her head from the fall she had taken, her hand reaching out to me, her desperate eyes.

"Breathe," Lolita reminded me again. "Let's move very quickly through the next few minutes, just observing. What happens?"

"She's bleeding. She's trying to leave us."

"And does she leave?" I sobbed and slumped forward in the recliner. "Breathe…"

"Nee-yaa-nu!" I shouted. "Nee-yaa-nu!"

"Does she survive?" Lolita probed.

"She's gone," I said, weeping.

"She's gone? I'm so sorry," Lolita offered. "What's happening now?"

"She's still bleeding. We both have blood all over us."

After a long silence, Lolita softly said, "I have a few questions. Can we look back into that lifetime to see Nee-yaa-nu?" Lolita asked. "See what she is like. Why she is so important to Ya-naa."

At that, the anguish torturing me lifted and was replaced by a calm peace. "What is she like?"

"Her braids are long, dark. They shine in the sun. She is so beautiful. She is my best friend. We want to make children together."

"And she was brought to you because you are the Medicine Man?"

I continued as if she hadn't asked a question.

"She is my new wife. We wrapped the blanket around us and danced around the community fire as they sang the Blanket Dance Song to my Nee-yaa-nu and me." I began to chant a simple tune:

> "See these two, who dance as one.
> See these two, who walk as one.
>
> Hear these two, who laugh as one.
> Hear these two, who speak as one.
>
> Under one blanket, under one blanket.
> Walking together, dancing together.
>
> Sharing words, sharing trails.
> Making certain, hearts are true."

"You and Nee-yaa-nu were husband and wife, newlyweds?"

"Everyone was at the Central Grounds: Chief Elder, our parents. She was so beautiful. We said our unison prayer, and we were escorted to the new home built for us. We had been married four days when they brought her to me with her injury."

"Such a tragedy for a young man," Lolita remarked. Then she asked, "Nee-yaa-nu, is she a familiar soul?"

"I don't understand."

"Look into her eyes. Feel her soul. Does it feel familiar? Do you recognize it as someone you know in your True lifetime?"

I looked puzzled, then shook my head.

"I promise to find her in another lifetime and be man and wife again."

"I see. And has that happened yet? Perhaps in your True lifetime?" I looked puzzled again.

"Doesn't seem so. All right, we will let Nee-yaa-nu rest. The others in your family, do you recognize any of them as someone you know in your True lifetime?"

"Biscolli. Grandfather Maa-pu is Biscolli." A broad grin covered my face and I enjoyed the reunion.

"Anyone else? Feel them. Take your time," Lolita added.

"My brother, Say-nu, is my friend Tara, and Anthony is my sister, Qu-nu-na." I smiled.

"Wonderful," Lolita remarked.

After a moment, I felt my full strength return and I spoke with pride.

"I wear the pouch. The Sky Way medicine is in me. I heal my people through the Gates in their bodies. There are six Gates, here, here, here," I said, touching the corresponding points along my body.

"The places you are touching on your body," Lolita remarked. "What do you call them?"

"Gates. There are six: the third eye, throat, heart, navel, reproduction, and rectum."

"Six? There are no more?"

"Yes, there are six higher ones, but they are only accessible through the third eye gate. Grandfather calls it the Wicket Gate. Not because it is bad, but because it is difficult to go through. They are spiritual regions—not nerve ganglia. I do not work with them, just the lower six energy centers."

"No seventh chakra?"

A puzzled look came over my face, but then I understood the nature of the question.

"No. There is a Life Force current moving through our body that originates between the rectum and the reproduction Gate, but it is not a true Gate."

"I see. And you use these Gates as a Medicine Man?"

"They serve the physical body and hold memories, past actions. They spin. The combined vibrations of a person's Gates give them a total vibration rate and total aura color. I read this. I use the Gates to match vibration rates for our harmony—our health. Everything has a vibration rate. If the things surrounding a person match their rate, they have health. If the things do not match, the person is sick."

"This is your medicine?" Lolita asked.

"Not my medicine. Sky Way." Lolita smiled at the correction.

"Ah. How do you do this? Lolita asked. "How do you match vibrations?"

"I match things to a person's vibration. I identify the elements, landscape, light density, and direction that have the same vibration rate as their own. I find the colors, fabrics, musical tones, tools, foods, essential oils, and crystals, which most closely align with their own energy, as well as the variety of wood, gems and stones, metals, botanicals, plants, and herbs. I help our people identify the work, tools, totems, animals, and even other people with a matching vibration rate.

"There are several varieties within each of these things, each with their own unique vibration. I find the match for a person. No discontent in vibrations means no sickness. I also locate the healing touch points on their body and identify their healing planets."

"So interesting."

"There are six times each day for healing. The sun sends different powers throughout the day, each with a unique vibration. At different positions of the sun, I heal different sicknesses. The sun's vibrational power must match that of the healing vibration for specific ailments. Healings are done for specific sicknesses at specific times of the year, days of the week, and times of the day. It all has to do with aligning energy, aligning vibrations."

"And you do this as Medicine Man? You heal your clan this way?"

"Yes. Our eye is on the sky, to know when each sickness can be healed."

"Interesting. How long are you the clan Medicine Man?"

"Until I am old."

"Let's move ahead to that time, the time before Ya-naa dies—when he is old. Three, two, one…" Lolita instructed.

"What are you sensing?" she asked.

"I'm satisfied with my life. I want to die."

"It's time?" I nodded. "Please move forward to your death. Move into it easily. Be aware of your impressions, and what you are aware of as you separate from Ya-naa's body."

"It is easy to leave."

"Easy to leave? Ah, you must have been ready. As you look back over that lifetime, what stands out? What was important to you?"

"The ancient medicine ways. Our people are healthy. They are content. This is because we are in harmony. We still our minds and listen to the audible life stream. We turned from those things that are bad medicine for us. We are healthy this way. It made my work much easier," I said, chuckling.

"Anything else?" Lolita asked.

"I was supposed to do something."

"What was that?"

"Father children."

"And, you didn't do this?"

"No, my work was my life."

"It looks like you are somewhat regretful. Are you?"

"Oh, yes."

"And why is it you did that? Chose work over a family?"

"I could not love another. My love was with Nee-yaa-nu."

"Ah, I see," Lolita said. "Please, let's go back to Nee-yaa-nu's death, and let's recall what you told yourself at that time." I cried. "What do you remember?" I whimpered. "What is the feeling?

"My heart is broken."

"Your heart is broken," Lolita repeated. "It's very hard to lose a lover, a soul mate. But not so hard when you remember that there is really no death. What was Ya-naa's understanding of death?"

"We cannot die."

"If that was your understanding, then what prompted your decision to remain single in that lifetime?"

"I was loyal."

"Ah, there's that loyalty again," Lolita remarked. "What do you think Nee-yaa-nu would have wanted you to do?"

"To grieve fully, then go on."

"And, what would that have been like?" Lolita asked.

"My heart is broken." I cried.

"Let's move now to in-between, after Ya-naa's death. Be aware of what you are still carrying from that lifetime as Ya-naa. Can you sense it?"

"Regret."

"Regret? Oh. What would heal this?" she asked. I sat silently in the recliner. "Usually the way to heal regret is to grieve. Some people say we shouldn't cry over spilled milk. I don't believe that. You shed tears over loss instead of holding onto it." Lolita watched me.

"What's that? What is happening?"

I felt my third eye open once again, and the Light grow within it.

"It's circles," I said, touching the bridge of my nose. "Circles. Three of them, circles. There," I said, touching it.

"You can let the regret go," Lolita suggested.

"It's gone," I replied, surprised.

"Good. Do you feel any obligation to Nee-yaa-nu, in your True lifetime?"

I drew my face up, puzzled.

"No? No obligation, no pain or hurt feelings? Nothing?"

I shook my head.

"Good. Ask your inner healer if there is any additional trauma or grief that needs to be let go of now."

Seeing that I was troubled, she asked, "What are you noticing? What is Ya-naa carrying?"

"He's so sorry."

"What is he sorry about?"

"He couldn't save her."

"Oh yes, of course. Because you are the Medicine Man?"

"Of all the people my hands ever touched, they could not save my Nee-yaa-nu. I'm so sorry."

"You can send her a message. Do you need to do that?" I nodded. "All right. Her soul can hear your words. Tell her."

"I'm so sorry," I cried.

"Nee-yaa-nu was fortunate to have you. You have a big heart and there are many opportunities to share it. Nee-yaa-nu does not want you in pain, to feel regret, or to hold onto her. I am sure the two of you will find a way for your love to continue. Are you ready to leave Ya-naa now?" I nodded.

"Good," Lolita said.

I quickly became aware of my surroundings.

"How are you feeling?" Lolita asked, her voice tender. "You've been through a lot, and you've worked very hard."

"Fine," I said. "I'm fine."

Lolita suggested I remain reclined for a few minutes. She excused herself and returned with a bottle of water for me. "Take all the time you need," she said, gently closing the door behind her as she left.

The energy within the room was magnificent. I raised my left hand to draw more of it in, and immediately sensed a presence nearby—a fast-vibrating energy, I thought.

Quickly, I turned toward the presence. For an instant, the veil separating the seen from the unseen thinned, and I saw my Guardian Angel. She was Light—radiant not just around her, but shining from within. A brilliant cloth framed her face, trimmed in fine gold. She brushed against my cheek before passing from my physical sight. I stroked my fingertips over the skin she had touched and wept.

# 20

## CANTINA

Biscolli was at the hotel when I arrived. He'd made the ride down the mountain with Russell, a digger who'd come to Chihuahua for a dental appointment. He hadn't eaten dinner, though confessed to having snacked on groceries from a small stash in my dresser drawer, after exhausting his own. I shook my head, pinched the corner of his shirt, and pulled him close. Being in his arms felt like coming home, and when we kissed, my legs went weak. I was happy he was back.

I had a whole new appreciation for Biscolli—lifetimes ago, he'd curated the knowledge and wisdom of a Sky Way Medicine Man. His soul still carried this wisdom. There was something else, too—our souls had loved one another before. It might have been as grandfather and grandson, but our love for each other was undeniable. I buried my head deeper into his chest.

"I missed you," I whispered.

"I missed you too." Biscolli kissed me and then smiled. "You would've loved the sight-reading we did on the solstice notch. I'll tell you all about it." He kissed me again. "Oh, and I did something I've never done before."

"Oh yeah, what?"

"Remember that little masculine-feminine talk we had in the car? Well, I must have swung so far to the feminine side, the girl diggers were looking for their feminine products."

"What are you talking about?"

"I wrote you a poem."

"You didn't!"

"I sure as hell did," he said, smiling and patting his back pocket.

"Oh Biscolli, thank you. Or maybe I should wait to hear it before I say thank you." He grabbed me, kissed me, and we laughed.

"Hey, I've got an idea. Are you hungry?"

"Yes. Starving."

"Let's go."

As we walked from the hotel onto the street, Biscolli told me that Polaris had been seen through the notch, but that its current position suggested a shift in the earth's axis had occurred sometime during the past 600 years. He did his best to describe the findings that he and his colleagues had uncovered, but after several blocks, the scientific jargon became a blur. I couldn't fully focus, as there was something else on my mind—something I wanted to share... Lolita.

Biscolli pulled the near-empty bag of sunflower seeds from his pocket and tossed a giant handful into his mouth, chewing on them during brief pauses in his narrative.

He wanted me to know everything there was to know about declination, solstice, and constellations. My head was spinning from the facts and numbers. Was he even remotely interested in why I wasn't at the sight-reading? I stopped in front of Rosa's Café, which stopped the monologue. Biscolli turned to me and frowned.

"Babe, I want to take you someplace other than Rosa's tonight—someplace where you can get a taste of Chihuahua." He squeezed my hand and we strolled past the café toward a cantina, already buzzing with the vibrant energy of a night in Chihuahua.

The cantina was a gaily lit narrow upstairs room with blue tile floors and open windows that spilled the vibrant beat of la música ranchera onto the street below. The colorful room was packed with two dozen tables, most occupied by locals seeking a bit of fun. Two waiters moved through the crowd with practiced ease—one navigating the tables while balancing platters of food on his arm, and the other, Tequila bottle in hand, pouring shots straight into the mouths of patrons as if he were feeding trained seals at a theme park.

The live music was cheerful but loud. The beat was coming from a couple of local musicians on guitar and trumpet—and a very large speaker.

The bar stretched along half the length of the room, a thick slab of wood sealed with a heavy varnish. It was lined with nearly as many occupied stools as were liquor bottles on the shelves behind it. I glanced at the labels, most of which I didn't recognize. So, this was Chihuahua on a weeknight.

Biscolli touched my arm and got my attention. A señorita greeted us as she darted past and pointed to a couple of chairs being vacated. She made up the third and final member of the wait staff covering the floor. It would be a long night. The possibility of sharing my news at the cantina appeared dismal.

Biscolli pulled a chair out for me and we crouched over a small table barely visible beneath the pile of dirty dishes and empty Corona bottles.

"Yeah, Biscolli, this is definitely better than Rosa's."

"Come on, Babe. The food at Rosa's is bland. I'm sure you've had a long day too. Just sit back and relax. You're in Mexico. The clocks run slower down here. Tell me you don't need to unwind."

I leaned back in my chair. He was right. My afternoon had been intense. It was time to lighten up. One look at Biscolli trying to squeeze himself around the little table did the trick—the blond giant looked totally out of place. He winked at me and excused himself to track down two menus, but he returned with the señorita instead. We ordered off of her suggestion and she cleared our table.

Moments later, the band set down their instruments and went on break, which raised my hope I could tell Biscolli about Lolita and Spirit Eyes. Our waitress offloaded our drinks as she passed by— two long-necked Coronas, sweating in the warm Mexican air for Biscolli, and a margarita on the rocks for me.

"Salud!" he called, raising the beer closest to him. That's when I got a good look at the torn tee shirt he was wearing. It read: "Duct tape can't fix stupid - but it can muffle the sound."

"What's with the shirt?" I asked, lifting my glass to toast him.

"You like it?" Biscolli asked, beaming.

"Oh yeah. Does someone send you these shirts and dare you to wear them?"

"No way, Babe. This is great stuff. You have no appreciation for a good, lived-in shirt," Biscolli said, setting down his bottle.

"Educate me. What's the difference between lived-in and worn-out?" I asked.

"Beats me. Though I'd like to see you in nothing but one of these worn-in tee shirts." He winked again.

"Soon enough, cowboy." I winked back. "I'm sure your shirts have been real chick magnets."

"Girls like a guy who is comfortable enough to wear what other men won't."

"That's your logic?"

"Well, it didn't stop you…"

"I'll have you know, Mr. Biscolli, that I could look past your blue eyes, that square chin of yours, those hundred-inch biceps, and these ratty-ass, chick-magnet shirts of yours. Yep, with me, it was professional all the way."

Biscolli started to snicker.

"It was your scientific brain that hooked me. I mean, one look at you in that laboratory, and my goose was cooked—I was all weak in the knees, cold sweats, fever… I about had to call the paramedics. 'Oh, come resuscitate me. No, wait… let the archaeologist resuscitate me.'"

Biscolli broke out into a full-on belly laugh, and I was right behind him.

I wiped tears from my eyes and recalled the banter and antics "Grandfather Maa-pu" and I had in Ya-naa's lifetime.

Biscolli then pulled a slip of paper from his back pocket.

"Now, True, don't laugh. This was my first attempt."

At that, Biscolli freed a pair of glasses that had been dangling from the neck of his shirt and slipped them on.

"Row after row of books.
But rare is it that you find one you can't put down.
Fine covers sell.
But it's what's inside that keeps you up to 1 AM.
You are that rare book for me."

"Biscolli, that's beautiful. That's really beautiful. Thank you. Will you read it again?" I asked.

Biscolli reread the poem and smiled. I was blown away by his willingness to be vulnerable and his ability to write. We kept dinner short and headed back to the hotel. I leaned my head onto his arm. We were near the hotel when I asked:

"Do you remember what made you want to study the Anasazi?"

He turned to me with a puzzled expression, perhaps not so much by the question, but that I'd chosen this particular moment to ask.

"Yes, I remember. My dad and I were exploring a kiva at Chaco Canyon in New Mexico. I was eleven. It was the strangest thing. We'd gone into the Kiva—not sure at the time what it was. I was awestruck and remember coming across a stone altar built into the wall. Dad had warned me ahead of time not to touch anything, but I felt compelled to touch it and I ran my hand over it anyway. A powerful sensation went through me, almost as though something had been detonated. It's hard to explain. Why?"

I could see he was reaching for words to wrap around the experience and explain it. "And that's when you knew?"

"Yeah, it was, only it took me twenty-plus years to act on it. But that's when I knew."

"Fascinating. You're not going to believe this," I said, then relayed my experiences over the past three days, including the one that'd led me to discover he'd been my grandfather and a great Medicine Man named Maa-pu in the Chacoan culture, some thousand years ago.

Other than a slight exaggeration here or there about how strong or good-looking Ya-naa was, I kept to the facts. It was a remarkable story to tell. He was intrigued with the idea of previous lifetimes and fascinated by the potential scientific and historical data that could be uncovered through reliving an Anasazi lifetime.

"Do you think I might be able to remember my life as an Anasazi Medicine Man?" Biscolli asked.

"Well, I don't know why not. All we can do is ask Lolita."

Biscolli and I shared a room that night. However, sleeping in the same bed with him after we explored one another, proved to be a severe challenge. He was as restless as I was tired. The lights came back on. He had a mountain of questions about my session with Lolita. I suggested he call her in the morning and ask her himself.

Moments later, I closed my eyes and sank into unconsciousness. I found myself running—rocks clattering beneath me as I flew over the bedrock. My cloth shoes pounded the loose stones, and the suede shift covering my body sailed in the wind. Someone was beside me, laughing softly. I turned, and running by my side was a man—a handsome man with black hair and eyes so alive they quickened my step even more. He wore a breechclout around his loins and carried a medicine pouch in his hand.

I brushed my hand over my chest, expecting to find my own pouch there. But instead, saw it was mine that he held in his extended hand, as if offering it back to me. We slowed and eventually stopped running. I opened the pouch and pulled out the three colored stones inside: black, white, and yellow. I glanced back at him. He became red and leapt into the pouch with the other stones.

I awoke, groping at my chest for a medicine pouch that wasn't there. The sheet was damp with sweat. I pulled myself off the bed and wandered down the dim hall to the women's restroom to splash water on my face.

# 21

# MEDICINE MAN

I couldn't have been happier that Biscolli forgot his coffee at Rosa's. He was wired enough without it, and though I was sure I'd had more sleep, he insisted on driving us to Lolita's.

He paced the room while we waited for the therapist. I noticed a large coffee stain on his shirt. Figures. It was the only shirt I'd seen him wear that didn't look like a rag. He'd obviously dressed up for the session—it was a button-down shirt. I spotted the little girl hiding behind a bookshelf, her dark eyes peeking through the shelves at the giant in her little house.

Lolita had been gracious, rearranging her schedule to accommodate Biscolli. At our scheduled time, she entered the room and found him pacing under a ceiling fan that nearly clipped his hair every time he lifted his head. I was seated on the couch, contently amused.

Leo admitted he was a bundle of nerves and asked if I could be present during his session. The professional frowned. He went on to explain that he'd come hoping to remember his lifetime as Maa-pu, with the intent of clearing up long-standing uncertainties about the Anasazi people.

It all sounded painfully clinical to me. It must have sounded that way to Lolita as well because she suggested they allow the information of the lifetime—if that's the one that comes forward, to unfold organically rather than to skim over it for the sake of collecting data.

The two scientists agreed, and Lolita consented to my attendance with an air of professional caution: I could say nothing.

A chair was placed for me behind the recliner and positioned so as not to inhibit the flow of dialogue during the session. It was a unique perspective and I was eager for the session to begin.

Biscolli took his time getting comfortable. As he fidgeted, I thought back to my session in the same recliner. My head had been spinning with uncertainty, caught between two worlds: hopeful and doubtful. Now there was no doubt as to the validity that I'd lived before.

Lolita was preparing herself a cup of tea. I took the opportunity to recall my own experience. My conscious mind had been put to sleep, and that allowed my subconscious to relive the lifetimes. It wasn't revisiting memories, but actually reliving events—events first experienced hundreds of years ago. What I hadn't been prepared for was reliving the sights, smells, and emotions of the lifetimes in total clarity, and I still had perfect recall of my session: finite details like cracks in the Iowa sidewalks, the smell of burning sage on the stone medicine altar, and the pattern woven into my Anasazi Medicine Pouch.

Lolita took a seat, and I redirected my attention to her. She spoke softly, yet distinctly, and soon completed her instructions to Biscolli.

From my perspective, I discovered that by following Lolita's expressions, I could vicariously interpret what she read on Leo's face. It was sort of like watching television through a mirror. I observed and listened in silence.

As information began coming through, we were told of a twelve-year-old boy whose name was Maa-pu. The year was 1101, and he lived with his parents in a village named Chaco. It was situated at the base of a rugged canyon whose steep walls towered some ninety feet above the progressive city. West of the village was Fajada Butte, where their solar calendar was located.

Maa-pu depicted Chaco as a major trade center with an extensive road system, accessing it like spokes on a wheel. He described roads 15 to 30 feet in width, direct thoroughfares radiating out from the trade Mecca to over one hundred other villages and extending south into Mexico and beyond. He described roads dotted with dozens of manned signaling stations, which were used to transmit information over long distances via fire, smoke, or reflective materials. This was the most expedient means of information exchange.

Maa-pu recalled living with his family in a three-room terrace at the northern end of the 600-room village. His mother was a skilled weaver and his father was a farmer in the community fields and a clan elder. We learned that his clan met their needs through societies of skilled craftspeople who produced enough for the village and exchanged excess goods. Though a major trade center, he said Chacoans met most of their own needs. No one was in need. He described growing up with a sense of community and cooperation.

The three-story terraces Maa-pu lived in were built alongside older ruins and were constructed of brick-sized stone, the residue of nearby canyon walls. He informed us that their terraces collected solar heat from the mammoth walls, which acted as solar reflectors in the winter, warming their community of five thousand people. In the summer months, the canyon walls shaded the village from the late afternoon sun.

Young Maa-pu remembered being scolded for dismantling a section of the sophisticated aqueduct system that directed scarce rainfall across their terrace rooftops to a check dam for storage. He then led us along a lower canyon wall that had been terraced into farming lots. He described the use of a digging staff, demonstrating with his hands, and pointed out overhanging ledges that watered the crops beneath them with seasonal runoff. It was delightful to watch him interact with his family. He was wildly animated. I smiled. Oh, how I loved this man.

The twelve-year-old then described his arduous Sky Way medicine apprenticeship, which had begun at the age of eight. The boy remembered the endless task of identifying each celestial body and constellation, along with the merciless all-night drills Medicine Man put him through, testing his knowledge.

At fourteen, Maa-pu became the Clan-Sky Watcher and was given the important job of informing the Chief Elder and Medicine Man of celestial movements. His skills were now being honed to integrate his sky-reading abilities, perception of vibration rates, and interpretation of aura colors into the health practices of his clan. He was delving deeper into Sky Way medicine. He beamed as he received word his Kiva ceremony would take place by his sixteenth birthday. That was when he would assume the Clan Medicine Pouch and officially become a Medicine Man.

Lolita asked Biscolli to move to the next significant event in Maa-pu's life, and we witnessed the birth of his first son, whom he named Qu-waa-nu. Maa-pu recalled chanting the Birthing Entry Prayer at his wife's side while burning cedar and sage on the altar to purify the space for the new life's arrival. A Medicine Woman assisted his wife with the birth, which he recalled occurring in 1125.

Close to that same event, he remembered seeing disturbing changes in the sky—changes that he described as sun flares. Maa-pu painted a frightening picture as he shared the details with us.

"Many troubles are in the sky—sun flares," Biscolli said. "Chief Clan Elder tells me they will take down Earth Mother's magnetic field for a minute and shift it."

"And how is it he knows these things in the year 1125?" Lolita asked.

"We have an understanding of astrophysics. It is a matter the Chief Clan Elder will take up with the Clan Council. Chief Elder tells me Earth Mother has a pattern grid of magnetic fields, running the length and width of her. He says sun flares tug at all the planets and their moons, upsetting their energy. The flares stir Earth Mother, causing volcanoes, earthquakes, and high water."

Lolita studied Biscolli's face. "What's happening now?" she asked.

"Chief Elder and I are chanting. We are calling to bring Earth Mother's energy back into alignment."

"Oh. And does this happen?"

"No, not until much damage has been done."

"This magnetic shift of Earth. Does it affect you? Do you feel the movements?"

"Only some. Most are far from us."

There was a long pause and then Maa-pu explained his understanding of magnetic fields. He informed us that our bodies, minds, and emotions are directly tied to—and influenced by—the magnetic pull of the sun, moon, and planets. He said water plays a significant role, and that the strong magnetic pull affects us positively or negatively, depending on such atmospheric conditions as elevation, humidity, temperature, and wind direction.

Biscolli's voice changed speed and took on a tone of delirious excitement as he began detailing what he understood as a healer.

"Humidity affects our chemical balance. Our bodies are more susceptible to illness in high humidity. Humidity accompanied by high temperatures and low elevation is the worst combination for health. Under these conditions, blood flow slows, creating circulatory problems and undue strain on our heart and lungs. Air pressure also affects blood flow and low barometric pressure produces similar hardships on our respiratory and circulatory systems."

"So, you're saying magnetic fields and atmospheric conditions affect our health?" Lolita asked.

"Yes, very much so." Biscolli continued, "Elevation drastically affects our respiration rate, metabolic rate, and blood chemistry. High elevations improve respiratory and metabolic efficiency and increase our overall energy and stamina. Our blood chemistry becomes more alkaline-based. All these factors contribute to overall good health.

"Wind can stir up trouble by increasing the number of positively charged particles our body is exposed to. Cold westerly winds exacerbate joint pain, stiffness, and muscle aches. Cold northerly winds intensify issues related to aging, diabetes, and gallbladder and kidney problems. Warm westerly winds aggravate blood and circulatory disorders, liver issues, cancer, tumors, migraines, and fatigue. Meanwhile, warm southerly winds worsen respiratory problems, allergies, insomnia, and depression."

Maa-pu told us these are the reasons Anasazi clans settled above 6,000 feet elevation in arid, mountainous areas with cool temperatures. These locations allowed them to harness the strong magnetic energy of the Earth. He went on to describe how his clan sleeps with their heads aligned to magnetic north, permitting Earth Mother's natural magnetic pull to draw energy up through their bodies and into their heads, rather than across their bodies or funnel it out through their feet.

Maa-pu remembered going to the Trade Center and admiring the shells, copper, and parrot feathers, which had arrived from Mexico. As he handled the strange items, he noticed that they gave him an uncomfortable feeling. He described trying an experiment: Cupping one item at a time in his hand, he would close his eyes and feel its energy. Maa-pu soon discovered that the items he was handling had vibration rates very different from his own. He went on to conduct the same experiment with foods and found his body responded negatively to foods grown outside his region. He became fascinated with the experiment and used it often as Clan Medicine Man to demonstrate vibration rates to his patients and to a young apprentice, named Ya-naa. Many learned the energy medicine.

All this had a familiar ring. It echoed nearly identical information that Spirit Eyes had shared with me during one of our conversations. I thought of her and an alarm went off in my head. Was her native blood Anasazi? My mind leapt ahead and I found myself wondering if she had, perhaps, been a Sky Way healer in a lifetime long ago. The sound of Lolita's voice brought me back to the session.

"It sounds like Maa-pu was a teacher. Is this correct?" she asked.

"Yes, when I was old."

"Ah. Let's travel through Maa-pu's life, to the time when he was a teacher. Can you do that?"

Biscolli nodded his head.

Lolita waited a moment and then asked, "What's the picture?"

"Altar. Cedar smoke…"

"Ah, an altar again," she commented.

"He is here with me."

"Oh? Who?" Lolita asked.

"My student," Biscolli answered.

Lolita grinned at the simple answer of an aging teacher.

"Just one?" she asked for clarification. He agreed. "Tell us about your student—an acquaintance or relative?

"A boy; a grandson," he replied.

"This grandson, why does he come to you? Do you teach him?"

"I try."

"You try what?" Lolita inquired.

"To teach him."

"Oh." Lolita smiled, amused. "And, does he learn?"

"Yes, he is a good pupil."

Lolita and I exchanged a friendly grin.

"What does your grandson learn from you, as your clan's Medicine Man?"

"I teach him Sky Way healing, but that is not all. He wants to know more. He is never satisfied."

"A curious boy, is he?"

"Yes, curious and mischievous," he replied, nodding his head.

"What does he want to learn from you, this grandson of yours?"

"I tell him of the beginning of our people, like most boys his age learn."

"And does that satisfy his curiosity, hearing it from his grandfather?"

"He wants to know what is to become of us."

"And you know these things?"

"Oh, yes! All the Elders understand the prophecy handed down to our people."

"What prophecy is that?" Lolita asked.

"We are guardians of the tablets foretelling the closure of the cycles of Earth Mother. Great Spirit entrusted them to our care until the day would come when their message should be told."

"What message?" Lolita probed.

"We made an oath to never turn away from Great Spirit."

"I see."

"Earth has passed through three cycles, each proceeded by purification. The Third Cycle ended with a great flood, and all life was renewed. Great Spirit asked those remaining to live with him on this clean land and not forget him. Should they forget him and the creation he made for them, a fourth cleansing would occur; this is what Ya-naa begs to be told of."

"And did you tell him?"

"I told him only of the tablets which contain the prophecy foretelling of that far-off day—tablets which also contain instructions on how to cure the ills of that time. In this way, the people can prevent the Fifth Cycle and the destructive events that will unfold as the Fourth Cycle comes to an end."

"Do your people know when the close of the Fourth Cycle will occur?" she inquired.

"This is the great secret. A corner of the tablet is not with us. It was broken off and is with our brothers. The Elders understand that we are the microcosm of the world because we hold the tablets. If our people remember Great Spirit, Earth Mother will stay her fury. If our people forget Great Spirit and Earth Mother's fate falls into the hands of greed rather than love, her cleansing will come quickly."

"And do your people remember Great Spirit in that far-off day?"

"I don't know," he said, looking bewildered. "But a time will come when the minds of men will become diluted to wise things and the promise made to Great Spirit will be ignored. On that day, the tablets will come forward and provide people with instructions, which will ensure the balance and well-being of Earth Mother and her creatures, if they choose to follow them."

My mind was spinning.

Images of Oliver, my boulder, Earth Mother, and her message about greed—about her balance and a secret in the desert, all flashed through my mind. Was the secret a tablet? Where was it?

"And your clan's name? What would we call your clan today?" Lolita asked.

"Anasazi."

"Thank you."

Lolita and I could have easily interrupted one another by asking the next question. My lips were already poised to say the words, but they were hers to ask.

"And your descendants? To whom you will pass these tablets, what will they call themselves?"

"Hopi."

This was it—the link we'd been looking for. It was a tablet, and it was with the Hopi.

Heat and adrenaline filled my body. What felt like a bolt of lightning shot through me and my composure unraveled to the point of explanation. Lolita lifted an eye towards me, but her expression remained unchanged.

The therapist knew nothing of the vision, nothing of the magnitude Biscolli's words carried. Sitting was a chore. I wanted to sprint from the room and track down the Hopi. Someone had to tell them they had a secret.

"Thank you," Lolita, said. This was killing me. I wanted Biscolli conscious so we could leave. The professional questioned Biscolli for a few more minutes concerning the Anasazi's acquisition of the tablets and the whereabouts of the brothers who possessed a broken corner of the tablet.

I knew I should listen to this—it must be important, but I felt like a kid being kept from recess. Finally, Lolita completed the session and Biscolli rallied. She informed him it was normal to experience a mild bodily cleansing following the regression, perhaps some vomiting or diarrhea. I just grinned, grabbed him by the hand, and made a mental note to get a room of my own at the hotel.

Biscolli was instantly animated and began what I knew would grow to become a lengthy narrative about the session and his life as Maa-pu. My first thought was to hop into the Mongoose and drive straight back to Chihuahua. Instead, I pointed toward the river, where we could have a bit of quiet.

Some children were kicking a ball in front of the Mongoose. Two were jumping from its enormous bumper while another swung from the driver's side mirror. Biscolli led, and we made our way along the streets until we came upon a path to the river.

Actually, it felt good to walk. Something had to be done with this adrenaline. The dirt path we were on gave way to some thick grass and stiff weeds. I fell in behind Biscolli and watched the heels of his boots until they disappeared in the brush. We found a clearing in the shade and pulled off our boots and socks.

It was the first I'd paid much attention to the grassy valley. El Sueco had always been a destination and the Rio Torreno River, was little more than a snake on a map. Biscolli turned towards me.

"You fish, don't you, Babe?"

"Yeah, a little." It was a lie. I fished a couple of times a month before moving to Mama's, had a membership at Grindstone Lakes in Central Oregon, and took a trip to the flats of Christmas Island each year.

"I thought so. I'm more into action sports. Fishing seemed about as exciting as bowling, so I never took it up."

"Not exciting? What are you talking about? When I'm in a deep green pool on a gorgeous stretch of river, with a nine-foot Sage rod straight out in front of me, and it trembles… that's excitement."

"Yeah, I guess so."

The brief diversion did wonders for me. Biscolli reached for my hand and I squeezed his. He turned towards me, smiled, and started talking about the road system in Chaco. I was tempted to ask if we could talk about the Hopi instead, but then I remembered the excitement of my own session and decided to listen. An hour wasn't going to make a difference one way or the other, besides, the passion in his voice was one of the things I most loved about him.

We found a flight departing Chihuahua at 9:30 the following morning. The last-minute booking, however, would bounce us around the southern half of the United States for seven hours, catching connecting flights and finally landing in Flagstaff at 7 PM. From there, we would drive the remaining two hours to the Hopi reservation. It sounded like a hellish day. I asked Biscolli if he could check on a charter flight. Twenty minutes later, he gave me a "thumbs-up."

We were in luck.

Of the three charter companies in Chihuahua, one had a flight leaving the airstrip at 8 AM. We'd arrive in Flagstaff by 1:30 PM, rent a car, and make the one-hundred-mile drive to the reservation, arriving by late afternoon. Biscolli reviewed the itinerary with me. I smiled, scooted onto his lap, and kissed him.

Though we were anxious to leave, we agreed that neither of us felt ready to say adios to Chihuahua without first saying goodbye to our friends.

Biscolli would head up the mountain to spend the day with the diggers, then clean out the pile of papers and food wrappers he'd let accumulate in the Mongoose. I decided to spend my final afternoon with my new friend, Spirit Eyes and walked the few short blocks to her home.

Her husband, Juan, greeted me warmly and led me to the porch, where I spent the rest of the day with my friend. We talked for hours. At noon, she served a light lunch of crackers, goat cheese, and grapes, and we continued to visit the afternoon away.

I reviewed my past life experiences with her and she shared many wonderful things with me—what she'd learned from forty-two years loving the same man, how she'd weathered loss, the wild and extraordinary journey of learning from plants, and what it was like to live with psychic abilities.

Toward sundown, when I mentioned I needed to leave, Spirit Eyes excused herself and returned with a tiny box that she said belonged to me. She unfolded my fingers and placed it in my hand. Then, she leaned forward, looked into my eyes, and said something I shall never forget:

"You were born for this. Who are you to not be brave?"

My hopes for a dry-eyed goodbye were doomed. I stood, slid my arms around this beautiful human, and hugged her.

I seemed to float above the streets on my walk back to the hotel. I felt completely seen, heard, and loved. How was Spirit Eyes able to be present—be so totally undistracted from me and our conversation? I wanted that for my life. I wanted to be able to be present with another person the way she'd been with me. I would practice that.

I arrived at the hotel and readied for bed. It felt wonderful lying there with nothing to do. I brought my hands to my chest and knew I was in love: I was in love with the Ancient Ones and the unity they shared with Earth Mother. I was in love with the humility, balance, gratitude, harmony, and peace they lived by. I was in love with Chihuahua; with the people I'd met here, and yes… I was in love with Biscolli.

It occurred to me that the whole crazy, convoluted trip to Mexico had nothing to do with Biscolli's Anasazi-Mogollon theory. It'd been a catalyst to land us in a place where we could learn of a promise made thousands of years ago—and the keepers of that promise in the present day.

# 22

# VERA

The passenger compartment of the chartered eighteen-seater aircraft was nearly full. I was delighted to see that Biscolli and I weren't the only Anglos on the flight. I was tired, and the thought of listening to several conversations spoken in a steady stream of Spanish for the next five hours didn't strike me as conducive to sleep. The interior was snug, but the plane was comfortable, and the promise of a coffee once we were in the air, made life instantly better.

Take-off was a bit bumpy, but the flying was relatively smooth. I stretched my legs and took a long look out the window to admire the countryside below. The early morning view was peaceful: rolling hills dotted with cattle, two wide rivers interwoven with a network of splintered tributaries, dirt roads winding through orchards, scattered outbuildings, and the majestic Sierra Madres in the distance.

I tried to pick out the road we'd driven up to Cueva de la Vasija, but it was impossible. I glanced at my watch. It felt odd to have it on again. I'd pulled it out of my pack this morning. It'd been on my wrist only twice since arriving in Chihuahua. I hadn't needed it. It was true, the clocks really did move slower in old Mexico. It read

8:12 AM. I knew the diggers would be in their rig, on their way to the cavern.

Beside me, Biscolli had drifted off. I knew the snoring wouldn't be far behind. So much for catching a nap myself.

We leveled off at a cruising altitude of 28,000 feet, and the fifteen passengers on board began to settle into the steady rhythm—and vibration—of the small aircraft. I accepted coffee when it was offered, then reached for my journal deep within the satchel Biscolli had crammed with snacks. I made an entry and then closed my eyes.

Moments later, I felt an eerie sensation. I opened my eyes enough to find an elderly woman with white bobbed hair staring at me from across the aisle. It was the sort of stare that can pull nails from a board, and it unnerved me. I glanced at her briefly and adjusted myself in the seat, hoping that would refocus her attention. I snuck a peek at her. She was still staring. I cleared my throat loudly enough to stir Biscolli and returned her gaze. She smiled coyly.

"Excuse me, miss," she said, finally. "I couldn't help but notice the Hopi symbol you're wearing."

The what? I wondered, and then it occurred to me I was wearing the medallion from the small box Spirit Eyes had given me.

"Oh. Is that what it is?" I answered.

"Why, yes, miss. You wear it, but don't know its meaning?" she asked, troubled by my answer. "How can you wear something and not know its meaning?"

To calm her down, I told the elderly woman the medallion had been a gift I'd received only hours earlier.

"If you wear it, you should at least know what it means," she adamantly stated.

I agreed with her, but couldn't figure out why she was making such a big deal about it.

"The Hopi shield symbol means: Together with all nations, we protect both land and life and hold the world in balance."

"What? Really? How do you know the symbol?"

"For many years, I came to Hopi land to attend the Bean Dance at Hotevilla."

"You know the Hopi?"

"Yes, or at least I used to. My dearest friends there were the elders in the village. I've often wondered if they're still alive."

She paused, her face taking on a distant, blank stare. Just then, I remembered my manners and extended my hand.

"Hello, ma'am. I'm True," I said.

"Vera Sinclair," she replied, placing her frail palm against mine and attempting to shake it. "I'm pleased to make your acquaintance."

"This is odd," I said. "See, my friend and I are on our way to the Hopi."

"Oh?" she said, raising her eyebrows. "Are visitors being allowed on the reservation again?"

My heart stopped.

"Visitors can't go to Hopi land?" I asked, praying she wouldn't say no.

"Well, my last visit there was in 1995. Like I said, it was the Bean Dance. By then, the Government had already squelched many of the ceremonies. And, of course, the Tribal Council and the Cultural Preservation people were there. They came by just to show everyone they were gaining control."

"I'm sorry, but you've lost me," I confessed. "I'm afraid I don't know much about the Hopi."

"And you want to go on their land?" she asked, in horror.

I felt embarrassed and wished Biscolli would rouse so he could back me up. I even elbowed him, but he winced and fell back asleep.

"Well, then," she said. "You've got a lot to learn. What time is it?" she asked, looking at my wrist.

I noticed Vera was not wearing a watch. In fact, she wore no jewelry. She was dressed in a lightweight cotton dress, which fit loosely over her slender frame. It was turquoise, which gave color to her near-translucent skin and complimented her coarse white hair, cut off bluntly at the chin and anchored back on one side with a white bobby pin.

The aged traveler then told me of her frequent visits to Hotevilla until, as she put it, "The Government began monitoring the tribe's activities and made it difficult for visitors to get onto the land."

Apparently, Hotevilla was being isolated from other Hopi villages and bombarded by the Government in an attempt to get the eldest of the Elders to agree to modernize their village. The Bureau of Land Management wanted to bring Bahanna (white man) schools, utilities, and conveniences onto the reservation.

Refusal by the Hopi Elders to change their traditional ways enraged the Bureau, and they launched an all-out campaign to break the Hopi into compliance. This plan had worked on neighboring Hopi villages, which had given in under the Agency's relentless pressure.

The Government systematically squelched the tribe's traditional patterns of life. They'd restricted ceremonies, imprisoned men without trial, and removed the village's children by force to send them off to Bahanna schools, where they dressed in uniforms and were punished if they spoke their native tongue. It was a vicious plan. Still, Hotevilla stood strong.

Then, Vera explained, a surprising thing occurred: the Government backed off, or so it appeared. The truth was, once the Bureau had achieved its primary goal of establishing hospitals, schools, and a quarry site in neighboring villages, they realized that the Hopi people, themselves, could do a better job wearing down the Hotevilla Traditionalists. At that point, the U.S. Government formed two agencies: The Tribal Council and the Office of Cultural Preservation. Then, they sat back and watched Hotevilla dismantle itself from within.

The second plan was even more devious than the first. Initially, Hotevilla knew their aggressor, but now, their neighbors, and even their own children, had been swooned into Bahanna's lifestyle. The Hopi's greatest fear had been realized; their people were turning away from the promise their Anasazi ancestors made long ago to Great Spirit. No one outside Hopi land knew the reason why Hotevilla held their ground, why it remained the last stronghold to exercise their father's traditional ways.

Sadly, many of the younger Hopi who had assumed the Bahanna lifestyle—called The Progressives by Hopi traditionalists, were now working with the council against their own Elders in an effort to modernize Hopi land. They wanted Hotevilla to become a modern society. This generation—taken from and schooled away from their tribe, knew little or nothing of their sacred vow.

Vera's face revealed the sadness she held for the Hopi people and the events her Hopi friends had faced. She, of course, knew nothing of the dialogue going on in my head as I listened to her. Part of me wanted to tell her why the elders at Hotevilla so adamantly refused to change, but I stopped short of saying it.

We drifted into silence. Vera stopped leaning towards me and settled back in her seat. I stretched my legs and looked out the window. I batted around the idea of speaking up again, unsure if it was wise to say what I knew. Then I thought of Spirit Eyes and the promise I'd made to follow up on intuition. I felt a nudge again, urging me to say something to her.

Vera had begun working on a crossword puzzle. I left my seat next to Biscolli—who was now snoring and dropped myself into the empty seat beside her. Vera looked up, surprised, and smiled.

"What's a five-letter word for politician?" she asked.

My inclination was to say, "could be bought," but I counted the letters and they didn't fit. So I shrugged my shoulders.

"Beats me."

She set the folded newspaper in her lap, removed her glasses, and looked at me. It was my turn.

From the beginning of our conversation, it'd been obvious that the Hopi elders meant something to her. I decided to start there.

"The Hopi are the descendants of the Anasazi," I said. "They are protecting an ancient tablet on their land." She listened with great interest as I proceeded to relay the story. When I had finished, she was nodding her head.

"That would make sense," she said. "The elderly elders adamantly refused sewer and utility lines on Hotevilla land. They claimed the backhoes would disturb their sacred land and unearth a promise it holds. It makes sense now. Their integrity always impressed me," she added. "But I'm afraid they are fighting a losing battle."

Her words hit me hard.

"The elders I knew back then were in their seventies and eighties. I don't know how many have survived to hold off the opposition. A few of their children were strong in traditional Hopi ways, but not many. Most had taken on Bahanna's lifestyle."

She paused, and then added, "Young lady, I hope you can get on the reservation. It sounds like you have important work to do."

I smiled. It had been a very long time since I had thought of myself as a young lady. But she was right about one thing, this was important.

"If we do manage to get on," I said, "is there someone you suggest we see? Someone you trust? Someone you believe would talk to us?"

"Yes, Denver Mahema. He is an elder in Hotevilla. He was in his late seventies when I was last there twenty-seven years ago. I don't know if he is still alive, but if he is, he will help you. Tell him you know me and, if you do find him alive, please tell him that he changed my life forever."

Vera then gently closed her eyes and leaned her head on the seat. The thought occurred to me that I may be tiring her, but in looking closer, I could see the lines on her thin face soften into a smile—she was visiting a memory. I covered her slight hand with my own. When her eyes reopened, they had filled with tears.

"They are good people," she said, as a tear slowly escaped her eye and rolled over her cheekbone.

"I know," I said, gently squeezing her hand. "If your friend is alive, we will find him. Can you give me an idea of where we should look?"

"It's been many years and a lot could have happened. You may find that you can just drive onto the reservation and ask for him. If the Tribal Office is still clamping down on visitors, tell them a dying friend of Denver's has a gift for him, and they asked that you deliver it personally."

The old woman bent over and pulled her purse into her lap.

"Here," she said, as she unsnapped a worn leather coin purse. "Give this to him. If he is dead, then it is yours, my new friend." Her fingers reached inside the small pouch and she pressed a token into my palm. I could see that it was very old, perhaps very valuable.

"Denver gave this to me many, many years ago. Return it to him and he will know you speak the truth and that I trust you." She cupped my hand closed around it and squeezed it with her small strength.

I must have dozed off in the seat next to Vera, because the next thing I knew, we'd touched down. I stirred awake, flashed Biscolli a thumbs up, then assisted Vera with a box that had been tied closed with kite string, and accompanied her to where her daughter sat waiting in the Flagstaff terminal. My thoughts were already on the Anasazi and their descendants, the Hopi—a nation once unified, now sadly divided by their own people. I wanted to be there more than anything else. Vera and I hugged goodbye and I told her I would be in touch.

I found Biscolli waiting at ground transportation. He puckered up and blew me a kiss as I approached.

"What gives with Grandma?" he called towards me. I shook my head, slid my free hand into his, and told him we could talk about it in the car.

While Biscolli was securing the rental car, I took the opportunity to locate Hotevilla on my phone. I was relieved we now knew which village to drive to, thanks to Vera. Apparently, the Hopi's land covered three mesas. Hotevilla was one of four villages on Third Mesa. We knew where we were going, I just hoped Vera's idea would get us on the reservation.

After loading our bags in the trunk, the reality that I was back in the States sank in. No, literally, I sank into the passenger seat, then slammed the door harder than I needed, forgetting it wasn't a World War II chunk of steel. It was another world, all right: power steering, power seats, Burmester stereo system, AC, Apple Car Play, and armrests. I glanced at Biscolli and wondered how on earth he'd adapt to a sedan. He looked up from the power seat control. He seemed to be doing just fine. He put his foot on the brake, started the car, and the adventure was back on.

## 23

## HOTEVILLA

The Hopi of Hotevilla were a tribe of people who lived very much like their ancient Anasazi ancestors. The traditionalists among them practiced dry farming techniques, lived without utilities, and performed the ceremonies and dances of their fathers. When they needed something, they made it. They grew their own food, raised their own sheep, and pumped their water from a well. They were tough, industrious people who often lived to be over one hundred years. And they preferred to be undisturbed on the land they occupied.

Within minutes of the airport, I told Biscolli of my conversation with Vera and the challenge we might face once we got to Third Mesa. According to Vera, getting onto the reservation was iffy. This had been the motivation behind her providing me with alternate directions.

"All right, then," he said. "We'll just have to take our chances."

I checked the outside temperature. It was seventy-nine degrees—unusually warm for the forested mountain country of Northern Arizona in May. We drove north, away from the cooler temperatures of Flagstaff, and into the mouth of the desert. The elevation loss made a world of difference. For the next hour and a half, the late afternoon sun chased us from overhead. I eased up the air conditioning and considered what Vera had shared with me.

The division between the Hopi Traditionalists and Progressives had me concerned. I didn't know what we were walking into. I was worried that we might not even get to see Denver Mahema. I thought about the critical state of the world and hoped we weren't too late—that the number of Hopi Traditionalists had remained strong. I shared my concerns with Biscolli.

"We're just two people. What can we do? What can we possibly do?"

"I don't know, Babe," Biscolli replied, and I could see he was turning and testing ideas in his head. With that, we fell into silence.

"What do we do if we find the tablets and learn the instructions on them?" I asked, thinking aloud. An answer didn't come, so I looked out the window at the desert. I felt small, like an insignificant speck landing on the edge of something big. In all my hurry, wanting to get here, I was now riddled with anxiety.

"You don't believe we would've come this far if there wasn't a way to do this, do you?" I turned towards Biscolli—to my man. I'd lean on anything he had to say right now. He'd know what to do.

Biscolli eased up on the accelerator and guided the car to the shoulder of the road. He slid the transmission into Park, unbuckled his seatbelt, and turned towards me.

"Look, I know you're worried. I've got a pit in my stomach as well." He reached across the console and touched my leg. "Hey Babe, look at me…"

I turned from the window and met his eyes.

"If this is ours to do, a way will open. Whatever happens, I want you to know I've got your back. Wherever you are, I'll be right beside you. Just keep that beautiful heart of yours open and keep communicating with me. Don't you dare go quiet, 'cause I need you too. It's okay to be scared... you're human. Now, we're going to drive onto that reservation, and one way or another, it's all going to work out. You with me?"

I nodded, grateful to have this good man beside me.

"Thanks, I feel better." I took a breath and slowly let it out. "Thanks. You're a good man, Babe."

As we neared the reservation the three table-topped mesas which identify Hopi Land, came into view.

"Do you know where we're going?" Biscolli asked.

I pulled out the paper I'd written Vera's verbal directions on. We'd be following landmarks she hadn't seen in over two decades.

I talked Biscolli through a couple of wide intersections that eventually led us onto an asphalt road that paralleled a street inside the reservation dotted with small, drab buildings. At Vera's suggestion, we steered clear of the fenced reservation and headed south to a remote entrance. I sat in the passenger seat, my eyes glued to the shoulder of the road, watching for a stack of rocks piled into chicken wire, that she'd mentioned. After a while, I spotted them. Sure enough, a section of fence was missing there.

Biscolli eased the car from the road and selected one of the animal trails to follow. Slowly we negotiated our way over the washboard land, lifting a heavy cloud of dust behind us which completely engulfed the car every time Biscolli dropped below ten miles an hour. We poked along on the bone-jarring path for fifteen long minutes.

"Well, it's no Mongoose," I said, and laughed.

"Thank God for rentals," Biscolli said, as he flipped on the windshield wipers to clear the layer of dust that had collected. After a mile or so of the dirt, he begged me for an answer.

"Are you sure this is right?"

"I hope so. Without knowing whether we could get on or not, Vera suggested this."

"Some route. Well True, if Grandma was feeding you a line, I'm sure she's laughing her knee-highs off right now. How much more of this do we have?"

"She didn't say."

"Swell."

I held onto the doorrest and tried to roll with the knocks. For another half-mile, Biscolli and I rocked in our seats and wondered where the hell we were going.

After clearing a low rise, Biscolli stopped the car and studied the landscape.

"What are you thinking," I asked. There had been no conversation during the bumpy drive. To talk meant running the risk of a chipped tooth. He pointed toward the horizon.

"I think we're here," he said. "A house. Do you see it?"

He was right. There was a house or at least, a building of some sort. Biscolli grinned, put the car in gear, and steered toward it. Dust billowed from beneath the tires and rolled downwind. It was a flat-roofed house, patched together of unpainted plywood sheets and tarpaper. A long white propane cylinder—rusted on top, sat to the side of the house. A man was working in an adjacent field against a backdrop of corn. As we drove closer, we found the man was actually standing in a field across a dirt-access road.

Biscolli turned to me, smiled, and crossed his fingers. "For luck," he said.

I crossed my fingers.

"For luck," I agreed, crossing the fingers of my other hand as well.

Apparently, the man in the field saw our dust cloud nef started walking toward it. Biscolli drove onto the access road, then eased up on the gas and guided the car toward him. The man looked to be about eighty and stood no more than five feet tall. Some sort of clothing covered every inch of his body, except his face and bony hands. The biggest portion of him was swallowed by faded coveralls. He adjusted a straw sunhat and leaned towards the driver's window. His face was tough as leather and dripping with perspiration. I noticed the tips of his fingers were swollen and discolored. Biscolli lowered the window and I said a prayer.

"Can I help you?" he asked.

"Yes, sir. My friend and I are looking for Denver Mahema. Are we close?"

He wiped his shirt sleeve across his face and pointed down the dirt road, adding, "Almost."

"Almost" was the most beautiful word I'd ever heard. Almost meant Denver was alive. Almost meant the old man knew Denver. Almost meant…

"Hey, True? Where are you, Babe?" Biscolli asked, touching me. From his expression, I could see he'd been trying to get my attention.

"Huh?"

"He says Denver lives about a mile down the road."

"Oh."

I leaned across Biscolli and thanked the man. He lowered his sunhat and took a step backward. Biscolli guided the car back onto the dirt road, and we drove another mile deeper into the reservation.

The corrugated road had smoothed out and the dust had settled. I looked over my shoulder to get the full effect of the land we had just traversed. It was every 4x4 owner's dream come true. All things considered, I thought we'd done a fine job crossing it in a sedan.

We came to a stop a few minutes later on a patch of dirt in front of a small house. The building was nearly identical to the one we had just left, except this home had a tin awning over the front door and an outbuilding had been constructed of plywood and some stones that strongly resembled the ones in the yard.

A man about forty-five was working the handle of a water pump beside the home. He finished filling a pail and then walked toward us. Biscolli and I got out of the car and met him halfway. The dry heat hit us instantly. Two black dogs rounded the corner of the house and came bounding toward us, barking and circling in the dirt when they reached our legs.

"Hello. We're looking for Denver Mahema," I said, lifting my hand to block the sun.

The man raised a thin smile and said, "I'm Clint. You would be looking for my grandfather. He's with his field right now. I wasn't aware he was expecting anyone."

"Well, we were told by an old friend of his, that he might be willing to talk to us."

"Grandfather enjoys company. I'm sure he will be glad you came to visit."

I sighed a deep breath.

"Oh, thank you, God," I whispered to Biscolli.

Clint stooped to pick up a second pail of water and Biscolli snatched the handle before he could pick it up.

"Where would you like it?" Biscolli asked.

We followed Clint through the front door, sidestepping the barking dogs the entire distance. The house was nothing to write home about. We entered through the living room and walked towards the kitchen area. Clint explained that they lived very simply. That was self-evident. As I panned the room I could see no appliances, no electric lights, or any of the conveniences most of the world considers essential. There was no sign of indoor plumbing and I figured the two pails sloshing in front of me confirmed it was true.

We stopped at the kitchen counter which was considerably lower than any I'd seen before. I assumed it had been built to match the Hopi's stature. Along one wall stood an old stove. Clint poured the water into a large basin and Biscolli followed in turn, then we backtracked into the living room. I looked around the sparsely furnished room and decided to sit on a Naugahyde Davenport. I had only seen one from a distance at the Smithsonian Institute. The seat cushions were covered with a thick wool blanket, and two bed pillows were stacked at one end. The rest of the room consisted of a potbelly iron stove, a brown upholstered recliner and a small primitive table next to it, and two occasional chairs—one yellow vinyl and the other wood. A beautiful watercolor of the three mesas hung from one of the walls that was painted a light yellow.

Clint remained standing and asked if we were comfortable. We thanked him for his hospitality. He offered us a cup of water and then excused himself to bring in "Grandfather." The dogs left with him.

"What do you think?" Biscolli whispered when we were alone.

"We'll see. At least we're in."

It was several minutes before we heard any sign of life. When we did it took on a distinct pattern of step-step-shuffle, step-step-shuffle. Moments later, a small-framed man with deep mahogany-colored skin entered the room. He stood upright, straight as an

Army sergeant, and had a full head of white hair, creased as though a hat had just been pulled from it.

Biscolli and I sprang to our feet. Standing in front of us in long sleeves, jeans, and boots, the elderly man couldn't have weighed more than one hundred pounds. He had a kind face and, had I been able to see his eyes beneath the sagging folds, I was sure a twinkle would have shown in them.

When Denver became aware that company was in the room, he swatted his hands on his blue jeans, which raised a puff of dirt from the denim. He smiled at us and stepped forward. Clint entered the room from behind the old man, then gently wrapped his grandfather's hand around his strong forearm and led him towards us.

"Grandfather, I would like to introduce my new friends," Clint said, bringing them both a stop. The frail man looked into his grandson's face and smiled.

"Do your friends have names?" he asked.

The room was silent and I realized we'd never introduced ourselves to Clint—he didn't know our names.

"I will let them introduce themselves," Clint answered. "I understand you have a mutual friend."

"Oh?" Denver asked. "Who is our friend?"

"Vera Sinclair," I volunteered. "I'm True North, and this is my good friend Leonard Biscolli."

We extended our hands to him, and then Biscolli poked me.

"Leonard?" he said, under his breath.

"Roll with me. He's an Elder," I whispered back.

The sound of Vera's name lightened Denver's slight frame another five pounds and raised a smile so broad that it lifted the sagging age that hung from his broad face like a burlap sack. I saw the twinkle in his eyes.

I told Denver that Vera was still traveling and she passed on her greeting. I then remembered the token buried in my front pocket, so kneeled beside the recliner where Denver had seated himself.

I presented the token to him, which he pinched between his fingers and lifted to the dark slits that hid his eyes. He smiled and then looked at me, not bothering to wipe the tear that had welled up and fallen onto a deep crease on his face.

What happened next is probably the closest I've come to witnessing a burning bush in my life. Denver closed his eyes and pressed the coin to his lips. It wasn't a big kiss, just a whisk. But it blended the two of them—Vera and the Elder. He cupped the little treasure in his hands and then we heard these words escape him:

> "My heart is your heart.
> My soul holds you dear.
> I pray for you.
> I care for you.
> Friend of mine.
> My special friend.
> May Grandfather keep you in his heart.
> My heart is your heart.
> Friend of mine.
> My soul holds you dear.
> My special friend."

Clint glanced towards us then back to his grandfather.

"My thanks to you," Denver said, looking up. "You have made this old man's heart very happy."

We looked on as he pulled a small pouch from his shirt pocket and carefully placed the token inside. I continued to kneel, and counted it an uncommon luxury to be with such a person. He possessed a mighty presence I suspected hadn't been put there by brawn, but through the peace that radiated from him. It was a sweet moment, and we reverenced it with the quiet it deserved.

Soon Denver's older son, Mark, and daughter-in-law, Eva, joined us. Both remembered Vera and had a dozen questions for me which, admittedly, I hadn't an answer to. I did volunteer that Vera looked healthy and happy, and I suspected, given the opportunity, she'd return to Hotevilla.

Talk of Vera led to the topic of visitors. Mark informed us that the Council no longer discouraged visitors, and the days of detaining or hassling them were history. It was reassuring to know Biscolli and I weren't looking at doing time for criminal trespass. The other bit of good news was that we could come and go freely, via the main road—surely easier on the car's suspension than the one we'd endured getting here.

Afternoon became evening and we were asked to stay for supper. Eva stretched a wonderful casserole of squash, lentils, and pinyon nuts between the six of us. We also enjoyed a flavorful side dish of roasted vegetables. What didn't stretch was the kitchen table, which undoubtedly was not made to accommodate Biscolli—but we managed.

With supper over, Eva excused herself to paint a kachina doll, which she would later sell to a crafts dealer. Clint cleared the table and brought out a box of playing cards. Evidently, a couple of hands of rummy after supper was a religious institution in the Mahema household. I scooted my vinyl kitchen chair to get some elbowroom, and let the ritual begin.

# ANASAZI VISION

At 43, I felt like a young pup sandwiched between an Elder, who'd made me guess his age and then told me he was alive in 1919, and Mark—a vigorous man thirty-four years my senior. Both were marvels that defied age, Denver for his mind—quick as a bullwhip, and Mark for his ceaseless vitality.

During our first hand of rummy, we learned that there'd only been a small number of men who—like Denver, carried a complete knowledge of the ancient vow made to Great Spirit. One by one, the other Elders had died, taking what they knew of the covenant with them, and leaving Denver the sole elderly Elder—the final taproot of a dying generation.

Denver had assumed leadership of his clan in late 1998, following the death of his lifelong friend Jim Ehema. In spite of Denver's advanced age he was the workhorse who drove his clan's political and ceremonial activities and was, according to Clint, the closest thing the Hopi have to a modern-day hero.

We learned that Denver was an adamant defender of the traditional Hopi ways and continued to do whatever was necessary to hold to the vow of his people. So enduring was he, that he'd survived six imprisonments, as well as numerous harassment and threats.

He'd led those resisting the destructive efforts of the Tribal Council, once even jumping into a utility trench and challenging the bulldozer driver to run over him. He was spunky, stubborn, and knew the sacred vow given to Great Spirit in its entirety.

Denver shuffled and dealt his deal with the precision of a watchmaker. Then once the cards were carefully divvied up, a gentle vibration came to his hands. I glanced at the hash marks on the scorepad and noted Biscolli and I were getting badly bruised in the game.

# ANASAZI VISION

It was the light receding from the room that alerted us to the time. Clint excused himself from the kitchen table and returned with a half-gallon can of kerosene to top off a lantern. He lit the wick and it raised a glow in the modest room. Time had slipped from us somehow, and a worry grew in my gut that Biscolli and I had made no arrangements for the night. The last town of any size was twenty-two miles away.

I hesitated to impose on our new friends. Besides, it didn't take much math to calculate that Denver's entire home could have fit in Mama's living room. I was also aware the home already slept four adults. From what I could see, Denver's home had only one bedroom. I was sure the bed pillows on the Davenport were there for a reason. I had no idea where we would sleep tonight. This dilemma, as it turned out, was to be my first real introduction to Denver Mahema.

The elderly man knew I was entertaining some kind of trouble. He said nothing at first—which I've since learned is his nature. Instead, he waited and he watched. When I didn't bring up the matter, he asked if he could have a conference with me in the living room. I graciously complied, wondering what would require the privacy. When we'd retired to the living room he matter-of-factly asked about my mood. Without going into details, I told him that I was concerned about the advancing hour.

"A woman with this much worry is not concerned with the light," he said.

I was in the company of a wise old man and he saw through me like a pane of glass. No longer dependent upon his gradually failing senses, Denver possessed the ability to read people with a clarity few acquire. He was 103. Time was not a luxury he could afford.

Perhaps this was why he didn't mince words and expected the same of others.

"We have no place to sleep," I said. Unexpected freedom accompanied the blunt declaration.

"You think we have no room?" Denver asked, inquisitively. I knew better than to sugar-coat my answer.

"Space seems to be a little tight."

Denver slowly raised his hand to my shoulder and smiled.

"Sometimes meetings go long and company stays," he reminded me. "There is bedding for two. Please, honor us by staying." I returned his smile, then bent towards him.

"Bet you're glad it's my shoulder and not Biscolli's."

He bellowed out a laugh that lifted heads at the rummy table in a synchronistic pattern. I swung my arms around his waist and tried to find it. The old man gave a fair squeeze. I fell in love when he did this and understood what Vera meant when she said Denver had changed her life forever.

A makeshift bed had been prepared for me on the hardwood floor alongside the Davenport. Biscolli's bedding was situated in the center of the room; the only place budgeted to accommodate his length. I dropped down onto a wool blanket, exhausted, and pulled the boots from my feet. One by one, Denver's family took their customary beds. It was a neat arrangement and reminded me of how everything will fit into a tackle box if one takes the patience to organize it. The six of us snuggled into our comfortable little nest and Clint dimmed the lantern.

Still more awake than asleep, I recalled some of the swanky places I had laid my head over the years; places I've paid a half-month's mortgage per night for a bed, just to find the place as cold and empty as the smiles working the front desk or carting around luggage. Visibly, Denver's home wasn't much, yet something about it, about this arrangement, was wonderfully soothing. The home was held together with love. A Four-Star Hotel can't manufacture that sort of thing.

It was quite a leap for my ego to imagine that, given the choice between monogrammed bath towels and a hardwood floor I preferred the floor. This ground, these people, they supported me - a complete stranger - with love. They had a powerful grace. Each decision in my life had been weighed by how much I would get in return. My top-shelf ambitions of success seemed so trivial. The Mahemas blended with the earth and sustained each other. A feeling existed here I had experienced nowhere else. Already I felt part of them, absorbed into the harmony and companionship thriving in this nest. I was in no hurry to leave.

### Thursday, May 26

"The days are turning into weeks. It's been two weeks since I left Grants Pass.—seems a lifetime ago now! We've met the eldest Hopi Elder—Denver Mahema. Apparently, he is the final living elder who knows the full extent of the vow his people made to Great Spirit—and he is ancient! I'm telling you, Earth Mother waited until the last second to get this job done. Though he is healthy and alert, he's 103, for God's sake!

He is an ancient gladiator and I love him already. When he passes from this world I'm sure all life will feel disoriented for a second or two. He's a humble warrior and I count myself among the lucky ones who will get to know this great man."

# 24

# CROWS

It was still dark when I came awake to the smell of musty wool and a low conversation of whispers. I rolled onto my back and opened my eyes. The floor had punished my body and I gave it a long languid stretch. Exactly how much rest I'd had I couldn't be sure, but I had surrendered myself to it completely and felt refreshed.

I tapped the mound beside me and called for Biscolli to wake. The room was void of light but there were steady signs it was time to clear the floor. He didn't move. I tapped harder this time. He cursed the air and pulled a blanket over his shoulder.

"What is it? I was dreaming," he said, moaning.

"We'd better get up," I whispered.

"Now?"

"Come on."

"Yeah, in a minute."

I got up and stretched a few more kinks from my body. The bedding was being folded by the men and turned over to Eva, who stood at a closet by the front door. I tickled Biscolli's ribs with my big toe and he came awake.

Eva received my stack of bedding with a smile and asked me how I had slept. I didn't know what kind of extra-sensory power she might have, so I answered honestly and told her I had a few kinks here and there. She grinned and led me to a washbasin behind a door jam partitioned off with a length of fabric. All the necessities were there and, though everything around me screamed "want," I felt like a queen—a queen in a strange, romantic land.

I quickly took a sponge bath and dressed. Biscolli staggered to the grooming area while I looked for Denver. In poking around, I noticed all of the men were gone. When I asked Eva about it, she told me they spent sunrise with their crops. I excused myself and stepped out the front door into the cool air. The familiar rattle of the doorknob raised life behind an outbuilding and the two mutts sprinted toward me with eager anticipation. I stooped to pet them. It was almost daylight.

The dusty road we'd traveled to get here divided Denver's house from his fields and sheep pens. Even with my meager farming experience, I could tell it would be a good year for the crop. A low-growing variety of corn filled a respectable portion of my view, and I delighted in the parade of light-green leaves waving in front of me as a breeze played with their new shoots. A flock of crows pecked and cawed as they patrolled a section of the field.

The men were nowhere to be seen, so I crouched on the front step, tied my boots, and set out for the fields with the dogs in tow. The morning air made me deliriously happy and whisked me back to mornings with my father in the fields of our Montana ranch. He'd sit me on the John Deere and promise one day it'd all be mine. Of course, none of that happened. We moved to Grants Pass, and a caretaker was brought in to maintain the 55 acres. With Mama's death, the property—and caretaker, were now under the stewardship of Dan and Linda. I never missed the ranch—never missed my family's dirt a single minute; until now.

# ANASAZI VISION

I stumbled onto Clint kneeling in a field. Though sure my clumsy approach may have startled him, he offered no sign he was aware of my presence. I withdrew a few steps out of respect, and let him finish his business, whatever that was. In the soft light, I strained to listen.

"O' Great Spirit,
Whose voice I hear in the winds,
And whose breath gives life to all the world.
Hear me.
I am small and weak.
I need your strength and wisdom.
Let me walk in beauty, and make my eyes ever behold the red and purple sunset.
Make my hands respect the things you have made, and my ears, sharp to hear your voice.
Make me wise, so that I may understand the things you have taught my people.
Let me learn the lessons you have hidden in every leaf and rock.
I seek strength, not to be greater than my brother, but to understand my greatest Enemy—myself.
Make me always ready to come to you with clean hands and straight eyes.
So when life fades as the fading sunset, my spirit may come to you without shame."

I was the one ashamed. Not at the simple words voiced by a farmer to the crop's creator, but that I'd lingered to hear their private conversation. I stepped backward and escaped into the crops, embarrassed, and feeling more a stranger than ever before. I was a tenderfoot in a foreign land with foreign customs.

I didn't pretend to know the rhythm of the Hopi. In fact, to assume I knew anything of these people was to perpetuate the naiveté of their ways. They were humble people with little ego. Not surprisingly, it had been Denver's family who'd been gracious enough to venerate a man much too humble to speak of himself. He was a rare gem.

Surely with his perception, the Elder must suspect that our visit constituted more than delivering a greeting from an old friend. Was he watching and waiting? I felt honor-bound to reveal my intentions to him. I came across Denver along a row of corn about mid-morning. He turned and greeted me warmly.

"We are having some trouble with the crows. They have forgotten our agreement."

"What?"

"The old ones don't peck at the seedlings, but these young ones, they forget the arrangement."

"You have an arrangement with the crows?" I asked.

"Yes, but it is time to have a conference with the young ones. Perhaps they will listen this morning."

"But how do they... how do you?"

It appeared I was about to find out. Denver looked out over his field in no particular direction and cupped his hands around his mouth. I looked on.

"I realize we must share this land," he stated. "So I'm offering an agreement with you that will meet both our needs. I am asking you to stop eating our crops. In exchange for this, I will see to it that you are fed and are not harmed in any way. Food will be left for you along the east field. I hope this is agreeable."

"That's remarkable!" I said. "And they listen to you?"

"We'll see. It has been a while since I have talked with the crows directly, but I often talk with the other creatures to be sure we understand each other. Unless we speak, I can't know what they will do."

"Really?"

Denver nodded then turned his attention toward the east field for confirmation his words had been heard. I observed in silence, not ready to pass judgment on something I didn't understand. Spirit Eyes came to mind. I wondered if she talked to creatures as she sang to plants.

"How do you do it?" I asked.

"I say words for my benefit," Denver replied. "The real talk is done through mind pictures. I put a picture in my head of what I want to convey and send it. They send one back, only their vocabulary is limited and their pictures are often very simple."

He turned towards me.

"Any animal can read your mind. They are very good at it. The secret is to speak on terms of equality and respect, with love and a willingness to learn from them. They have taught me much." He then nodded, confident the crows were agreeable to his proposal.

Denver led me through the crops to a patch of squash, just beginning to send out runners. Using a long stick to steady himself, he knelt to the ground and began to pull weeds.

"We all get along if no creature, including myself, believes the land is theirs."

I dropped to my butt, and we sat among the vines pulling weeds until the sun had climbed high above us. At times, I stopped just to watch the Elder's nimble fingers work a weed free of the tough soil. It was hard to believe he was a century old. As we labored among the vines, I recalled the vision I'd had at Hovenweep and the urgent message Oliver had delivered for Earth Mother. It was time to share the experience with Denver.

He listened with interest and when I had finished, he looked up from his weeding.

"It is a fulfillment of the prophecy. The season has come to share our message of prophecy, peace, and harmony with the world.

"My new friend," he continued. "Just as we knew Bahanna would come to America, we have known the secret that enables us to blend with the land must one day be shared with our brothers and sisters. I am old and the last of The Elders. In my prayers, I have asked Great Spirit to send messengers who would take the sacred teaching to our brothers and sisters of the other three races. I have been expecting you."

At that moment, I realized I'd never considered the elder's response to the vision. My entire focus had been on finding the right person to share it with. I spent the afternoon pondering how—after thousands of years protecting the covenant, Denver could be certain now was the time to share their people's sacred knowledge. And, I was terrified at the possibility that I had anything to do with this.

# 25

## TURTLE ISLAND

The following day, Elder Denver Mahema addressed a modest gathering of Hopi. Five months earlier a meeting held to discuss the construction of Bahanna schools on Hopi land had filled the lodge to capacity. Today, the room was occupied by dozens of vacant wooden seats, a sign more Hopi were siding with the Tribal Council. In attendance were Hopi Traditionalists from Third Mesa—the land mass Hotevilla was built upon, and a handful of fence-sitters. All totaled, including the "two white strangers," we were thirty-six in number.

Denver moved freely among the small crowd and everywhere he went, he was received with affection. Men clasped his hand and presented him with tobacco, women smiled and waited for their turn to hug him. They talked of crops and children and of those no longer among them. All looked to their leader as a spiritual good-luck charm.

Biscolli and I didn't go unnoticed, though, it'd be safe to say Biscolli couldn't have remained anonymous had he wanted to. We were greeted with sincere friendship by cheerful people—stout women with children in tow and muscular men in work clothes.

Mark and Clint look pleased. Daily chores had been set aside to notify residents and prepare for the gathering. Still, both knew that

Denver had put forth the most effort to convene the group. Those in attendance had an idea what was to be presented, but that was not why they were here. Elder Mahema had called a meeting and that was reason enough to be present.

Denver took his rightful seat at the head of the room. When the voices had died down, he stood.

"I am glad to have this time with you, my friends. We are celebrating a point in our history that is both filled with joy and sadness. For thousands of years, we Hopi have lived in villages by a pattern established by Great Spirit, whose teachings go all the way back to the dawn of time."

He gazed across the room. Two babies cried.

"All the prophecies are being fulfilled, including the one that says one day the secret that enables us to blend with the land and celebrate life, will be shared with all people who truly deserve to hear it."

He paused.

"This secret for happiness was never intended to be a secret—for it has always been Great Spirit's intent that it be shared. We Hopi have faithfully been keepers of the covenant. It has been a long road and is far from complete. I want you to be aware that I have seen this day when we share our knowledge. Thank you for coming. I will take your comments."

I panned over the small sea of mahogany-colored faces and wondered what they must think of the news.

I was not Hopi. I could not know what struggles they'd endured or what battles they'd fought to keep the tablets safe and to defend their right to practice its contents.

Much of what the Elder had said was as foreign to me as the bottom of the ocean, and yet, I understood its significance. It was a profound statement, perhaps the boldest words to date, to come from the aging Elder's mouth. But not everyone was smiling.

The meeting ran well into the evening. Mothers nursed their infants. Children curled up on their father's laps. There were many questions and concerns raised from the close-knit group. This was to be expected. At times the discussion grew tense and, in the end, three refused to side with the others. This, I found out later, was not an uncommon theme in clan meetings, since so much division among their people had already occurred.

Denver waited until the last of the opponents had voiced their concerns, then, he raised his hand in peace and told them he respected each of their respective opinions and personal decisions.

If there was anyone a Traditionalist the Hopi could trust, it was Denver Mahema. He was the most knowledgeable among them. He alone knew the covenant in its entirety. Their underlying belief was that if the Elderly Elder felt the time had come to share the responsibility of Earth's stewardship and fate with the world, they would support the effort to bring it forward. A vote was taken at 9:35 PM: thirty-one to three.

I was told by Denver the following morning over a breakfast of porridge, that ten thousand people comprise the entire Hopi tribe—thirty-four were in attendance at the meeting. Twenty-eight Traditionalists were left of an entire Hopi nation. Collectively, they had chosen to share the contents of the tablets entrusted to their care since the Great Flood.

It was explained to us that Biscolli and I were to spend the next five days in school. It was not much time to learn the Hopi way, but that's what occurred. Denver's home became a schoolhouse. The Mahema fields became a laboratory.

Each morning following Denver's private time with his crops, we plunged into our elementary lessons at the kitchen table. In the afternoon, we retreated to the fields and were instructed in the traditional dry farming techniques of the Hopi people. Evenings, after a couple of rounds of rummy, the elder spun our imaginations with the tale of how the Hopi came to be Keepers of the Covenant.

I took on the responsibility of recording the contents of our lessons in my journal. I learned soon enough that this record would comprise the only written account containing the full extent of the ancient prophecies. There was little time to absorb the impact of what was occurring. Biscolli held me in the evenings, before we drifted off to sleep.

**LESSON 1: The Emergence**
**Sunday, May 29**

"The story begins long ago on the floor of the Grand Canyon," Denver explained. "Just below the canyon's floor is the Womb of Earth Mother, the World of Spirits; a place where pieces of the Creator, called souls, await the opportunity of life on the earth's surface. When the emergence of souls to the earth's crusty layer began, Great Spirit gathered the human beings together on an island which is now beneath the water, and said, 'I am going to send you in four directions and change you to four colors.'

"During the cycle of time, I am going to give each of you two stone tablets with my life plan and teachings on them. These you will call the Original Teachings. After four cycles on the earth: one of mineral, rock, plant, and animal, you will come back together with each other, and you will share these teachings so that you can live and have peace on earth, and a great civilization will come about."

"Now," Denver said, leaning forward onto the kitchen table, "There seems to be a mystery surrounding the great Kivas of our Fathers and of our people. I will clear this up for you."

Biscolli was instantly electrified and poised himself like a hungry robin waiting for the first worm of the day.

"In the center of a Kiva floor is a small circular recess. This hole has long puzzled man. The recess, called a sip-pa-pu hole, symbolizes the passageway from the womb below the canyon's floor to Earth's surface. Each year our people gather to the Kiva and reenact the emergence story, just as our fathers and grandfathers have done from the beginning of time. Kivas always sit below the earth's surface because they symbolize the womb of Earth Mother, from where all life emerges."

Biscolli beamed and scribbled a few notes in longhand on a piece of borrowed paper. I remembered Spirit Eyes telling me she had come from the Wide Canyon.

"Great Spirit Creator made the earth in perfect balance where human beings spoke one language. As they took on bodies, they drifted further and further away from their Source, and a harmonious existence of peace and love was lost. They willfully misused their spiritual powers for personal gratification and did not follow nature's rules. Eventually, the world was cleansed by sinking it."

He continued.

"Earth has completed three cycles: mineral, rock, and plant. It is now in its Fourth Cycle, the cycle of animals, which will end someday and give way to the cycle of human beings. Great Spirit says the Fifth Cycle is a time when humans will live and have peace on earth—and a great civilization will exist. But for now, we experience what it is like to be an animal without peace on this earth.

"Preceding each cycle is a purification. Earth's last purification was a flood, which destroyed all but a few humans who asked for—and received, permission from Great Spirit to live with Him on this new land. 'It is up to you if you are willing to live my poor, humble, simple way of life. It is hard to live according to my teachings and instructions. This is my life and this is my way,' Great Spirit said, showing them his only material possessions: a digging stick, a container of water, and a pouch of seeds. 'This is how I live and create. If you never lose faith in the life I shall give you, what you gain shall never be lost. But you have two ways to choose.'"

I reflected back to my conversation with Spirit Eyes and the principle of duality we had discussed. I also remembered Roger saying Earth was a place of love and fear.

"Before Great Spirit hid himself again, he made the people four colors, as he had promised one day he would. He placed before the leaders of the four groups, different sizes and colors of corn, and asked them to choose their food in this new land. The red-skinned leader waited until last and picked the smallest ear of corn. At this, Great Spirit said, 'You have shown me you are wise and humble. For this reason, I will place in your hands my sacred tablets and call you people of peace. I will place in your jurisdiction all land and life to guard, protect, and hold in trust for Me, until I return to you, for I am the First and the Last.'"

Denver interlocked his trembling fingers.

"This is why the Hopi is ordained the keeper. Truly, the earth and all living things are placed in our hands to steward and protect.

But this is not all—to each color of people he gave a Guardianship. Each was to care for and learn the fundamentals of their guardianship and then, at an appointed time, all four colors were to come together once more and share their knowledge and live in peace with each other.

"To the yellow race of people, he gave the Guardianship of wind and sent them to the south into the land now called Tibet. They were to learn about the sky and breath, and how to pull air within ourselves for health and spiritual advancement."

"To the black race of people, he gave the Guardianship of water and sent them to the west into the land now called Kenya. They were to learn the teachings of water—which is the height of elements; the most humble, yet most powerful and intelligent of them all. I understand it was a black man who discovered blood plasma. Is water not in blood?" He asked.

"To the white race of people, he gave the Guardianship of the fire and sent them to the north into the land now called Switzerland. The creations of the white race often have fire at their core—the light bulb represents their fire, while their cars and airplanes are powered by a spark. If you look at the center of their spacecraft, you will find fire. Fire consumes and moves. This is why it was the white race that moved upon the face of the earth to reunite us as a human family.

"To the red people, he gave the Guardianship of the earth and sent us to the east to the land now called America. We were to learn the fundamentals of the earth, the plants that grow from the earth, the foods that can be eaten, and the herbs that are healing, so that when we come back together with our other brothers and sisters, we can share this knowledge with them.

"Something good was to happen on the earth. This was the plan at the beginning of the Fourth Cycle."

Denver's simple explanation of mankind made sense and it occurred to me that truth often comes packaged in simplicity.

## LESSON 2: A Digging Stick and Seeds
Sunday, May 29

Following a lunch of stew and vegetables, Denver led us across the road into his cornfield.

"A Hopi man cannot see himself as Hopi without farming," he explained. "Of all other spiritual practices in our culture, farming is the most sacred. It is the ultimate test of our faith. Will an individual accept Great Spirit's way of life or not? It is the final spiritual discipline, for farming requires ultimate acceptance that mankind—that means you and me, are really at the mercy of nature."

He placed a finger on each of our chests.

"In order to benefit, we need to respect Earth Mother and blend with her. That is what it tells me." Denver then lifted the staff I'd often seen him with. "This is my digging stick," he explained. "Everything, at least in our family, is done with our hands. We hoe, plant, weed, and harvest with our hands. Our water comes from the clouds. We blend with the ground we work. It is something we have done all our lives. It is something we enjoy. It makes us feel good and helps us understand farming's role in the ceremonial part of our culture. The two go hand in hand," he explained.

I glanced around his field. It appeared endless.

"It is for both man and Earth, bringing balance to each. For the man, it is a place to escape to find peace, meaning, and tranquility. For Earth, it holds its sacred balance in place and rewards the man in the same spirit with which he tended it. A Traditionalist farmer undertakes their work without the use of machinery. How can a man blend with his land when his hands are not in it? No—he must gradually blend with his land. That way everything works in harmony. Our hands are in the dirt; we understand our land, and it understands us. This is why Hopi can grow crops where no one else can.

"I tell young men: Never call yourself Hopi. It is for others to decide if they deserve to be called Hopi. If they still farm as their father and grandfather did; if they accept the Creator's life way, maybe they are Hopi."

Denver led us to a dry, caked patch of soil. It appeared to have been untouched for some time. Its surface was hard and cracked from lack of rainfall. Biscolli and I were taught to drive Denver's digging stick into the earth. The staff—about four feet long, was worn smooth, brought to a fine gloss through a lifetime of repetitious stabs in the dirt. I didn't underestimate the talent it took to bury the staff into the caked soil, and took great care in learning the technique from Denver.

I accepted the digging stick and took a stab at the earth. At first, the soil only splintered, but it eventually yielded under my persistence, and I dug a hole roughly a foot wide and six inches deep. When sweat ran down my face, I'd hand the staff to Biscolli, who, in turn, would hand me a handkerchief, and I'd wipe my face. As I dug, Denver explained that a digging stick is the only tool of a Hopi farmer.

"A farmer's digging stick comes from a straight branch of a hardwood tree. It will last many years. Any tree will work. We grow wild desert oaks here," he said.

"Corn is planted in rows, five steps apart. The same goes for melon and squash. Beans and other crops are planted two steps apart."

I continued to dig holes twelve inches deep and just as wide. After half a dozen holes, Denver checked my progress.

"Fine," he said, "but where will you put the seeds?"

"In the hole?" I asked.

My answer must have struck Biscolli as funny because he let out a chuckle.

"Now, now. Wait a minute," he said, stretching his hand toward Biscolli. "Your friend is half right."

Denver placed his sure hands over mine.

"We'll dig a recess in the bottom, like an Emergence hole. See here?" he said, sending a stiff jab to the bottom of the hole. "Imagine the large hole is a sacred Kiva and the seeds come up from the small emergence hole."

"There, that works fine," he said. "If it were early April, we would put ten seeds in the recess, then fill the hole with earth to within two inches of the ground surface. This way the seeds have their shared energy to emerge. When the young shoots are a foot high, we thin them to four or five stalks per hole," he explained.

"A Hopi farmer depends only on rainfall to water his crops. We'll leave a two-inch lip here," he said and created one for one of my holes. "This permits rain to accumulate in the hole, which, in turn, seeps into the soil. Do you understand this?"

"Yes," I said, nodding my head.

"Planting every two to four steps allows moisture in the soil to distribute evenly to each plant. Our field is not over-planted so there is sufficient moisture."

After a long while, I stopped my digging and studied the three additional holes I'd put in the earth. They looked pretty good. I handed the stick to Biscolli and spat onto my hands. The work had raised blisters on them. I wondered if Hopi men ever wore gloves.

Biscolli had a much harder time mastering the tool, which fit neither his height nor his hands. He dug his own holes. I supervised with my hands crossed over my chest.

"You'll have to make your own digging stick," I mused. "Denver and I will share this one."

Denver grinned and admired the holes the two of us had created. Biscolli and I stole a glance at one another, hoping our work for the day was done. Denver must have caught our look, as he gave a knowing nod before turning and heading toward the house.

I thought I'd wait for Biscolli until I turned and found he was digging the dirt from the bottom of his boots with his fingernail. I laughed and ran to catch up with Denver.

That night, sunburnt and blistered, I crawled into our makeshift bed and nestled into the cocoon of Biscolli's arms. Before I could breathe "good night," I was asleep.

# 26

# GUARDIANSHIP

**LESSON 3: The Migration**
**Monday, May 30**

Our Fathers agreed to the simple life of Great Spirit and received the two tablets of stone. As instructed, each of the four races migrated to their portion of the clean earth. When the red people arrived on Turtle Island—now called the Continental United States, Great Spirit visited them again and divided the set of tablets between the two sons of our leader. To the older brother was given a corner of the tablet, and told to go eastward toward the rising sun of Tibet. Upon reaching his destination, he was to immediately start looking for his younger brother on Turtle Island.

"The younger brother was given all but the missing corner of the tablets and instructed to migrate throughout Turtle Island, marking their footsteps as they traveled so the older brother could track him. Both brothers were told that a great white star would appear in the sky when the elder brother had reached his Eastern destination and had begun his search for the younger. When the star appeared, the younger brother was to stand fast and settle whatever land he happened to be on, remaining there and following the covenant, until the older brother found them, shortly before the next great purification.

"The younger brother traveled throughout Turtle Island—to forests, lakes, jungles, lands of ice and northern lights, settling and migrating until the great event in the sky. Our fathers were Anasazi, and Third Mesa in The Rocky Mountains is the land they stood fast upon and settled when the star appeared. Hopi became our name. It means 'Peaceful.'"

Denver adjusted himself in the kitchen chair and continued.

"At Third Mesa, our people scratched out a simple life with digging sticks and pouches of seeds, just as Great Spirit had instructed. The land blessed us tenfold.

"Our Fathers were also told that one day Bahanna—or white man, would come to Turtle Island and try to take our land and lead us into their ways. Great Spirit told us to always hold on to our ancient knowledge and to our land—and always without violence. If we succeed in doing this, Great Spirit promised that the renewal of Earth Mother would begin here, at Third Mesa, and radiate outward, infusing a spirit of love and peace over her as it spread.

"My friends, I will tell you again so there is no mistake—just as we knew the day of Bahanna would come, we knew the day to share the knowledge in our protection would come. In my prayers, I have asked Great Spirit to send two messengers who would radiate outward the teaching to our brothers and sisters of the other three races, that they might remember and reclaim their responsibility to Earth Mother once again."

Denver extended both of his hands across the table to where Biscolli and I sat.

"Thank you both for listening to your hearts and coming to assist us."

The Elder's words landed like a chunk of cement on the table. I searched for Biscolli's leg under the table with my other hand, then squeezed it. He glanced towards me. His pupils were dilated.

**LESSON 4: Communication with Plants**
**Monday, May 30**

After lunch, school reconvened in the field. As we took the short walk across the road, I said a quiet prayer. I really didn't want to dig any more holes today. I was sure my hands—and their blisters, couldn't hold up to another beating. Once we were deep in the cornfield, Denver tapped his digging stick into the ground.

"A Hopi farmer knows the spark of life is in all creation. Spirit is in plants like it is in us. We see every tiny green life as an individual creation, and we hold it in deep regard and affection. In turn, it rewards us with bountiful crops.

"We will start with energy," Denver announced, situating Biscolli and me so we faced one another.

"Come on, stand close to your friend. I know you two like one another," he said. "Now, let your hands touch." he instructed, "And close your eyes.

"A man's eye captures most of the information his senses send to his brain. We must still the senses to feel energy." As his voice trailed off, we did as we were asked. I could feel the weight of Biscolli's hands pressing against mine.

"Now friends, ever so lightly, pull your hands from each other. Eyes still closed," he added. "Go to the point you feel the energy pull away, then merge with it again. Feel your energies."

I felt Biscolli's hands lift off mine. At first, all I felt was the weight of them leaving, but then, as he brought them close again. I felt it!

"Did you feel that?" I asked, excitedly.

"Just a sec… I want to play with this."

We began intentionally moving our hands, feeling the energy flow in waves, corresponding directly to our movements.

"Friends, do not confuse energy with Spirit. It is Spirit that enlivens the body and gives it its spark of energy. What you feel is energy—the River of Life, not Spirit itself."

"Wow! That's wild," I said. "So is the energy responding to our intentions?"

"Yes," Denver confirmed. "Now, open your eyes. Still, feel it?"

"No," Biscolli said, disappointedly. I shook my head in agreement.

"You will with practice."

The Elder then placed his hands on either side of a long, slender corn leaf. "Now let's try it with this life."

"Whoa," I exclaimed. "Won't that be harder?"

"What's the difference?" Denver asked.

"Nothing I guess."

"All right, I'll try," Biscolli, said.

I watched as he placed his hands along either side of a leaf and closed his eyes. After a moment, he grinned, but then, the smile left his face and he opened his eyes.

"I thought I felt something. Though, I'm not sure. If there is something there, it's much weaker."

"Ah, your friend is a smart man," Denver said, looking at me. Biscolli grinned, then winked at me.

"Communication goes on between living things all the time. It is how life supports life. What affects one life form affects others. How can I believe as a man that I am the only life form with energy, feelings, and intelligence? No. Great Spirit has plenty to go around. Animals have it, and so do plants, just lesser amounts."

I nodded my head.

"Every life on this land depends on my attention," he continued. "Plants can grow with soil and rain just as a man can grow with food and water. But to flourish, they too need love and attention. Each day we spend time together. I touch them, I talk to them, I pray over them and I sing. Always, I sing," he repeated.

Biscolli grew excited. "I've read about experiments done on plants! They respond to voice, music, meditation, and prayer. Seems I remember seedlings grew fifty percent more when prayed over."

"Really?" I said, and thought of my many orchids, and how I talked to them each week as I set ice cubes in their pots. Did some part of me know to do this?

"Yeah, I guess the high-frequency electromagnetic waves of voice and music stimulate the tiny pores on a leaf's surface. Apparently, it opens them and the plant can absorb more nutrients."

"I don't know about all that," Denver replied, shaking his head at the scientist. "I just remind them they are healthy and beautiful and full of nourishment. I ask them to be plentiful and to feed my family. In return, I sing to them—I share a story or a new joke. They always mature early, give us great yields, and are full of flavor."

Denver began to slowly walk, extending his hand to touch the tender leaves of the young corn. We fell into tow behind him.

"I treat everything alive as my equal. I take them into my confidence. I learn what I know by watching, touching, and loving them. I sing to them and pray over them."

He stopped and turned to face us.

"The life spark is in the plant—I just love it into abundance. The secret of life is that we are all interconnected. Plants are alive. They experience life with roots and leaves. They feel the wind brush against them, the rain bathe them…"

"Dogs that piss on them," Biscolli added, nearly choking in his hurry to make a joke.

"Dogs piss on them," Denver repeated, laughing.

We played with the energy we detected amongst the plants and ourselves for the next hour, and then Denver encouraged us to find a field where we could be alone with the plants to sing to and pray over them.

I'll admit, I was self-conscious at first. I'd only ever talked to orchids—and that was in private, but noticed as I prayed, the energy around me increased. Before long, I was talking about my kids, and—once all inhibition had blown to the wind, I entertained the corn with my version of Keira Knightley's, "Lost Stars."


**LESSON 5: Microcosm of the World**
**Tuesday, May 31**

"So the four races went their four directions to learn their Guardianships. When they arrived at their destinations, Great Spirit visited them and gave them instructions that would enable them to blend with the new land and celebrate life. He also gave the four races a handshake, so when they met again, it would be a sign to the other race that they had remembered his teachings and had come to share the knowledge they had learned of their Guardianship with the others.

"Great Spirit said, 'Your pattern of life is to become so infused with Earth Mother that you became One with her. You are not to waste or abuse her in any way, but walk gently upon her face and resolve life issues in such a manner, as you do not inflict pain or abuse on your brothers and sisters. You are to live in fellowship and harmony with all life. Look behind you as you step, and leave nothing along your trail that will scar or harm Earth Mother or each other.' This was Great Spirit's instructions.

"It was further explained to the red race that we were the Keepers of the Covenant, and the piece of tablet we had, was to be reviewed often so generations would remember our vow of simplicity and jurisdiction to guard, protect, and hold all land and life in trust, until Great Spirit returns.

"As people in the four directions repeated this pattern day in and day out, through the months, years, and centuries, peace resided in our hearts, and Earth Mother was held in balance.

"We understood from our tablets, that the first visitors to our village would come as turtles crossing the land. One morning our people woke up and looked out across the desert sunrise. As we did, we saw Spanish Conquistadors coming, covered in armor—like turtles across the land. This was the fulfillment of a prophecy, so we went out to the Spanish man and extended our hand hoping for the handshake that Great Spirit had given them. Instead, they dropped a trinket into it.

"We knew they had forgotten the handshake and the sacredness of all things. This told us hard times were ahead for the earth and its people, so we turned to the prophecy on our tablets. It said that if we could remind them, then there would be peace on earth. If, however, they did not remember and gather with us to share our Guardianships by the time the other races came to Turtle Island—and before a black ribbon stretched from east to west across the land, then Great Spirit would grab the earth with his hand and shake it."

Denver looked at our faces. I suppose he was checking for alertness or questions. He appeared satisfied and continued.

"Two things happened. First, treaty efforts were unsuccessful. Rather than bonding with this race, we were separated from them, which resulted in further isolation of our races and more forgetfulness. Second, a transcontinental black ribbon (road), running east to west, was completed. These became a sign to our elders that the First Shaking of the Earth was about to occur.

"The prophecy said that the First Shaking of the Earth would be so violent, that a bug would be shaken off the black ribbon into the air. There, it would begin to move and fly, and by the end of this shaking the bug would be in the air around the world. Behind the bug would be a trail of dirt that would eventually fill the sky of the entire earth, causing many diseases.

"So we know the bug moving on the land was the automobile, and The First Shaking was the First World War. In that war, the airplane came into wide usage for the first time. That was the bug moving into the sky."

I turned towards Biscolli at the moment he turned towards me. There was recognition in his eyes.

"Our Fathers heard of a peace attempt on the west coast of Turtle Island. They heard there was going to be a League of Nations in San Francisco, so our Elders gathered in 1920 and wrote a letter to Woodrow Wilson, asking if the Indian people could be included in the League of Nations.

"The League of Nations circle had a southern door—the yellow people; a western door—the black people; a northern door—the white people; but the eastern door was not attended. At that time, the United States Supreme Court held that reservations were separate and semi-sovereign nations, and not considered part of the United States; only protected by it. So they did not invite us, and the Native people were left out of the League of Nations. The circle was incomplete. Our Elders knew that peace would not come on the earth until the Circle of Humanity was complete—when all four colors sat in the circle and shared their teachings. Only then, peace would come on earth."

Denver paused.

"My father was an Elder by then. We knew this was a sign that things in the world would speed up, culminating with an end to the Fourth Cycle. A cobweb would be built around the earth and people would talk across this cobweb called a telephone. We knew when this talking cobweb was built around the earth, a sign of life would appear in the east, but it would tilt and bring death, and it would come with the sun.

"The sun itself would rise one day, not in the east but in the west. So, when we saw the sun rising in the west, and we saw the sign of life reversed and tilted in the east, we knew that a Great Death was to come upon the earth. This was a sign that Great Spirit would grab the earth in His hand a second time and shake it. This time, the shaking would be worse than the first.

"The sign of life reversed and tilted, we call the Swastika, and the rising sun in the east was the rising sun of Japan. These two symbols are carved into our stone tablet. When we saw these two flags, it was a sign to us that the earth was to be shaken again."

Denver paused again.

"Let me say here friends, that the grossest misuse of the fire Guardianship by the white race is called the Gourd of Ashes—the atom bomb. The prophecy says that the gourd of ashes will fall from the air, making people as blades of grass in a prairie fire, and that nothing will grow on land it has touched for many seasons.

"Now, we wanted a conference with the United States concerning the gourd of ashes when we first understood the meaning of this prophecy back in 1920. We were given no such audience. Had we been allowed to enter the League of Nations, we would have foretold its coming then. Our people tried to contact President Roosevelt and ask him not to use the Gourd of Ashes because it would have a great effect on the earth and perpetuate greater destruction at the Third Shaking of the Earth—a Third World War.

"The prophecy said after the Second Shaking of the Earth, a House of Mica would be built on the east coast of Turtle Island. It said that it would be a house where all the nations and peoples of the earth should come. It was called the House of Mica because the building would shine like the mica on our desert. We knew the United Nations was the House of Mica, and that all the peoples of the earth should go to it. So our people met and discussed this.

"In 1949 we wrote Woodrow Wilson and did not receive a response, so we agreed we would go to the House of Mica because we thought if we did not go, things might get worse. So, in 1949, a number of us drove to New York City. We went to the United Nations front door and said, 'We represent the indigenous people of North America, and we wish to address the nations of the Earth. We offer you four days to consider whether or not we will be allowed to speak.'

"Four days later, we came back and they voted to let us in and hear what we had to say. The United States is one of five nations within the United Nations with a veto power, and they were concerned because our sovereignty was strong, so the United States vetoed our entrance. This action told us other happenings described in the prophecy would occur on Earth.

"We knew the United Nations would not bring peace on earth, but that conflict would continue and deepen world confusion. We knew little wars would worsen and become more plentiful. We knew we would see a time when an eagle would fly high in the night and land on the moon.

"We knew when this happened, many of our Native people would be sleeping—they would have lost their teachings as if they were frozen. We knew the eagle flying high would bring the first light of a new day; the first thawing of spring for the Native people of Turtle Island.

"The Eagle landed on the moon in 1969. When that spaceship landed they sent back the message, 'The Eagle has landed.' When we heard those words, we knew this was the start of a new time and a new power for Native people," Denver said with conviction.

"The prophecy says when the eagle lands on the moon, power will begin to come back to us. Within seven days of Eagle's landing, the Freedom of Indian Religion Act was introduced into the United States Congress. Eventually, it was passed in 1978."

Denver looked into our faces again.

"I understand this is a lot in one spoonful. What I am sharing with you is contained on our tablets. For there to be an understanding of how we got here, is important. Later, I will share how we get through the Narrow Gate of Time we are in, but first things first," Denver said. He waited for our confirmation and then continued.

"The prophecy says there will be two great uprisings by black people to free themselves. We have seen one in 1965. There is a second, more violent one. We are witnessing that today. The black people will be released then, and this is also going to have an effect on Native people—a good effect, for we are brothers.

"These are the physical manifestations of the spiritual prophecies that we have," Denver explained. "Now, you are going to see things speed up. People on the earth will move faster and faster. Grandchildren will not have time for grandparents, and parents will not have time for children. It will seem like time is going faster and faster.

"I advise you, that as things speed up, you two should slow yourselves down. The faster things go, the slower you two should go.

"Great Spirit has shaken the earth two times to remind us that we are a human family, and to remind us that we should have greeted one other as brothers and sisters. We had a chance after each shaking to come together in a circle that would have brought peace to Earth, but we missed that opportunity.

"The sign for the Third Shaking of the Earth is what we call the House in the Sky. A house will be built and thrown into the sky. When you see people living in the sky permanently, you will know Great Spirit is about to grab the earth again, this time, not with one hand, but with both hands. In 1973, Sky Lab was launched. It fell to earth in 1979. A second space station now orbits above us.

"Great Spirit has warned us twice, but the third time we stand alone. We have had two warnings to sit as four races and share the truth of our Guardianships, but we are alone in the third.

"We say at that time, there will be cities in this land so great that when you stand in them you will not be able to see out. In the prophecy, these are called Cities of Stone. At the center of each and every one of these cities will be Native people, and they will walk as hollow shells. We said hollow shells because they will have lost their traditional understandings, they will be empty within.

"After the Eagle landed on the moon some of our people began to leave these cities of stone and come home to take up some of the old ways and make themselves reborn. But many did not.

"Now I will say one last thing," the Elder said, weary. "Over time, the races in the four directions began to forget their responsibility to Earth Mother. One by one they began to take up foreign ways and be lured into selfishness and greed.

"What I am saying, is that Hopi Traditionalists eventually assumed the entire burden of world balance. Now our numbers are dwindling. You saw our number at the assembly the other evening. These are the ones who work to keep Great Spirit's life way alive. Without it, the balance tips, and the Fourth Cycle closes.

"Now, listen closely." He said, earnestly. "Hotevilla has become the microcosmic image of the world. What changes or violations take place here, are reflected and amplified in other parts of the world. To predict what will happen in the world, you need to look no further than this village. If our rights are being abused, if the land is taken or spoiled, if an affinity for influence or greed manifests itself in Hotevilla, be sure it will happen elsewhere. This is why we so firmly refuse to take on Bahanna's ways.

"Do not push us," he said, raising his trembling finger to us and looking into our eyes as though we represented mankind.

"Our men have been forced to fight your wars. We have been forced into your schools. We work in your factories and become dependent on your economic system. We have taken your vaccinations. Leave our reservation, our fields, and our promise alone! Can't you see, we hold to our ways as much for you, as for our own people?"

I couldn't hold back my tears. This was too much to swallow. I scooted back my chair and excused myself from the kitchen table. My heart broke for these people. I couldn't begin to know what'd been imposed upon them for generations—all they'd endured for our sake. I felt ashamed for any thought I'd ever entertained about the meager means of Native Americans. I'd always respected how close they were to the land but had no idea the promise behind it.

I went outside and sat on the front porch step. Bahanna—my ancestors, came to Turtle Island and insisted these people take on our socially acceptable ways. We scorned, harassed, and jailed them into conforming. All the while, never bothering to ask why they didn't want to become "white."

We'd jinxed ourselves—the joke was on us. We'd succeeded in bringing about our own demise by diminishing the number of Traditionalist Hopi who, alone, have held the balance of the world on their narrow shoulders.

I heard the door behind me open... and close, then saw a handkerchief. I closed my fingers around it, and Biscolli lowered himself to the step. He swung an arm around me and leaned me towards him. I sobbed. He pulled the hairband from my long braid, freed my hair, smelled it, and then kissed my head.

It had been a long, heart-wrenching morning and we all needed a break. Ancient prophecies etched on stone tablets had been thrown at Biscolli and me like hot coals. I kissed Biscolli, rose to my feet, and let him know that I needed a moment. He squeezed my hand and I turned toward the dirt road. It felt good to move. I wanted desperately to think of anything else but the prophecies. It was too sad to consider. My son, Stewart, popped into my head and I visualized him pounding away on his keyboard in London and managing a team of software developers. I wondered if he missed me.

On previous trips to the desert, I'd spend a few days in Santa Fe, New Mexico before the drive to Albuquerque and the flight home. On both trips, my kids thought to have a fruit basket waiting in the hotel room for their mom. I'd kept in touch with them during those trips—and they knew when and where I'd be enjoying a bed and long soak in the tub, after fishing the San Juan for a week or more.

It dawned on me that my kids had no idea I was on the Hopi Reservation. I'd last contacted them after my session with Lolita. So much had happened—so quickly, since then. They knew better than to worry about me—I'd taken retreats before. This trip was closing in on three weeks though. I'd told them—and Linda, two weeks. Another day or so without checking in and they'd be worried. I'd try to see if there was a cell signal out here, but chances are, they'd just have to wait a couple more days to hear from Mom.

I heard an awful racket up the road and picked up my pace to check it out. About sixteen crows were scraping and pecking away at a pile of corn cobs, kitchen scraps, and weeds. I put my hands on my hips and shook my head. The old man did it. The arrangement with the crows worked!

Lunch was in full swing when I returned to the house. I soon learned that in the Mahema household, it was customary for everyone to be present for meals. A place had been set for me, so I took a seat and dished up a serving.

**Tuesday, May 31**

"This is going to be short. I've been writing all day—taking notes on everything Elder Denver is teaching us. A hand massage would be nice, right now. Anyway, I wanted to jot down a couple of highlights of the day so they're handy.

When the Spanish Conquistadors came to America it was a fulfillment of prophecy. They'd forgotten the handshake given to them by Great Spirit. This tipped off the red-skinned people that the knowledge of their promise to the creator had been forgotten by others, and they knew sorrowful things would begin to happen.—It's fascinating how they had prior knowledge of a transcontinental highway, the automobile, and airplane, both world wars and the atom bomb. Which makes me wonder what they know of a Third World War—and what that would look like.

Denver predicts it will occur if the four colors of people don't come together and share the knowledge of their guardianships, restore balance to Earth, and live in fellowship and harmony.

The plight of these people—of all of us, is more apparent—and urgent, with each successive lesson by the Elder. God help us."

# 27

# DIGGING HOLES

**LESSON 6: Blending**
**Tuesday, May 31**

We began our afternoon session on a patch of ground we'd not yet visited. It was an area near the sheep pen. Within the pen, about eighteen sheep wandered about. There didn't appear to be much to graze on, so I assumed there must be an adjacent field for that purpose. Not that I was trying to second guess my elderly instructor, but this setting had all the earmarks of talking to the livestock.

When Denver knew he had our attention, he cleared his throat.

"I have had my travels. As issues arise, I have traveled from Hotevilla to bring about some resolution. When I was in the east, Bahanna said to me, 'Look here, a soft bed. Look here, a television. Look here, restaurants.' Then they led me to a telephone and said, 'Look here a telephone. You can call anyone on it.' Now tell me friends, who am I going to call?"

I burst out laughing and Biscolli about split his shorts. It did sound pretty ridiculous. When the humor passed, Denver continued to walk and led us over a knoll. Sure enough, it was an open range where the sheep grazed. We hiked a ways further and then Denver stopped us. When he had done this, he closed his eyes and became very still.

I recalled many times I squeezed a little shut-eye in my day, so waited as the elder rested. He was very old and I wondered if resting was one of the things he came to his fields to do as well. Another moment passed and Denver said with closed eyes, "A hawk is in the southeast sky."

Biscolli and I looked at one another, puzzled, then looked up. Sure enough, gliding ever so effortlessly above us, was a red-tailed hawk. Denver opened his eyes.

"You knew he was there, didn't you?" Biscolli asked.

"Yes, I felt him."

"How do you do that?" I asked. "How do you see without using your eyes?"

"Everything alive is part of everything else alive. I feel him," Denver said, then retied the red bandana he'd wrapped around his white hair—bluntly cut straight at his cheeks, then walked us to a shady spot under a snarled oak tree. We sat.

"Great Spirit's instructions to all people were to become so infused with Earth Mother, that we became One with her," Denver explained. "In addition to these instructions for all, Great Spirit gave earth Guardianship to the red race."

The Elder paused and turned to me.

"Describe 'One'."

"One is all there is. No more, no less," I answered.

"You learn this in your Bahanna schools?"

I'd given thought to my response and it seemed reasonable enough, so I stood by it. Not a wise move when you're in school with the last remaining elderly Elder, whose people have been told to BE One.

"One is not something you have. It is something you are. To Hopi, Oneness means there is nothing but that which you are. It is total awareness there is only you—yet, the moment a Hopi realizes this, they cease to be One, for they have stood beside themselves to observe their own Oneness. Oneness is no separation. Hopi do not have a relationship with Earth Mother; they are Earth Mother."

"Now, when I tell you I have left this land to travel, it is only half true. A Hopi never leaves the land, because he is the land. This is not something we think about. It is not something we can try and make happen. It is a gift as he lives Hopi."

"I think I understand," said Biscolli. "You're saying you are the dirt."

I thought that was a rude way of putting it, but apparently, Denver found the humor in it.

"Yes, that is right. I am dirt." He smiled. "A Traditionalist Hopi follows the simple path because it is Great Spirit's way. We know this way is what has kept the world in balance. We will continue, but Great Spirit asked all to blend and infuse with Earth Mother. We will see what your spirit remembers, all right?"

Denver took my hand and led me into the sunlight. He explained that he was going to walk about twenty paces from me and move about in a circle. My instructions were to point in the direction I felt him to be.

Before he turned away, he had me close my eyes and focus on becoming very still. I recalled my own "brain-dumping" exercise and tried to let go of my thoughts and direct all my attention to my third eye—just above the bridge of my nose. I nodded my head when I felt prepared.

Denver said nothing as I tried to pinpoint his whereabouts. It was hard and I failed. We did the experiment another nine times. I was wrong more than I was right. I returned to the shade tree. Biscolli was then led to the same area and given identical instructions. I saw the two of them grin a couple of times in the distance and assumed Biscolli must be catching on. When they returned to where I rested in the shade, our lesson continued.

"In the wind are airborne specks of everything it brushes against. Listen carefully to the wind. It can become your eyes."

Denver led me back out to the range. This time, he led me to various spots and asked me to describe, by the sound of the wind, what surrounded us—where the trees, rocks, hills, and grass were. I couldn't do it.

"With practice, you will do this thing. We can become more aware with our eyes closed than open. All life is to be loved and respected by other life. Blending is more than sharing a planet. The true nature of blending is only realized when there is no separation between us. We are one of The One—circles of The Circle."

Walking back toward the house, I thought of Spirit Eyes, and heard her words in my mind, "If Señora practices this stillness, she will become familiar with Great Spirit."

After dinner, the table was cleared for rummy. Clint brought out the cards and I played until I couldn't keep my eyes open. I crawled into our bed of blankets not understanding how these people could get by on so little food and even less sleep. Back home, I was a nine-hour girl.

**LESSON 7: The "IF" Factor**
**Wednesday, June 1**

"There are three parts to the tablet: its prophecies, its warnings, and its instructions," Denver explained. "Great Spirit gave us many prophecies to pass on to our brothers. All, including the House in the Sky, have come to pass. In 1998, a permanent space station was put into operation after the first sky lab fell to earth in the late seventies. This is how we knew the time had come to reveal the last warnings and instructions to mankind.

"We were told to settle here in Hopi Land, which is on the backbone of America—where we would meet with Great Spirit and wait for our older brother who went east, to return to us. When he returns to this land, he will place his stone tablet beside ours to show that we are true brothers.

"When the Guardians of Fire invented their Gourd of Ashes and the House in the Sky was fulfilled—when leaders turn to deceptive ways instead of Great Spirit, then we are told the Fourth Cycle will end if they do not heed to the Original Teachings that instruct all races to become so infused with Earth Mother that they become One with her.

"My friends, we are told of three helpers commissioned by Great Spirit to help the Hopi bring about peace on earth. We are told they would come to help us and that we should not change our ceremonies, our homes, or our hair, otherwise, the helpers might not recognize us as Hopi. So, we have been waiting all these years for our helpers.

"Prophecy says if the three helpers fulfill their sacred commission, even if only one Traditionalist Hopi remains who is living the ancient religion of our Anasazi fathers, then the scales shall be tipped and the Fifth Cycle will begin without the cataclysmic purification. This is because the people will have learned to be One—to be human beings with peace, rather than animals with no peace.

"Earth Mother will renew itself as it was in the beginning—flowers will bloom, wild game will return to barren lands, and there will be an abundance of food for all life. This is because selfishness and greed will have turned from the hearts of mankind. As you know friends, there is enough now, but selfishness and greed stand in the way of a new world.

"If the three helpers either refuse their commission or fail, the Fourth Cycle will quickly come to an end and Earth Mother will renew herself without our volunteered assistance. If that occurs, there will be mass destruction just as there was at the close of the Third Cycle.

"Now, I have said all along that the teachings of Great Spirit were never intended to be a secret. The flood survivors who were turned to four colors and went their four directions, originally held Earth Mother in balance. As long as they practiced the instructions of Great Spirit, the balance of Earth Mother was maintained.

"At this time in our history, the Traditionalist Hopi have assumed the entire responsibility of maintaining the balance. This will no longer be the situation when the three helpers arrive to assist us. The responsibility will then be shared."

Denver leaned forward on the table and in all soberness said, "Our three helpers are first—the yellow race of people, the ones with the Guardianship of wind who were sent to the south into the land now called Tibet. You will note Tibet is in the mountains where magnetic energy is most powerful.

"Second—the black race of people, the ones with the Guardianship of water who were sent to the west into the land now called Kenya. You will note Kenya is in the mountains where barometric pressure is low.

"Third—the white race of people, the ones with the Guardianship of the fire, who were sent to the north into the land now called Switzerland. You will note Switzerland is in the mountains where the air is thin.

"These are our helpers in the closing days of the Fourth Cycle. We invite our brothers and sisters to remember the promise made to Great Spirit by their fathers who survived the flood, and return to the Original Teachings of the Guardianship they received, and each to send a helper to our land."

## LESSON 8: Gratitude
**Wednesday, June 1**

Denver trudged across the dirt road like a man on a mission. Meanwhile, Biscolli and I waddled along behind like a couple of ducklings out for an afternoon excursion. When we eventually caught up with the elder, I knew exactly where we were, and I didn't like the looks of it. We were back at the holes we'd dug on Sunday. I inspected my blistered hands. They were barely scabbed.

"Do you remember your words?" Denver asked. The question jarred something from my memory. We'd been given homework.

"What were those words?" I pleaded with myself. I turned to Biscolli, hoping to be rescued. He was biting a corner of his lip and staring at me. We're in for it, I thought.

"First word: Attitude," he said, reminding us.

When he said the word, it sounded vaguely familiar. I searched my mind for a second word and came up with gratitude. Yet, when I repeated it to myself, it sounded so close to the first that I doubted myself.

"And the second?" Denver inquired. I was about to admit I didn't know when the word popped into my head again.

"Gratitude?"

"Yes, gratitude."

"Whew," I sighed. And then looking down at the dozen-or-so holes we'd dug in the ground, I couldn't figure out what gratitude had to do with holes.

"When a Hopi plants, he must be in good humor," Denver stated. "He should have no unpleasant thoughts, certainly no anger. A Hopi farmer sings and talks to the seeds he has hidden in earth's womb. He encourages them to come to the earth's surface. If his heart is heavy, he will convey this to the tiny lives in his care and protection, and they will not be filled with joy.

"Whatever attitude an individual has when he tends his crops will affect his crop's health and yield. I tell Hopi, 'Begin your day with Great Spirit, and offer up gratitude each morning before you begin your work.' After a morning talk with Great Spirit, it is easier to carry out his wishes for the day. It is easier to find goodness in everything."

The Elder handed me his digging stick.

"Let's dig a hole with a heart grateful for this land, the corn it will produce, and the happy bellies of those who will eat the corn," he offered.

I didn't want to do this—anything but another hole, I confessed to myself. I even tried to hand the stick back to Denver, but he refused. There's a certain tragedy in knowing a hundred-year-old man could do the work that deflated each of my petty excuses.

Reluctantly, I took a firm hold of the thing, counted to three, and rammed it into the earth. The staff refused my entrance and sent a vibration up its shaft and into my upper body that rippled through my arms and shoulders. The air went deathly silent. I took another hasty jab at the dirt. She held her ground.

From behind, I heard Denver whisper to Biscolli, "We'll let her work it out for herself."

I turned in time to see the two of them disappear from the field.

"Well, that's just great!" I said loud enough that I hoped they heard it. I dropped to my butt and sat in the dirt. A blister was oozing on my palm. I wanted to be anywhere else but here.

"Damn it," I said aloud, "I don't want to dig another damn hole. This is senseless. It's not like we're going to put seeds in them or anything. We're just digging damn holes!"

I was anything but grateful to be digging this hole and could think of a hundred better things to be doing besides beating up the ground—such as fishing.

I sat there in the heat of the afternoon, my shirt stuck to my back, trying to forget digging sticks by visualizing a slow river and a graphite fishing rod in my hand. I tried to forget holes—deep, dirty ones that an old man would expect to see when he returned, by making love to a deep green fishing hole. I sat and forgot, and forgot until all that remained was an exhausted fantasy and a plot of dirt with an angry girl, a digging stick, and two measly chips put in it.

I pulled myself to my feet using Denver's digging stick and let the blood work the tingle out of my leg, then walked to the end of the row to see if I could see signs of Biscolli or Denver. Clint was standing beside Biscolli, who was busy ramming a digging stick into the ground.

I dragged myself back to my patch of dirt and stared at it. The air had found my open blister and my hand stung.

"God," I cried, "What do you want? You want this for me, is that it? The life these people live is a hell of an existence, and I'm not so sure I'm cut out to live it. What do you want me to do? Dig this dirt? Sell my house and live in some hut, carve a digging stick, and dig holes the rest of my life? Is that what you want from me?

My eyes filled with tears. My hands stung. What'd God want from me anyway? God was riding my Montana hide like a wild stallion he aimed to break.

This was it—it was all over. I was done. The week of Mama's diarrhea seemed like a ride at the county fair. I'd worked long and hard for the life I had—put myself through school, served my country, raised four kids, and buried their father, I'd scratched out a decent life—a good life. I called the shots, traveled when I pleased—and fished.

At that moment, the good life struck me as kind of a painful melancholy. Beneath the layers of fear, frustration, and confusion driving it all, was a simple girl searching for peace.

I looked up at the sky, but all I saw was blue. I realized my answer wasn't in the sky. If Great Spirit was part of everything, then It was as much a part of me as it was the sky. I sat in the dirt, wondering what it'd all been for—all the books and retreats and workshops; all the purchases and latest technology and deals too good to pass up. All the boyfriends and prettying up for them, the bodybuilding, the moves, and the parade of jobs. Even my vision quest. What had I been looking for in them? Could I answer that? What have I been looking for? Was a part of me missing? Is that what I was trying to find? Why would I feel I wasn't whole... like something was missing? What sick, perverted message had I been feeding myself?

If all this was a part of me—if I was One with it, could I still tell myself something was missing—that I wasn't enough, wasn't good enough, didn't have enough? What part of me could be missing, anyway?

I picked up the digging stick and rolled the shaft of it back and forth in my open palms, then closed my hands around it. I looked back into the sky. Was I looking at myself? Could I believe that?

I began to cry, but not in a sad way. I'd melted, softened, yes… surrendered. The thing my parents could never get me to do. I'd dug in my heels all my life, staking off—protecting something I felt I had to defend.

Today, I had met my ego—had stared it in the face. I'd stared it down. It was a façade. In defending the identity that I thought I needed in order to know who I am, I'd kept the very thing from me that I was: All of this.

I WAS all of this.

I sobbed. Finally home. Finally at peace with myself. There was nothing to defend.

I felt a strength rise up in me. I felt supported in a way I never had before. So this was peace. It filled me until I felt I might drown in the beauty of everything around me—the sun, the wind, the rocks, and the earth. I heard Spirit Eyes' voice:

"Señora cannot believe until she accepts she is part of all that is, this includes her magnificence. Then she will know all things are magnificent, real, and possible."

"I'm sorry. I do love this land and I love you, Great Spirit, and I'm grateful to be here in the middle of this miracle. Even if it doesn't seem so right now, I am. I just don't understand how I'm supposed to make a difference—how I can help ease the burden of these people, of this land, and do my part. What do you want me to do?"

A thought filled my head—a simple, clear one.

"I'm not saying everyone should pick up a digging stick and scratch out a living on the land. That is the Hopi way. Just look at your life and see where you can simplify, come home to yourself, and welcome and respect all life as part of you. If everyone does their part, the impact on Earth will be greatly decreased. All she asks of you is to blend with, respect, and care for her. That's all."

I dug my hole.

### Wednesday, June 1

"It's been a very good day. I see how the prophecy fits together now. All of us from the four corners of the globe have the opportunity and responsibility to bring the world back to its original state of peace. And that starts with ourselves.

It is safe to say I'm having an awakening here at Denver Mahema's small ranch. The information is a timely miracle for our planet and to be on Hopi land to receive it is, well… as it should be. Hotevilla is an amazing place. It's infused with spiritual energy. I understand that this energy can be enlivened anywhere people love, blend, nurture, and sustain the land. People do not need to, and should not come to Hopi Land. This is their sacred home.

Denver has given me much to consider. He calls Biscolli and me messengers, but I find the work here is impacting my life in a dramatic way. I got an attitude adjustment this afternoon and when I spoke to Denver about it later, he said he could feel my spirit ask for it. Well, all I can say is thanks!

He also shared a little about their ceremonies. Though some are very sacred and not for me to know, he did say Hopi life IS attitude and gratitude. He gave me a couple of suggestions, which I'm noting so I can contemplate them:

Live simply.

Live as self-sufficiently as possible.

Lift a prayer of gratitude morning and night.

Touch Earth Mother with my hands; plant and maintain something alive and interact with it daily.

Step outside first thing in the morning, and take in the early sunlight, breathe deeply, and take in the air.

Before eating, thank the plant or animal that has given of itself to sustain my life.

Develop my own style of blending with the earth that encourages balance, moderation, and harmony.

Regularly contemplate Earth Mother and all life. Pray people will remember and renew their vows with Earth Mother. Honor the vows myself.

Practice sustainable living by limiting my consumption, reusing what I can, simplifying my wants, recycling, using up, and wearing out before I replace things.

Upon my departure from Hopi Land, I will do everything in my power to ensure Traditionalists and the Elders are left alone and untroubled to continue their jurisdiction in peace.

Well, Biscolli and I will leave Hotevilla tomorrow and return to Cortez. It's a five-plus hour drive. Perhaps we can discuss how best to distribute the information from the tablets. Guess I should contemplate that too, huh?

**Note:** Denver requested we meet him in his field at sunrise for our field lesson. I wonder what's up?"

**LESSON 9: Medicine Water**
**Thursday, June 2**

After we'd folded our bedding, Biscolli and I accompanied Denver outside to where Clint and Mark stood waiting for us by the road. The twilight air was chilly and raised goose bumps on my exposed arms. We were greeted by the dogs, but they soon lost interest in us and returned to their blankets behind the outbuilding.

Denver was the first to speak. He explained that typically, each man would head off in their own direction to pray to Great Spirit and visit with their crops. Today, however, the five of us would remain together for a sacred ceremony. I felt honored to be included in their early-morning ritual. I'd be lying if I said I didn't wonder what they did during their early morning alone time. And then I remembered our first morning here when I'd happened upon Clint as he was praying. Is that what we would do?

I knew this was time sacred for the men. I glanced at Biscolli. His squirrelly hair was especially wild this morning. He'd dressed in shorts, boots, and a wrinkled tee shirt that read: "Exercise? I thought you said extra fries." Rather tame, I thought. He looked tired and wondered if he felt the reverence among our group this morning. He returned a glance, and I could detect a similar sense of wonder growing within him. We smiled at each other.

Denver's digging stick—which was as much a part of his attire as the red bandana or work boots he wore, was nowhere in sight.

Instead, he had an empty quart-canning jar in his hand. Mark and Clint each had an empty Mason jar as well, which only added to my curiosity.

Denver led our small posse to the water pump where we'd first spotted Clint upon our arrival here seven days ago. He held his clear jar under the spigot and asked if Biscolli would work the handle. Biscolli gave it a few plunges, and a surge of water gushed into the mouth of the jar. Mark and Clint followed in turn. Their movements were slow and methodical, and I found myself mimicking their slow actions. The air was still. Not a word had been spoken other than Denver's instructions. As Clint's jar was being filled, Mark leaned over and whispered to the two of us.

"We will pray over the water and make medicine." This ought to be interesting I thought.

We fell into step behind Denver and formed a little procession, the men carefully steadying the open containers of water. The elderly man led us through the dark morning air to a cornfield. When we stopped, I recognized it as the spot where I'd stumbled on Clint's worship. Each took their jar of water and set it upon a small wooden produce crate. That done, they stepped back from the makeshift altar and knelt. Biscolli and I followed their lead and knelt in the dirt beside them.

Before long, the darkness we'd made our preparations in began to lift, and long fingers of virgin sunlight stretched across the land. And then, as if on cue, Denver sang.

"Great Spirit, who gives us this new day. Renew us with your strength. Touch these waters with your power. Gift them with your strength and light. Make them flow with shabda's life. To bless and heal all lives they touch."

The men remained in their reverent posture, suggesting each were having private time with Great Spirit. I took the opportunity to have my own conversation with God. One by one, heads lifted. When the sun had completely cleared the horizon, the men retrieved their jars and we returned to the house. It was Clint who offered an explanation.

"For thousands of years, our people have depended on Great Spirit's power to create medicine. One of our medicines is water touched by the rising sun. As Father Sun rises in the morning, the vibration it sends to the earth is strongest. This is when new life springs forth. This is when Great Spirit's power is closest to Earth. We make our prayer to Great Spirit as the sun begins to appear, and when we see the bottom of Father Sun clear the horizon, the strong vibration ends. Now we have fresh medicine."

"Clint?" I asked. "Your grandfather said something about shabda life. Did I hear that right? What's shabda life?"

He smiled.

"Shabda is the creative force found in all life. It is the current that extended from Great Spirit and formed all life. It is the unspoken language through which Great Spirit speaks to all Its creation. It exists everywhere and is in all things, enlivening them daily. Great Spirit does not watch Its creation from some far-off place, but Great Spirit is in each creation, and this part watches. It sees all, experiences all, having spread itself throughout the entire universe. Shabda is in the soul of every rock or mineral, every insect, plant, or animal. Every human."

What Clint was saying sounded familiar. Could this be the same power Spirit Eyes spoke of?

"On this current rides all truth, and is the intelligence carried in the elements—in water," Clint continued. "Because shabda is everywhere, so is truth. Within the makeup of each creation is truth in its entirety. With nowhere to go and no time separating man from Great Spirit, all exists in this single moment. Here and now is all there is. People run everywhere looking for truth. The secret is to stop all seeking to find it. Shabda is what we listen to when we still ourselves."

"I see. That's beautiful and makes so much sense. Thank you, Clint."

"If you would like, we can have a conference about our water," Clint said.

"Yes, that would be wonderful."

Clint motioned for me to follow him to the living room. I tugged on Biscolli's shirt and waved for him to join us. When we were seated, Clint began to share his understanding of water.

"We are all creators. Great Spirit continues to create through us. Water is the connector. Water connects plants, animals, birds, humans… all living. It circulates through us—all of us. I understand some of the water on our great mother is as old as 4.5 billion years. And, friends, that has been circulating—constantly recycling through all life.

"The idea that there is a separation between races, nationalities, or species is erased with this awareness. We are all one living consciousness connected by water."

"And there's no life without water," I added. I'd always had an affinity for water, and was happy we were having this conversation. Clint nodded and continued our conference.

"You may have noticed the planet is going through changes—we are going through changes as well. All will adapt. We live and are connected to Earth Mother, and share a consciousness with her. Water is her blood. It seeps deep into her soil and is purified by her rocks. It then surfaces, is picked up by the wind, and carried to the clouds to circulate again."

I could see Biscolli nodding out of the corner of my eye.

"The wise thing about circulating water is that everywhere it flows, it collects information. The water you pumped into our jars this morning, is intelligent. There is nowhere water has not been. If you pay attention, it will share its information with you. Think about it, if water is in you—and it is, this information is in you as well."

I knew it! I knew water was special. I certainly didn't know any of this, however.

"One more thing," Clint added. "Water is alive and responds to human emotion. We are peaceful around water and treat it with respect and reverence. Unkind emotions are unhealthy to water. If we were to pour three glasses of water and each wrap our hands around our container, each water would hold a different emotion."

"Fascinating," Biscolli responded.

"Now, consider we humans are containers of water. Do you think emotions—ours and others, do not affect us? Unhealthy water can be restored again, with kind emotions intentionally sent to it. This is especially helpful before drinking water—perhaps bless it with your love."

**LESSON 10: The Close of the Fourth Cycle**
**Thursday, June 2**

When breakfast dishes had been cleared from the kitchen table, Biscolli and I sat back down in our chairs and I joined Denver for our final day of school. It was a bittersweet moment for me, knowing we'd be leaving for Cortez today. I set my journal on the table and prepared to write down today's lesson.

"As I said yesterday, the remaining Traditionalists work to keep Great Spirit's life-way alive and maintain earth's balance. Without it, the balance tips, and the Fourth Cycle closes.

"Now these are the nine signs that will occur before the closing of the Fourth Cycle: White-skinned man will come to Turtle Island. They will take land that is not theirs and strike their enemies with thunder. The land will see a spinning wheel filled with voices cross her face. A strange beast with great long horns will overrun the land. The land will be crossed by snakes of iron. The land will be crisscrossed by a giant spider web and rivers of stone that make pictures in the sun. Seas will turn black and many live things will die because of it. Men will become women, women will become men, and youth will wear their hair like our people. Man will learn the code for life and make two where there was one. And, there will be a dwelling place above the earth, which will fall from the heavens with a great crash, appearing as a blue star when it falls. These are the signs that a cleansing is pending. All have occurred."

Biscolli and I turned toward one another at the same moment. I could read the concern on his face.

"Two separate but equal happenings are on the horizon. First, the close of the Fourth Cycle. Second, is the Third Shaking. The close of the Fourth Cycle has begun. Our tablets clearly showed two paths the end of the Fourth Cycle could take. One led to physical cleansing of earth's surface by way of her elements: fire, water, and air—and the destruction that must inevitably occur. The second led to a vibrational cleansing, by way of our global family moving from low vibration energy of fear—and intentionally raising it to love. Either way, Earth Mother would cleanse and restore herself, and raise her vibration.

"In 2020, our people understood that a tipping point had been reached. The COVID assisted in that. Humanity slowed down and had time to contemplate the state of their lives. Collectively, humanity made its choice. The path of vibration had been chosen, and the cataclysmic events of a physical cleansing had been diverted. Earth is now being cleansed of corruption, cruelty, injustice, and anger. It does not happen overnight."

"Elder Denver," Biscolli said, "Excuse me, but nothing in this world even remotely suggests we've been moving the needle in the direction you're talking about. In fact, things seem to have become worse since 2020."

"You are correct in your observation, my friend, but are overlooking the fact that a large ship takes a tremendous amount of ocean to make a turn. Established ways of being and attitudes have been in place for thousands of years. What you are witnessing is the rising of corruption, cruelty, injustice, and anger, so it can be dismantled. That is how a vibrational cleansing occurs. Chaos is the first stage of rebuilding. The energy of old things becomes free."

Denver paused.

"When the shed for our sheep became fragile, we had to take a hammer to it before we could build a strong new structure. Earth has moved into a period of chaos. The old structure is being torn apart as a new one is being built simultaneously. This new structure will be the one we have envisioned was possible. At its heart is love, respect, and equality.

"We may not like it, but chaos will exist for years—decades. It will be a time of challenge, as old structures dismantle themselves. But, no matter the outer appearance, the fate of Earth Mother and her inhabitants is peace. New solutions and resources will rise. I think that we are all in agreement a vibrational cleansing is far more desirable than a physical one using Earth Mother's elements."

"I pray to God you're right," Biscolli replied. "Your people know this for certain—we've diverted cleaning the earth through natural disaster?" But there are still so many natural disasters—in fact, they've increased in number and intensity. It seems there is no hurricane or fire 'season' any longer. We're just pounded by storms, rain, floods, earthquakes, eruptions, and fires."

"Earth Mother is clearing her density. Natural disasters, as we call them, are her way of clearing density and rising in vibration. Remember, the close of each cycle is a complete cleansing. Individuals, governments, lands, and cultures, are all clearing their density, and leaving behind the cycle of animal with no peace. Earth Mother will be thorough in her cleansing. Still, I think we can agree, it is better than total destruction by her elements."

We all took a deep breath—Denver, I suppose, from explaining a lifetime of knowledge to two newbies, and we, from the magnitude—and implications, of what was being discussed. I excused myself and got a glass of water. Biscolli winked at me, so I pulled a second glass and filled it as well.

Denver was silent for a long time. He then leaned forward onto his elbows. This had become his position for serious news. I leaned forward as well to fully grasp what he had to say.

"I am old and will soon move on to rest my bones with my ancestors. I have waited only for the message to be carried to our brothers and sisters. I can now go. It is fortunate for us that Earth Mother spoke to you, dear True," he said, looking at me. "Much movement can take place in the hearts of mankind when they receive this message."

"Now my friends, when the blue star fell, it signaled a Third Shaking would visit the earth. The offending nation will come from the west and her symbol will be red. It will be cataclysmic, but many will survive.

"Listen carefully," he continued. "Remember war is a choice. A body of thought carries a strong vibration. It is thought made into action. Any death will be a choice on the individual's part, and one made before their birth into this life. Never confuse death as an accident, mistake, or misfortune. It is the choice of each spirit.

"Do not despair if you are among those who perish. You have lived through death before—as spirit, none of us die. Life is a cycle of birth, death, rebirth. People may lose their body, but never their spirit. They will come back.

"Always remember, the prophecy says if the three helpers fulfill their sacred commission, then the scales will be tipped in the favor of peace. Our brothers and sisters have the responsibility to remember their guardianships and come together to share their knowledge in peace. It appears mankind is forced to ask the question: Will we remember our sacred promise to come together or will we choose war?"

I tried to take in the gravity of what the elder was saying. I wanted to be sure I understood, so asked for clarification.

"Denver, are you saying that a third world war is imminent if the yellow, black, and white races do not come together and share the knowledge of the respective guardianships they were given?"

"Yes. If we could have come together back in 1920, we could have had a great civilization by now, but it didn't happen. At any time along the path of these prophecies, we could have come together. We still could!" Denver exclaimed.

"The three helpers that Great Spirit said he would send, need to be told we are waiting for them. They need to remember their commission and step forward—they need to slow down and come together so we can share our guardianships and live by the Original Teachings that balance Earth Mother and balance all life that lives on her.

There may be a squabble, but they can cushion the Third Shaking of the Earth and make the transition into the Fifth Cycle easier on all of us.

Biscolli placed his hand on my back and gently moved it between my shoulder blades. He then removed it and leaned forward onto the table. The three of us—eldest elder of the Hopi people, a six-foot-three inch archaeologist, and a mom of four, eye to eye. What now lived between us was an understanding. It was a sober moment. Each now knew what was at stake—and what we must do.

There have been times in my life when I haven't wanted to do something—a thesis in college, tracking down financial or legal documents, elective oral surgery. I've procrastinated, pushed deadlines, and made my share of excuses. When I assumed care for Mama, that all changed. There was no putting off anything. My mantra became, 'You can do this, Sweetie,' and I'd just go ahead and do it.

On the table in front of me was a journal. I'd picked up the journal with a green paisley print on it, for my vision quest. It had now become the one written testament of a 103-year-old Traditionalist Hopi, holding together a handful of committed people, and a planet. His shoulders didn't look near broad enough for such a feat.

As if right on cue, Spirit Eyes' words visited my mind: 'Who are you to not be brave? You were born for this.' I slid the journal to the center of the table and placed my palm on it. Biscolli turned to me, then placed his hand on top of mine. Our eyes met Denver's, and he placed his strong, mahogany-colored hand on ours.

"When you two leave here," Denver said. "ask every person regardless of who they are, young or old, native or non-native, to wake up and learn everything they can about the Teachings, and then act on them. Can you do that for my people?"

Biscolli and I gave our word of honor to the elder.

**Thursday, June 2**

"Though I have recorded the prophecy in its entirety in this journal, I thought it wise to make a list explaining the symbols found on the tablets for reference and clarification. Okay, here goes:

Thunder = guns

Spinning wheel = covered wagon

Voices = pioneers

Long horns = longhorn cattle

Snakes of iron = locomotive train

Giant spider's web = phone and power lines

Rivers of stone = highways

Pictures in the sun = heat vapor rising from highway

Black seas = pollution

Men will become women, women will become men = sex changes

Youth will wear their hair like our people = youth revolution

Code for life = DNA

Make two where there was one = cloning
Blue Star dwelling place = space station
Third Shaking = World War III
Three helpers = the black, yellow, and white race"

We've also learned that the tablets are buried somewhere on Third Mesa. Oliver's message makes sense now. He said the land held a secret, and it'd been protected because people saw this place as worthless miles to cross. Indeed, people's blindness had protected the tablets and the people who'd been living its covenant since the great flood. Wow!

Denver Mahema is an extraordinary man. He has tangoed with time and has beaten the odds against longevity on the mesas. With each successive year, he has built a remarkable storehouse of knowledge and wisdom, which he has readily shared with anyone who has been willing to slow down enough to listen.

His sight is receding, yet he sees with a clarity few ever achieve, and he can dance the pants off anyone given a deck of rummy cards. He has kept his mind quick and his laughter alive. He knows when to speak and when to hold back and let life speak for itself.

The old one has a power and strength about him that comes up from the dirt he knows himself to be. He is a rare man, indeed."

When the last of the clothing Eva had so generously cleaned for us, was tucked into our bags. Biscolli and I knelt by Denver's kitchen chair and said goodbye to our dear friend. His white hair glistened in the room's afternoon light and lifted the familiar twinkle in his dark eyes. Eva pulled her hands from behind her back and put a woven pouch about the size of a coin purse, into our hands.

"I have been weaving these for you two. Now you have your own medicine pouches," she said.

Mark explained every Hopi has a medicine pouch. In it are the things most dear to him, a feather, a rock, a crystal, things dear to his heart.

"Like a token from a friend," I said, remembering my first moments with Denver.

"Yes," he said with a grin.

We squeezed hands once more and then Clint and Eva walked us to the front door. I scanned the sparse three-room home once more and thanked Eva for the gift. Biscolli and I got a robust hug from the short, gray-haired woman, and then Clint walked us out to the car. I thanked him for picking up the slack around the ranch so his grandfather could spend time with us. He leaned into me and whispered, "He has been praying and waiting for you. We all have. Please, get us some help."

We embraced then he leaned back toward me and said, "Thank you, friend, for wearing the shield around your neck. The shield symbol with its four circles in the four quadrants, means, 'Together with all nations we protect both land and life, and hold the world in balance.'"

That said, the soft-spoken Hopi turned and walked away. All at once, I knew it was true. Spirit Eyes was Hopi.

# 28

# PROPHECY

The car engine stopped and I came awake. "What? Where are we? Are we here?" I asked, rising from the reclined passenger's seat.

"Highway 160," Biscolli answered, unbuckling his seatbelt. "We're still two hours out of Cortez. Just stopping to take a leak, Babe."

The drive from Hotevilla, Arizona to Cortez, Colorado was a long five-and-a-half-hour trip. I had to take a leak, as well. We were in the middle of nowhere, so why not? I raised the passenger seat from its reclined position and looked out the window. Sure enough, nothing but desert for miles in all directions. Directly in my line of sight was Biscolli relieving himself; but beyond him, off in the distance, I could make out the hazy outline of mountains. Was it the San Juans?

I freed myself of the seatbelt and took the opportunity to squat and relieve myself on the shoulder of the road. I giggled to myself… just me and my man, peeing in the middle of BFE. I giggled again. This was nothing new, I'd squatted nearly a thousand times hiking the Pacific Crest Trail.

Biscolli studied the landscape and finally said, "I thought that once this turns into Highway 64, we'd stop for something to eat. Sound good?"

"That'd be great," I said, pulling up my wrinkled shorts. We piled back into the car and I refolded the shirt I'd been using as a pillow.

"Hey Babe, are you planning on sleeping all the way there?" he asked, pulling the car back onto the lonely highway.

"I don't know," I answered, recalling that Biscolli had slept both directions of our Chihuahua flights. "I've just felt wiped out since we left."

"It's the energy there," he said. "Remember when Denver said Hotevilla was the microcosm of the world? Well, he said it with good reason. Clint told me that uranium mineral beds beneath Hopi land have served as one of the electromagnetic anchors of the world for millennia. When the uranium decays it releases alpha particles which interact with air molecules, knocking off electrons and creating ions in the process."

"Hold on!" I interrupted. "I don't know what you just said. Reign in the scientific jargon, please. What does that mean?"

"The land they sit on literally anchors the planet so it remains on its axis. If that land gets disturbed the planet will do just as Denver described, and shift its axis."

"No way!"

"I'm serious as a heart attack, Babe."

"I thought they didn't want backhoes in there to protect the tablets and to keep utilities off the land. You're telling me, they're trying to protect radioactive mineral deposits?"

"That's right! But remember, there used to be a coal mine in one of the other villages."

"My God, you're right! I remember Clint saying that."

"The land was seriously disturbed. In addition, the water used to run the slough for the mine lowered the water table. That's why Denver's pond had no water."

"Why didn't you point that out to me when we were there?"

"What good would that done?"

"Biscolli, that's for me to decide; please don't just not tell me things, okay?"

"All right. Point taken."

As if the situation at Hotevilla wasn't already bad enough, now there was this to consider. Biscolli added another comment, but I didn't hear it. I was thinking about the situation that the Hopi—and the rest of us, were in.

"Is this a good time to talk about the prophecy?" Biscolli asked.

"The what? I said, still lost in thought. "Oh. Oh, yeah. Sure. Now would be great. Thanks."

"Have you thought how we're going to distribute the message?"

"Hum… I'm not sure. I've been wondering about it a lot, though. I'm glad we're talking about it."

"Yeah, me too."

I mentally scoured my contacts, trying to come up with a friend or client who was an author or publicist—someone who could be trusted. Whomever we used—if we went that route, they couldn't exploit the Hopi or incite a caravan of people onto their land. I opened my phone and began to scroll through my contacts.

As I did so, it occurred to me that we'd been riding a giant synchronistic wave of events. I stopped scrolling and thought about it—I panned over the events that'd landed me in the passenger seat of a car returning from Hotevilla. I felt certain that we were going to be okay. And that's what I chose to share with Biscolli.

"Yes, I agree. I don't think we have to have all the answers, but we should at least have a direction."

"Considering everything that's happened to get us this far, I suspect something's formulating as we speak," I said. "We know what we want—to get this out there. How about I jot down all the ideas that pop into our heads, knowing any one of them may be the route? What do you think?"

"Yeah, that's a good idea," Biscolli said, as he glanced towards me and smiled.

We pulled up to a funky little diner at a wide spot in the road. Someone had haphazardly nailed old barn wood halfway up the front of a building sadly in need of paint. A hand-painted sign hung above the entrance. I eyed Biscolli, who was easing into a parking space. Apparently, we were going to eat at "Ace Tavern." It was rough, at best.

The only sign of life at the road junction was two eighteen-wheelers idling to the side of the diner in an open side lot. As we walked toward the screened door, Biscolli waved his hand toward the big rigs.

"Truckers. That's a good sign."

It was a dark, grimy place that smelled of rancid grease and liquor. There was no evidence of overhead lighting, just half a dozen windows shaded by red gingham. A couple of neon beer signs raised a glow on what must've been the remainder of the barn wood from outside nailed to the interior walls. Above us, the dingy white tongue-and-groove ceiling was covered with hundreds of soiled baseball caps. If there was overhead lighting, it'd most likely been swallowed up in the mass of caps. My bet was that customers took off whatever cap they were wearing at the time, and the hottie behind the counter over there, tacked it to the ceiling.

I wanted to hear the story behind the caps—I'd ask her; but for the moment, all I cared to know about the greasy spoon was that it had a place to wash up. I returned from the ladies room and found a booth. While Biscolli fed the jukebox with quarters, I took the opportunity to call Linda.

"Tell me you're alright," were her first words. I assured her I still had all ten fingers and asked if she could pick me up at the airport on Sunday afternoon.

"You sure know how to stretch out two weeks. Where have you been? Are you still in Mexico?"

"Sorry Sis, No, I'm in Arizona. I've been off-grid," I said, trying to calm her down. She asked if I'd send my itinerary, which reminded me I also needed to give my departure info to Biscolli. We'd return the rental car and stay at the Archaeological Campus when we returned to Cortez, so I'd need a ride to Durango to catch my flight.

I hung up the call and heard country music coming from the jukebox. It was Old Dominion's 'Do It With Me.' I smiled, then scoured the place to find Biscolli. He was at the counter talking with the hottie, who was holding a ball cap in one hand and a staple gun in the other. I located the bareheaded trucker the cap came off of at another booth, wiping his beard with a napkin.

I figured Biscolli was just as curious as I was about the ball caps, and was getting the scoop. I leaned back, outstretched my legs on the padded bench, and passed my time by reading logos on the dusty ball caps overhead. I couldn't help but occasionally glance at the counter and watch Biscolli. I had to admit, he was a damn handsome man, and it was fun to observe him at a distance. At last, the staple gun hottie sent him back to our booth with two plastic food trays. He handed me the yellow one.

"I ordered your burger without mayo. I know you're watching your waistline," he chuckled. "By the way, aren't you a little on the light side for a soldier-bossing fitness trainer?"

"COVID. It took its toll on me," I said, lifting the dry bun from the meat to see what I was eating.

"Ohhhh…"

Just then, Hottie delivered our drinks. "How ya doin' here?" she asked, her eyes on Biscolli.

Since I was invisible, I let him answer for both of us. Her flirtatious giggling went on for a few seconds, and then her boss wised up and jerked her short leash. Moments later she was propped behind the counter again, pouting.

I busted out laughing. She was so predictable. Biscolli tried to hide his laughter—I supposed not to add insult to injury. Eventually, even he couldn't contain himself, and it took minutes before we settled down enough to choke down our food.

I looked up at Biscolli.

"You do realize I'll be flying home. What are we going to do with this?" I asked, gesturing my hand between the two of us.

"I know…" He met my eyes. "I know." He paused a moment, then stared into my eyes.

"Have you done a long-distance relationship before?"

"Yes. It's not ideal. But…"

"Well, it's what we've got. I'm in Cortez… that is if Eric doesn't fire me and Collier doesn't 'off' me."

"Well, that sounds cheery," I said. "That's not a real possibility, is it? I mean, the Center is your life, and Collier wouldn't be that stupid, would he?"

"I don't know what I'm walking into, Babe. We'll find out soon enough." He reached for my hand. "Look, fate brought us together. We can create whatever we choose to create. I'm in if you are."

I got up from my side of the booth and scooted next to him. I set my hand on his leg, and then, in one swoop, he lifted and set me on his lap.

"Whatever you decide, I'm good," he said. I kissed him, then lowered myself back onto the seat beside him. Miss Hottie walked up and slammed our check onto the table, gave a huff, and marched off. Biscolli and I turned to one another and broke out laughing.

**Friday, June 3**

"Biscolli and I are en route to Cortez. As I write this, I'm struck with the realization that this journal contains the Hopi's message—and is the only record we have of our lessons with Denver. I'll feel a whole lot better when we get it copied and into the hands of a publisher or whomever we're supposed to work with.

I'm actually excited to return home—it's time. I miss the mountains, river, and trees. Biscolli and I had a talk about us. Do I want a long-distance relationship? I don't know. I do know he's planted in my heart.

The truth is, I keep thinking about Nee-yaa-nu. I know it's silly. I just wonder if he's alive and looking for me. Spirit Eyes said I'd know it when I met him. If Biscolli is Grandfather Maa-pu, that means, he's not Nee-yaa-nu. What am I supposed to do?

I still wear the medallion Spirit Eyes gave me. She's Hopi. I'm sure of it.

I got a text from Dan—something to do with Mama's house. Hope it's still standing when I get back. Anyway, soon enough! Guess that's it for now."

It was about 8 PM when Biscolli rounded the final bend of the three-quarter mile dirt driveway into Red Rock. He swung into the graveled parking lot as though he had done it a million times. The dust raised by his speedy entrance was still floating in the air as we got out of the car. I stretched and then took a look around. The grounds were quiet.

It was only my second visit to the campus, yet it felt uncommonly familiar. Perhaps it was because it was home to diggers like Biscolli and André, or maybe it was just one step closer to my own home. Either way, I was glad to be here. Biscolli was off doing something, so I walked to the edge of the property. The view at dusk was exquisite.

I heard footsteps and turned to find Biscolli. He'd used the men's room in the mechanic's shop. He explained that most of the students were long gone.

"Spring term just ended. It'll be a week or so before we get a new rotation of students... happens every year. We use the first week of June for annual cleaning, so the labs are in shape for summer. That's when it gets crazy around here. We get a new round of students and a flood of volunteers. They should be cleaning this week," Biscolli explained.

We grabbed our bags and walked to the front door. It was locked. We walked to the other set of doors. They were locked as well. We dropped our bags by the door and walked to a side entrance. Locked. There were a couple of additional cars in the parking lot but, oddly, no one was here. It appeared everything but the combination gate Biscolli had used to get into the maintenance shop, was locked up tight.

"What the hell?" asked Biscolli as he rattled on the final set of double doors we tried.

"What do you think is going on?" I asked, becoming concerned.

"Beats the hell out of me."

"Well, do you have a key? Can we get in?"

"No, I don't have a key! Why the hell would I need a key to this place when I'm in Mexico?"

"What should we do?" I asked. "Can we call Eric?"

"Babe, Eric lives here."

"Oh… I'm just trying to help."

"I know… I know."

Biscolli looked at me. I could see he was searching for answers.

"None of this makes sense. Even with Raven Creek closed someone should be around. Hell, the staff live here."

"We can still call Eric. He could meet us here."

"Hum… you know, you're right."

"Good. Let's call him."

"Shoot, my phone is dead."

"What? You could've charged it in the car."

"Well, I never figured we couldn't get in when we got here."

"I knew we should've called before we drove all the way out here. What do we do now? You can use my phone. Do you know his number?"

"Come on, Babe. Do you know your boss's phone number?"

I was really tired, but for Biscolli's sake, I held my tongue.

"There's the mechanic's shop."

"Look, you sleep on the greasy shop floor if you want. I'm getting a motel. We can settle this in the morning when we've had some sleep. Aren't you tired? You did all the driving."

"Yeah, you're right. I just can't figure out what the hell's going on."

"We're not going solve this tonight, Honey. Let's get some sleep. It's only thirty-five minutes back to town."

"Let me at least leave a note so Eric knows I'm back. We'll stay at that motel… the one you stayed at."

"White's"

"That's the one. Hey, Babe, do you have something I can write on?"

I opened the glove box and pulled out a meal receipt. Biscolli scribbled a note and wedged it into a doorframe.

We pulled into Cortez as the sun was ready to set. Shadows were fading, much like my patience. We were back in Cortez—back to fast food, ATMs, and traffic lights. It'd been a long day and I was overdue for a bath and a firm bed. I was sure Biscolli was spent too.

I woke to the sound of Biscolli stirring in the motel room. "What time is it?" I asked, still groggy.

"About five-thirty," he answered. "I can't sleep. I'm going out for coffee."

"Is everything okay?" I asked, only half-concerned.

"Yeah, I've just got a lot on my mind. Sorry, I disturbed you," he said and kissed me.

I pulled him back for another kiss, then grabbed the pillow from his side of the bed and covered my head. At about seven-thirty, I got up, dressed, and put on a bit of makeup.

Biscolli wasn't back yet, so I thought I'd walk to the coffee shop and meet him. I assumed he'd chosen the one just catty-corner to the motel, so I strolled over to it. I recognized it as the cafe I'd had coffee in the morning I hurried out to Red Rock. I looked around to see if Claire was on—she was. I asked the hostess to seat me at one of her tables.

"Hi Claire, remember me?" I asked, fully expecting she wouldn't remember me from any other tourist.

"Yeah! You're the pretty lady with the five-dollar tip. Am I right? Are you still around here?" she asked, sliding the breakfast menu into my hand and pouring a cup of coffee.

"No, back again."

"As I remember, you were looking for Leo. Am I right?"

"Right on two counts. Claire, you're one sharp gal."

It took that long for me to register the word "Leo." When I had, I abandoned my chit-chat with Claire and turned my head to scout the room for Biscolli. There were no blondes seated in the diner.

"Claire," I said looking up. "Is Biscolli—I mean, is Leo here?"

She smiled back at me and took a quick sweep of the room. "No Darlin' He was here earlier. He sat at one of Marie's tables. But I don't see him now."

"How long ago was that?" I asked.

"Well, I came on at six, and he was here then. I'm not sure… business has picked up. I can ask Marie if you'd like."

Normally, I would have let it slide, but we hadn't coordinated when we'd leave for Red Rock. I assumed he was probably getting in touch with someone who could let us into the Campus. Maybe, he'd even gotten a ride out there? No, he wouldn't have left without me. Besides, I recalled seeing his bags in the room when I left.

"Yeah Claire, that would be great if you wouldn't mind."

"Have you had a chance to look over the menu? I can drop off your order when I go back to the kitchen."

"Sure, your special," I replied, without bothering to look at the menu. "No hash browns."

"Be right back," she said pulling the menu from my hand with a big smile.

I tapped on the door of the men's room and peeked inside while waiting for Claire to return. There was no sign of him. I sank into the booth. Within moments, Claire stepped up to the table accompanied by a waitress in her late twenties.

"Sugar, this is Marie. Go ahead Marie, tell her what you told me." I wondered what all this was about.

Marie slid a pen into her ponytail and said, "I thought it was kind of funny that Leo left in such a hurry. We let him run a tab here, but he never leaves without saying goodbye."

"What? Where was he sitting?" I asked.

"Right over there at number twelve," Marie said, pulling the pen from her hair and gesturing toward a booth about six down from mine.

"Mind if I look?" I asked, already starting to get up.

"No, go ahead."

"And how long ago was this?" I asked, feeling a knot growing in my stomach.

"Twenty... maybe thirty minutes max."

"Damn," I whispered under my breath.

"I haven't cleared the table yet," Marie called toward me. "We've been a little busy."

By now, other customers were looking on. When I arrived at the correct booth, Marie called out, "Stop." I poked around the messy table. Sure enough, it looked like Biscolli had eaten here. Table scraps were everywhere. I happened to glance at the floor. There was a book. I crawled over the seat and fished around the floor. It was a book all right—the one I'd read in Chihuahua. My boarding pass for our flight was tucked between the pages.

'What the hell?' I wondered.

I returned to the two waitresses, who by now had their own worry.

"Did he leave with anyone?" I asked Marie.

"Like I said, one minute he was eating breakfast, and the next I knew, he was gone. No tip—that's not like him. Do you think something happened to him?"

"Now, don't let your imagination run wild," I said, trying to keep them calm as my own mind was searching for an explanation. "He probably got ahold of Eric," I said.

"Eric from the Campus?" Claire asked.

"Yeah."

"I don't think so," she said, shaking her head. "Eric was in here… what do you think Marie? The day before yesterday? They all came in—the staff, I mean. He said they were headed to Utah. Leo wasn't with them."

"No, he wouldn't have been. He was with me on… ah, vacation."

I called Biscolli's phone. The call went straight to voice mail. Ugh… I couldn't remember if he'd charged it last night.

A dozen dark scenarios raced through my head, each progressively grimmer than the previous. I had to get out of here. It suddenly occurred to me that the last time I'd been here, I'd left

Claire with unclaimed food. I slipped her a twenty-dollar bill and asked her to box it up. She handed it to me under the meddling glances of impatient customers.

"Thanks," I said, and she shoved a coffee to-go cup into my hand. A second later, I was out the door.

I had ground to cover.

The Malibu was still parked in front of the motel room. I unlocked our door. Nothing in our room had been touched. I called Biscolli's phone again—our room was quiet, so assumed he had his phone with him. I hurried over to the office to check if Biscolli had been by, but all I got was a blank stare from Mr. White.

I didn't want to cause a stir, but at the same time, I needed answers. The Campus was locked up tight, Claire knew nothing, and the desk clerk was absolutely no help.

I called Biscolli's phone again and left a message, then left him two notes: one inside our room and another taped to the door's exterior—in case he didn't have his room key with him. The note said to stay and wait for me here. Once the notes were in place, I drove to the coffee shop to check with Claire and Marie again.

Nothing.

I called Biscolli's phone again. Nothing. I hated to alarm the ladies but knew I needed directions to the police station. I asked the first face I saw on my way out the door, and they pointed down Main Street towards the second traffic light. I hopped into the car and sped off.

Just then, I thought of Cowboy Earl at the gas station, so drove the extra three blocks to the Chevron. It was closed.

Damn.

And I'd been in such a good mood when I woke up.

I growled... if I discovered Biscolli was just dinking around somewhere, I'd be pissed when I caught up with him. I tried to remember everything about this morning. What had he said before he left the room? What was he wearing? What did he have with him? It was all a blur—I'd been too groggy.

The only thing that stood out in my mind was hearing him say, five-thirty and that he couldn't sleep. Thoughts of Dan Collier entered my mind. I tossed them out, but they came back. I didn't want to believe Collier had gotten a hold of him. God, not that!

I pulled up to the Cortez police station, said a quick prayer, got out, and marched down the sidewalk toward the door.

Within seconds of mentioning Collier's name, I had the attention of a barrel-chested man wearing sergeant stripes. He sat me down in a chair and I covered what I knew with him. Biscolli had been gone from the diner less than an hour, and there wasn't much to go on. Collier or no Collier, I could see the interest drain from the sergeant's face.

I was adamant that he listen to me. Reluctantly, the sergeant filled out a report. I told him about the death threats and the video Biscolli had made of Collier and his men digging up the infant. He was aware of the video, they had a copy on their computer and a backup locked in their evidence safe.

The sergeant gave little credence to the death threats. It was evident Leo's name didn't carry much weight. I concluded that if it were Dan Collier the donut-dunker was looking for, he would've gladly given up a day's filing to search for him. But as for some digger who couldn't find his way home? Fat chance.

I did find out that Sheriff Turner had tracked Collier and four accomplices to Monticello, Utah. But that's where the trail ended.

The Monticello office received a tip that Collier had been spotted in Moab, just north of there, but that turned up nothing.

Sheriff Turner was getting fed up with the dead ends he kept running into. Collier was operating in his jurisdiction, and the fact he couldn't be caught was putting a serious damper on next November's election. The cocky front desk sergeant assured me they were in daily contact with the Grant County Sheriff in Utah. All believed Dan Collier wasn't stupid enough to hang around Cortez, even if he did believe Biscolli was in town. He promised to send a patrol car out to the Archaeological Campus, and I explained it was vacant.

"Well then, it looks like all we can do is poke around Leo's regular hangouts and see what we can dig up. Where are you stayin'?"

I'd heard enough. I got up from the fake leather chair, tossed him the motel receipt that Biscolli had stuffed in my pocket last night, and slammed the door behind me, exasperated.

"We'll be in touch," he called after me.

"Yeah, like hell you will," I mumbled under my breath. I left the building, climbed into the car, and leaned my head against the headrest to think for a minute.

Biscolli couldn't be far away. It'd been no more than ninety minutes since Marie had last seen him. I looked down Broadway Street, neatly trimmed with its wide sidewalks. Cortez was coming to life and it made my heart sink. Images of Biscolli came to mind—his head of unruly hair, smudged glasses, quick smile, and hearty laugh.

"Where are you Biscolli?" I called out.

It was almost nine o'clock. I put the car in reverse and backed out of the parking lot. As I drove from the police station, a terrible sense of dread hit me. A knot in my stomach followed. At the red light, I stopped, leaned into the headrest again, and closed my eyes. A headache was coming on fast. When the light changed, I took a left and pulled over. Was I getting sick? I sat for a moment and realized I was sweating. Closing my eyes again, a terrible thought hatched and burrowed itself in my brain. Something was wrong. Dead wrong. Was it Biscolli?

I pulled myself together and drove to the edge of town, then wove my way back to the motel, slowly crisscrossing the main drag. While passing through the City Market parking lot, I remembered Biscolli had once mentioned a woman in Cortez. He'd called her a friend but had never given her a name. Could he be there? I cursed him and swore if he turned up at her place after putting me through this, he'd wish he had been kidnapped. Or worse.

I checked the motel again. No Biscolli. Both notes were untouched. Twice a thought tried to surface, but each time I tried to grab onto it, it receded into my growing headache.

Where was he?

I scoured through the incidentals Biscolli had emptied from his pockets the night before. Nothing unusual. I grabbed his duffle bag and rifled through it. I didn't have a clue what I was looking for, but something compelled me to look just the same.

Still nothing.

What was eating at me? I dropped to the corner of the bed, baffled. What was it?

And that's where it hit me.

The fire started in my head—at my temple, and spread fast. In an instant, everything in the room began to sway. I was crazy on fire, burning. I tried to stand but the world began to spin. Life moved in and out of focus. The world went small—then big again, until it crushed what was left of me.

I was dead. It was dead. We were dead.

"Oh God!!" I cried. "The journal!"

I leapt from the bed and threw duffle bags, loose clothing, and magazines onto the beds. It wasn't here. I shook the bedspread, rifled through my pack, and pulled open drawers. I flew out the door and unlocked the car.

Nothing.

I popped open the trunk and ravaged through fishing gear.

"Oh sweet Jesus, help me!" I tried to retrace my steps. Think rationally, I reminded myself, but my mind was too consumed to think clearly. The journal… where did I put the journal? Think!

I was terrified. My journal wasn't here. It was…

"Oh, sweet mother of…" It was in Biscolli's satchel. And the satchel wasn't here.

'That's right,' I thought… the book I'd been reading was in the satchel—the same book I found under the table at the coffee shop!

The satchel had my journal in it, and the satchel was gone— my journal was gone! Oh, sweet Jesus, not the Prophecy!

Wait! Biscolli had the satchel. Where was he? Where?

NO, it couldn't be… No, he wouldn't have taken it… taken it and bolted. No, he couldn't have. He wouldn't have. Not Biscolli. I know him. I know him, right?

I slammed the trunk closed and staggered into the motel room. The moment the door closed, a sharp pain shot through my body. The harder I tried to get to the cool water in the bathroom, the faster the room started moving. The last thing I remember was the floor giving way under my feet and seeing the dresser pass by.

## 29

## JOURNAL

I became aware of a voice echoing in my head. It was muffled at first, then it took on a distinct voice and pitch. It was a stream of Spanish. It was in a woman's voice and she was hysterical. My head hurt and I couldn't see. I tried opening my eyes but they felt glued shut. A different voice—deeper in tone, then filled my ears.

"She's coming to."

I turned toward the deep voice and the Spanish began again, only this time it sped up. I winced at the sound of it. My head was pounding. I reached up to grab my head and managed to open my eyes. It was a woman—a dark-haired woman—the housekeeper, and her mouth was pelting me with Spanish. I closed my eyes and her face disappeared, but the punishing sound remained. Someone touched my face.

"True, are you all right? Hey, Sweetie... that's it, open your eyes."

I reached my hand up and banged it on something hard. Where am I? What stopped my hand, started my memory. I panned my eyes from the ceiling to the two faces above me, trying to figure out what this place was. Everything was hazy.

"Welcome back. How you feeling?" the voice asked. "It looks like you've been out for a while. Housekeeping found you. How you feeling, Babe?"

I tried to put a name to the voice. Biscolli? In an instant, it all rushed back and I remembered the satchel, the journal, and Biscolli.

"Biscolli? Biscolli? Is that you?"

"Sure, who else would it be?"

"What the hell happened to you?" I said, trying to sit up. Biscolli moved to accommodate me and leaned me into his body.

"Looks like you hit your head when you passed out. She says you gave her quite a scare," Biscolli said, turning to the source of the Spanish, which had thankfully stopped. "When I got here, we managed to move you to the bed. What happened?"

"What happened?" I responded. "What happened to me? What the hell happened to you?"

Biscolli turned to the housekeeper and said something in Spanish. I watched as the woman snatched up towels with one hand and grabbed a vacuum with the other. As she passed by the bed, dragging the vacuum behind her, she spilled out a steady stream of Spanish again and then pulled the door closed behind her with her foot.

"Unscramble this mess for me, will you Biscolli?"

"First things first," he said." Are you all right?"

"I'm fine! Now, where the hell have you been?"

"Well it's been a rather interesting morning," he said, leaning himself back against the headrest of the bed—with me in tow. "I couldn't sleep last night… wondering about the Campus. So when it got to be a decent hour I stepped out for something to eat."

"I know that!" I said impatiently.

"Please, may I continue?"

I lifted my head slightly and adjusted it higher on Biscolli's chest. It felt like a tree trunk. "Sorry. Go on."

"I'm eating my breakfast when, out of nowhere, this guy slides into my booth and shoves a pistol into my side. I think to myself, 'Oh shit. Here we go, one of Collier's boys.'

"The bastard tells me we're going outside. I figure, okay, get the jerk outside so no one else gets hurt. I grab my satchel and we go outside. It starts to look like he's taking me around the corner, so I make it look like I'm swinging the satchel onto my shoulder, and I go for the gun. It flies. Where? I don't know. I crash against the building and get slugged in the gut. Then out of nowhere, comes a punch under my jaw. I never saw it coming.

"Anyway, he somehow ended up against the wall. That's when I got in a couple punches. The blood started. He grabbed my arm and twisted, so it turned into a kicking match. Damn SOB had cowboy boots. I got my arm back but had no strength to punch, so I slammed him into the wall once, twice maybe. He was on the ground when I left. I headed back here but couldn't find my key, so went to Kamela's to tend to the cuts."

Biscolli was breathing hard as he recounted the fight, and I found myself nearly out of breath as well, just listening to him. He wrapped his arms around me.

"Now, what happened to you?" Biscolli asked. I tore from his arms, turned, and glared at him.

"I've been tearing Cortez apart looking for your sorry ass. Do you know the cops in this town don't give a rat's ass about your measly hide?" I stopped myself short. "Where's the journal?"

"I don't know. Why are you asking me? You're the one who writes in it. Where'd you put it last?"

"In your satchel!"

"What the hell did you do that for?"

"That's where I keep it. That's where I've always kept it! Tell me you have it."

"I had the satchel when I came out of the coffee shop. After that, I lost track of it. I don't know, True."

My head felt weak again.

"Cause if you don't have it… we're screwed!" I cried.

We stared at each other, feeling the gravity of the situation, but not wanting to believe the nightmare… not yet.

I scrambled from the bed and the room began to spin. Biscolli grabbed me and set me on my feet. I read the terror in his eyes, and it wasn't because I was dizzy. So, it was true. The Hopi's message was gone.

"Maybe it's still there," I shouted. "Let's go!"

Moving gently, Biscolli helped me across the street, and we combed the sidewalk in front of the diner and checked the back alley. Biscolli climbed into the dumpster and shuffled through breakfast scraps, napkins, and runny eggs looking for the pack. We drove to Kamela's.

The redhead looked immortal in the pressed white men's dress shirt hanging loosely over her curves—its sleeves rolled to her elbows. I wasn't sure Biscolli owned a white shirt—or ever had. I ran my eyes up and down him and then her again.

Kamela couldn't materialize the satchel and I liked our situation even less. There was no blaming Biscolli. Besides, he had troubles of his own. The guillotine had fallen, and my head was in the basket. I dropped to her sofa, closed my eyes, and thought about crying. I'd lost the only copy of a document that might save the Hopi—save our planet from catastrophe, for that matter. I asked Kamela for some aspirin and buried my face in my hands.

"Let's have another look around the back of the coffee shop," Biscolli chimed, trying to resurrect some hope.

I looked at him blankly. Forty-five minutes ago I might've suggested it myself. Now the idea seemed a fruitless use of energy. Something deep inside of me knew I'd never see the journal again. I swallowed the aspirin and closed my eyes again. The journal was gone.

I agreed to lunch with some misgivings. Biscolli swung into the Chevron station to gas up the car, and Cowboy Earl was right out to greet us. I didn't feel like visiting. My patience was spent.

"People talkin' about you," he called, walking towards the gas pump.

"Oh," Biscolli replied.

"They're saying you wer' in-a fight. Is dat true?"

"You know how people talk," Biscolli answered.

"Sounds like you did a fair job sendin' 'em to County Emergency."

"What'd you say?" I interrupted.

I could see Earl's mind scramble and try to pin an identity on the woman in Biscolli's passenger seat. I saw the light go on.

"You're da kooky tourist who chased Leo 'round da corner. Funniest damn thing I ever seen."

"Yeah," I replied, thinking I'd just as soon have Cortez folks forget I'd once chased "God" in a dirty white van. "Did you say he's in the Hospital?"

"Not no more. Sheriff's got 'em locked up. County put his nose back together," he said, turning his attention to Biscolli and jabbing him in the shoulder while, under his breath, saying, "Good job." He eagerly continued his narration, "Didn't take Sheriff Turner long to realize he had one of Dan Collier's boys right there in County. You didn't know dat?" he asked.

"No. Now how could I have known that?" Biscolli volunteered. "They've arrested him?"

"Yep. The sheriff went out to da Campus lookin' for you."

"There's no one out there," I offered.

"Oh. Well, then I'd be findin' Dale Turner." Earl then paused, and I could see he was doing some math in his head. "Maybe dat Collier boy with the knocked up nose is da one who's been comin' round askin' fer you?"

"You could be right. Good thinking, Earl." Biscolli said, handing him a twenty for gas. "I'll mention that to Turner. Thanks."

I turned to Biscolli.

"What do you think?"

"Let's eat, then we'll find out. Collier's boy is going nowhere," he said and started the car.

After lunch, we drove to the courthouse. Sheriff Dale Turner was in his office. We sat on cold plastic chairs in the lobby. A uniformed officer covering the reception desk excused herself and poked her head into the doorway of a glass-walled room to announce us. Between mini-blinds, I watched a dark-haired man tighten the knot of his tie, put out a cigar, return it to his mouth, and bite down on it. I felt sorry for the guy—living in a fishbowl.

The public servant then placed a black cowboy hat on his large head and, once he'd dressed for company, motioned through the glass for us to enter. The room smelled of cheap cigars. He rose from his wooden chair and it rolled backward, hitting a bookcase along the back wall. Its shelves were cluttered with mounted softballs and family photos. From the number of little heads in the pictures, it looked like he'd fathered a slew of kids. He extended his hand like a true politician.

The elected official was on the fast track to middle age and clearly didn't care. Biscolli informed him of our business and he invited Biscolli to stay. I paced the waiting area, then the parking lot. Did you know that takes three paper cups of water to raise an air bubble in a water cooler, and there are thirteen parking spaces in front of the Montezuma County courthouse? After pacing outside, I stepped back inside and sat in a plastic chair. Biscolli finally emerged from the fish bowl.

"Well?" I asked impatiently.

"It works," he said with a big grin. "I used thought vibration."

"What are you talking about?"

"Well, when I couldn't sleep last night. I decided to give this stuff we're learning a try. I focused all my energy on Collier. I visualized him being stopped at a roadblock, and then arrested. I played it out in my mind, as though I were watching a movie. I spoke to my guardian angel and said, 'Angel, if your job is to help and protect me, I could use you now,' then explained exactly what I needed—protection and Collier captured. I asked my angel to work with Collier's angel to generate whatever it'd take to get him into custody. After all, it's in everyone's best interest. Collier's too."

I nodded and thought of the sites, the lives, and the history he'd torn up.

"When I had a clear image of his capture, I held it in my mind, gave it all my attention, and felt how relieved and thankful I was he was finally captured. I did the same thing with the four guys that work for him. It took most of the night, but it worked. All five were arrested at a roadblock this morning.

"Wow, that's incredible. And what about the one who beat you up?"

"You mean the guy whose ass I kicked? Well, I'm not gonna pretend I liked fighting him. At least, I had some size on him. Still, I'd rather visualize a peaceful resolution than fight… damn cowboy boots." Biscolli winked. "Think about it, Babe. I'm no worse for the wear, Collier is behind bars."

"That's amazing. You visualized it? That was brilliant. I'm impressed."

"I just held the thought, gave it my attention, and was thankful—as though it'd already happened."

"Well, it's a good thing, 'cause I don't ever want to go through a day like this again."

"Yeah, I thought you'd appreciate it. It works, Babe! I tell you, it really works!"

"Yes, I guess it does."

"We should do the same thing to find your journal."

"I don't think so. I've come to the conclusion it's gone."

"How can you say that? It's somewhere. How can you give up?"

"I'm not giving up. I'm being realistic."

"Listen to yourself. You're giving up. Collier's arrest was no accident—I'm sure of it. He's been on the loose for two decades, and we both know where he's sleeping tonight. You're never going to convince me it's mere coincidence. It's a matter of perception. Check your perception, True."

He was starting to irritate me now.

"Hell, I'm more afraid your attitude will ensure the journal stays lost. Don't you want to see the Hopi message get out? I thought it was important to you."

"Will you back off?" I barked. "Look, I'm not the one who lost the journal. You go visualize it." As soon as the words left my mouth I could feel their sting. I knew they weren't meant for Biscolli—he wasn't to blame. I was mad at myself. He had poked a stick at my trouble—challenged me, and I had a lot to think about.

"Look, I'm sorry. It's not your fault," I said. "I just wasn't prepared for something like this to happen. I thought the wind was at our back like we were in the good graces of God, or Earth Mother. Oh, I don't know… I'm rambling now. I just want you to know that I don't blame you."

"Well, I take responsibility for my part. If we can agree we're both partly responsible for the whereabouts of the journal, at least we can move ahead unified, instead of undermining our strength. I think we need each other, now more than ever."

Biscolli took a step closer.

"Look at me, True."

I couldn't look, not yet—I knew I'd cry. I was a jumble of emotions. My nervous system was a wreck. I wanted to blow off steam as much as I wanted to drop to my knees and surrender. I knew I'd cry if I looked into his eyes. I had to be strong… I had to be.

"Sweetie, I know you've had to do things on your own, and that's a brave and honorable thing to do." He took another step closer. "I'm just going to say this because it needs to be said. I don't know what broke your heart, where you decided you couldn't trust, but you have to believe that I'm here. You may have broad shoulders, but they're not broad enough to carry this on your own. There are two of us for a reason."

Biscolli took another step and reached out his hands.

"Look at me, Sweetie. I have a handkerchief…"

I laughed and then beat my fist against his chest.

"This is so hard for me. People have either left or died. My grandma died. My husband died. Whose to say you won't leave… I'm surprised you haven't."

"First of all, look at me."

I took a breath and then looked up at the man I loved. The first tears fell from my eyes. Damn it…

"Now, listen to me. I'm not going anywhere. Whatever cosmic forces brought us together, are here to support us, but we have to believe that."

I took another long, measured breath, and composed myself.

"Okay. I know you're right. It's just a lot."

"I know, and we're going to do it together."

I leaned my weight into Biscolli and laid my head on his chest. He wrapped his arms around me.

"Babe, I have an idea. All you have to do is stand here. I'm going to slip my arms under yours, and I'd like you to give me all your weight. Don't hold yourself up… just let me have all your weight."

Biscolli bent his knees and slid his arms under mine. I then leaned completely into him, and then, still keeping my feet on the ground, gave up holding myself upright—let him have all my weight.

As I did so, I felt myself take back some control, until Biscolli whispered to me that he had me. I then fully let go and detected a sense of weightlessness. That remained for a moment and then, the strangest thing happened. The best I can describe it is my nervous system went offline—like rebooting a computer. When it came back online, there was a marked difference in the way I felt. The buzziness I'd just experienced had been replaced by calm. I'd been unplugged. I felt still. Quiet. I felt... amazing.

"I don't know what you just did, but I feel incredible."

"I don't know, maybe I still have a bit of Sky Way medicine in me? I just felt the urge to do it. What happened?" I described to Biscolli what I experienced, and he kissed the top of my head.

"Thank you. I love you," I said.

"I love you too."


While we hoped for the best, Biscolli and I took steps to duplicate the contents of the journal before it faded from our memory. We purchased paper and retreated to the seclusion of our motel room, ordered in Thai, and methodically went through our lessons day by day, painstakingly recalling and charting everything we could recall of our daily lessons with Denver. The prophecy, warnings, instructions, and field exercises were relatively fresh in our minds, and we replicated them in detail. It was well past midnight before we were satisfied the material represented the essential message the elder sought to convey to the world. I also visualized every detail of the unremarkable-looking journal and saw it as safe, protected, and on its way back into our hands.

# 30

# CEASEFIRE

I stirred awake to the sound of an emergency vehicle passing the motel and found Biscolli, fully dressed, staring at me from the armchair he was sitting in.

"Cutting it kind of close aren't you?" he said, obviously perturbed about something.

"What are you talking about?" I asked, pulling back the covers.

"This itinerary sitting here says your flight to Oregon leaves at 10:05 AM," he said, pinching a piece of paper on the table.

"Yeah. Well, I wasn't planning on catching the flight," I replied, as I got out of bed.

It took my response half a second to catapult the 220-pound man from his armchair and land him in front of me. Now, anyone who's had to pee really bad will tell you that an argument standing between you and the bathroom door is one of life's most disagreeable experiences. And when that argument is with Leo Biscolli, it makes for a sour way to wake up. But that's what stared me in the face not two minutes after coming awake.

I insisted that I wasn't leaving Colorado without my journal. Biscolli reminded me we'd replicated the lessons, and I was taking the flight. He stepped around me and grabbed my backpack. I took a step back and sat on the bed. He tossed my pack onto the bed and, like a madman, began grabbing anything within reach that was mine. I snatched the pack. As fast as Biscolli shoved my socks and shirts into the pack, I pulled them out. From the cursing and the flying panties, it was hard to tell who was actually winning. That's when Biscolli grabbed the document we'd compiled the night before and hurled it toward the backpack.

"Take the copy and go!" he yelled. "There's no reason for you to stick around. I can find the journal. Go home. Trust me.

I glowered at him and then began picking up the loose sheets of paper strewn across the room.

"You stubborn…," he shouted, "Sometimes I just want to…" He stopped short of what he was about to say and then knelt on the floor to help me.

I glanced up, wanting to punch a hole in his throat.

"Come on, Babe. When haven't you been able to trust me?"

It appeared we were circling our wagons around the trust fire again. Did I have an issue with trust, or did he?

"Plenty of times. Try Cueva de la Vasija, your cute little Kamela, and the journal…."

Biscolli held a neutral expression.

"Sorry to be the one to tell you this Babe, but each of those times, you concocted some story in your head and told yourself it was true. Look, we covered this last night. Either you trust me, or we're nowhere."

There was a long pause. I knew he was right, again. I'd jumped to conclusions before talking with him. I sighed.

"I'm sorry. You're right."

"Damn it, True. It's not about being right. It's about trust. You've got to decide if we're a team. Sorry if it hurts to hear that, but it's true. Either what we have is built on trust, or…"

"Okay, okay… I hear you. I do. I appreciate your honesty. I can always count on you for that," I said and sat down with the papers in my hands. "Yes, you've been honest with me. I just want the journal in my hands before I go home."

"I know. I'd probably feel the same way. But, that may or may not happen. The point is, I'm here. If it can be found, I'll find it."

"I don't know what to do," I confessed.

Biscolli knelt, then sat cross-legged on the carpet, a stack of papers in his hand.

"Look Sweetie, stay if you want to, but don't stay because you're worried. It's a reason, but it's the wrong reason. Come on, it's fear-based, and you know it. I get it… you think you're doing something if you're worrying—but what you're actually doing is giving your power to fear… a wise old elder taught me that. I'd say a force bigger than us is asking you to trust on this one. Worry is a clever lie that pretty much says, 'Hey Universe, I don't trust you… or that dapper blonde you're with," he added.

I shook my head at him, then smiled. He leaned forward and kissed my forehead.

"Remember the day we met at the gas station? I thought you were with Collier. That next morning, you showed up at Campus and I nearly blew you off again. Babe, if I'd let worry get the best of me, look at all I would've missed," he said, raising the stack of papers in the air.

I thought of all we'd been through and laughed. "Yeah, you're right."

"See, I learned something when Collier was arrested. I learned God wasn't kidding when he said we could create. Now I know whatever I give my attention to long enough, will eventually manifest. It's a law—it's how the universe works. Now, that's power and we've got it."

He set down the papers.

"Sure, I can use that creative power for my own petty interests and accumulate more junk, or I can decide to do something with it. Truth is, I don't need a lot, but I do need you." Biscolli reached for my hand. I smiled and took his.

"We know the outcome we want. How it happens isn't up to us, Sweetie."

I placed my hand on Biscolli's leg. We got up from the floor. It was 6:08 AM. We smiled. I stepped into the shower first. It was a bittersweet moment, knowing our remaining time together was thin. Somehow this gorgeous man and I had found our way home—together. My heart was his.

We made the drive to Durango. Biscolli insisted on upgrading me to First Class. He claimed I needed to "take a load off." I concluded I'd done enough arguing with him, so said thank you.

Once we'd climbed to our cruising altitude, the flight attendant served me an espresso and omelet. I'd forgotten, that First Class had its perks. I reclined the seat, sipped my coffee, and watched Colorado slowly fade. Before long the clouds swallowed the plane and the vast desert beneath us was gone completely.

It was hard to believe I was actually going home. It was one thing to live among the Hopi, and quite another to step back into a world of 24-hour everything. I rolled around the earplugs in my palm and then slid them into my pocket.

The document we'd created was in a legal-sized manila envelope. On the outside, I'd printed the words: For Earth Mother. It sat on my lap and I stared at it a long time. This was it. The envelope represented the past three weeks of my life. Still, that was nothing compared to the countless millennia it represented for the Keepers of the Covenant. On its pages was the Hopi's plea to the world. Carefully I lifted the seal and slid out the pages. I ran my eyes across the lined sheets of paper, reading random words written on them again and again.

I recalled my night on the boulder, the hunt for Biscolli, our trip to Chihuahua, and the events that led me to Spirit Eyes, Lolita, and the Hopi. I thought of Biscolli—how wrong I'd been about him, and how I loved him. I smiled, glad for it all.

How on earth could I tell this story?—tell people about this whole, crazy, wonderful experience. I laughed to myself. Only the message in this envelope mattered. This was a labor of love for Earth Mother.

It would take some time to settle back into life. I closed my eyes to rest them. Biscolli and I would talk tomorrow and determine how to go about distributing the document in my lap. Oh well, that was tomorrow. No sense robbing this moment by gobbling it up with tomorrow.

I requested a pillow, lowered the window shade, and then slept most of the three hours it took to fly to Medford. The nap was only disturbed when a flight attendant tapped me on the shoulder and requested that I put my seat upright. From the overhead speaker, the pilot announced our pending arrival. I raised the shade and admired Mount Shasta in the distance. Its northwestern-facing glacier glistened in the mid-day sun. The majestic beauty rose 14,000 feet above the densely forested green hills of the Cascades. We were close.

From above, I watched the town of Ashland come into view, and then Medford, Interstate 5, and a network of roads swarming with cars. The buildings shimmered in the light and I spotted my favorite family-owned golf course. Boats were on the Rogue River and its banks were dotted with dark specks I knew were families sprawled on bedspreads, dining on chicken wings, potato salad, and chips.

At last, we veered west. Mount McLaughlin came into view and with it the runway. Within minutes we were on the ground. There was relief in touching down. Though it was a poignant relief. I was a far different woman than when I left. I retrieved my carry-on and exited the plane.

Linda smiled as I approached her in the terminal. She looked overjoyed. So was I, actually.

"Sis! It's good to have you back," she said, hugging me.

"Thanks," I answered. "I'm surprised you're in the terminal. I thought you'd pick me up curbside." She reached for my fly rod case and backpack. "Thanks, Sis," I said, offloading them, then swinging my travel duffle over my shoulder.

"Well, I wanted to welcome you back. How was your trip? Got some sun, I see. Catch anything?"

"Didn't even use my rod after the first day."

"Really? You must have gone stir-crazy. I know you said you went to sit on a rock for ten days. It must've been hard, knowing the San Juan was right there and not fishing it."

"No, not really. You wouldn't believe me if I told you what happened," I replied.

"Well, I want to hear all about it. When you called from Mexico, I thought maybe you'd booked yourself a fishing trip down there, or something."

"No, not exactly," I answered, as we stepped onto the escalator. "And that'd be nice. I'd like to tell you about it."

"Do we need to stop at baggage claim?" Linda asked.

"No. This is it."

"Well, that's good. For two years they've been remodeling this airport—now they've got baggage claim torn apart. I try to get by with just carry-on too."

For some reason, Linda was chatty. She talked about the great weather they'd been enjoying and filled me in on work, home, and her pets. Then she said something that stopped me in my tracks.

"Did Dan tell you someone offered cash for Mom's place?"

"What?" I said. "It's not for sale."

My sister stopped and turned towards me.

"I know Mom left it to you, and you can do what you want with it. But, the last Dan knew, you said this was Mom's town, so assumed you'd be open to selling it."

"Wait? What are you talking about? Yeah, I got a message from Dan. He said to call him—something about Mama's house, but he didn't say a word about someone wanting to buy it. What's going on?"

"Well, about a week ago, Mom's neighbor called Dan and said they had friends up from Los Gatos who were looking to buy in Grants Pass. Apparently, the couple saw Mom's place, and from what he says, they fell in love with it. Maybe they looked in the windows… I don't know. Dan has the details."

We walked to Short-Term Parking. Linda popped open the trunk and I set my backpack, duffle, and fly rod case inside.

"You know as well as I do, the river, alone, could sell that place… and it's got that beautiful yard. They want to know what you'll take for it. I've got their number at the office. We can swing by work before I take you home if you want."

"What's gotten into you?" I asked as I walked towards the passenger door." No, I don't want to swing by your work and get the number! Mama's house isn't for sale."

"I don't get it, Sis. You said you didn't want to live there. Did you change your mind while you were gone?"

I stared at her.

"At least think about it." she said "Who's to say when the market might tank again? Look, if it were mine, I'd jump on it before they find something else. Besides, it's more house than you need now that the kids are gone. How often do cash offers come along? You shouldn't sit on this."

"Alright already, a person would think that you were the one trying to buy it."

"Just looking out for my Sis."

"Yeah, like I need someone looking out for me... As I said the words, I started to laugh. It was pretty funny. Maybe my sister was right—I needed some looking after. "I appreciate it, Sis. But for now, I think I'll stay in the house."

"Okay, but if you do decide to sign, Dan and I are expecting a finder's fee," Linda said, grinning.

"Get in the car," I said and laughed.

The house was still. Light from an outdoor porch lamp softly filtered through the sheers covering a set of French doors on the far side of my bedroom. Seeing the hanging crystals above my bed, brought a happy smile to my face. I'd missed this room—my sanctuary.

Outdoors, a breeze played with a willow in the backyard and tossed a swirling shadow onto my bedroom wall. The bamboo water feature in the living room was still, and I supposed Linda had unplugged it. Wind chimes hanging from a far-off grape arbor, swayed in the wind, sending a melodic song into the night. I tossed the throw pillows from my bed, and fell onto it, exhausted.

But the indoor air was stagnant and I couldn't sleep, so I eased back my covers, got up, and opened the bedside window for a little fresh air. The breeze on my face felt delicious, so I opened the French doors and stepped onto the porch. Surrounding me was a wonderland. The magnificent yard was my mother's imagination brought to life. Its care had been hers until her leg became infected. That's when a gardener took over the task.

That'll have to change, I thought. There was no way I could handle the yard when I'd had the responsibility of Mama, but now I was anxious to get my hands in the dirt. I could spend time with the live things in the yard. I'd plant corn, I mused. Next to Mama's prize begonias would be perfect, I chuckled to myself. Maybe they'd even get a song out of me.

As I examined the grounds around me, I was struck by the realization that in the hands of the landscaper, it'd been maintained out of commitment. I wondered what a little love might do for it. Granted, it wouldn't look quite like this, but the plants would certainly get the love and attention they deserved.

I stepped from the porch into the yard, touching leaves and remembering my lesson on energy in Denver's cornfield. I paused at the red geraniums and pulled a weed. I looked forward to this.

A slight dampness hung in the air. I'd experienced enough desert for a while, and the weather here would soon turn hot. Late Spring rains can visit the northwest in June, and I hoped for one—a light shower anyway. I turned, entered my room, and closed the door.

Once settled, bed became a bit of heaven. It was good to be home. I lay there and allowed the past three weeks to settle—to sink in.

In the security of my bed, the past three weeks seemed larger than life. So much had happened. I thought of Denver and his devoted family, of Spirit Eyes and Biscolli. I wondered what they were doing. I thought of my missing journal—and the full message of the Hopi people that was recorded on its pages. It was somewhere. The handwritten document I'd brought home had to be safeguarded until it could be copied and shared. I then thought of Nee-yaa-nu and wondered where he was—who he was in this lifetime.

The truth is, I loved Biscolli and knew he loved me. And yet, my Nee-yaa-nu was out there, somewhere.

I closed my eyes. Perhaps Nee-yaa-nu wasn't in this world. Perhaps Biscolli was my guy. He was a good man, he understood me and he made my heart happy. He had his moments, but then, so did I. Was Nee-yaa-nu on the other side of the veil, loving me from there? Or was he alive and seeking me? I couldn't know.

# 31

# THE VOICE

I have done a lot of hiking in my life—including all but 365 miles of the 2,663-mile Pacific Crest Trail, sections of the Appalachian Trail, and hundreds of day-hike miles. Two of my favorite places on the planet to hike are Tryon State Park and Forest Park, both in Portland, Oregon. Another favorite place is right here in Grants Pass. I found Cathedral Hills almost by accident, but it quickly became a favorite hiking spot, for its variety of trails—some flat, some with elevation, but all with views and vistas of Southern Oregon's evergreen-laden hills and lush valleys.

I've logged many miles in Cathedral Hills. I love to hike and trail run there, especially in Spring and Autumn. It is a sanctuary for me, and I would sneak there every chance I could during the year I cared for Mama. I missed Cathedral Hills while I was away. I missed hiking.

My intent for my first day home was to unpack, get a load of laundry done, sort mail, make some calls, and hike. At about 11 AM, I made the short drive to Cathedral Hills, slipped on my trail shoes, and began the hike.

Early June in Southern Oregon is glorious, and today was exceptional. The trailhead was a gateway into a world I sorely needed. A dense forest of madrone trees and evergreens towered overhead, and a thicket of underbrush, alive with wildflowers, carpeted the ground.

Hiking is many things for me. It can be a meditation, a way to calm stress; to exercise, a time to think and incubate ideas, or simply to take in the beauty around me. Today I needed to think. The Hopi document was sitting on my bedroom dresser, and I needed an idea of what to do with it.

Biscolli and I had brain-dumped several ideas, but I hadn't gotten a "Ya" for any of them. We were to talk later today, and I hoped to have at least one idea that had "legs," to share with him.

My hike took me up a ridge that overlooked the small town of Grants Pass. I paused at a vista point and attempted to locate familiar landmarks in the valley below. Beyond the vista point, the trail then leveled off, before winding its descent to the parking lot. I'd just left the vista point, when a movie, of sorts, played out in my mind. I didn't recognize the story, the characters, or the scenery, but it appeared so vivid and clear—so real, that I did nothing to censor or control what I was viewing. I just watched in my mind's eye as I hiked.

In the "mind movie," I observed a man and a woman. They were hunting for something. After much searching, they found themselves at a natural spring flowing with clear water. Near the spring was a massive rock. The rock had a flat side, and on it was a petroglyph. A second man appeared, and escorted the couple to the rock, whereupon, he explained the petroglyph in great detail. He then drank from the spring and offered the couple a drink of the water as well, and the three of them became doves and flew away.

A strange urgency accompanied the mind-movie, and I had a feeling that I shouldn't let it slip from my mind, so ran the remainder of the trail to the trailhead, unlocked my car, opened my phone, and made a verbal note of the story.

It was an odd experience.

I drove into town and enjoyed breakfast at a delightful outdoor cafe, bought groceries, then drove home. After the groceries were put away, I sat down to listen to my voice recording of the mind-movie. As I listened, I had a strong impression to write it down, so listened again and again, until I had captured the mind-movie on paper.

When Biscolli called, I confessed that I hadn't gotten a firm "Yes" to any of the ideas we had tossed around. I told him I was using the belly test I had been taught by Spirit Eyes, and he seemed to feel it was reasonable to wait until something became a firm "Yes."

"This is too important to have misgivings," he said.

I asked him how he was doing, what was happening at the campus, the state of Collier's trial, and how the new students were taking to the program.

He said that with Collier's arrest, he was back to work, and was grateful for it. All of their focus was now on Yellow Bar, which was great for the site because it had always played second fiddle to Raven Creek. He asked if I would be open to him flying up for a weekend.

"I thought you'd never ask," I said, and we made plans for him to visit the following weekend. I have to admit, my heart fluttered at the thought of seeing him again.

I spent the balance of my day reading the document Biscolli and I had drafted. I wondered if we had left out anything important. We never imagined we would lose the journal, or access to the full extent of the Hopi's teachings, prophecies, and lessons. I was seriously concerned something may be missing.

After reading all that we had written, I placed a hand on the stack of papers in front of me.

"This is yours to have, Earth Mother. This has never been about me. It's never been about Biscolli. It's never even been about Oliver or the desert. By the grace of God, we've gotten this far. Please tell me if anything is not here that should be—anything that you want people to know. Thank you for your help; and for guiding us every step of the way. I couldn't see the forest for the trees, but you've known all along how to get us here.

"Show us what to do with this—how to best serve the elders holding the balance of the world on their shoulders—how to bring the three helpers to them and divert war. Show us how to encourage stewardship of you. I am yours. I'll do what you say. Please be absolutely clear in your messaging, so there is no confusion, mistake, or misinterpretation on my part. Thank you."

I got up from the table, slipped on my flip-flops, and walked to the river. Once there, I lay on the grass and let my body rest on the ground. Sunshine shimmered on the cottonwood leaves, dancing above my head.

I drew in a deep breath. There was no way I was selling this place. I needed to be here. I could make Mama's home, my home.

I continued to lay on the grassy riverbank until the sun dropped below the branches. I then stepped into the river's current up to my knees. Standing there, I thought of my Uncle Claud and took the opportunity to give my cares to the water flowing past me. I smiled, stepped from the water, slipped on my flip-flops again, and returned to the house.

I retired early that night. The trip had caught up with me, and I was tired. I turned off the light and was instantly pulled into sleep.

At some point, I stirred awake to a voice. Only, this wasn't the voice I was used to. You know the one—the one that reminds you to grab your keys before shutting the car door. The one that reminds you to turn off the stovetop, or to stop binge-watching Netflix and go to bed.

I'm used to that voice in my head. This wasn't that voice. In fact, it was very different. It had a quality; a richness and texture to it. It was smooth, clear, and metered—as smooth as Spirit Eyes' voice. In fact, when I first heard it, I thought I was hearing her voice in a dream. This was not a dream, however. I was awake.

I wasn't sure where the voice was coming from. It felt as though it was in my head—but it wasn't being generated by me—and my listening to it felt almost telepathic. In other words, the voice was inaudible.

I can't recall what it said. I only remember the feeling of love, presence, and compassion that attended it.

I fell back asleep.

I woke again. This time I checked the hour. It was 3:33 AM. Numerology suggests that the number three symbolizes optimism, communication, growth, and freedom. It's considered to be a perfect number—the number of harmony, wisdom, and understanding. This morning it showed up in all its force, as a triple three.

The voice was back, and, this time as it spoke, I could recall everything that was being said. It was as though a part of me was recording it. It was the oddest thing.

I lay there in the dark as it spoke in full sentences. I'd now become witness to a conversation between the voice and—what I could only assume, was my soul (based on the over-the-body, floating experience I'd had in the River of Trust). It was kinda cool.

I felt that I should pay attention to the conversation, and when I did, what I heard astounded me. The voice was telling the story I had seen on my hike today.

It was bizarre—but that's what was happening.

I got out of bed, and the conversation continued. I turned on the light. The conversation continued. I washed my face. The conversation continued.

I decided to conduct a test and listened for the normal, day-to-day voice in my head. It was still there—and the new dialogue continued alongside it.

I thought it best I not lose what I was listening to, so attempted to write it down. It became impossible to keep up with its pace. I sat down at my desk, opened my laptop, and damned if I didn't start typing what I was hearing word for word. It was the craziest thing. That continued throughout the day. Except for meals and personal breaks, I was at my desk, listening and writing all day—literally taking dictation.

That evening when I went to bed, an even stranger thing occurred. The voice stopped. Then, during sleep, I then slipped INTO the mind-movie. I actually found myself WITHIN the story itself. As I moved around within the story, I realized that I could interact with the scenery and the characters. It was bizarre.

The first significant event that occurred in my nighttime movie, was I saw the woman I'd seen in the story on my hike—and she was standing on a boulder.

As I moved within the mind-movie, I realized that I knew this place. It was Hovenweep. What was the woman doing at

Hovenweep? I wondered. I studied the boulder. I knew that boulder. It was MY boulder. What was she doing on my boulder?

The next morning, I rolled out of bed and scrambled to keep up with the stream of dialogue I was receiving. Immediately, I realized that what I was typing was a total recall of what I'd experienced the night before in my sleep.

My fingers were flying across the keyboard, and I was making a lot of mistakes trying to keep up with the pace of the voice. In my frustration, I called out.

"Can you just slow down?"

And it did.

I then discovered that I could communicate with the voice myself, and ask it to pause, repeat something, or to clarify what it had said.

That day I wrote about a woman arriving at a ranger's station, speaking with a female ranger, loading four jugs of water into a pack and hiking to a boulder.

It was odd to be taking dictation about this "mind-movie woman" doing what I had done.

That evening, I found myself in the nighttime movie again. This time the woman was fumbling for a flashlight under a full moon, terrified she was about to be eaten by a beast. She looked up, and…

What?

What was Oliver doing here?

A moment of clarity came over me, and I realized this was no mind-movie woman—this was me.

The voice was relaying the story of me—and my experience, at Hovenweep.

I relaxed into the mind movie again, and, sure enough, there he was—Oliver.

I heard his message to me from Earth Mother. I watched him vanish into the night. I watched myself scour the desert, looking for a sign of the little old man.

In the morning, I rolled out of bed and typed what the voice dictated—which included everything, word for word, that Oliver had said that night—things I'd even forgotten in my state of panic.

The next evening, I found myself in the nighttime movie, in a wet sleeping bag, then pouring out three gallons of water in preparation to hike out of Hovenweep. I witnessed myself arguing with the sky and vowing to return to finish my vision quest after finding some archaeologist that I'd probably fabricated in my head.

In the morning, I typed everything the voice dictated.

The story progressed night after night. Each night I would relive events in detail, and in the morning I'd begin typing what the voice communicated.

"The Voice" was capturing everything.

When I became tired, I would ask the voice to stop. Our interaction became personal, conversational, and friendly. The Voice and I spoke as though you and I were carrying on a conversation.

This became my life, progressively reliving the events of my life over the past three weeks in intimate detail, at night, and in the daytime, dictating the recollection of what I had experienced the night before, as dictated by The Voice.

Biscolli arrived ten days into the process. He didn't know what to make of it, but it had become apparent to me, that the story I'd seen on my hike that day was Biscolli and me, and the second man was Denver Mahema. The rock was the ancient tablets, and, in the end, peace prevailed.

## ANASAZI VISION

Night after night the past three weeks of my life played out in intimate detail. Nothing was lost or left out. Mama's death, fishing the San Juan, CJ and Smurf, holding a bottle of cream soda, Miss Brunette and Cowboy Earl, the campus library, two infants, the site notch at Cueva de la Vasija, André, the Mongoose, Spirit Eyes, Lolita—all of it.

Knowing now, what was unfolding, I eagerly awaited the point in the story when Biscolli and I would arrive in Hotevilla and begin school with Elder Denver Mahema.

I witnessed myself at the side of the elder, delivering the token from Vera, and Biscolli beside me, engaged in our school lessons. I witnessed myself in Denver's cornfield digging holes.

Through the series of nighttime movies and daily dictation, the entirety of the lessons Denver had fervently and patiently taken us through, revealed themselves.

I was recording the entirety of our journey—the entirety of the ancient covenant, and it would be for the world.

It was a glorious weekend with Biscolli. We stayed close to home; cooking, talking, walking, and spending time at the river, reveling in all we'd been through in a mere three weeks. Our lovemaking stirred awake something within me that was as sacred as it was wild and untamed.

Earth Mother had found her own way to ensure the message was in its entirety. It was all there. She is a marvel, and I trust her completely.

The Voice continued day in and day out, for seven weeks. At the close of that time, the voice stopped.

There was a manuscript. This manuscript.

# EPILOGUE
## THE STORY BEHIND THE STORY

I stood in the presence of an old Hopi elder. The cameraman I accompanied to Hotevilla, Arizona, had just completed an interview with the elder and left the room. During the filming, I had been holding a large light reflector, and as I prepared to leave, the elder caught my attention and motioned for me to come closer. It was a dream of mine to visit the Hopi, but never occurred to me that I might actually meet a traditional elder who held onto and lived by the old ways. Yet, here I was, alone with one.

Less than a week earlier, I had been on a movie set in Ashland, Oregon. One of my best friends was a publicist for the movie and asked if I would visit her because she wanted to introduce me to someone. That someone turned out to be Kent Romney, a cameraman, and he was temporarily leaving the set to complete the final interviews of a documentary film. He was on his way to Hotevilla to interview members of the Hopi, including several elders. I asked if I could tag along, perhaps carry camera equipment, and that's how I happened to be at Hotevilla, one of four villages on Third Mesa in northern Arizona.

The elder's eyes and mine locked. We shared a moment in silence, and then a generous smile rose on the aged man's mahogany-colored face.

"Dear," he said. "This is not the first time we've met." His dark eyes were warm and kind. He continued. "You know that vision quest you did?"

Of course, I remembered and thought back to the vision quest I'd done eight years earlier. I had carved ten days out of my busy life and dedicated them to venturing into the wilderness and being alone; fasting, praying, and meditating; drumming, dancing, and creating ceremony, all in an attempt to call in a vision that I hoped to God might provide some clarity and answers for my life. I was desperate to understand who I was and what direction to steer my life.

"Yes," I answered, wondering how on earth the elder knew that I'd done a vision quest. "That was me," he said with conviction. "I was the one who came to you."

Now, I've come to believe that anything is possible, but that doesn't mean I wasn't shocked and confused by the elder's first words to me. I recalled the vision that I received late one night. I'd memorized every word and detail of the little man who visited me in a vision. He'd identified himself as Oliver. Was the elder saying that he was Oliver? Is that what I heard? Really? Wait. What? How could that be?

"You know me as Oliver. Thank you for coming, True. We have much to talk about."

My thoughts were spinning and my heart was pounding. I felt inwardly disheveled, as if I had just dropped a tray, and my sense of reality was strewn about the floor. I looked into his eyes, seeking something to anchor me. His eyes remained on me, warm and steady, and his smile grew.

"I don't understand," I confessed.

"Well, you see when I was a lad and had come of age, I was presented with two ways I could help my people. I was given a choice. I could become a medicine man or I could choose to be a shifter and move from place to place. I was clever enough to know that medicine men can be up all night and rarely get any rest, so I chose to be a shifter, and it's been a fair decision. This is how I came to visit you."

"You're Oliver?" I asked.

"Yes, and you know that story you wrote? It is not time to publish it. You're not ready. The world is not ready, and there is information you do not have. You will know it when you do. Confirmation will come. You can add the additional information and then publish."

I was stunned. How could the elder know that I had written a story… this story?

The morning after receiving my vision, I took a hike. It was during this short hike that a story filled my mind. It played itself out in its entirety as I walked, and I quickened my pace, eventually running back to my campsite, grabbing a pen and journal, and outlining the bones of the story. Upon arriving home from my vision quest, I began hearing a voice. I heard it as I slept and watched two individuals interact in a story that progressed nightly. Upon waking, I would roll out of bed and scramble to keep up with the stream of dialogue I was receiving. This continued for seven weeks, and at the close of that time, the original draft of Anasazi Vision was complete.

This was a wholly new experience for me. I'd heard of such things and experienced spurts of inspiration when writing poetry, but nothing like this. This dialogue was clear, consistent, and communicated in full paragraphs. Interestingly, the voice wove several of my own personal experiences into the story, and the tale became an intriguing tapestry of events that I experienced either via the voice or in real life.

The scenes of the book came as a series of experiences I interacted with nightly as I slept. I entered the book's scenes and interacted with the characters, like virtual reality. Awake or asleep, I was living the literary journey unfolding in front of me. What is most interesting—and I must admit I enjoyed this immensely, is that the voice, which became my companion for nearly two months, was friendly, caring, and communicated as if you and I were enjoying a conversation. And, it was patient with me as I tried to keep up with its pace. When our exchange ended, I sincerely missed its presence.

Kent and I remained in Hotevilla for a second day of interviews with tribe members. I met with the old Hopi elder again, who guided me through a rudimentary understanding of Hopi ways, traditions, and customs. He escorted Kent and me to Prophecy Rock, to the spring that provides water to the village, and to his field, where he practices the ancient technique of dry-farming. He sketched images and symbols that made no sense to me at the time. He told me I would understand their meaning later, and that more information would come in the years ahead.

I went on with my life, all but forgetting the manuscript until the pandemic when I detected information surfacing that belonged in the book. By late 2023, the most significant piece of information was acquired, and the sketch now made sense. It was then that a dear friend told me of an upcoming cosmic event that involved Third Mesa. I took it as a sign that the time had come to rewrite the manuscript; to change the protagonist from a man to myself, add the additional information, and new chapters, and publish it. What you are holding in your hands is a decades-long collaboration from both sides of the veil.

As you will read in the second book, Return To Third Mesa, the voice came to me again, briefly. My experience of the rewrite was as different as one sibling is from another—yet, every bit as remarkable.

I knew nothing of the Ancestral Puebloans or the Hopi before this book took me on a deep dive into their worlds. In the years leading up to my vision quest, I'd done two personal retreats and was no stranger to spending time alone. At the time, I was living in Portland, Oregon, having ended up there after graduating from college. The truth is, I was as lost as I was found. The "found" part of me had a fresh degree in journalism, but the majority of me was as lost as ever. It took six years to earn my degree because I played hopscotch with majors—a direct reflection of the hopscotch I played with my life.

My family was deeply religious, and though it served me well growing up—helped lay a foundation of faith, and standards, and, much to my parents' relief, steer me clear of partying, promiscuity, and prison, I began to question everything as I entered my 30s. I wasn't sure the direction organized religion laid out for me was the direction I wanted to go. I wondered how much of my life I'd adopted and how much of it was intrinsically my own. Something was festering deep within me. I had to know what I believed— not what I had been told to believe. Thus, I began the great unraveling of my life.

# ANASAZI VISION

I know everything happens for a reason and, in hindsight, I'm grateful I took the time to yank back the curtain and see what was guiding my life, but it was damn scary at the time, and I wasn't alone during my years of searching. I was the mother of four children, and they rode my coattails, hanging on through the ride as I endeavored to clean and learn to read my internal compass—while still trying to do right by them. I was also a recent widow, grieving a man I deeply loved, and having very few tools to navigate the murky waters of grief. I joined the Army National Guard. It seemed the logical thing to do. Religion and marriage had sheltered me. I was clueless about what I was capable of. I'd taught fitness classes but had few marketable skills. Entering the military was the toughest thing I could think to do that had no backdoor or safety net. I'd either grow up and grow a set of legs to stand on, or forever wonder what I was made of. It was the right decision for me and started me on a path of personal and spiritual growth, education, and opportunity.

A decade later, I thru-hiked the Pacific Crest Trail, a 2,663-mile "long trail" that stretches from Mexico to Canada, following the crests of nine mountain ranges. I hiked 2,300 miles of it, 1,200 miles of it solo. Looking back, it was my time on the PCT that helped me build a history of resilience and perseverance with myself. I didn't know it then, but I'd need every bit of it. One of my greatest challenges was still ahead of me, and that's where this story, Anasazi Vision, begins.

# AFTERWORD

Anasazi Vision is a fictional novel. I am most certainly not connected to the Hopi or Hopi Prophecy in any way, and they request that visitors refrain from visiting the Mesas that comprise their land. The true events of this story have been dramatized to assist in its telling, and the order in which they occurred has been considerably rearranged.

The original manuscript was written immediately following my vision quest, years ago. When I returned to Hotevilla a second time, the Hopi elder informed me that it was not time to publish; I was not ready, and valuable information was not contained within it—that would be forthcoming.

In reflection, I hadn't yet lived the experiences that would become the bedrock and context of the events and emotional fabric of this tale.

In 2024, the manuscript was rewritten to incorporate the new information and the updated characters. This revised story and characters feel true to the experience of the vision I was given, true to my heart, and in great honor, respect, and gratitude for the Hopi people I dearly love.

— True North, 2024

# ACKNOWLEDGEMENT

READERS: Sesha Ward, Linda Cole, Kathi Duckworth, Lidija Diller, Tara Ott, Maelani Darcy
FIRST DRAFT READER: Marie Stevenson
STORY STRUCTURE CONSULT: Joshua McDaniel
WRITING PARTNERS: The Voice and my spiritual guides, who usually started speaking at 3:30 AM. What a profound experience. Thank you.
DRAFT EDITORS: Chuck Boyle, Sharen Schneiderman
LINE EDITOR, PROOFREADER: Annie T
COVER PHOTO: Credit and gratitude to respective photographer.
PUBLISHING COACH: Tina Konstant

# SPECIAL ACKNOWLEDGEMENT

JERRY HONAWA: Hopi elder. Thank you for your instruction and trust in me.

SHELLY VAUGHN: Chapter One grew its lungs in your beautiful space. Thank you.

TARA OTT: My fellow nature sister and steward of Mama Gaia, thank you for sending the text that initiated the rewrite. I love you.

KEN & LIDIJA DILLER: You saw me through the final stretch before publication. I love you, my chosen family. "Zivelee!"

CREATIVE'S ROUNDTABLE: Laura LaJoie-Bishop, Lucia Evans, Joshua McDaniel, Mark Courtman, Shelly Vaughn, Cedar Love, Antoinette Elam, Ray Snedaker

GEORGE KING, ERIC ROSE, and MAMA: who provided inspiration for the new characters of the 2024 rewrite.

SARAH BLONDIN: Your meditations literally saved my life, sister.

MY CHEERLEADERS: Kathi Duckworth, Gail Sinclair, Linda Cole, Lisa Schneiderman, Emma Silvera, and my children: Cedar, Denver, Stewart, and Clint, for holding the space for this beautiful tale since day one. I love you.

# BOOK CLUB TOPICS FOR DISCUSSION

Earth as a Living Breathing Organism

Communication With Plants

Water Intelligence and Water Memory

Activated Water - Infused With Love, Gratitude, Intention

Life Lessons - Repeating Patterns / Issues - a Clue to Life Lessons

Trust / River of Trust

Life Path

Death

Grief and Loss

Inner Peace

Accepting Change

Everything is Energy - Can't Be Destroyed

Reincarnation

Coherence - Heart Coherence

Nervous System - Affects of Being Held and of Holding

Energetic Anatomy- Human & Earth's Chakras, Meridians

Third Eye - Energetic and Spiritual Eye

Prayer and Meditation in Mass Number

Vibration and Frequency

Law of Frequency - Match Rate of Desire / Intention

Law of Creation / Law of Attraction - Visualizing & Feeling Outcome

Co-Creating Our Reality

Gratitude and Its Role in Creation

We Choose the Narrative that Creates Our Reality

Collective Consciousness

Higher Self / Soul

Higher Self's Perspective - Knows All, Its Access to Akashic Records

Life Purpose

Trusting the Universe Will Provide

Integrated Attachment Theory - Being Securely Attached

Sky Way Medicine Disciplines

Frequency and Sound Healing

2020 Trigger Point - Tipping the Scale / Enough Humans With Elevated Vibration

Close of Fourth Cycle To Be Vibratory Shift Not Cataclysmic Event

Chaos

Diverting World War Three

The Three Helpers: Yellow, Black, and White Races

Fear and Love

Transmute Fear

Guardians / Stewards of Gaia (Earth Mother)

Building "New Earth" - What is Our Vision of New Earth and the New Human?

Caregiving and Caring for the Caregiver

Responsibility

Commitment, Integrity

Vision Quest

Ceremony and Ritual

Fasting

Breath / Focus on Breath

Synchronicity and Coincidence

Bargain With the Crows - Ask for What You Want / Need

Setting Boundaries

Turtle Island / America

Hopi Prophecy

Repressed Emotions, Feeling & Expressing Them

Saying "Yes," then Leaning In and Trusting

Our Shared Human Experience

Organized Religion / Spirituality

Needs of Children - Feel Loved, Encouraged to Pursue Interests

Ancient Civilizations

Listening, Being Completely Present With Another

Channeling

Soul Families

Spiritual Team: Angels, Guides and Ancestors

Masculine Container

Divine Masculine - What Does That Look & Feel Like?

Masculine - Feminine Energy / Attributes & Flowing Between Them

Conscious, Intentional Relationships

Strong, Competent Women With Gentle Core

A Woman's Yumminess - Our Feminine Aspects

Women's Circles

Personal Transformation, Growth, Empowerment

Vulnerability, Transparency, Authenticity, Alignment

Self-Love

Inner Child

Sovereignty

Psychic Mediumship

Hypnotherapy

Past Lives

"Other Side" of the Veil

Belly Test (Ya / Na) - Testing for Your "Yes"

Intuition - Internal Compass

Perceived Upper Limits - Doubt, Limitation, Worth, Feeling Insignificant

Health Essentials: Sleep, Morning Sunlight, Earthing, Activated Spring Water, Clean Nutrition, Movement, Emotional Connection, Time in Nature

Pure Awareness - Our True Essence

Blending & the Various Blending Exercises - Feeling Energy

Earthing / Grounding

Plant Medicine, Herbal Remedies

Numerology

Oneness

# TRUE'S PLAYLIST

Khan - Trevor Hall
Closer - Samuel J
Mother - Trevor Hall
Daughters - Stephanie Schneiderman
Vuela con el Viento (Mose Remix) - Ayla Schafer & Mose
Open Doors - Trevor Hall
Grandmother (I Am the Earth) - Ayla Schafer
Chapter of the Forest - Trevor Hall
Lost Stars - Keira Knightley
Remember - Omkara
Yeah Noha - Sacred Spirit
Water Song - Ayla Schafer
Do It With Me - Old Dominion
Moon / Sun - Trevor Hall

I created and listened to this playlist no less than three hundred times while rewriting Anasazi Vision. These songs became my North Star. If this book had a playlist, this would be it. Thank you to these artists for nourishing my heart. I share your love for our dear Mama Gaia.

# BISCOLLI'S TEE SHIRTS

If women are from Venus, why don't they go home?
The Seven Habits of Highly Defective People
I tried being normal once. Worst two minutes of my life
Duct tape can't fix stupid, but it can muffle the sound
And yet, despite the look on my face, you're still talking
In my defense, I was left unsupervised
Just because I'm awake doesn't mean I'm ready to do things
Beer is the reason I wake up each afternoon
Exercise? I thought you said extra fries
That's a horrible idea. What time?
Tourists go home, but leave your pets behind
I have selective hearing. Sorry, you weren't selected today
I may be wrong, but I highly doubt that
I'd love to explain it to you, but I don't have any crayons
Hold on, let me overthink this
Admit it, life would be boring without me

# ALSO BY TRUE NORTH

## ANASAZI VISION - RETURN TO THIRD MESA
*Release Date: Winter 2025*

The Fourth Cycle is closing and the recalibration of Earth's vibration—and all life upon her, is well on its way as the Fifth Cycle prepares to open. True North and Leo Biscolli return to Third Mesa and discover deeper secrets, including the arc of events preceding the Fifth Cycle, and how best to navigate them. They are sent back with tools from wise elders, on how to navigate the planetary reset.

## THE ANASAZI VISION COMPANION - NAVIGATING THE 30-YEAR RESET: A GUIDE TO THE LESSONS AND TOOLS
*Release Date: Winter 2026*

A companion guide to the Anasazi Vision series, compiling in one place, the lessons, tools, and wisdom to navigate the 30-year reset of human consciousness, and the pathway to peace in the Fifth Cycle.

Printed in Great Britain
by Amazon